THE SLICKROCK

PARADOX

Stephen Legault

TouchWood
Editions

TouchWood Editions
touchwoodeditions.com

LIBRARY AND ARCHIVES CANADA CATALOGUING IN PUBLICATION
Legault, Stephen, 1971–
The slickrock paradox / Stephen Legault.

Also issued in electronic format.
ISBN 978-1-927129-39-5

I. Title.

PS8623.E46633S55 2012   C813'.6   C2012-902550-X

Editor: Frances Thorsen
Proofreader: Lenore Hietkamp
Design: Pete Kohut
Cover image: Stephen Legault
Author photo: Dan Anthon

We gratefully acknowledge the financial support for our publishing activities
from the Government of Canada through the Canada Book Fund, Canada
Council for the Arts, and the province of British Columbia through the
British Columbia Arts Council and the Book Publishing Tax Credit.

MIX
Paper from
responsible sources
FSC® C016245

The interior pages of this book have been printed on 100% post-consumer
recycled paper, processed chlorine free, and printed with vegetable-based inks.

1 2 3 4 5 16 15 14 13 12

PRINTED IN CANADA

For Jenn
For Silas and Rio
For Ann and Paul
With gratitude to Ruth and Frances
For Cactus Ed

1

SHE WAS NOT THERE.

Standing on a slab of naked sandstone, the fierce, dazzling light of midday bearing down on him, he thought this was the kind of place where if you lost something it would be hard to find again. Especially if that something was a person.

Silas Pearson stood with his hands at his sides, his fingers curled slightly as if attempting to hold onto something slowly slipping from his grasp. His face, brushed with graying whiskers, was shaded by an oversized, sweat-soaked, wide-brimmed hat, encrusted with red dust and faded from too much sun. He faced east, his shadow a slender disk at his feet.

He slipped his pack from his back and crouched on the coral pink stone, pulled a water bottle from the bag and unscrewed the top. He drank, a few precious beads of water trickling down into his rough beard. The water was cool and sweet; he'd frozen the bottle solid the night before, as was his routine, so that at midday it was still cold, the ice long gone. He tightened the lid before slipping it into his bag. He fiddled with the ring on his left hand, pulling at it, and noticed his hands were so swollen the ring would not move.

He stood and fished a worn and tattered topographic map from his shirt pocket. The reflection of the sun made it difficult to look at the white paper for very long. He regarded the map for a brief moment, looking up at the landscape to get his bearings, and then used a pencil to mark his route. He folded the map and put it away.

Silas set out again, walking over the corrugated sandstone, the soles of his light hiking shoes gripping the 100-million-year-old slickrock like Velcro. The earth tilted upward, so he pressed his legs into service to ascend a hump of barren stone. At the top, the landscape leveled out and the stone gave way to a sandy arroyo. There were trees here, though not the type Silas had become accustomed too in the dry upland forests of his recent past. These trees were stunted and tortured, growing a few feet each decade, existing more on hope and dogged perseverance than water or the desert's thin, dusty soil. Pinyon pines, their thick, bushy boughs decked with tightly whorled cones that the searing heat would soon pop open. And Utah juniper, deformed trunks bare and gray, twisted like an old man's body, their roots seizing the naked stone, drilling deep into the earth in search of moisture, tattered limbs clutching at the azure sky.

Silas scanned the undersized forest before him and began circling back and forth across the sandy rill. He stooped and peered in the shade of each bunched-up pine and in the lee of every juniper, slowly making his way eastward. Sweat soaked his shirt and hat and the waistband of his pants. He pushed away the trickling beads as they seeped through his eyebrows and burned his eyes. He wore no sunglasses despite the wicked glare, because he missed things that were in the shadows at midday if he wore them. It was too great a risk to take.

He widened his circling and took in a broader sweep of the folded landscape, finding a narrow defile in the tableland that promised shade, and he hunched at its edge a moment, consulting his map again. The contour lines bent slightly here, but otherwise the slot canyon didn't appear on his topographic sheet. Silas's sunburnt finger hovered over the place on the map, tracing the gorge's path east, toward the edge of the map. He'd have to check it. He slipped his pack off again, retrieving the water bottle. After a cool drink, he stepped to the edge of the crack and peered into its depths. It was a narrow crevice in the stone, impossible to tell if it was twenty or one hundred feet deep. This gorge *might* have offered the promise of shade, he reasoned, had it been sought. He put his feet on either side of the opening in the earth and stared down into the darkness, but could see nothing. Tucking his hat inside his pack, he set the bundle next to the cleft. He pulled out a small headlamp from his bag and strapped it on.

Silas drew a sharp breath and pressed himself between the stone walls, then slipped beneath the desert.

It was cooler in the cleft of naked rock, but it was very narrow and almost immediately he wished he hadn't started this descent. Below him the darkness seemed to pull at his feet with its cool, inviting depths. He wedged his shoulder against one side of the fissure, hands and feet against the other, and continued down. He glanced up after a minute to see the sky a thin white line above him. He edged downward again, his face was only six inches from the wall opposite him, the sky now gone.

Some people do this for fun, he thought.

Silas's breath came in sharp staccato gulps, in part because of the tight fit in the iron lung of stone, in part because of the claustrophobic grip the earth had on him. He turned his head to regard the darkness all around him. It was possible that a person might fall into such a rent if they were not looking where they were going. Possible, but improbable; you could step over such a crevice and hardly notice it. He was suspended thirty feet or more below the surface now, and an unknown distance from the bottom. He began to shift himself eastward, his senses alert to any sound that might lead to a discovery.

He found the going strenuous. Three and a half years ago his body, more adept at standing at a university lectern, would have given out. But in the ensuing years he'd grown both strong and adept at this sort of subterranean exploration.

He pressed his hands flat against the cool surface of the sandstone before him, his back grating over the stone behind, his feet moving back and forth, finding what purchase they could on the grit of the rock. He continued inch by inch along the length of the narrow defile, the tiny light from his headlamp catching cracks and fissures and folds in the sinuous earth.

In a few minutes he came to a place where the defile opened a little and he found himself pushing the opposite wall with his arm fully extended. Sun trickled down from the grotto's opening far above and the stone glowed with an ethereal light. If he hadn't been obsessed with his morbid task, Silas might have appreciated, even taken pleasure in, the suspended moment in time there in his narrow slot.

Another twenty feet and the canyon constricted again, and this time he felt a jumble of basketball-sized chock stones beneath this feet. He rested for another moment, his light raking the bottom of the crevice, searching for any sign that told of previous human passage. There was none; there was nothing there. Stone, red dust suspended in the arc of his light, the middens of pack rats, nothing more. He drew a deep breath, his body nearly touching either side of the slot. He forced himself farther eastward along the rocky bottom, his face turned sideways so the light would lead him onwards. He looked up and could see no sign of the world beyond.

There came a moment when the walls pressed so closely together that Silas felt he might not be able to take another deep breath. He was a slender man, what might have passed for lean, except that his arms and shoulders and back were well developed from carrying a pack these last few years, his legs corded with long, sinuous muscle from thousands of miles trudged over canyon country.

Another twenty yards and Silas came to another complication. His light caught the lip of the canyon floor where it disappeared. Silas inched forward, his breath coming sharply. Despite the coolness of the canyon, sweat leaked from his thatch of gray hair, hanging in a drip on the end of his hooked nose.

He peered over the lip of the drop-off and could see the floor of the canyon continue twenty or more feet below. But the walls here were slickrock, the sandstone hollowed out and polished smooth by the purge of intermittent floods and coated with a fine dust. Too wide for him to reach across. He could likely put one foot down on the small stone protruding five or six feet below, then climb down the slickrock, but could he climb back up? The fine grit and light dusting of powder that coated much of the surface of the canyon country made these slabs, shoots and pour-offs deathtraps. What was often easy to descend could become perilous to ascend or vice versa; such was the paradox of slickrock country. Men died that way in the canyonlands, he reasoned. Women, too. He stood for a long moment, evaluating his prospects.

He could not count the number of times over the last three years that he had come to some lip, some corner, some precipice and weighed the odds: to continue his lonesome search and risk becoming like that which he sought, or turn around and live to search another day. He could climb out of the grotto, retrieve the harness and rope from the car, rappel down the overhang and then use his jumar—a small tool used to mechanically ascend a rope—to climb out again. But that would take several hours, and he was already tired. It seemed highly improbable that he would find what he was searching for here. He began his solemn ascent.

In fifteen minutes Silas reached the top of the breach and pulled himself onto the tableland. He retrieved his pack just half a mile away. He fished his water from the bag and drank greedily. As he consulted his map, he traced his underground passage with swollen fingers and sighed deeply. He rubbed his face.

Hat back on his head, the pack on his back, Silas turned east again. He walked his zigzag traverse until there was no earth left to walk upon. He stopped on the rim of the canyon, the Wingate sandstone dropping five hundred feet straight down into a narrow talus slope, and then down again, a thousand feet to the canyon floor. Below him was the Middle Fork of Shafer Canyon, and farther on the East Fork, rising up abruptly to the plateau of Dead Horse Point. Though not visible from where he stood, just miles to the southeast the Colorado River twisted through the earth below, doubling back on itself in the vicinity of the Gooseneck.

She was not here. It was a fact.

Silas retreated to the meager shade offered by a solitary Utah juniper on the cliff edge. He found his GPS unit and calculated the day's progress: a mere five and a half miles, not including the narrow slot. More than a thousand feet of up and down.

Despondent, he pulled up the totals for his three and a half years of journeying: 4212 miles. Had he been walking across the United States he could have strode from San Diego, California, to Bangor, Maine, and halfway back again in that time. He did the calculation for elevation: just over three hundred thousand feet, up and down, up and down. He could have climbed Mount Everest ten times. He put the GPS back in his pack, weary with accumulated effort.

He sat in the refuge of the juniper's shade and surveyed the scene. It was not uninviting. In fact, Silas knew that it was beautiful. Beautiful in a terrible, reaching, agoraphobic sort of way.

But for Silas, it was not beautiful. It was not repulsive. It was empty.

2

SILAS DROVE BACK ACROSS THE Island in the Sky mesa, a can of Molson Canadian tucked in his crotch, the windows of his dusty 2008 Subaru Outback rolled down, the early evening air still oppressively hot. He had bought the car new, off the lot—cash—when he had moved to Utah from Flagstaff, Arizona, to begin his search. The odometer now read 109,000 miles. He was on his third set of tires, his fourth windshield and his fifth set of headlights. He'd stopped trying to keep up with the cracks in the fog lights, which were too low to the ground, and the innumerable chips, dents and scratches on the body. The car looked like it had done two tours in Desert Storm, complete with a real bullet hole in the rear hatch from when he'd strayed too far onto private property.

In Canada, when you wandered too far onto private land, he mused, they took you in and fed you and then showed you where you had taken a wrong turn. In Utah, they shot at you. It was one of a thousand things he had resigned himself to never fully understanding, despite these dozen years living south of the border.

Silas pulled off his sweat-stained hat and put it on the passenger seat next to him. He ran his fingers through his gritty, gray hair. It stood on end with the dirt and grime. He scratched his beard.

Business was always slow in Moab in the middle of the summer. Most people were smart enough to stay out of the desert during the inferno of the season. Silas had taken all of this week off from his sporadic, irregular schedule at his bookstore to devote himself to this futile search. He had scarcely been home. For three nights he'd slept in the back of the car far out on Bureau of Land Management land. Every single day of the last seven he'd paced a transect covering some anonymous section of the region. His body felt worse for wear. Seven days of hiking across the tableland through temperatures that topped 115 degrees. Three times he'd been caught by torrential thunderstorms that pounded the parched earth with rain, forcing him to find refuge, but leaving the earth as dry as it had been.

He drove with one hand on the wheel, the other bringing the can of beer up to his eager lips. Hard to find a decent canned beer in Utah. In the grocery stores it was all Budweiser and Coors, and to add insult to injury, 3.2 per cent, for which no redemption would ever be possible. He turned to his native Molson's—now owned by Coors anyway—for the solace of the familiar.

Soon Silas descended off the plateau and into Nine Mile Canyon. He flipped his second empty beer can onto the floor behind his seat, buckled up his seat belt and turned onto the highway.

Within range of Moab, he checked his cell phone for messages. Few people had his number. His two grown sons never called. Robbie, twenty-four, and Jamie, nineteen, both lived in Vancouver, British Columbia, close to their mother, his second wife. The only other people who had his number were Grand County Sheriff Dexter Willis and the FBI Assistant Special Agent from Monticello, Dwight Taylor. They never called either. He flipped the cell phone shut and put it back in his pack.

Before he could retreat to his private sanctuary near the top of the Castle Valley, Silas would have to brave the not-so-private world of Moab. A week away from the Red Rock Canyon bookstore and the town of Moab meant his supplies were low and his mail was piling up.

Tucked between canyon walls and situated near the banks and slew of the Colorado River, Moab had first been settled by white people in 1855 when the Elk Mountain Mission of the Church of Jesus Christ of Latter-Day Saints built a fort in Spanish Valley. They forged a tenuous peace with the Utes and Navajo Indians who had been traveling to this location for thousands of years. When that peace broke down, and several Mormon settlers were killed, Spanish Valley was abandoned until the 1880s, when ranchers returned. In 1884 the settlement was named Moab, a biblical reference to a dry, mountainous area east of the Dead Sea and southeast of Jerusalem. By 1920 the area was synonymous with the uranium industry, and by 1955 it was the uranium capital of the world.

That boom was short lived, and as the Cold War cooled, so did the demand for uranium. By the mid 1960s, Moab's mines had laid off hundreds. It would be two decades before a fascination with a different kind of rock—slickrock, and the national parks and recreation areas that surrounded the town—would supplant uranium's dominance.

He piloted the Outback down the broad Main Street, its art shops and bars flooding light onto the widened thoroughfare, and then turned up Center and down South 400 Street. Silas's Red Rock Canyon Books was not Moab's premier bookshop. That distinction belonged to Back of Beyond Books, which had graced the town's busy Main Street for more than twenty years.

Silas parked his car in front of his shop on the nearly deserted street. The narrow adobe building was tucked between two shotgun houses that squatted on the double-wide lot. Next to one of the houses spread an ancient and enormous cottonwood tree, its stalwart arms reaching across all three buildings. At the front door he swept up the pile of flyers and newspapers that had accumulated there. He checked for spiders or scorpions inside the ceramic pot that doubled as a mailbox and grabbed the handful of bills and junk mail. Everything was coated with a fine red dust. He balanced all of this under one arm while he unlocked the glass-fronted door with the other.

The sign on the door read, "Red Rock Canyon Books. Open when I'm here. Closed when I'm not."

Once inside, he found the switch and flipped on the bank of lights that ran down the center of the narrow building. The room was oppressively hot. Silas flicked on the wall-mounted air conditioner as he made his way to the back of the shop. The two long, low outside walls were lined with bookshelves weighed down with thousands of titles. Pot lights created pools of illumination on the narrow, red carpet that ran the length of the store. The ceiling boasted hundred-year-old pine joists, the thatched adobe ceiling visible between them. At the back of the store was a small, ornate wooden desk with a computer on it that doubled as the sales counter, in case someone bought a book.

Silas threw the flyers in the trash and put the papers down on the desk, amid piles of other paperwork. He sat down heavily in his leather office chair—liberated from his final teaching post at Northern Arizona University—and turned on his computer. While the machine grumbled to life, he scanned the area newspapers' headlines, including the *Salt Lake City Tribune*, for relevant stories concerning a mysterious discovery, a crank call to the police about something—anything—turning up where it shouldn't. There was nothing about a body.

He checked his email, deleting almost everything without reading it. There seemed to be no trace whatsoever.

Feeling suddenly weary beyond words, Silas turned off the computer, switched off the air conditioner and the lights and left the store in darkness. He made his way to the City Market for a stack of frozen dinners, then to the state liquor store for a case of Molson Canadian. He left Moab via Highway 191 north. Thirty minutes and he'd be home.

For a moment Silas slipped into a familiar wistful reverie: He was driving up the narrow, looping road that led from Flagstaff, Arizona, to his home in the woods below the San Francisco Peaks. The sun was setting and the forest was full of long shadows; the vanilla scent of the pines was intoxicating, invigorating. As warm as the days of the autumn semester could be, it was always cool in the evening deep in the woods along the base of Humphrey's Peak. Soon he'd be home. They might sit on the wide porch a while, sipping gin and tonics; maybe he'd retreat to his library, as he often did, to review notes for the next day's lecture.

His wife, however, did not await him at his new home in the Castle Valley. It had been three and a half years since Silas had seen Penelope. It had been three and a half years since she had gone for a hike, somewhere within a day's drive of Moab, never to return.

Lost in his dream, Silas took the turnoff to his small ranch house too fast. He kicked a spray of gravel and sand into the defenseless weeds and cactus before driving the track to a single-story, wood frame house that sat pressed against the fifteen-hundred-foot sheer wall of Porcupine Rim. His lights swept across the front of the house as he came to a stop, a cloud of dust swirling up and then settling in the dense evening air. He turned the engine off and sat for a moment, feeling tired and thirsty and numb.

Hunger soon won out over fatigue, and he stepped from the car, carrying as much of his gear as he could to the front door. The house was hot and airless. He went first to the kitchen and opened the fridge to let its cool air spill out. He took the last cold can of beer from the fridge and opened it. Without stopping for a breath, he downed half of it, then put the new case in the nearly empty icebox. He tucked the dozen frozen dinners, save one, into the freezer, and popped the remaining meal into the microwave. The four water bottles from his dusty day pack he rinsed and refilled, then placed in the freezer next to the dinners.

Silas closed the fridge door, went into the living room and turned on the central air conditioner. He carried the rest of the gear to the second bedroom, which he had turned into a gear room, and plugged in his GPS. Next he went to his bedroom. A small chest of drawers sat against one wall next to the open closet. Beside the bed stood a nightstand with a lamp, a clock radio, and a single framed picture, and on the walls hung half a dozen large-scale road maps of the region.

At the back of the house, next to the bathroom, was the utility room, with a back door that led to a picnic table and hammock beneath a thatched pergola. With the lights off, he stripped naked next to the washing machine and put his sweat-stained, dusty clothing directly into the wash. He padded to the bathroom and took a cold shower.

By the time Silas was finished, dressed, and had dinner ready, the house had begun to cool. He sat in the darkness at a small, square table at the center of the room and looked out the floor-to-ceiling windows at the world beyond. His view was dominated by the conical form of Round Mountain, and beyond that the steep precipice of the Adobe Mesa. In the faint light cast by the stars he could just make out the mesa's edge, its forested crown looking like the bristles on a wire brush.

He ate half of the cardboard meal and finished the beer and sat back in his chair and regarded the darkness. There was one more task to complete and then he could fall into bed, perchance to sleep.

He turned on the lights in the living room. The walls were filled from floor to ceiling with a series of topographic maps. The 7.5 minute quad-rangles were arranged end to end: the entirety of the Canyonlands and Arches National Parks; the Manti-La Sal National Forest, stretching south to Natural Bridges National Monument; and farther south still through the Vermilion Cliffs and the Grand Canyon. Then west to Glen Canyon,

Dark Canyon, and Paria Canyon; the Arizona Strip; and then, on another wall, the vast expanse of the Kaiparowits Plateau and the Grand Staircase-Escalante National Monument. On a third wall were trail maps of various national monuments, state parks and national forests scattered across the American Southwest.

Silas moved to the sheet that showed the vast tableland called the Island in the Sky, spread out over several maps pinned next to one another. He took a colored pencil from a box on the floor and found the location of his day's exploration. Carefully he hatched in the five-mile-long and half-mile-wide section of terrain he had traversed. He indicated on the map, with a black pencil, the narrow defile he had explored with a dashed line. He stepped back and regarded his progress.

Much of the Island in the Sky area had now been hatched to indicate he had searched the area once. Other sections, more easily accessible, had been shaded in, indicating a second exploration. Large areas of the vast region along the Green River and down through the more remote sections of the Needles district and the Maze still required examination. He looked up and to the right, where he had indicated that most of Arches National Park had been searched, as had much of the La Sal Mountains. Looking around the room he could plainly see that despite his tiresome tromping of three years, so much country remained to be searched. At his current pace he knew it would be the work of a lifetime. He put the pencils back in their box and turned out the lights.

In the bathroom, Silas regarded himself in the mirror. Disoriented, he retreated to the bedroom, where the bed was the only piece of furniture he had kept from Flagstaff. He reached to turn out the bedside light, letting his fingers trail over the framed picture that rested there.

She smiled back at him, as she always did in his memories, her midnight hair pooled like the waves on a river where they break over stones just below the surface; at once soft yet strong. His fingers traced the line of her cheek and then trailed down her mouth and chin. A tear ran from his bloodshot eyes and he brushed it away. He turned out the light, and into the emptiness of the night whispered the first words he had said all day: "I miss you."

3

THEY SAT TOGETHER AT THE dining room table. The room was illuminated by two candles flickering in their brass holders. Silas held her hand. Outside, in the dark woods that ringed the San Francisco Peaks, the snow lay deep and cool. It felt good to be cool again.

Dinner had been cleared away and they sat facing one another across the end of the long antique table she had inherited from her Mexican grandmother. He topped up her wine, then they raised glasses and drank. She smiled at him, the same smile he had first fallen in love with more than a decade ago when he was a visiting professor from the University of British Columbia. She had been an associate in the Department of English at NAU. They had different tastes: he chose Wallace Stegner, Bernard DeVoto; she liked Edward Abbey and Cormac McCarthy. They had argued long into the night. It had been like that, in the beginning; he was drawn to her youthful vitality and she to his experience.

In that candlelit room the passion was still there.

He felt her hand drawing back and felt the hot flush that always accompanied that retreat. Not this time. Not this time. *Please don't go*, he thought, holding her large brown eyes. "There is water in Sleepy Hollow, Si," she said, calling him by his nickname, her fingers tightening around his hand.

I don't understand.

"That's where you'll find what you need." Her hand slipped away. He stood up, the table rocking, the candles flickering, sending shadows swooning across the blackness of the room. *Please wait. I don't know what you mean.*

He made his way from the dining room into the study with its wood-paneled walls and tall bookshelves crammed with tomes. He found what he was looking for, always seemed to be searching for, and rushed back, the book in hand, flipping through the worn, dust-stained pages. But she was gone.

"Penny!" He turned in a circle. He felt the cool wind sweep through the room and the candles blew out, casting the house into blackness. "Penny!" He ran for the door, dropping the book. The front door was open, the winter chill sweeping down the hall, snow and leaves on the floor.

He stepped out onto the broad front porch. The moon was up and full and cast its hollow light down on the ponderosa pine forest that ringed the house and crept up the slopes of the peaks above, the winter trees like skeletons in the blue light.

"Penny!" he yelled again, but she was not there. The tracks led off into the woods, and in his stocking feet he ran after her into the black and white landscape, but the tracks led on and on and he could never follow them far enough.

HE WOKE WITH a start. He had dreamt that he was cool once again, but it was the same dream as ever and he was sweating, naked on top of the sheets. He rolled onto his side and looked at the clock. It was almost five. There was no light outside from stars or moon or the first rays of the sun. He tried to remember everything about the dream; the way her hand felt in his, the soft gaze of her beautiful eyes. The sound of her voice. "There is water in Sleepy Hollow," he said aloud. The dream was the same but this time she had spoken to him. He sat up in bed. From a small drawer in the bedside table he found a notebook and pen and jotted those words down. He knew those words.

When the sun finally splashed across the bold face of Dome Plateau and Dry Mesa to the north, he was sitting at the small table, surrounded by his maps. A cold cup of coffee rested in his hand, a pile of books open before him.

Is it possible he could have missed something? He stood, placing the coffee down on the table, and picked up the book again, walking with it to the map of Arches National Park. He traced his finger down the long, winding path of Courthouse Wash. It had been one of the very first places he had searched. That was three and a half years ago. He had looked there even before retiring from NAU, before selling the Flagstaff house and their possessions and moving to the Castle Valley to be closer to her last known location. He had searched again shortly after moving: the cross-hatched length of Courthouse Wash had been colored in.

It was a ten-mile stretch of arboreal canyons that cut across the western edge of Arches National Park and emptied into the Colorado River just outside of Moab. He opened the book to an essay called "Cowboys and Indians" and, with his finger on the map, read, *"There is water in Sleepy Hollow, a big pool under a seep in the canyon wall, fenced off from the cows. We paused for a few minutes to drive and refill our canteens, then moved on. No time for a swim today . . ."*

The book was an original 1968 edition of Edward Abbey's *Desert Solitaire*, chronicling three summers in which the iconic desert writer worked as a park ranger in what was then an off-the-beaten-track national monument attracting a few thousand adventurous tourists each year. The book was a requiem for the desert, for the canyons and for America's national parks. Silas had disdained it throughout his career as a professor of comparative western literature. Now he had much of the book's text memorized.

"'There is water in Sleepy Hollow.'" He tossed the book onto the table and headed for the gear room.

IT WAS 7:00 AM when Silas parked his Outback at the old trailhead for Courthouse Wash. He had bypassed the new park entrance and chosen instead to drop into the canyon as near as he could to where Abbey would have begun in *Desert Solitaire*. That meant driving along the rough track that wove between Seven Mile Canyon and the upper reach of Courthouse Wash to where Arches National Park began and the road ended.

He set off on foot, past an old stock pond, and down into the canyon. Weaving his way down the wash, he pushed through every grove of alder, looking beneath each tangled mass of tamarisk. The branches pulled at this hat and scratched his face so that by mid morning he looked as if he'd been in a fight with a cat.

At midday, the canyon opened up into a broad valley, and he knew, from his previous searches of Courthouse Wash, that he would soon pass under Park Entrance Road. Through waves of undulating heat he made out the distinctive shape of the Tower of Babel, its perpendicular walls rising a thousand feet above the sandy flats below. Another ten minutes of trudging through the dust and the Courthouse Towers hove into view.

There were still several miles of Courthouse Wash, including Sleepy Hollow, yet to search. He passed under the park road's bridge, lingering in the shade, drinking from his second water bottle before plunging back into the liquid heat.

The day grew hotter still, and soon he could see, where the canyon ran east by northeast, the daily collision of clouds forming high over distant plateaus. Sleepy Hollow was just around the corner, so he pressed on, pushing through the suppurating morass of quicksand that pulled at his boots and made him light-headed with expended effort. He reached the opening of the side canyon where Abbey had found water during his cattle drive, and where hikers often found solace from the intense afternoon sun.

Silas headed up the canyon, its walls narrow and in places overhung, the black stains of desert varnish extending from rim to canyon floor. In places the sandy bottom was wet, and as he strode on, pools appeared, stagnant but lovely in the brutal heat. He cupped water with his hands, splashing it against his gritty face. He took off his sagging hat and submerged it in a pool, then put it back on so that the evaporation would cool him. In less than ten minutes it would be dry again.

When he finally reached the spring, he sat down on a slab of sandstone that had peeled off from the canyon rim. The slab was in the shade of the overhang, next to the pool of water that seeped from a fissure in the canyon wall. He drank from his water bottle and lay back on the stone and fell into the chasm of an uneasy sleep. He woke with a start a few minutes later, blinking, trying to remember where he was. He searched the area around the spring. Crawling on hands and knees through the tangles of alder and willow, he found nothing. "There is water in Sleepy Hollow," he said out loud, his voice sounding weak. "But nothing else . . ."

He stood and shouldered his pack and decided to walk out the rest of the narrow gulch to where it boxed up in another mile, just to be certain no stone was left unturned. If Penelope had come this way on her last hike into canyon country before vanishing three and a half years before, she would be plainly visible to all.

Maybe the naysayers were right. Maybe she would never be found out here amid the rocks and canyons. Maybe she had simply disappeared of her own volition and was living now in the south of France, on a desert island, in a cabin somewhere in the Maine woods, perhaps not alone.

Silas shook his head. He may not have been the most attentive husband in the world, but he knew that his wife would never leave him. Not for another man. Not without telling him why.

Three and a half years of doubt swelled in him as thunderheads roiled over the Windows section of Arches National Park.

As he moved farther up the canyon, away from the spring, the quiet in the canyon grew deeper. He walked through a world reduced to the barest of elements: sun, sand, slickrock, and silence.

Distracted and weary, Silas didn't notice the earth moving beneath his feet until he heard the deep growl from ahead in the canyon. He stopped. He squatted down and put his hand on the canyon floor, then on the sandstone wall next to him.

"Fucker," he cursed.

He turned and began to run down the canyon, shedding his pack. Drained as he was, he ran for his life, the sound in the canyon growing with intensity. In a short moment the ground beneath him started to quiver, the sand became saturated and he was suddenly splashing through ankle-deep water. He knew that if he made the mouth of the Hollow where it met Courthouse Wash he would be okay. He risked a glace back over his shoulder. That was a mistake.

The torrent of water raging down the canyon was half as tall as he was, and surged up the ruddy wall in a thick, gelatinous meniscus, heaving from one side of the chasm to the other as it rounded each corner. A short, intense thunderstorm in the Windows area of the park had dumped a month's worth of rain inside of ten minutes, and it was all racing down Sleepy Hollow, with Silas between it and the Colorado River. He turned again and ran hard, but before he reached the spring he was overtaken by the thick slurry of the flood and swept away.

IT WAS EVENING when Silas awoke. He knew he should be dead. He could see stars, and realized he was lying on his back. He tried to move but could not. His immediate thought was that his back must be broken. He tried his arms and found that the left arm could move and he reached across his body. He was covered in a thick, soupy muck, buried except for his left arm and face. He clawed at the stuff, trying to push his arms and legs free. In a moment, he had pulled himself from the mud and lay down on his face, vomiting. He pushed himself to his knees and tried to stand. His left ankle gave away and he fell again into the ooze. Scratching and clawing for purchase in the watery mess, he pulled himself toward the trunk of an uprooted cottonwood log and lay there a moment.

His pack and hat were nowhere to be seen, his shirt was in tatters. He imagined his body to be covered in cuts and bruises and he did what he could to feel for rents in his flesh. Having survived the flood, he didn't want to bleed to death there in the quagmire.

His watch had cracked and stopped. The canyon here was broad and deep, so he guessed that he had been pushed out into Courthouse Wash proper. He studied the stars and guessed it was sometime after midnight. Maybe as early as three o'clock. He felt nauseous again and hunched over, gripping the cottonwood for support.

When the retching passed, he lifted his head and regarded the changed landscape around him. He'd seen flash floods before, and had even survived one previously. Their power still surprised him. The canyon floor had been perceptibly altered. Two or three feet of quicksand, mud, rock and wood now covered Courthouse Wash's floor. He regarded the size of some of the boulders lodged in the muck. Had one of those come in contact with his head on his precarious journey down Sleepy Hollow, he would be dead now. The trees too, and the water itself—the list of things that could have killed him during his flight was long. Branches of cottonwoods stuck out of the muck like daggers. His eyes were drawn to one branch close by, and he struggled in the starlight to see it better. This branch was unusual. He moved as much as his body would permit and blinked the grit from his eyes.

Silas crawled on his belly a foot or two, stopping just a few inches from the protrusion. He realized that he was not looking at the branch of a cottonwood: It was a skeletonized human arm that jutted from beneath the sand.

4

SILAS PEARSON WAS UNCONSCIOUS WHEN they found him. The sun had been up an hour. The young man turned to his female companion and pointed in the direction of the prone figure in the wash. "Is that a . . . person?" he asked, starting to walk faster.

"Carlos, be careful." The young woman was hanging back.

"It's a man," he clarified over his shoulder as he got closer.

The body was on a sandy bottom, lying on its side, legs bent behind him in an awkward contortion. The young man could see the marks Silas's legs had made where he'd crawled along the canyon floor.

"Silvia, I need your help here," Carlos said as he hurried to Silas's side and stooped down. "Hey mister! Hey mister!" He put his hand on Silas's shoulder and rocked him gently. Silvia came up beside him.

"Is he alive?"

"I don't know."

"Check his pulse."

Carlos put his fingers on the man's neck. "I can't tell."

"Hey mister." The young man looked around him, then took off his ball cap and knelt down. He pressed his ear against Silas's back to listen for breath.

"Hey mister." He looked up at Silas's face. "I hear something . . ."

"Is he breathing?"

"Quiet," the young man said, and his companion straightened and crossed her arms, a look of fear on her face.

"He's alive, I can hear his breath. Help me roll him on his back."

"You sure?"

They rolled him on his back and Carlos cleared the man's mouth of sand. Silas choked and spit and his eyes blinked open, encrusted with sand and tears. To the two young people, he looked like Tom Hanks's stunt double in *Castaway*, his clothing was so tattered.

"You're going to be okay," said Carlos. "You're okay."

"She's dead." Silas whispered so softly that Carlos had to lean in to hear him better. "She's dead," he said, more audibly.

"Who is?"

"Back by Sleepy Hollow. Under a cottonwood. She's dead." Silas closed his eyes. Carlos took out his water bottle and pressed it into Silas's hand. Then he looked up at his companion.

"Silvia, go back to the road and get help."

"What are you going to do?"

"Sleepy Hollow is half a mile from here. He's fine. Just banged up. I'm going to have a look."

WITHIN AN HOUR there were two park rangers on the scene. Silvia led them to where Silas lay, and Carlos, his face ashen, took them to where the skeletonized arm protruded from the mud beneath the cottonwood tree. There were the usual questions about disturbing the site of the body, to which Carlos simply answered, "We didn't touch a thing."

Silas refused to be evacuated by the seasonal park rangers, neither of whom he'd met. He wanted to be there when the skeleton was exhumed. "It's just a sprained ankle," he told them, feeling better after drinking some of their Gatorade and sucking on a few energy gels. "A few bruises. It can wait." He asked for Grand County Sheriff Dexter Willis and was assured he was on his way.

Another hour and the sheriff arrived, along with his chief deputy and two others. Deputy Sheriff Derek Penshaw from San Juan County was acting on behalf of the Medical Examiner for the State of Utah, and Stan Baton was the chief ranger for Arches and Canyonlands National Park.

"Silas, you're looking well," said Willis.

"Hi Dexter," acknowledged Silas, leaning against a boulder in the wash while one of the rangers put a splint on his ankle.

"You're going to need to go to the hospital, Silas."

"It can wait."

"You're going to need X-rays." The sheriff pointed to Silas's ribs through the torn shirt. The left side was black and blue.

"I found her."

"We'll see, Silas. We'll see. Tell me what happened." Willis squatted on his boots in the sand.

Silas told him everything except the dream. Willis was silent throughout the telling. The park ranger finished his work on the ankle and then handed Silas a cold pack to hold against his side.

"Can you walk?" Willis asked.

"Maybe."

"Help me here, Stan," Willis said to the chief ranger, and they helped Silas to his feet. With one on either side of him they made their way down the now crowded wash.

DWIGHT TAYLOR WAS at the beginning of what promised to be a very successful career. He was thirty-four years old and was already Assistant Special Agent in Charge for the FBI field office in Monticello, Utah. He was an ambitious yet practical man. At the age of eighteen he'd enlisted in the Navy and had trained as a Seal, serving mostly in the Gulf. Twelve years later, Taylor had accepted an honorable discharge from the Navy to study criminology, and to begin work with the FBI's agent training program in Quantico, Virginia. Born in Harlem, New York, Taylor was beguiled by the desert. He might have been more comfortable with a posting to Los Angeles or Chicago or New Orleans where he wouldn't be the only six-foot-four black man, but he would never consider complaining about his station. He was a career agent now, and would serve where he was assigned.

Taylor was driving from Monticello to Moab at seven-thirty in the morning on Tuesday, August 17, to respond to a call from the Park Service that a body had been found in Arches National Park. It was likely, in fact probable, that the body was that of a hiker whose disappearance had never been reported for a variety of reasons. The body was found on federal land, in the national park, and therefore posed complicated jurisdictional questions. In any other state, the FBI would have had exclusive or at least concurrent jurisdiction. But this was Utah. Here the FBI had to vie for jurisdiction with state and local law enforcement everywhere except on Indian reservations and military bases. Silas Pearson had discovered the body and that made the situation more interesting, and gave the FBI clear reason to assert its authority.

Riding with Taylor was Special Agent Eugene Nielsen. A Utah native, Nielsen had served most of his thirty-year career in the Monticello Field Office, so he knew the canyon area well and he had a good relationship with local law enforcement. Behind them in a second vehicle was the Monticello Evidence Response Team: Agents Janet Unger and John Huston. Together they constituted the Critical Incident Response Team for the region.

"Want me to put in a call to make sure there's a chopper on the deck in Salt Lake?" asked Nielsen.

"May as well," said Taylor.

Nielsen opened his cell phone and placed the call. They were approaching Moab. Taylor slowed the ubiquitous black SUV as they entered the city limits, his thoughts on what they might find in Courthouse Wash.

Taylor had met Silas Pearson just six months after taking on the Monticello Field Office. It was a missing person's case that spanned state lines, which brought the FBI into the equation. The husband had called almost five days after his wife had left for what was supposed to be a three-day backpacking trip into an undisclosed location within a day's drive of Moab. That meant a vast swath of territory covering all of the Navajo Nation, southwestern Colorado, much of the canyons of northern New Mexico and northern Arizona—including the Grand Canyon—and all of southern Utah. It had reportedly taken a call from Penelope de Silva's hosts in Moab for Pearson to realize that his wife was missing in the first place.

Pearson had behaved as you might expect after he reported his wife missing. He had driven through the night from his home in Flagstaff to Moab, where he had been deluged by local and federal law enforcement agencies. When, a few months later, Pearson relocated to Utah and made the unusual move of opening a business in Moab, Taylor grew increasingly interested in the husband's role in the disappearance of his wife. More than three years had passed, and Taylor knew that Silas Pearson spent most of his time prowling the canyons rather than selling books. The agent was curious as to how this discovery in Courthouse Wash would play on Silas Pearson's already addled disposition.

The pair of SUVs sped out of Moab and soon made the turn into Arches National Park, bypassing the entrance gate and speeding up the steep switchbacks of the entrance road. The early morning light caught in the ramparts and domes near Park Avenue, and Taylor slipped on a pair of sunglasses.

There were half a dozen police and park ranger vehicles pulled up along the shoulder of the road where it spanned Courthouse Wash. A uniformed ranger waved the vehicles to a halt as they approached and pointed to a spot where they could park. A Grand County sheriff's deputy stood waiting for them. All four agents assembled there, the two Evidence Response Team members wearing backpacks and carrying suitcase-sized Pelican cases.

The ranger pointed them in the obvious direction, and the sheriff's deputy led the way. Taylor walked silently with the deputy. They arrived in time to see Grand County Sheriff Dexter Willis and Chief Park Ranger Baton hefting Silas Pearson to his feet and setting off down the wash. Taylor quickened his pace, sweat forming on his broad brow, and reached the trio a few hundred feet down the canyon. "Sheriff Willis," Taylor called.

The trio stopped and all three men looked back over their shoulders. "Looks like we'll be turning you over to the feds," Willis said to Pearson, only half joking.

THE HALF-MILE WALK down Courthouse Wash was a solemn, painful trip. Silas, assisted by Willis and Baton, limped his way forward. He had no memory of crawling from the confluence of the wash with Sleepy Hollow the night before, nor could he remember passing out again in the darkness of the canyon, to be awakened by the anxious young couple a few hours earlier.

What he could not forget was what he had found. He was certain it was her.

It took more than half an hour to travel the distance he might walk in ten minutes on a healthy foot, but when the morass of the flood came into view, they all stopped. "Jesus, Silas, you're a goddamned lucky fellow. You could have been killed," said the chief ranger. "You were in that?"

"Yeah. I guess I rode it for a mile or more."

"Guess?" asked the sheriff.

"Don't remember. Think I hit my head."

"Let's have a look at what you've found, shall we, Mr. Pearson?" asked Taylor.

"There." Silas pointed to the earthbound cottonwood. The Sheriff's Department had partitioned off the core crime scene area with yellow tape, strung between a patch of willows and some rabbit brush.

Agent Taylor stepped forward. "You say the flood came down this way?" Behind him agents Unger and Huston were beginning their preliminary walk-around of the scene.

"That's right."

"How far up were you?"

"Pretty much at the top. There's a box a ways up, just past a spring that is tucked in along the canyon wall."

Taylor pushed his hands into his pockets and looked around him, taking note of the sheer cliffs of Courthouse Wash. On the walk down the wash he and Sheriff Willis had agreed that the FBI Evidence Response Team would provide support for the recovery of the body.

"Okay, Mr. Pearson," Taylor said, looking Silas in the eye. "Let's see the body."

Silas pointed toward the log. "She's over there." Taylor turned and motioned for the two members of the team to begin. They stepped past the assemblage of men and walked toward the log.

Unger slipped off her pack and opened the top and pulled out a hardshell black case. She took out a small handheld digital video recorder and turned it on. Beside her Huston removed a camera and began to take photos of the mouth of the wash and the area surrounding the log. When he was done, Huston looped the camera over his shoulder and took out a sketch pad and made a drawing of the area. "We're going to want to extend the crime scene perimeter back at least another hundred yards up Courthouse," he said. "With the flood moving everything around, we don't know what's evidence and what isn't."

Meanwhile, Unger focused her video camera on her companion, who spoke into the lens: "August seventeenth, Special Agent John Huston, location Courthouse Wash, Arches National Park . . ." He looked at this watch. "9:42 AM. Present are . . ." When he had finished the introduction to the video, he said, "Okay, let's go."

He and his companion approached the log, recording their short walk. "Mr. Pearson," said the first agent, "reports having dragged himself from this scene after sustaining injuries during the flood." Silas watched as they slowly approached the skeletonized arm.

The lead agent sunk up to his shins in the mud and quicksand. "Goddamn it."

"What's the matter, Agent Huston, get some mud on your shoes?" asked Taylor.

"Very funny." Huston turned to look at Taylor, then continued to record his observations. "From where I'm standing, I can see depressions in the mud that lead to and are adjacent to the protruding radius and ulna. There appears to be no carpus present." He took two more steps toward the log, the thick, heavy mud sucking at his feet. "Janet, see if you can get around behind the log, please." Unger, still filming, side stepped the worst of the mud and circled around to get a better view of the arm. Huston bent down to get a better look.

"Definitely human," he noted. "Agent Taylor, I'm going to remove some of the top layer of recently deposited mud so see if we're dealing with full or partial skeletal remains." As Unger continued to film, Huston took from his pack a small trowel and began to remove, half an inch at a time, the uppermost layer of recently deposited red earth.

Penshaw stepped forward, too, photographing the scene for the Medical Examiner's office. "I'm not seeing the signs of any insects." Penshaw bent a little so his face was closer to the exposed arm. "Nor do I smell any decomposition."

Silas felt a wave of nausea starting to build in his stomach. His whole body felt as if it were shaking. After all this time, here he was, watching the arm of his wife being meticulously unearthed by these strangers. He turned his head away and felt his legs go out beneath him.

"Whoa." Willis reached for Silas as he started to sink to the ground. "Grab him there, Stan. Let's sit him down." The sheriff nodded toward a boulder. "There, come on, Silas, let's get you sitting down. Stan, you got any more of those energy gels in that pack of yours?"

Silas's head was swooning. How ironic, he thought, refocusing his eyes, that Penelope should be unearthed with this cadre of strangers standing around, all of their clinical eyes watching.

"We've got the humeral trochlea," said Huston.

"That's the elbow," said Willis. Silas nodded, drinking more Gatorade.

"We've got the humerus," said Huston, sitting back and wiping a thick layer of sweat from his forehead. He looked at Unger. "We've got most of the arm, but it appears to be extending straight down. That could mean the rest of the body is buried under a few feet of this sand and possibly this cottonwood. We're going to need to more than my kid's trowel to unearth this one." He turned and looked at Agent Nielsen. "Special Agent, we need to bring in an excavation team. We'll want Agent Rain to come down for this."

Silas had managed to follow the proceedings up to this point. With the agents' shift in focus—he had been hoping for quick confirmation—he finally let go and felt himself slip into the blackness of unconsciousness.

5

SILAS BLINKED AND TRIED TO force his eyes open. His eyelids felt like sandpaper. The room was dark, with only a thin thread of light coming through the curtains. He could make out a shape standing by the window, arms crossed.

"Where am I?" he asked. He could smell a strong floral scent intermingling with something antiseptic.

"Agent Taylor," he heard a male voice say, "he's awake. You're at Moab Regional Hospital."

"Who . . ."

"It's Special Agent Nielsen, Mr. Pearson."

"Penelope?" Silas blinked again and the room started to shift into focus.

"Let me get the Assistant Special Agent in Charge," said Nielsen as he stepped away from the window and went to the door. He swung his body out, holding onto the frame, and Silas heard him say, "Mr. Pearson is awake, Dwight."

A moment later, Taylor entered the room, with Nielsen close on his heels. A nurse followed them in. The two FBI men stood by the window while she checked his vitals, made notes on a tablet computer, and then asked about his eyes.

"Hurt like hell," he said. She administered some drops and the pain eased. "Thank you." He closed his eyes, savoring the relief.

"I'll be back to check on you in a few minutes," she said, patting his hand.

Taylor stepped forward. "How you feeling, Mr. Pearson?"

"I'm alright. Is it Penelope?" he asked, his voice rough.

"It's too early to tell, Mr. Pearson. We have a forensic anthropology team on site now. They've been on the ground for maybe . . ." Taylor checked his watch. "Two hours now."

"What time is it?"

"It's 7:00 PM."

"Have you exhumed the skeleton?"

"Our team is in the process of doing that right now."

"Is it all in one piece?"

"We're not able to say."

Silas swallowed and felt the bitter coarseness in this throat. He opened his eyes and looked around for a glass of water. There was a pitcher on the small wheeled bedside stand and he reached for it, but his right arm had an intravenous tube connected to it. Taylor stepped forward and handed him a cup. Silas drank from the articulated straw. The water tasted better than anything he had ever tasted in his life. When Silas was done Taylor put the cup back on the table.

"What do you mean, you're not able to say?" Silas asked when he had swallowed again.

"Let's go over a few of the details of how you found this body, Mr. Pearson," said Taylor.

"I told you everything when we were in Courthouse Wash," Silas said, the annoyance in his voice obvious.

"Let's go over it again."

Silas exhaled loudly. "There's nothing more to tell. I was looking for Penny. I wanted to search the upper part of Sleepy Hollow. I hadn't been there in three years. I wasn't paying attention to the weather. There was a storm over the Windows section of the park and I got caught in the flash flood. I must have hit my head, maybe on that big cottonwood log." Silas reached up and felt the bandage that was coiled like a white snake around his head.

"When you came to, what did you see?"

"I've told you all this. I saw what I thought was a branch of a cottonwood sticking out of the mud. But it wasn't. It was bones. Looked like an arm to me."

"Did you disturb it?"

"I didn't touch it."

"How was it that you happened to be in Courthouse Wash when a flash flood uncovered these remains, Mr. Pearson?"

Silas looked from Taylor to Nielsen. He was dumbfounded. "You think I could predict a flash flood, Agent Taylor?"

"It seems very . . . interesting that you would happen to be in that location when the remains were unearthed."

Silas shook his head. It ached. He reached up and touched the bandages again, his eyes pressed shut. "Mr. Taylor, I don't know what they teach you in Quantico, but maybe your colleague could educate you on the random nature of flash floods in the canyon country in the summer."

"How long have you been looking for your wife, Mr. Pearson?"

"Since she went missing. Three years, five months, six days . . ."

"Since five days *after* she went missing," interrupted Taylor.

"She was backpacking. It wasn't unusual for Penelope to spend a few extra days on the trail," said Silas. His voice betrayed the defensiveness that haunted him.

"Mr. Pearson," said Taylor, "why was your wife backpacking alone?"

"We've been through this a hundred times," Silas replied wearily.

"Let's do it again."

"She was a very experienced backpacker. She didn't always go alone, but she liked being in the desert and the canyons that way. She sort of scorned other people when she was in the backcountry."

"You never went with her?"

"Once or twice. But it wasn't my thing."

"But now it is?"

"Now it's different. I'm not out to appreciate nature. I've been trying to find my wife."

"You've told us you think she was looking for something when she was hiking. Do you have any idea what that might be?"

"I have no idea, Agent Taylor. I've told you before. Penelope often went hiking in places that were threatened with some kind of development: mining, logging, a hydro development. She would document what she found and use it to fight whatever threat there was."

"But you don't know what your wife was looking for when she went missing?" Silas shook his head. Taylor continued, "So here we are, the middle of August, and you just happen to be hiking in a canyon where a body has been buried and somehow, miraculously, there is a flood that churns up enough of the canyon floor to expose it?"

Silas looked from one agent to the next. "Agent Taylor, am I a suspect in some sort of crime?"

"So far there is no evidence of a crime."

"You won't tell me if these . . . remains . . . are those of my wife?"

"Not *won't*: can't. We won't know ourselves until our team recovers the body and has time to examine it in detail."

"You know." Silas pushed himself up onto an elbow so he could see Agent Taylor better. "When Penelope disappeared I had to beg local law enforcement to get involved in finding her. People said . . . they said that Penelope had likely just left me. Would turn up in Maine. In France. When *you* got involved—the FBI—the first thing you did was investigate *me*. At some point in all of this, I'd like somebody to take the disappearance of my wife seriously without accusing me of being involved."

Taylor pushed his hands further into his pockets. "When a person is murdered by an intimate, a husband, a boyfriend, a brother, and that person is buried, there is sometimes a deep psychological need for the killer to lead authorities to the body. It brings them closure, even satisfaction."

"They teach you that at bullshit at Quantico?" asked Silas, laying back down and closing his eyes.

"You want us to help you find your wife. For most of the four years I've been in Monticello this file has been open on my desk. Every time you and I talk, Mr. Pearson, I come away feeling that while you say you want us to help you find Ms. de Silva, all you do is throw up roadblocks. Every lead we chase down brings us to a dead-end. Every interview we conduct circles back to where we started from. Every theory of the crime we construct that doesn't sound like something from a movie leaves us with only one conclusion."

"And what is that?"

"One third of all women murdered in the United States are killed by their husbands." A long moment passed and then Taylor spoke again. "Like I said, we don't have an ID on the body in Courthouse Wash."

The nurse came back at that moment and checked Silas's vitals. "Let's let him get some rest," she said.

"Get some sleep," said Taylor, pulling his hands from his pockets and turning to leave.

"It's Penelope," said Silas, his eyes pressed shut, tears forming at their edges. "I don't know why she was there, or what happened to her. She was my wife. I loved her. Maybe I didn't give her everything she needed . . . but I would never have . . ." Silas's voice trailed off.

Taylor suppressed the urge to say "That's what they all say." Instead he said, "We'll call you when we know the ID of the remains." He walked out of the room, Agent Nielsen close behind him. The nurse finished her work, touched Silas's arm gently and left as well, leaving him in the darkness of the private room.

6

SILAS WAS RELEASED FROM MOAB Regional Hospital the following day at noon. The doctor told him that he was in remarkably good shape for a man who had gone through what he had. He stood up from the wheelchair at the door to the hospital, facing the glare of the midday sun with his eyes closed. The temperature hovered around 100 degrees. Using the cane he'd rented from the hospital dispensary, he took a few tentative steps on his sprained ankle, then set off toward 5th Street West.

He guessed the walk would take him twenty minutes, but with his ankle in a tensor bandage and his head still aching from his concussion, it took him nearly an hour to walk to Kane Creek Boulevard and the small two-cabin bed and breakfast that backed up against the sudden cliffs of the Moab Rim. It was where his wife often stayed on her many trips to Moab. He slipped through the gate of the residence and hobbled down the path that led to the rear of the main house.

The central adobe structure was two stories tall with thick roof beams supporting an elegant, traditional design. The exterior was painted a rosy pink, blending at sunrise and sunset with the hue of the salmon-colored cliffs. The neat, rectangular windows were framed with heavy wood, and baskets of flowers hung from the trusses that supported the veranda. The garden path was lined with Parry's agave, fragrant verbena and lush thickets of purple autumn sage. He felt his legs weakening as he made his way down the perfumed walkway.

Behind the main building were two small adobe replicas that served as the guest houses. He reached the door of the first one and bent to retrieve the key he knew was hidden under the stone next to the entrance. He unlocked the door.

It hadn't occurred to him that the room might be rented, and when he saw a suitcase on the bench at the foot of the four poster bed and several sundresses in the open closet, he hesitated. But the space soon compelled him inside, the memory of Penelope drawing him forward like a moth to the flame.

"Hello?" he called out.

There was no reply. The room was empty. He stepped in and closed the door behind him. It was like stepping into a dream.

"WHY DON'T YOU come here more often?" Penelope asked. She was lying on the four-poster bed. The windows were open and a breeze blew through the room, ruffling the gauzy canopy so that it looked like undulating waves on the ocean.

He was lying next to her. He rolled over and put an arm behind his head. "I don't know. It's a long way?"

She laughed. She had the sort of laugh that song birds envied. "It's not that far. Seven hours. Six, the way you drive . . ." She rolled over and put her hand on his naked chest. Her fingers played with the patch of graying hair.

"The university, it's busy. There's this push on for publications . . ." She kissed his face and he stopped.

"I know how busy you are, Silas. I know. Your work is important."

"It's really important that I focus on publishing now."

"I know. All I'm saying is . . . I love it here. And I wish you could come here more often. That's all."

"I'll try," he said, smiling sadly.

HE PRESSED HIS back against the door behind him. That had been more than a year before she vanished. It was the last time he'd been with her in Moab.

Silas went to the bed and sat down, his thoughts far beyond the violation he was committing. The room had been made up that morning and the elegant, patterned bedspread was pulled taught. He fell backwards onto the spread and closed his eyes. It was as if she had just been here. He reached up and pressed his knuckles into his eyes. They still burned from the scouring they had received two days ago in Sleepy

Hollow. Dresses hung in the closet and there was lipstick on the counter by the sink; in the miasma of his daydream it felt as if Penelope would walk through the door any moment. The night before she left on that final hike, she had stayed in this very room—as she had so many nights while visiting Moab. And now, after so long, she had led him to her corpse. He felt tears again; the warmth of relief. He lay down on the bed and fell asleep.

He jolted upright at a knock on the door, his head feeling as if it had been struck. He tried to speak. "Who's in there?" barked a rough voice at the door.

He opened his mouth to reply, but the door flew open and a man with a pistol stood there, backlit by the searing afternoon sun.

"Jesus fucking Christ," the man said, lowering the pistol. "What the fuck are you doing here, Silas?" It was Kenneth James Hollyoak, Silas's only true friend in Grand County.

THEY SAT UNDER a pergola adorned with honeysuckle that scented the air. Silas rested his hand on his cane and with his other, reached for a glass of ice tea. The ice clinked as he raised the glass to his lips. He drank half of it. As he wiped his mouth with the back of his hand, he looked at Ken sitting across from him. His friend was dressed in light cotton pants and a matching shirt that hung open, exposing his bulbous belly and the scar that traced the length of his sternum.

"Trish is in the house, fixing you something to eat," said Ken. Silas silently reached for the glass again. Ken did the same. "We were heading to the hospital, but they said that you had been discharged. We were going to drive you home. What the hell are you doing walking a mile on that goddamned cane, and in this heat?"

"They found her, you know."

"You don't know that, Silas. Jesus Christ. Listen, it's all over the news. I heard it on KZMU this morning. It's even in the Salt Lake papers but you don't know that it's Penny. It could be anybody—"

"It's her. I know it."

"How do you know it?"

Silas regarded the man a moment. "Ken, you're going to think I'm—"

"You're what?" Ken interrupted. "What? Crazy? Jesus Christ, Silas, I *know* you're crazy. You gave up a tenured position at Northern Arizona University so you could open a bookstore four blocks off the beaten path in Moab. That's crazy. You've been walking around in the desert, staring into the sun, willing Penny to materialize from behind a juniper, for how long?"

"Three—"

"Three and a half years." Ken scratched the scar on his chest. "I don't think you're crazy, Silas. I *know* you are."

"I had a dream."

"You and Martin Luther King, Silas."

"No, I had a dream, Ken. She was in it."

Trish emerged from the house. She was twenty years Ken's junior, in her early fifties and beautiful in an understated, eloquent way. She carried a plate of sandwiches and a jug of ice tea on a silver tray that she placed on the table between her husband and Silas. "Would you like anything else, Si?" she asked. Besides Penelope, she was the only person who ever called him that.

"No thanks, Trish, this is fine."

"Sit down, darling," said Ken. "Silas was just about to recite Martin Luther King." She sat down and smiled at him.

"I had a dream," Silas began, reaching for the jug to pour them all ice tea. As he began to speak, his hands started to shake and he stopped pouring. Looking down at the tea, he described the dream.

Trish reached out and put a hand on Silas's. She took the glass from him and put it on the table. "Sleepy Hollow . . . ?"

"Is in Arches. Courthouse Wash. That's why you went there," said Ken.

"Yes. I'd been there twice before. You know my pattern. Every place gets two passes. It was one of the first places I looked."

"Because of Abbey," said Ken.

"Yes, because of Abbey. Every place he wrote about I go out and search. I have no idea what Penny was up to when she went for that hike, so searching Edward Abbey's haunts is the best I can do. She was obsessed with him. I went back to Sleepy Hollow. I thought she was telling me something. Leading me to her. It turns out she was right."

"It was a goddamned dream, Silas. Unconscious mind intruding on the conscious world. Nothing more. Your wife was not trying to lead you to her body—"

"But I found her!" he said, pressing his fists into his legs.

"You found *something*, a body for sure. And nearly got your fool self killed in the process."

"Ken," said Trish, touching Silas's hand again.

"What did the sheriff say?" asked Ken.

"I haven't talked much to him. Taylor showed up from the FBI. They and the sheriff are sharing proprietary jurisdiction, but the feds are playing the state line card."

"Have they told you anything?"

"No. They said that they would contact me when they have an ID on the . . . on the remains."

"Could very well be a hiker gone missing. Could have been from fifty years ago by what the news says."

"Could be. So why the dream?"

"Because you are crazy," said Ken, laughing.

"Ken," said Trish, scowling at him.

"He is!" said Ken, and Trish slapped him on the arm playfully.

"If she wasn't leading me to her own grave, then why lead me there? Why there, and the flood, and the body? It's too much to just be a coincidence."

Trish picked up the tray of sandwiches and passed it to Silas, who took one and passed the tray to Ken. "So," Silas said after a bite, "who's staying in the room?"

"Nobody you know," said Ken, "and you are damned lucky the young lady wasn't in her birthday suit when you let yourself in. I'm going to have to find a better hiding place for that goddammed key, I guess," he said. Crumbs fell onto his bare chest as he bit into his sandwich.

"She's a nice young woman from Boston," said Trish. "You should stay for dinner. I think she'll be back."

"Thanks, Trish, but I don't think so. Not *today*." Silas took two more bites of his sandwich and made an appreciative sound. He asked, "Did Penny ever have a man here with her?"

"Jesus, Silas, not this again."

"Did she?"

"No. For God's sake, no. Penny never had a man here."

"It's just that, you know, people talk."

"Who, Jacob Isaiah?"

"Him and others."

"Jacob Isaiah is a snake. He's the king of snakes. I should take a god-damned shovel and cut off his fucking head," said Ken.

"Ken, darling . . ."

"I know I know," he said, tapping the scar on his chest. "But it just makes me so goddamned angry, people talking like that about Penny, and getting poor Silas here all worked up."

"She loved you, Si," Trish said. "She loved *you*. And she loved the canyons. And she's gone. You're going to have to let go."

"Not yet," said Silas.

Ken laughed and sat up in his chair, "You didn't think it would be as easy as that, did you darling?"

"What do you need, Si?" asked Trish.

"I need a ride. I need to get my car. I want to go home."

"Let's go then."

"YOU WANT ME to come over and stay the night?" asked Ken as they passed the entrance to Arches. "We could have a bachelor party. I might even be convinced to drink one of those Canadian beers you keep in the fridge."

"That's just what I need. Trish pissed at me because you break the rules and drink."

"What she doesn't know . . ."

"Women *always* know," said Silas. "The car's down there," he added, pointing down the dusty road that led to the trailhead where he had left his Outback two days before. Ken steered his Lincoln Navigator down the dirt track. "Looks to be all in one piece," said Silas.

"You call that all in one piece?" asked Ken. "That car looks like it's never seen the inside of a car wash. Why don't you let me buy you a new one?"

"So I could trash it too? Thanks, Ken. Keep your money. I don't need anything fancy."

Ken stopped next to it and they both got out. Stepping from the air-conditioned, cooled-seat luxury of the Navigator to the glaring furnace of the mid-afternoon desert was jarring.

"Nobody should be out on a day like this." Ken put a wide brimmed hat on his head. Silas looked at his Outback.

"Might be a little hot in there."

"Witch's oven," said Ken. "I'll follow you to the turnoff. Then you're on your own."

"You don't need to do that, Ken," said Silas.

"It's not an option," said Ken.

IT WAS LATE in the afternoon when Silas turned off the road and into his driveway. He had driven back from the trailhead with the air conditioner blowing full blast. He turned the car off and retrieved a shopping bag from the back of the car. The half a dozen cans of beer were hot to the touch.

He reached his front door and limped into the empty house. The light through the vaulted front windows in the living room lit up the kitchen. He pushed the door shut with his shoulder, and dropped his gear on the floor. He opened the fridge door to exchange the hot cans with a cold one. He popped the tab and drank the whole can, then reached into the fridge for another.

Can in hand, Silas confronted the maps lining his living room walls. As he stood in front of the map showing Arches National Park, he took a long pull of beer. He reached out and traced with a split fingertip the line of his march down Courthouse Wash. The canyon had been the subject of two previous searches. It was also a busy part of Arches National Park. That her body had gone unseen for more than three years was surprising.

Silas stepped back from the map. He drank the rest of his beer staring at the dizzying scale of his work over the last few years. On the small dining room table, the worn copy of *Desert Solitaire* lay open to the chapter called "Cowboys and Indians." He sat down on one of the wooden chairs and held the book gently in his hands: "*There is water in Sleepy Hollow, a big pool under a seep in the canyon wall, fenced off from the cows. We paused for a few minutes to drink and refill canteens, then moved on. No time for a swim today . . ."*

Silas read the passage three more times and nothing new emerged from the page, except that he, of course, *had* taken a swim on the previous day, though it wasn't the sort that Edward Abbey alluded to. He then read the entire chapter again.

There was nothing new there. Silas put the book down and remembered why he didn't like Edward Abbey: the tendency toward hyperbole. He and Penelope had fought about it often enough. She had loved Edward Abbey, had loved every word he had written. Silas had dismissed her argument as a schoolgirl crush. She had chided him for being jealous of her passion for the man's writing, citing Silas's failure to write anything more than academic texts condemned to mediocre journals.

In the end she had won the argument, taking the last word with her, it seemed, to the grave. It was fitting that the burial place was Courthouse Wash. He threw the book down on the table in despair. Taking his cane, he pushed himself up and went to the kitchen to get another beer—one last cold can behind a jug of pickles and a bottle of ketchup. While he heated a frozen dinner, he clomped down the hall to the utility room where he gingerly stripped naked. Hanging his cane on the bathroom door, he stood in front of the mirror to contemplate the damage done by his wild ride down Sleepy Hollow. There was almost no part of his body that wasn't covered in bruises and cuts. Two of them still had gauze pads taped to them, which he carefully peeled off to reveal two-inch-long abrasions sewn together with black surgical thread. He looked exactly like he felt: as if he'd been through the wringer. He swallowed three ibuprofen tablets with the last of his beer and turned the shower on.

After his shower Silas ate his dinner and then retreated to the hammock under the pergola. He lay down and listened to the end of the day: cars on the road leading further up the valley, poor-wills in the willows, and somewhere, a canyon wren's tremolo tripping down the harmonic scale.

And his Penelope, found at long last, seemingly, inexorably, by her own will. He jolted and twitched toward sleep, the hammock gently swaying, his last thoughts on his long-lost wife.

THE TELEPHONE WOKE him. Silas struggled to free himself from the hammock. Around midnight he had woke, chilled, and found a thin blanket in the house and returned to the cooler out-of-doors. Wrestling to free himself now, he came down hard on his damaged foot and winced. He bent over to find his cane, but the phone stopped ringing. He rubbed his face and stood awkwardly, then made his way into the house. There was a cordless handset in the bedroom and he went to see who might be calling him at 6:00 AM. As he picked it up it rang again.

"This is Pearson," he said. His voice was raw and gravelly.

"Mr. Pearson, this is Agent Taylor. Would you please come to the Grand County Sheriff's Office this morning? As early as you are able?"

"Is this about my wife? Have you identified the . . . have you identified her?"

"It *is* about the body found in Courthouse Wash. I need you to come into the Sheriff's Office. You know where it is?"

"Yeah, East Center. Can't you tell me what you've found over the phone?"

"Will you be here by 7:00 AM?"

Silas shook his head. "Yes, yes, I will," he said, then hesitated. "Do I need a lawyer, Agent Taylor?"

"That's up to you," said Taylor.

7

IT TOOK SILAS A SURPRISINGLY long time to leave his Castle Valley home to make the drive to Moab. For some inexplicable reason he couldn't decide which shirt to wear. For the longest time he'd dressed in whatever T-shirt fell to hand, but this morning he kept thinking, *What would Penelope want me to wear?* When he was teaching at NAU she would dress him most mornings before he left for class; those mornings that she was away, in canyon country, his students would take note of his shabby attire. It had become a running joke between them.

As he drove down Hal Canyon the Colorado River was visible through the tangles of invasive tamarisk and native willow; it reflected the orange glow of the adjacent cliffs in near mirror-like perfection. It was a good morning, he thought, to put this business to rest. The thought that his manic search might have come to an end gave him some comfort. He almost allowed himself to feel relief.

Almost. Doubts plagued him as he neared the junction with 191 and the turnoff to Moab. If the body had in fact been that of his wife, why hadn't Agent Taylor simply said so? Was there some official Bureau procedure that had to be followed around notification? Maybe he had to be present to receive the news so it could be witnessed. Maybe they would be watching him for his reaction. He wondered if he should call Ken and ask him to join him at the sheriff's office. In his prime, Hollyoak had been a fire-brand defense attorney until a heart attack had sidelined him a decade ago. He decided that if it became necessary, he'd make the call. Silas parked in front of the red brick building housing the County offices and turned the car off, then just sat in it with the door open.

"You coming in, Silas?" a voice said and he looked up. Sheriff Willis was standing in front of him on the sidewalk. Silas realized that the sheriff had probably been waiting for him. He got out of the car and followed the man into the building.

"You like coffee?" asked Willis.

"No thanks," said Silas, his mouth dry. "A glass of water maybe."

"We can do that." They stepped past the reception area and the sheriff used his pass to unlock a door marked "Authorized Personnel Only." Silas had been in this area on several occasions, to file the missing person's report, and later, to be updated from time to time on the search for Penelope. It was unnerving to think that this was where the search would finally come to conclusion.

Silas drank the water Willis handed him and tossed the paper cup in the garbage. Silently, Willis led him through another set of doors and into a conference room full of people. Taylor stepped forward, towering over the rest of the crowd. He extended his hand.

"Thanks for coming in so early," he said. They shook. "You know Special Agent Nielsen and Deputy Derek Penshaw, who is representing the Medical Examiner. And this is Special Agent Janet Unger. She's a member of our Evidence Recovery Team. You might remember her with the video camera. That's John Huston, also with ERT, and Stan Baton, with the Park Service."

"The gang's all here," Silas said dryly.

"This is Dr. Kathleen Rain," continued Taylor, indicating a woman who rose from the conference table, notepad in hand, and came to shake Silas's hand.

"I'm with the FBI's Forensic Anthropology program. We're a new subgroup of the Trace Evidence Unit."

"Silas Pearson. I own a bookstore."

"You found these remains?"

"Yes."

"Okay. Well, the deceased does not match the description we have on file for your wife, Mr. Pearson."

Silas felt his vision grow dim. He looked around and spotted a chair next to the wall, but his legs wouldn't respond. The sheriff moved the chair under him just as he started to sag against the wall. He sat down. Dr. Rain crouched down so that she was at eye level.

"I've only been able to do a preliminary examination here. Thanks to the morgue at Moab Regional, and with the tools I brought with me from Salt Lake City, I've been able to determine a few facts. When the remains are transported back to the Medical Examiner's lab in Salt Lake, we'll undertake a more thorough examination, but here's what I can tell you. The remains you discovered in Arches belong to a woman, but one who is no older than twenty-five. I'd say closer to twenty-two or twenty-three. She was five-foot-four, give or take an inch, and weighed maybe one hundred and ten pounds at time of death."

Silas was focusing on Rain's face. He struggled to hear what she was saying. He blinked several times as she spoke. "How do you—"

"There are some relatively straightforward means for determining these things. First, we were able to exhume nearly a complete skeleton. We're still looking for other bones in Courthouse Wash. There were several smaller bones missing, but all of the larger bones were there. I can take measurements and determine height and approximate weight. We add a few inches to allow for soft-tissue loss. It's not that difficult a calculation.

"As for age, the last bone in the body to stop growing is the collarbone," said Rain, indicating her own. "That usually happens in the late twenties. In the subject you found in Courthouse Wash, there was no indication that this bone had reached maturity. No fusing, no deterioration. There are also several fusion points in the skull," she continued, touching the back of her skull, "where ossification occurs at different times. Finally, dental wear. This young woman had pretty good teeth. Very little wear. It all adds up to someone in her early twenties.

"Sex is easy to determine. Wide hips, an open pelvic bone, for childbirth. So what we have is a woman, say twenty-two to twenty-four years old, to be on the safe side, five-foot-four, and one hundred and ten pounds."

"Penny was—"

"Older, taller, a little heavier. If the remains had been of your wife, we would certainly have seen early signs of calcium deterioration. By age thirty the bones start to lose density. By forty we see notable bone loss."

Silas, who was in his mid fifties, thought of his own bones and the miles he'd put on them over the last few years. He closed his eyes and rubbed his hands across his face.

"There's a little more, if you're willing to hear it. This young woman was murdered. We have conclusive proof. We don't always get it from a set of remains this old, but in this case there is no doubt."

"Mr. Pearson," Agent Taylor interrupted. "You understand, you're being told this in some confidence. We need your help here."

"How can *I* help?" Silas asked, looking away from Dr. Rain to the FBI agent.

"You found the body. I have a couple of questions," said Rain. "When you discovered the remains did you get the impression that they had been there for some time, or that they had been washed down in the flood?"

Silas cleared his throat and looked around the room. "It was hard to tell. I'm not an expert—"

"I just want your impression. It may be important later on," said Rain.

"I got the feeling that the flood uncovered them, that they had been in Courthouse Wash. The force of the flood had unearthed them, maybe from under the cottonwood log."

"That's how I felt when I came on the scene. We have an agent working with the Park Service and the National Meterological Service to determine if there have been any additional floods in the area over the last two years."

"You say two years?" asked Silas.

"Yes, two years. The condition of the remains suggest that this young woman was killed no more than two years ago. The loss of some of the small bones and the generally good condition of the larger bones suggests that time frame. We're obviously checking national missing person files and will be able to check dental records shortly. I believe we'll have a positive ID in another day or two."

Rain continued, "Did you happen to notice anything else that might have been associated with the deceased, Mr. Pearson?"

"It's 'Doctor,' by the way," said Silas, looking down at his hands.

"I'm sorry?"

"It's *Doctor* Pearson. I have a PHD in Comparative English Literature from the University of British Columbia. I was a tenured professor at NAU until Penny disappeared . . ."

"Of course, I'm sorry, Dr. Pearson—anything?"

Silas shook his head. "I didn't see anything at all. No clothing, nothing."

"It's *possible* in two years, especially if the body had been buried near the stream bed, for the clothing to rot away entirely," said Rain, standing up and looking around the room. "Gentlemen, I don't have any further questions at this time for Dr. Pearson."

Silas felt dizzy. He needed to get outside and out of the clinical room with all these faces glaring at him. He stood up and steadied himself with his cane. He turned to make his way to the door.

"Oh, Dr. Pearson," said Rain, pushing her hands into the pockets of her white lab coat.

He turned to regard her. She had an intense, almost troubling gaze. "The deceased was Native American. You can tell by the teeth."

The room was silent a moment. Then the sheriff said, "I'll show you out. We'd like a few more minutes of your time, Silas, but you look like you could use some air."

"Don't be long," said Agent Taylor. "*Doctor* Pearson and I need to have a chat."

8

SILAS DRANK A SECOND CUP of water, and when the sheriff offered him coffee he accepted. Willis brought back three cups, and he and Silas and Agent Taylor sat together in an interview room.

"This is a murder investigation now," Taylor noted. "We have to do this by the book. The Park Service has ceded jurisdiction and this is to be a joint investigation by the Grand County Sheriff's Office and the FBI."

"Do I need a lawyer?" asked Pearson.

"Do you *think* you need one?" asked Taylor.

"You're not a suspect, Silas." Willis earned a sharp look from the FBI man.

"You're not a *prime* suspect, Dr. Pearson," said Taylor. "But surely you must understand that whoever finds the body does make the list of people who need to be interviewed. If you want a lawyer, feel free to call. The sheriff won't mind you using his phone, I'm sure."

"Not at all," said Willis.

"I don't think I need a lawyer." Silas raised the coffee cup to his lips with shaking hands.

"I'm sure this must be hard on you, Dr. Pearson, but we have to ask you some additional questions."

"You think this is hard on me?" Silas looked up.

"I'm sure it must be—"

"You're sure it must be what?" Silas interrupted. "Difficult? I thought I found my wife in Courthouse Wash. I was almost killed, and when I came to I was lying next to bones I believed were my wife's. And you think that was difficult? I went to sleep last night thinking I could stop looking, that there might be some closure. And now, it's what . . ." He looked at his watch. "It's 8:30 in the morning, and you're telling me that the bones I found were from a stranger, and someone who was murdered at that. No, Agent Taylor, that's not difficult at all. But thanks for your concern." Silas put his coffee cup down and crossed his arms in front of him. The sorrow he had felt over the last two days had ebbed and anger had taken its place.

Agent Taylor watched him a moment, his dark eyes inscrutable. "We have a few questions," he said again after a moment. "Do you have any notion of who it was you found in the wash?"

"I have no ungodly idea."

"None whatsoever?"

"None at all. I've been a little preoccupied over the last few years, Agent Taylor, doing for myself what my government could not, which was trying to find my wife."

"In all your efforts, you didn't come across a missing person's report about two years ago that caught your eye?"

"I read half a dozen a day, Agent Taylor. Nothing in this area caught my eye. At least not that I remember."

"When were you in Courthouse Wash last?" asked the sheriff.

"I'd have to check my notes," said Silas.

"Estimate?"

"I'd say late in the fall, over three and a half years ago, then again early the next spring."

"You had already moved here?"

"You have that in your files."

"Would you answer the question?"

"I had just moved from Flag to the Castle Valley when I visited Courthouse Wash the second time. I had bought my place there, had set up my search. The local S&R folks and the Park Service gave me a grid of where they had looked. Courthouse was on that sheet, but I went back to look for myself."

"Did you find anything?"

"I wouldn't be sitting here if I did, would I?"

"That's a no?"

"No, I didn't find anything. The first or the second time around."

"What made you look again two days ago? Why go back if you'd searched it twice already?"

Silas looked down at his cup of coffee. "I had a hunch."

"A hunch?" said Taylor.

"Yes, slang for an intuitive feeling . . ."

"I'm familiar with the word, Doctor, but what I don't get is how a hunch led you into this location at this *time*. I mean, the middle of August seems like a hell of a time to go setting off into a canyon in the middle of Arches."

"When you have nothing else to go on, Agent Taylor, you use what you have. I follow my intuition."

"And your intuition led you to Sleepy Hollow?"

"It did."

"The young people who found you, they said you kept saying that you had found her."

"That's right. I thought I had found Penelope."

"You said *her* but all there was visible of the skeleton were the bones of the arm. How did you know it was a woman?"

Silas looked from Taylor to the sheriff and back. "Are you serious?" Neither man said a thing. "I just told you I believed I'd found my dead wife. I thought the . . . my hunch had been right. I was looking for my wife: *a woman*. What kind of asinine question is that?"

Agent Taylor ignored Silas's protest. "You said there was a flash flood, that you got caught in it. Has this ever happened to you before?"

"Yes, once. In Dark Horse Canyon, but it was minor, a foot or two of water. Nothing like this."

"You're lucky to be alive."

"You're making me feel otherwise."

"What the agent is getting at, Silas, is that surviving that big a flood is, well, rare," said Willis. Silas felt anything but lucky, but he didn't say anything.

"You say you blacked out?" asked the FBI man.

"I did black out. I got hit on the head. I have the lump to prove it," said Silas, pulling aside some of his wiry hair.

"When you came to, you were next to the cottonwood."

"That's right."

"Do you remember it being there when you went up Sleepy Hollow?"

"I'm pretty sure it was. I remember checking it, but it moved in the flood. It was up against the canyon wall when I went in, and when I came to, it was in the middle of Courthouse Wash. It's a big log, and there aren't that many of them just lying around."

"Do you think that the remains you found were under the cottonwood?"

"When I found them they were off to the side. A few feet away."

"What about when the cottonwood was along the canyon wall, as you describe it?"

"I have no way of knowing."

"You don't remember ever having seen anything . . . peculiar there in the past?"

Silas looked at the FBI agent. "I think this conversation is done." He pushed himself up.

"I have a few more questions, Mr. Pearson."

"*Doctor* Pearson, and no, you don't. You're trying to tie me to this somehow, and that's the most insulting thing I think I've ever experienced from the FBI. Let me tell you, having dealt with you and other agents for the last three and a half years, that's saying something."

"We're just trying to eliminate you as a suspect, is all," said the sheriff. "Why don't you sit down and we can finish up."

"Thanks, Dex, but no, I don't think I will. I believed I'd found my wife, and now I have to accept that all I found was some random stranger, and someone who got murdered on top of that. My ankle is killing me, my head is pounding and my ears are ringing. I keep feeling as if I've been put through the tumble cycle in an old-fashioned washing machine. I'm going home. I'm going to sleep and I'm going to try and forget all about what I found in Courthouse Wash. If you want to interview me again, I'll bring a lawyer. Otherwise, I'm washing my hands of this. Good luck, Agent Taylor," Silas said, looking at the man, who was still seated. "I hope you do a better job finding this young lady's killer than you have done finding my wife."

Silas walked to the door and tried to turn the handle but it was locked. He looked at Willis. "Dex, would you open the goddamned door, please?"

Willis walked over and knocked. One of his deputies opened the door. Silas walked past the maze of cubicles that amounted to the Grand County Sheriff's Office and into the growing heat of the day.

9

SILAS SAT IN THE OUTBACK until the heat became oppressive. He decided to go to his Red Rock Canyon bookstore instead of home. He drove through the stifling streets and soon arrived at the store. Inside, he dumped the mail and the newspapers on the desk and sat down at his computer. He wanted to look at the various news sites for anything on Penelope.

A story in the *Salt Lake Tribune* caught his eye: "Body found in Arches NP by hiker." He'd grown so accustomed to scanning for such a story that his eye was naturally attracted to it. But the bones weren't Penelope's and *he* was the "hiker" noted in the story. He scanned the article and felt a wave of relief that he hadn't been named. The story noted that the FBI had been called in and that the circumstances surrounding the death were suspicious, but that a murder investigation hadn't officially begun yet.

Yet. Silas knew that within a matter of hours, or maybe days, the FBI would announce that the young Native American woman had been murdered. He read the rest of the story and considered for a moment how he would feel if it was Penelope's body he was reading about. He felt a strange kinship with whoever had lost this young woman only to have her turn up murdered. When the FBI identified the skeletal remains, they would send someone to find this young woman's husband, or her parents, or maybe her siblings, and inform them of her murder.

Silas sat at his desk and considered the case for a moment. The body had been hidden—likely buried—under the cottonwood, for a long time, Dr. Rain had said. Any trail leading to a killer would have grown cold in the intervening years.

Silas shook his head and continued his online search. There were more stories about the corpse in Courthouse Wash, but nothing else that would lead him to his wife. He shut his computer down. The ring of the telephone at his elbow startled him and he waited for a second ring to compose himself.

"Hello?" he said into the receiver, forgetting to add the name of his shop.

"Silas, that you? It's Ken."

"Hi Ken."

"I've been trying to call you all morning!"

"I think my cell phone is dead. Literally dead. Got a little water and sand in it."

"Of course. Did they ID the . . . the remains?"

"It's not Penny," said Silas. "I was wrong."

"Who is it?"

"They don't know."

"Then how do they know it's not Penny?" Silas explained to Ken what Rain had told him that morning. "What are you going to do?"

"Go home. Get some sleep."

"No, I mean about the remains?"

"What do you mean?"

"*You* found it."

"Ken, this isn't a kid's game. It's not finders keepers. The FBI will handle it."

"Like they handled Penny," said Ken, echoing Silas's own doubt-filled sentiments.

"It's not my problem. I'm going to go home, sleep, rest my ankle, and as soon as I can, I'm going to start looking again."

"Silas, don't you think you found that young woman for a reason?"

"What the hell are you talking about?"

"Your dream."

"You said so yourself, Ken: a product of an over-active imagination. Too much sun. Not enough water. Delusions. There's nothing more to it. So don't go all Sedona on me. I got enough of that when I was at NAU. I don't need it from you."

"Easy, Silas, easy. I'm just saying that you were all convinced that Penny had led you to her . . . to her body yesterday. You had *me* convinced—and I think New-Age hippies should be used for cord wood in the winter!" He laughed at his own joke. "But you had me convinced. And now, you're just going to ignore it."

Silas was shaking his head. "Ken, it was a dream. Nothing more. I dreamt about my wife, because—"

". . . you miss her, amigo. Listen, do you want to come by the place? We'll fix you a big dinner tonight. You can drink that Canadian beer you like. There's nobody in the second cabin. You could stay the night. We'll sit out and howl at the moon. What do you say?"

"I'd like to, Ken, but not tonight, some other time. I need to go home and—"

"And what? Stare at your maps?"

"Maybe that's what I need to do. Right now I just want to sleep. I'll be fine. Kiss Trish for me and tell her some other night."

"¡Hasta luego!" said Ken.

"See you soon," said Silas as he hung up the phone.

HE TOOK THE long way home. He wasn't ready to face the emptiness of his house, but he didn't want company either. Silas drove his Outback south on Highway 191 and took Spanish Valley Road on his way into the La Sal Mountains. He wove along the dirt roads until he'd left the inferno of the canyon country behind and had passed into the cool sub-alpine area. Here and there the tangled forest opened up and sweeping meadows stretched across the rolling earth like a soft green sheet across a lumpy mattress. Cows dotted the hillsides, grazing their way down to the quick.

At Miner's Basin, in a grove of trembling aspen, Silas killed the engine and got out of the car, stretching his back. He took his cane and walked a few yards from the car to stand among the quivering trees.

The La Sal Mountains were omnipresent in the Canyonlands; one of four great laccolithic mountain ranges that ringed the region. From forty miles distant, in Moab, or from a hundred miles away, from Island in the Sky in Canyonlands National Park, their triangular facades appeared dark and barren. But venture up out of the Spanish Valley and up to eleven thousand feet above sea level and you exchanged the oppressive heat of summer for an eternal spring or perpetual autumn.

The temperature was a modest eighty degrees as Silas walked slowly along the cattle-worn path through the aspens. A breeze gently ruffled his hair, and Silas wondered why anybody in their right mind—and here he included himself, first and foremost—would spend a single day in the scorched earth of the canyons during the summer. He walked for half a mile, leaning heavily on the cane for support, until his ankle ached. He sat down on the leaf litter at the edge of a clearing below Mount Waas. He leaned back on the stout trunk of an aspen and closed his eyes.

Penelope had taken him here once, some years ago—five, six? He couldn't recall now. She had brought along a copy of *Desert Solitaire* and read to him the chapter called "Tukuhnikivats, The Island in the Desert" about a hiking trip Abbey had taken in the La Sal Mountains to escape the heat of Arches during one of his seasons in the park. At the time Silas had criticized the writing, saying that anybody who talked about pissing, eating, and drinking as much as Abbey could not be taken seriously as a writer. Upon reflection, Silas now thought it was one of Abbey's finer moments in *Solitaire*, reminiscent of one of his own favorite bits of prose, *The Sound of Mountain Water* by Wallace Stegner. He wished Penelope was with him to hear his confession. He drifted off to sleep listening to the wind's harmony in the branches above.

When he woke it was late in the afternoon, and he was hungry. Silas rose stiffly, his ankle sore and swollen, and limped back to his car. From the trunk he took a bag of granola bars but when he looked at them he felt he would rather wait. He started the motor and began backing down the narrow lane.

With a shock he found himself suddenly hitting the brakes, stalling the engine, to avoid a collision with another vehicle. Not five feet from his rear bumper, partially obscured by a tangle of alder along the side of the track, was a gunmetal-blue Jeep Wrangler. He started the Outback again and revved his engine, but the Jeep didn't move. He turned the ignition off and opened his door.

"Hey there," he called. There was no reply. "Hello?" Nothing. Silas walked to the end of his wagon and looked at the Jeep. There was nobody behind the wheel. He went to the driver's door and looked into the cab. An open can of beer sat in the holder next to the gearstick and there was a six-pack minus two on the passenger-side floor. In the back were several oversized duffle bags and two large water-tight surplus ammo cans, the sort that rafters used to keep their food and belongings dry when running the Colorado River.

"Help you?" came a voice from behind him. Silas turned, his ankle protesting, and saw a man not twenty feet away, partially concealed by the foliage.

"This your Jeep?"

"Yup."

"Mind moving it?"

The man approached. He was short and powerfully built, thick across the shoulders and broad in the arms. He wore a heavy beard and his hair fell in long curls, nearly touching his shoulders in the back. "Don't mind at all. Just had to take a piss."

"What did you do, walk all the way back to Moab to do it?"

The man laughed, showing a set of bright white teeth. Silas guessed that he was thirty at the oldest. "Just went off in the woods. Got distracted by a bird."

"That's what you call it, eh?"

"You Canadian?"

Silas's speech had betrayed him again. "Yes."

"I'm Josh," said the man, thrusting out a heavy hand. Silas regarded it momentarily and then shook it.

"Silas Pearson."

"Good to meet you. Want a beer?"

"I'm actually just heading home."

"Whatcha doing up here?"

"Just getting out of the heat."

"Yeah, I know what you mean, man. Hot as fucking hell down there. Nice to be up in the trees. I got a place up here, just over by Oowah Lake. Don't tell the fucking rangers on me."

"You live up here?"

"Sometimes. In the summer. Winter I head down into the canyons."

"Sounds nice," Silas said. "I won't tell. Do you mind?" he said, pointing to the Jeep.

"Sorry, fuck. Let me move my machine." Josh jumped behind the wheel. Silas noticed a heavy revolver tucked in the waistband of the man's khakis. America, he mused, home of the heavily armed. Josh gunned the engine and deftly navigated the trail in reverse. Silas followed at a more cautious pace. When he reached the T-junction a few hundred yards back, Josh had pulled over and cut his engine.

"Come up for a visit sometime?" he said when Silas leaned out his window.

"How will I find you?"

"I'll find you," Josh said with a wolfish grin.

Silas turned around in the narrow track and drove down the trail. He glanced in his rearview mirror and saw the young man leaning on the front of the Jeep. Silas hoped he wouldn't see him again.

THERE WAS A message on his machine when he arrived home. He dialed the number to play back the message and stood in the dark by the big picture windows, the last light draining from the Adobe Mesa.

"Dr. Pearson, this is Kathleen Rain calling. I wonder if you'd be so good as to give me a call. I'm heading back to Salt Lake in the morning and I have a few questions I'd like to clear up before I go. No lawyer necessary. Okay, give me a call. Here's my cell . . ."

Silas thought he detected a hint of a laugh when she made the crack about the lawyer. Obviously the team had debriefed his interview that morning. He jotted the note on a slip of paper by the fridge and took out a frozen dinner and a can of beer. Back in the living room with the food, he picked up the phone and dialed.

"Rain," she answered on the third ring.

"Not much here in the desert," he said, deadpan.

"Dr. Pearson?"

"Returning your call."

"Thanks. I hope you don't mind. I've got a few questions I could use your help with."

"I don't mind. That's why I called back."

"I know this might sound foolish, but I'm trying to reconstruct the original grave and I wonder if you could help me with something."

"I can try."

"How much water do you think came down Sleepy Hollow when you were caught in the flood?"

He laughed.

"You may think it's a stupid question, but I'm trying to estimate how deeply she was buried, and how far the grave site might have moved."

"I can't see why that makes a difference."

"It might help us estimate how long ago she was buried."

"You mean, if she was buried right after she was killed, or if she was moved there sometime later?"

"Exactly."

"Well, Sleepy Hollow is about thirty or forty feet wide at the most, so you've got to assume a wall of water, what . . . ?" He paused to think.

"One hundred and fifty, maybe sixty, feet square?"

"Sure. Of course. But it wasn't square. It went on for some time. Certainly five or six minutes' worth of water. Can you do that in your head?"

"No, I'm an anthropologist, not a hydrologist. I'll touch base with the USGS. But that helps."

"You said you had a couple of questions."

"Yes. What time of day did this all take place at? The report doesn't list the time of the actual flood."

"I'd say four in the afternoon."

"And you were found at eight or so the next morning?"

"That's right. I came to sometime around three or four that morning and started to, you know, crawl out."

Rain was silent. "Okay. Again, that's helpful."

"Is your boss getting anywhere on this?"

"Who, Taylor?"

"Yeah."

"God, he's not my boss. I report to the head of Trace Evidence back in Virginia. Taylor, is like, three steps down the pecking order from where I sit. I exist outside of the hierarchy for the most part. There are only three forensic anthropologists in the entire FBI, and I'm the first one to work out of a state field office. The others are at Headquarters."

"Lucky you. Salt Lake City."

"I like it there."

"Takes all kinds," said Silas.

"It does."

"Anything else?"

"No. Thanks for calling back. Listen, I'm going to tell you something that maybe I shouldn't. You have a right to know, I think."

"Taylor isn't coming to arrest me, is he? Is this a trap, you keep me on the phone while he breaks down the door?"

"You watch too much TV, Dr. Pearson."

"I don't own one," he said, looking around the austere room. "What do you want to tell me?"

"Kayah Wisechild."

"Who's that?"

"The young woman you found."

Silas was silent. He sat down on one of the chairs at the tiny table at the center of the room.

"Are you there?" she asked.

"I'm here."

"She was twenty-four years old. A graduate of Northern Arizona University with a degree in anthropology. She was from Third Mesa."

"The Hopi Reservation."

"That's right."

"Have next of kin . . . ?"

"Yeah, we reached her mother and father this afternoon. Not married, three siblings, all living on the reservation."

"You do quick work."

"I try. Anyway, I thought you'd like to know."

"Thank you," he said.

"Thanks for your help, Dr. Pearson."

"It's Silas."

"Okay. Silas. It's Katie. And thanks again."

Rain hung up the phone and Silas sat in the dark. He drank his can of Molson's and watched stars pop out of the firmament above the Mesa. She thought Silas would like to know the name of the woman he found and had believed to be his wife. She had a name and a family. But Rain was wrong. He wished she hadn't told him. He wished that he could be left in peace to look for his wife and not be troubled by the murder of a young woman he had never met.

10

ON FRIDAY MORNING SILAS WAS determined to restore some semblance of normalcy to his life. He intended to go into Moab and open the Red Rock Canyon bookstore for a few days, and he wanted to plan another week of searching for his missing wife. His sprained ankle was healing quickly. It might not allow rugged desert hiking, so he thought he would take the last week of August off from the bookstore and search a new section of the canyon country. By nine-thirty he was in Moab, flipping the sign on his storefront to "Open" and settling in behind his desk with a store-bought Americano and a muffin. An email from his oldest son, Robbie, popped up:

> Hi Dad. I saw the headline in the Salt Lake paper. Yes, I am keeping tabs. I guess I would have heard from you if it was Penelope. I just want you to know I'm thinking of you. Things are fine here. Summer has been pretty laid back. I've been working for a security company, mostly doing criminal record checks and background research. I start my master's in the fall at Simon Fraser University in criminology.
>
> Jamie is well. He's "taking a year off" to consider his options. I think he wants to study English but doesn't want to seem like he's following in your footsteps. He'll come around.
>
> Anyway, I just wanted you to know I was thinking about you and hope that the news coming so close to home didn't upset you too much.
>
> —Robbie

Silas sat back. Robbie was keeping tabs on him, or at least on his search for Penelope. That gave Silas some comfort. Neither Robbie nor his younger brother, Jamie, had liked Penelope much. They had only met her twice, and both times the week-long rendezvous near Flagstaff had felt strained. Silas knew that both boys blamed her for the breakup of his marriage to his second wife, their mother. The truth was that their relationship had never really worked. The mechanics of producing offspring was reasonably simple; the means by which you create a life with another person much less so. When he had accepted the teaching position at NAU twelve years ago, he believed that his marriage to the boys' mother was already over. A year into his tenure he met Penelope and officially filed for divorce.

A year later, when Robbie was fourteen, and mature for his age, Silas and Penelope got married. Jamie was just nine, and fragile. He focused his anger on his father's young wife. It made for very uncomfortable gatherings the following two summers. So much so that after the second time they decided not to do it again. Penelope was game, she claimed, but Silas was not. Twice a year he flew solo to Vancouver and took the boys sea kayaking or mountain biking or camping on Vancouver Island, and that was the extent of his parenting. For the last three and a half years, he hadn't even done that. Silas had been distracted.

The bell chimed on his front door. He looked up to see who had gotten lost or was looking for a bathroom. It was Jacob Isaiah. He walked down the long center aisle of books. Isaiah had been a broad-shouldered man in his youth, but age and an angry life had diminished him. He had neatly combed hair that was almost as white as snow, a clean-shaven face, and a wide but malevolent smile that showed off perfect teeth.

"Silas, good morning," he said, extending a huge, twisted hand. Silas half stood and shook it. Jacob Isaiah's physicality radiated from him, and though Silas stood two inches taller than the man, he always felt diminutive in his presence. Isaiah was a powerful force in the community, having been the local real estate developer for nearly forty years. Silas forced a smile and then sat back down, nodding toward the chair used by the occasional customer.

"Have a seat if you like, Jacob."

"Don't mind if I do," said the elderly man.

"Would you care for something to drink? Tea, coffee, a soda?"

"No thank you," said Isaiah. He was still smiling, looking around the store. "How's the book business?"

"Quiet," said Silas.

"You picked the quietest part of town to open shop, you know."

"So you tell me."

Silas could tell there was something on Isaiah's mind, but they would have to chit-chat for a while before he would spit it out. Normally Silas had little patience for that, but today, unable to hike, and disturbed by his discovery in Courthouse Wash, he almost welcomed the distraction.

"Slow part of town. Nobody's ever made a go of this location. You might consider moving to Main Street. Give Back of Beyond a run for their money."

"I'm pretty happy here."

"You're not really in it to sell books, though, are you?"

"I sell the occasional volume."

"It's a pretty eclectic mix you got here. And none of the touristy stuff."

"I cater to a particular crowd."

"True story? These are all your books you brought with you from Flagstaff?" Silas didn't say anything. "It don't matter," Isaiah continued, waving his hand is if shooing a fly.

"What can I do for you, Jacob?" Silas's interest in being distracted had only lasted two minutes. Now he wanted Isaiah to get to the point, and then get out.

"So I hear that *you* found that body, out in Courthouse Wash up in the park."

"Where'd you hear that?" Silas asked. His name hadn't been in the news.

"Oh, word gets around. It's a small town, Moab. Still a small town. Word travels fast, you know. Is it true that you found that woman?"

Silas looked around the store.

"What the hell were you doing out there Silas?"

"Going for a hike."

"I'd have credited you with more brains than that. It was a hundred and ten on Monday, and fixing to thunderstorm. It true you got caught up in a flood?"

"I did."

"Jesus, Silas, you're going to get yourself killed if you keep this up."

"Man's got a right to enjoy the country, doesn't he?"

"Well, sure he does. But you're looking for something, ain't you?"

"That's no secret, Jacob," Silas responded.

"Did you know this girl, the one you found in the wash? They printed her name in the papers this morning."

"Never even heard of her," Silas said.

"Never? She was big news two years ago, Silas. Goodness, you living under a rock?"

"I don't remember her. Did she live in Moab?"

"On and off. She was an archaeologist. Worked with one of them consulting firms that look for bones and bunnies. Local outfit called Dead Horse."

"If my memory is correct, Jacob, they've done plenty of work for you, haven't they?" asked Silas.

"I believe they have. I think we had them in to do some work out near Blanding, or maybe it was over in Cortez. I don't get involved with the details, Silas. I just say, 'Let's get this thing done!' and golly, my boys just get the thing done." He smiled and slapped his knee.

"Must be hard to keep track of all your money, Jacob," said Silas.

"Now don't be like that, Silas. A man's got a right to earn a living."

"No argument from me, Jacob. I just don't like the way you lord it over everybody in this town."

"I don't hear my employees complaining. They seem to like having jobs just fine."

"Did you ever meet her? This girl, Wisechild?" asked Silas.

"I seen her around the office once or twice. Said hello to me with a sweet smile. Nice Indian girl."

Silas felt the bile rise in his throat, but he swallowed it back. "*You* knew this girl?"

"I didn't know her, Silas. I knew who she was. What *were* you doing out there?" asked Isaiah.

"Like I said, I was on a hike."

"You were looking for Penelope, weren't you?"

"Listen, Jacob, I don't have time for this. As you can see, I'm run off my feet here today."

The man's bright smile faded a quick as a wink. "That wife of yours, your Penelope de Silva, you are not going to find her here no matter how long you look."

Silas felt a wash of heat race up his neck and spread across his face.

"She ain't here is what I'm telling you."

"How would you know, Jacob?"

"I know. I know these things. Some people around this town like to talk. Talk, talk, talk. And you know what the talk about your lovely wife was, don't you, son?"

Silas had heard it all before. He didn't say a word.

"Well," said Isaiah, "the talk was that she had herself a boyfriend."

Silas picked up his cane and stood.

"I know that the truth can ouch, son," said Isaiah. "But I'm just trying to keep you from getting yourself killed. And you keep up this nonsense, crawling around all over this goddamned desert, and that's what's going to happen. You are going to end up just like that poor little girl you found down there in the rocks. Dead."

Silas walked to the front of the store. Isaiah remained seated. Silas looked back at him. "We're closed," he said, flipping the sign.

"Are you now? And here I was just fixing to buy me a book." Isaiah stood up, brushing his pants and straightening the collar on his shirt. "Well then, suppose I'll just have to walk over to Main Street to see about getting me something to read there. Goodbye, Silas," he said.

He stopped and put out his hand. Silas just looked the man in the eye. There was a malicious light there, something dark and spiteful behind the guise of mirth. He didn't take Isaiah's hand.

"Very well then," Isaiah said, and walked out the door. Silas closed and locked it behind him.

11

SILAS DROVE NORTH ON 191 and turned west on Highway 279, past the Moab Tailings Project, and drove along the banks of the Colorado River. For almost thirty years, from 1956 to 1984, the Atlas Mill processed fourteen hundred tons of uranium, day in and day out. All of it within a stone's throw of the lifeblood of the American Southwest: the Colorado River. The US Department of Energy stepped in with this new project to move 16 million tons of uranium tailings from the banks of the Colorado River to a permanent disposal site thirty miles north, near the town of Crescent Junction. Every day two trains, each up to twenty-six cars long, transported highly radioactive waste away from its burial site along the river.

The landscape that surrounded him was unimaginably grand and spectacularly beautiful, but of all the environments on earth this one was among the least tolerant of fools and their mistakes. The uncommon and exceptional wealth it made for a few brash men and women had even led to murder on occasion. Most often, however, what killed a person was their own foolishness.

Silas called it the slickrock paradox: While the stone was innocent enough to look at, once you tried to get a grip on it, it took your feet out from under you.

He stopped the Outback a couple miles down the river, at a place recently converted from a random camping site to an organized day-use area and tent campground. There were only a few vehicles so he parked close to the river. He sat on the bank of the Colorado and watched it flow. He recalled of one of his favorite pieces of Western literature, Norman Maclean's *A River Runs Through It*, and the much-loved passage, "*I sat there and forgot and forgot, until what remained was the river that went by and I who watched. Eventually the watcher joined the river, and there was only one of us. I believe it was the river."*

Now *there* was a great American writer. He only wrote two books, but they stood up. Silas counted Maclean among his favorite "river poets": Stegner, Maclean, and Ellen Meloy, the latter having passed much too soon.

When he had met Penelope she told him he was missing the best: Abbey and his pieces on the Green, Colorado, Dirty Devil, San Juan, and Dolores Rivers. The jewel, she told him, was his eulogy for the Colorado River where it had carved out Glen Canyon. Abbey floated down it, she told him, just months before the completion of the dam, and had included the piece in *Desert Solitaire*. Silas read it. He read it all, but remained unconvinced. He did admit—though only to himself—that when the famous desert rat wrote about rivers, he was at his middling best.

Silas watched the Colorado River as he would a telephone waiting for it to ring. He wanted answers. Silas wondered why Jacob Isaiah was suddenly so interested in him, and more important, why Isaiah was so interested in Penelope. The man had never been particularly neighborly toward him, nor had he ever been so openly hostile. Something had changed in his attitude toward Silas with Silas's discovery of Kayah Wisechild's body.

How was it that Isaiah knew *he* had found the body? None of the newspaper reports identified Silas; they all just said that a hiker discovered the body after a flood. Maybe the young couple who found him had told their story, but *they* didn't know his name. Maybe the doctor or the nurses at Moab Regional finked him out, but that too seemed unlikely. The only person he figured who could have given him up to Jacob Isaiah was Dexter Willis, sheriff of Grand County. He would have to find out.

And lastly, Silas wanted to know why it was that his wife wanted him to find Kayah Wisechild. Silas had feigned steadfast resolution against Ken Hollyoak's idea the other day, downplaying his dream and its portent. He hadn't, in fact, stopped considering its possible meaning for more than a few minutes since learning the identity of the corpse. The direction this dream sent him on was as obvious as if there had been a road sign on 191 pointing him down Courthouse Wash. Penelope often appeared in his dreams, but she was usually mute. He felt that *she* had sent him to Sleepy Hollow. She *wanted* him to go there. She wanted him to find Kayah Wisechild. He simply had no ungodly knowledge as to why.

"I DON'T THINK you ought to come by the County Office," said Dexter Willis. "The feds are still all over this place. I'm lucky to still have my desk."

"Can you come by the store?" asked Silas. He had his new cell phone to his ear while he geared down coming into town.

"Don't see why not."

"Do me a favor, Dex. Don't tell Taylor you're coming to see me, okay?"

"What's going on, Silas?"

"Nothing. I just need to ask you a few questions without getting the third degree."

"I'll come by in ten minutes."

Silas was unlocking the door to his bookstore when Willis strolled up the sidewalk. They greeted each other and Silas opened the door.

"You got a soda in that little fridge of yours?" asked Willis.

"Should have," said Silas, walking the length of the store and opening the fridge. "Dr Pepper do?"

"Perfect."

Silas motioned toward the chair that Jacob Isaiah had vacated just a few hours before and handed the sheriff his cold drink. "I'll get right to the point. Did you tell Jacob Isaiah that I was the one who found the Wisechild woman?"

Willis looked taken aback. "It wasn't me, Silas. What happens while I'm on duty stays there."

"He knew it was me in Courthouse Wash. He made a pretty big deal about it." Silas told the sheriff about his conversation that morning.

"Leave this with me, I'll look into it. You know that uttering threats is a crime."

"People get riled. I just can't understand why now."

"What else did he say?"

"He said if I kept poking around in the rocks looking for Penny, I'd end up like the Wisechild girl. Dead."

Both men sat in silence a moment. "Did you get hold of this girl's folks?" Silas finally asked.

"The FBI did. They found them yesterday afternoon."

"In person?"

"They don't have a phone. Nearest one was at a crossroads store thirty miles from where they lived up on Third Mesa. Real middle-of-nowhere country. I believe the Hopi Tribal Police visited the residence."

"How did they take it?"

"I don't know. Even though the tribal police are overseen by the Bureau of Indian Affairs, communication between departments isn't so good."

"Did you know that she worked with Dead Horse Consulting doing archaeological surveys for our friend Isaiah?"

"Yes. Did Isaiah tell you that?"

"He did. First he comes at me as if the girl's disappearance two years ago was headline news on CNN and then he acts as if he's never heard of Dead Horse Consulting. He's had them on the payroll of his various development schemes for as long as I've known him."

"He's a big player, Silas. He's got two dozen people working for him. Maybe he just farms it out and they hire who they want."

"Maybe."

"Listen, we're working with the feds to chase this thing down. You've got to let us do our job."

Silas held up his hands. "Say no more. I'm just curious."

"Careful with that, Silas. You know what they say about cats and all." He stood up and offered his hand. Silas took it. "Listen, Silas. Jacob Isaiah, well, he's a serious man and serious about his business. He's been here since before they started pulling uranium out of the ground back in '54. He's likely to be here after both you and I are buzzard bait. I make it a point to stay out of his way. It's just some friendly advice from me to you."

"I appreciate it, Dex. I do."

Silas closed the door behind the sheriff. He had every intention of getting in Jacob Isaiah's way if it meant understanding what connection the Wisechild girl had to his missing wife. He looked around the store. He hadn't sold a book in a month; maybe he wouldn't wait for the following week to resume his search. There was a lot of country on the Hopi Reservation that he could search by car.

12

SILAS WAS OUT THE DOOR by eight the next morning. Now, at midday, he was on the long and nearly empty stretch of highway that ran across the northwest corner of the Navajo Reservation. He drove down the length of Black Mesa, where in order to understand the roots of Penelope's environmental activism in the American Southwest, Silas had turned early in his search for her. What he thought of as her "college-student" fascination with the work of Edward Abbey had led her to this part of the Colorado Plateau many times. It was only a couple of hours from Flagstaff, and it was here in Abbey's novel of malcontent, *The Monkey Wrench Gang*, that the band of eco-saboteurs had struck at the nerve center of the coal industry that was ripping into the heart of the Hopi and Navajo lands. Since the 1960s the Peabody Coal Company, one of the largest coal companies in the world, had been digging into the rich deposits of coal found on Black Mesa.

He couldn't see them from Route 160, but just south and east were some of the largest man-made holes on the planet. It was here, when Penelope first started to get involved with conservation work, that she came. When Silas asked her what she hoped to accomplish, she said that it was enough at first to "bear witness." He had returned to marking his papers, and she had returned to the Hopi and Navajo Reservations many times.

Silas wondered if the Wisechild woman and Penelope had known each other. Or maybe Penelope's disappearance was somehow linked to the work that Kayah had been doing when she was murdered?

He drove on, his mind buzzing with questions. It was early in the afternoon when he turned off Route 160 at Moenkopi and headed into the heart of the Hopi Reservation, a smaller reservation completely surrounded by the sprawling Navajo Reservation. They were different people, with different cultures, but they were inextricably linked by geography. He steered the Outback up the southwest side of the incline of Black Mesa and into the Fourth World of the Hopi. According to Hopi creation myths, the previous three worlds of the Hopi had been destroyed by the creator when witchcraft led their people to do evil. The Hopi emerged through a crack in the earth—believed to be at the heart of the nearby Grand Canyon—to the Fourth World, where they now dwelled.

The landscape that greeted him on the Mesa was open, wide and far-reaching, the color of milky tea. Russian thistle, the invasive plant better known as tumbleweed, blew across the road. Cows dotted the landscape, their ribs and hips jutting like invitations to the turkey vultures that soared high above. The panorama of dust was flat, with reefs of stone on the horizon surrounded by a tan landscape dimpled with flat-topped mesas, and otherwise starkly barren.

It was nearly four o'clock when Silas drove into the tribal seat of Kykotsmovi Village, or K-Town, as it was known locally. After a bloodless feud in 1906, those who wanted to foster closer ties with the outside or white world had settled here to create the modern Hopi government. It was located on the Second Mesa, and though Silas knew he'd have to backtrack to find the family of Kayah Wisechild, the only person he knew on the Hopi Reservation lived near K-Town.

He followed a narrow winding track that wove down through the sage and rabbit brush to a double-wide trailer sitting on the edge of a dusty arroyo. This was Roger Goodwin's place. Goodwin was a professor of cultural anthropology at Northern Arizona University. He also taught courses in the university's groundbreaking Applied Indigenous Studies Program, which focused on the Hopi. He was an Anglo, and one of the few outsiders who had been accepted into the Hopi clans.

There was no vehicle in the yard and no lights on at the house. Silas stepped out of the car, went to the back and opened the hatch, and took a can of Dr Pepper from the cooler. Alcohol of any kind was prohibited on both the Navajo and Hopi Reservations. He walked over to a sickly cottonwood and sat down on a broken lawnchair in its shade and waited. An hour passed when a pick-up truck finally came barreling down the road. Silas waited in the shade of the tree as the rusting 1970 Ford came to an abrupt halt next to the trailer. Two people were riding in the back and three in the front. The two in the bed of the truck had kerchiefs over their faces and sunglasses on, and as the truck skidded to a halt, they hopped out, grabbing packs. He waved to them and raised his can of Dr Pepper and they waved back. The driver's door opened, its hinges popping loudly, and Roger Goodwin stepped down. He paused when he saw Silas reclining in the shade.

"Been here long?" Roger asked, as his two passengers unfolded themselves from the bench seat and headed toward the trailer.

"About an hour."

"Can you wait five more minutes while I shower?"

"No trouble. Want a soda?"

"In a minute. Let me drop my stuff." The lanky man grabbed a rucksack from the back of the truck and followed his passengers into the trailer. Silas heard the generator roar to life, shattering the stillness. Ten minutes passed and the man emerged. "You said something about a soda?"

Silas was about to push himself up on his cane when the man waved his hand. "I'll get it. You want another?"

"Back of the car. Yes please." Roger went to the Outback and returned with two cans of Dr Pepper.

"It's good to see you, Roger. Got yourself a new batch of vassal laborers, I see?"

"We call them graduate students, Silas. Maybe you remember them? Eager, willing?"

"I remember grad students alright; handy for getting your research done, as I recall. I see you're working them even on a Saturday."

"Billed as a cultural anthropology hike . . . What brings you to the Fourth World, Silas? It's been, what, two years since I last saw you?"

"I need some help," Silas said. "I'm looking for someone."

"For Penelope, Silas, I know. Every one of my students has a picture of her in their pack."

"That's kind, but no, a local girl. I'm looking for her family. Her name is Wisechild. Grew up on the Third Mesa. Did an undergrad degree with you."

"Yes, of course." Roger spoke in Hopi and then translated for Silas, "'Her breath has passed from her body.' She was found up in your neck of the woods. It's been all over the local papers."

"I know, Roger. I found her."

THEY SAT ON the tailgate of Goodwin's truck. Silas told him the whole story, including the dream. The anthropologist was silent for a long time after Silas had finished his tale.

"Death is a strange thing for the Hopi," he finally said. "When a person dies in the Fourth World, their spirit lives on and descends into the world below, where they can carry out their day to day lives. This happens on the fourth day after death, when their *soona*, or substance of life, is released. There are many different beliefs around this on the Mesas. Some believe that when this happens, a person's spirit can play tricks, trying to convince others to join it on the journey."

"How do the Hopi manage when a person has died but the body has not been found?"

"About as well as we do, Silas. Maybe a little worse. These people have very ancient beliefs in the katchina, their gods, and in many different entities of the underworlds. These include some very unsavory characters, taking the form of witches. When a girl like Kayah Wisechild goes missing, they believe it is the work of these dwellers of the underworld. They move among us, sometimes taking human shape, and sometimes causing all manner of trouble among people."

"Will there be some rest now that her remains have been recovered?" asked Silas.

"There will be a ceremony. I was under the impression that the FBI would be transporting the bones back to Salt Lake for further study."

"I don't know the answer to that question. I can make some calls. Can there be a ceremony without the body?"

"There will be some ritual, but nothing final. Given the nature of her death, there will be no rest," said Roger.

"Do you know her family?"

"Oh yeah. They're good people."

"Can you point me in their direction? I'd like to talk to them."

"Sure, I can do that. And then send someone to find you after a week of driving around the Mesas. How about I take you there in the morning? It will help if I'm with you."

"To translate?"

"Yes, but also for more than just the language. More as an ambassador."

"I'd appreciate it."

"You want to come inside? It's Rachael's turn to cook tonight. She's pretty good."

"I need to find a place to camp," said Silas, looking around as if a Big K Campground might materialize out of the desert scrub.

"You can camp here. Come in, talk with the students, eat our food, then pitch your tent wherever you want. In the morning we'll drive over to Third Mesa."

Silas nodded. Roger hopped down from the tailgate and offered Silas a hand.

BY EIGHT THE next morning they were in Goodwin's truck, bouncing up the rutted track to Indian Route 2. They drove mostly in silence, Goodwin from time to time pointing out a cultural or natural feature and commenting on its significance. In a little under half an hour they turned north onto a dirt track and then again onto a two-lane, rutted path that wove across the top of Third Mesa.

"Anything I need to know?" Silas asked.

"Just like anywhere else. Respect. That's the place there," Roger said, pointing to a trailer parked against a small sandstone butte. A tiny, dry wash snaked across the scrubby field, several rain tanks next to it. "Down the wash a ways the family grows corn. It's about their only source of income besides the government." Roger and Silas continued on the path and noticed that in addition to a dilapidated Chevy pick-up in the yard, two dusty but new Yukon SUVs were parked by the trailer.

"Stop here," Silas said forcefully. Roger stopped in the middle of the tracks.

"Friends of yours?"

"I don't know. They look like government vehicles."

"Nobody out here drives a truck like that," agreed Roger. The two men had stopped a quarter of a mile away, the butte partially obscuring the trailer and concealing them from view. Silas reached into the pack at his feet and pulled out his Nikon binoculars.

"Definitely government," he said, looking at the plates. "Don't know who's driving them. Oh, wait a minute . . ."

A man stepped out of the trailer. "Agent Dwight Taylor. Assistant Special Agent in Charge," said Silas.

"This going to be trouble?" asked Goodwin.

"I don't know. He's from the Monticello office. He's leading the investigation into Ms. Wisechild's murder. I've been dealing with him for the last three and a half years, you know, with regards to Penny."

"So you're old buddies then?"

"Something like that."

Three more people stepped out of the trailer. "I see two more FBI men, including Taylor's partner, a Utah man named Nielsen. I don't recognize the fourth man."

"Let me have a look." Goodwin trained the binoculars on the men. "The feds are pretty obvious. I don't know why they all look alike, but they do. Even the yokel-looking guy is clearly a G-man. The guy with the white shirt and the tan slacks, I don't recognize him. He's certainly not Hopi."

Silas took the binoculars back. "We'll find out in a minute." The two SUVs were bumping along the pitted track toward them. Goodwin put the truck in gear and steered so that his left wheels were in the outside track, leaving room for the SUVs to do the same. They came up to the duo slowly and stopped when the lead vehicle's window was adjacent to Goodwin's Ford. The window of the black Yukon slid down. Agent Taylor was behind the wheel. The man Silas didn't recognize was in the passenger seat.

Agent Taylor said, "Hello, Dr. Pearson, funny meeting you here."

"I was thinking the same thing, Agent Taylor."

"We're conducting a murder investigation."

Silas asked, "Who's your co-pilot?"

"This is Charles Nephi. He works for Senator C. Thorn Smith."

"*US* Senator," said the man sitting next to Taylor. "He's currently in Washington on the nation's business, so he asked that I come to offer his condolences to the family."

"Senator Smith represents Utah," said Silas. "This is Arizona."

"Yes, but the remains were found in our state. The senator thought . . ."

"I see," said Silas. "Nice gesture to make."

"What brings *you* here, Dr. Pearson?"

"Same as Mr. Nephi. Paying my respects."

"And who is *your* pilot today?" asked Taylor, smiling.

Goodwin extended his hand and Taylor shook it. "Roger Goodwin, from NAU."

"Somebody else I have to call 'doctor,' I presume?"

"Roger will do just fine."

"You're not getting involved in this investigation, are you, Dr. Pearson?" asked Taylor.

"I'd say I already am, wouldn't you, Agent Taylor? I just want to tell them how sorry I am about their daughter and let them have some closure. Nothing more."

Taylor regarded them a moment. "Good enough. Please don't over-step your boundaries, Doctor."

"How do I know what they are, Agent Taylor?"

"When you overstep them, I'll let you know pretty quick."

Silas said, "Goodbye Mr. Nephi. Tell the senator hello. My wife is—was—a big fan."

"I'll do that," said Nephi as Taylor rolled the window up. The two SUVs passed on down the track. Silas watched them disappear in the cracked side mirror of the Ford.

"Penelope really a big fan?" asked Roger.

"Are you kidding? C. Thorn Smith is the senator who killed every single piece of environmental legislature brought before the Senate. If the environmental movement has an arch enemy, he's it. I don't know anything about his minion there, but I doubt he's any more sympathetic than his master. Maybe even less so."

"You think he knew who you were?"

"I doubt it. Taylor is probably filling him in. I wonder why he felt it necessary to come all the way out here. I mean, nice sentiment, but usually a letter will do. Seems a little odd to be riding along with the FBI."

"Budget cuts," said Goodwin. "Maybe they're carpooling." He put the truck in gear and crept on toward the trailer. They parked outside for a minute while dogs sniffed and then peed on their tires. After a moment a young woman appeared at the door to signal that they had been noticed and that they could approach the house.

"That's Kayah's older sister, Darla. She lives at home to take care of her folks," said Goodwin. They both opened the doors and stepped out, Silas taking his cane. There was a breeze blowing across Third Mesa, and the air was lightly scented with sage. It was hot, but not oppressively so.

"*Um waynuma?*" said Goodwin as he walked up to the trailer.

"*Um pitu?*" said the woman. She was about five-foot-two, with a lean face and long dark hair. Silas immediately wondered if this was what Kayah Wisechild had looked like.

"*Owí*. This is Silas Pearson," said Goodwin. "We've come to pay our respects to your mother and father. May we speak with them?"

"You can come in. They will be happy to see you."

"The government men were just here," said Roger, walking up the wooden steps to enter the trailer.

"They told us not to worry, that they would find whoever did this to my sister."

Silas looked at Roger and twisted his mouth to indicate his skepticism. The two men stepped into the trailer. It was small and clean and smelled like freshly cooked corn. A couple in their late fifties sat in the living area on twin floral pattern chairs next to the open kitchen. Silas and Roger stopped. Roger said, "*Owí, nu' waynuma.*"

"*Um pitu?*" said Mr. Wisechild.

"*Owí,*" said Roger. "This is Silas Pearson. He is the man who found your daughter. He's come to bring his condolences."

The man and woman looked at one another. "Do you want to have coffee?" the man asked after a moment.

"Yes, coffee would be good."

"I am Leon, and this is my wife, Evelyn. You've met our eldest daughter, Darla."

"We've met." Darla went to the kitchen and plugged the coffee maker in.

"Sit, please," said Leon, pointing to a matching couch. Both men sat.

"What did the FBI men tell you when they were here?" asked Goodwin.

"They said that they would catch the evil man who did this to our daughter," said Leon.

"There is a witch at work," said Evelyn. Leon nodded his head. Silas could see that Darla in the kitchen was less convinced. She rolled her eyes in exaggerated disbelief.

"We are glad that you found our little girl, Mr. Pearson."

"It's Silas," he said. "I'm very sorry for your loss."

"Now her *soona*, her soul, can travel to the underworld. Now she is no longer just *qatungwu*."

"Lifeless, a body," translated Goodwin.

"I hope it brings some peace," said Silas.

"How was it you came to be in that place, where you found her?"

Darla brought strong black coffee on a tray and handed them each a cup. Silas sipped his. It was hot and delicious. "I was looking for my wife," he said. "She has been missing for three and a half years. I thought that maybe she was in that place, but instead I found your daughter. There was a storm, and a flood, and when it was over, I saw her. Under a cottonwood tree."

"Is that what happened to your leg?" asked Leon.

"I was caught in the flood. It's on the mend."

"And why were you looking there? In that place. It's big country," asked Leon.

"I've been searching for over three years. I've looked everywhere. She went on a hike, within a day's drive of Moab, and never came back."

"Third Mesa is within a day of Moab. Did you look here?"

"I did. Almost three years ago. Around the Peabody mine. She was . . . an environmentalist, an activist. She worked here on the mesa for years trying to stop the mine."

Darla said, "There are only so many white women who come to Hopi. Maybe I have seen her. Do you have a picture?"

"She was half-Hispanic. Her mother was from Baja," Silas said, digging out his wallet. He showed the picture to Darla, Leon, and Evelyn.

"Have you seen her?"

"I don't think so. Lots of white people have been trying to stop the destruction on Black Mesa, but only a few come and talk to our people about what *we* want," said Leon.

"I expect that Penelope did. That's the way she was. I can't help but think that somehow maybe . . . I don't know, that my wife would have wanted me to find your daughter." Silas drew a breath. "I had a dream. The night before. In it, my wife told me to go to this place. The place called Sleepy Hollow. It's where I was when the flood came. It goes into Courthouse Wash, in Arches Park. It's where I found your daughter." The stillness that followed was interrupted as the wind rattled the metal trailer.

Outside a dog barked. Leon sipped his coffee, drew a long breath and exhaled quietly. "You will keep looking for your answers. My little girl, she has some of the trickster in her, some of the coyote. Maybe your wife does too. One or the other of these women has been tricking you, Mr. Pearson," said Leon. "When a person dies, they do not go to heaven as your people believe, but instead live on, as spirit, in the rocks and in the corn. In the sky. Sometimes they play tricks. Sometimes they get into our heads, and even our dreams. I don't know if it was our little girl who got into your head, or maybe it was your wife, your Penelope. One of them wanted you to find Kayah. Whichever ghost led you to my daughter wanted you to find her because Kayah will help you find your wife. You go and do what you have to do to learn what happened to our little girl, and that will help you find your Penelope."

Silas sat in complete motionless silence. He felt his heart racing and his breath coming in staccato pulses. He put the cup of coffee down on a tiny end table and stood up.

"You don't have to be afraid," said Leon, pushing himself up. "Our daughter's *soona* is soon at rest. She won't play in your head anymore." Leon put out his hand and Silas shook it and went to the door.

"Thank you for the coffee. Again, I am very sorry about your daughter. Now, if you don't mind, I'm going to get a little air," he said. He opened the door and stepped out into the desert.

Ten minutes later Darla came out onto the porch with Roger. Silas was sitting in the cab of the truck. He hadn't moved since coming out of the trailer. Roger and Darla walked over to him.

"You okay?" asked Roger. Silas said he was, and Roger continued. "You should hear this. I asked about who Kayah was friends with, if she had a boyfriend, who she was working with. The FBI asked the same questions, I guess. Darla just told me something that she didn't tell the feds."

"Why not?" asked Silas.

"They didn't show any respect to my father and mother. And they didn't ask me, just my parents."

"Darla says Kayah got a job working with Dead Horse doing archaeological surveys. Mostly for the sake of the Archaeological Resource Protection Act, in advance of some building or development."

"About two months before she disappeared," explained Darla, "Kayah came home for a long weekend. We stayed up one night talking, you know, the way sisters do. She told me about a man she worked with, about how they were . . ."

"Involved?" asked Silas.

"Yes, involved."

"Who was it?" asked Silas.

"A man named Peter Anton."

"Yeah, Anton was a hired digger for Dead Horse Consulting. I've heard his name around," said Silas. "Anton must have been forty years older than her."

"*And* he was married," Roger added. "He was also a professor at NAU."

"It's bad for the Hopi to do this," continued Darla. "The katchina don't like this sort of behavior."

"When she went missing, was this known to the FBI?"

"I don't know. I didn't speak with them. Just my mother and father, and they didn't know about this Peter man. It would have been very bad for them to know. Maybe I should have said something, but I was embarrassed . . . If Kayah showed up, well, it would have been very bad for her if people knew about this. If she was dead . . . Well, what good would it have done?"

"Where is Anton now?" asked Silas.

"I don't know," said Darla. "I've never met him."

Silas looked at Roger.

"I don't know either. He left NAU around the same time that Kayah disappeared. He got a gig overseas, in Saudi Arabia. I don't even know if he's back in the country. What are you going to do?" asked Roger.

"Find Peter Anton," said Silas.

13

THE SIX-HOUR DRIVE BACK FROM Third Mesa gave Silas a lot of time to consider what he'd learned from his visit to the Wisechild family. The evening sky was shot through with lightning. Thunderheads hung over the tableland of the Colorado Plateau like so many anvils, threatening to crash to earth. Near Kayenta the heavens opened up and Silas, back in his car after returning to Roger's trailer, parked on the side of the road while rain fell to earth as a single wave of water. Ten minutes later the storm had passed and moved on across the desert.

The most troubling thing he had learned was that Kayah Wisechild may have been romantically involved with Peter Anton. Did the FBI miss this when they were investigating Wisechild's disappearance two years ago? Had they missed it again, now that the case was officially a murder investigation?

There was the business of witchcraft Leon Wisechild mentioned. It was always present among the Hopi and their neighbors, the Navajo. Silas was too pragmatic to believe that a witch had led him to the body in Courthouse Wash, but he was hard-pressed to explain how a nighttime vision of his wife was all that different. Try as he might, he couldn't shake the words that the elder Wisechild had imparted to him: *"Follow her."* The words of a desperate father hoping someone—anyone—would find the person who killed his daughter? Or was there something more to his plea to Silas?

Silas knew that he had to talk with Peter Anton, but he had no idea where the man might be. Saudi Arabia was a long way from Moab, Utah. He also knew that he should inform the FBI of what he had learned, though doing so would create another entanglement with Taylor, something he was anxious to avoid.

Finally, he knew that he had to learn what it was Kayah Wisechild was working on at the time of her disappearance, and death. It might be conceivable that at some point in the past the young woman knew Penelope. If they had worked on a project together—possibly a campaign to protect important archaeological sites?—Silas might find out more about what his wife was doing when she disappeared.

It was nearly midnight when he drove through Moab, too late to make his inquires, so he pressed on for home. When he finally arrived, he collapsed on top of his bed, delaying his slumber only long enough to touch the face of his wife in the photograph next to the bed on the nightstand and tell her that he was trying to understand.

WHEN HE WOKE, he took his morning coffee, along with his portable phone, outside to watch the sunrise over Castle Valley. He dug a scrap of paper from his jeans and dialed the number he had scrawled there.

"Salt Lake Office, Bureau of Investigation, Trace Evidence Unit."

"Dr. Rain, please."

"One moment, let me see if she's in." There was a silence, then a familiar voice came on the line.

"This is Rain."

"It's Silas Pearson, Doctor."

"Hello, Silas. You know, if you want me to call you Silas, you're going to have to at least call me Kathleen; Katie would be preferable."

"We'll see about that. Listen, this is a little unorthodox, and you can tell me to go fly a kite, but I want to ask you something."

"Is this with regards to Ms. Wisechild's remains?"

"In a way. It's about the investigation."

"I'm not a part of this investigation team, as such. I'm auxiliary to the core unit. Are you sure you don't want to talk with Assistant Special Agent in Charge—"

"No, thank you. If what I have to talk with you about proves relevant, I'll leave it to you to decide if Agent Taylor gets involved. I assume you have access to the investigation records?"

"I do, but I'm not at liberty to share them with you, Silas."

"Well, let me run this by you. There is some evidence to suggest that

Kayah Wisechild was in a relationship with someone she worked with when she disappeared. A man named Peter Anton. He was married at the time, likely still is. He's a good forty years her senior. He's adjunct at NAU and a consultant with the firm that Kayah was working with, called Dead Horse. They're based here in Moab. Does the Bureau know about this?" He could hear keys tapping and assumed that Rain was accessing the FBI's internal files on the investigation.

"How did you come by this information?" she asked.

"I visited with the family—"

"Yesterday," she said, cutting him off.

"That's right. You've got notes there?"

"Yes, Agent Taylor noted that he passed you and another man while departing the Wisechild home."

"Does he mention Peter Anton, or any suggestion of an affair?"

"Let me . . ." Silas assumed she was scrolling through the notes. "No. Nothing. He says he questioned the parents about boyfriends and co-workers, but they didn't say anything about an affair."

"They likely didn't know, and he likely didn't know how to ask. The man I was traveling with speaks Hopi, and he knew the family. There was trust there. And he asked Kayah's sister, Darla. *She* knew. The parents didn't. In the Hopi tradition, that kind of behavior is considered taboo, the work of witchcraft."

"It's pretty much taboo everywhere, isn't it?" asked Rain.

"Do you think it's important?" asked Silas.

"I'd say so. I'm not the lead investigator, though."

"No, but you are FBI. Do you want to bring it to Taylor's attention?"

"Taylor will already be following up with the employer, this Dead Horse Consulting company. That's standard. He might learn about this Anton fellow there. He'll certainly ask. He's likely to turn up this same information on his own. If I send him this information, he's going to scream about you interfering with a federal investigation and obstruction of justice. That's going to end you up in an interview room at the Grand County Sheriff's Office, if not a trip to Monticello. I don't think you want that, do you?"

"No, I don't."

"And that's likely not going to help you find your wife." Silas was silent. "Are you still there?" Rain said.

"Yes," he said after a moment.

"Here's what I'm going to do. I'll monitor Taylor's notes and if in the next day or so if this doesn't come up, I'll ask about it. The cause of death would lead me to believe that this was a very personal crime, perhaps a crime of passion, though not necessarily between lovers. I suspect that somebody had a grudge against this girl."

"Can you tell me how she died?"

"No. It would prejudice the investigation. Frankly, Silas, you're still a suspect—excuse me, a person of interest—until Taylor says otherwise. He makes a notation that your being at the Wisechild residence yesterday is considered suspicious. If *you* had information about how the girl died, it could be difficult to establish guilt or innocence. That would lead to trouble, for both you and me."

"Okay, I appreciate what you're doing."

"Let's hope that I'm not wrong and that you prove to be trustworthy."

"I guess it could mean your job."

She laughed. "No, I'm not worried about that. I'm one of only three people doing this work for the FBI. And there's only eighty board-certified forensic anthropologists in the entire United States. I won't get fired for this conversation. I might get a letter on my file, but nobody will care so long as I keep leading our people to the bad guys. What I am worried about is finding this killer, and I'd very much like you to find your wife. It's why I got into this line of work."

Silas felt a strange sense of relief. It had been a long time since anybody but his closest friends had offered him help. Mostly people just avoided him, or in the case of Jacob Isaiah, scorned his efforts. Here was a complete stranger, and someone in a position of considerable authority, offering him encouragement and assistance.

"Thank you" was all that he could manage.

"I'll call you if anything turns up. You do the same. Goodbye, Dr. Pearson," she said, and he could tell she was smiling.

"Goodbye, Dr. Rain." He broke the connection.

SILAS HAD NEVER been to the offices of Dead Horse Consulting, but he had driven past them heading south on 191 many times. Located in an industrial complex near the BLM and Park Service Headquarters south of town, Dead Horse was a broad-based business, specializing in environmental assessments, planning, design, and archaeology.

On Monday morning he drove from his home in the Castle Valley and stopped at the bookstore. He wanted to read up on the company online before he headed out there.

When he finally set out for Dead Horse's office, he had learned that the person he needed to speak with was Jared Strom. Silas parked next to several white four-door, extended cab pick-up trucks, all with the Dead Horse logo artfully displayed on the front doors. When he had visited the company's website, he found that the logo wasn't at all what he expected. It did not involve a horse, but rather a stylized motif from the ancient Pueblo art found in Dead Horse Canyon.

Silas entered the air-conditioned office. The receptionist behind the long, faux-maple counter looked up as he approached. "May I help you?"

"I'd like to see Mr. Strom, please."

"Do you have an appointment?"

"I don't. Will that be a problem?"

"No, as long as he's here. What was your name?"

"Silas Pearson."

She picked up the phone and spoke with someone. "You're in luck. He's in the back. His assistant is paging him."

A moment later a broad-shouldered man with a ball cap covering a mostly bald dome entered through the door. He reached out a meaty hand to Silas. "Jared Strom," he said.

"Silas Pearson."

"What can I do for you?"

"Is there someplace we can talk?"

"Sure, follow me." Strom turned down the hall at a brisk pace, and Silas, cane in hand, had to hurry to keep up. Strom led him through a warren of cubicles and partitioned offices to the rear of the building.

He stopped at a doorway and turned, noticing Silas several steps behind. "Sorry," he said. "Sometimes I think I only have one speed."

"I banged up my ankle last week. Otherwise, I'd be fine."

"Hiking?"

"Something like that."

"Let's sit in my office," he said, opening the door to a windowless room. He closed the door behind Silas. Strom reached down and moved a pile of files and folders and maps from a black leather chair and motioned for Silas to sit. "Do you want anything? Ice tea? Or something hot?"

"No thanks. I won't take much of your time. I want to ask you about something. It's a little sensitive." Strom waited.

Silas continued, "*I* was the one who found Kayah Wisechild's body."

The man paled. He leaned back in his chair and folded his hands together.

Strom said, "The FBI and the Sheriff's Office came by yesterday morning. I had heard it on the news. They are saying the body was found by a hiker."

"That was me."

"I see," said Strom.

"I want to ask you about Kayah Wisechild, if I may. You see, finding her body has been, well, troubling me."

"No doubt it has."

"How long did she work here?"

"Two summers. The first one was three years back. She was a senior at NAU, finishing her degree. We hired her as an intern. The following spring, when she was looking for work again, we found her a full-time position."

"What did she do?"

"How much do you know about what we do, Mr. Pearson?"

"Not much, I'll admit. You seem like a going concern."

"We're a full-service environmental and archaeological consulting firm. What that means is if you want to do something around here that would trigger any kind of environmental assessment, or anything to do with the Archaeological Resources Protection Act—we just call it ARPA— then you hire us. We do any field work and report writing that's needed to satisfy the BLM, the Forest Service, or the Park Service."

Silas had heard Penelope talk about such firms many times. She had painted them as eager to green-wash any project so long as the pay was sufficient. Silas had dismissed this as his wife's typical one-sided bias. "What was Kayah doing for Dead Horse?" Silas asked.

"She worked for me. I run the archaeological services side of things. Kayah was young, and a little naive, but she was a solid technician. For example, if someone wanted to build some condominiums up there on the bench above Moab, or out near Canyonlands, or anywhere else around here, they'd hire us to tell them how to do it so they don't mess up the environment and don't disturb ancient Pueblo sites of significance. In such a situation, Kayah would work with one of our senior archaeologists at the proposed site and make sure there was nothing of significance there. If there was, we'd advise our client on how to develop the site without violating the various pieces of legislation, the National Environmental Policy Act and ARPA, or sometimes even tell them that they couldn't build where they wanted to."

"That happen often? Where you'd have to say no?"

"Well, we just advise. It's up to the BLM and other agencies to say yes or no." Silas couldn't remember many situations where someone had been told no by the BLM.

"Did Kayah work with a man named Peter Anton when she was here?" Silas watched for a reaction. If Strom had any, he didn't show it.

"She did. They worked together on a couple of projects."

"Where is Anton now? I heard he was working on a project in the Middle East."

"I don't know. Peter was only ever with us on contract. We haven't used him in the last two years."

"Don't you think that's a little strange?"

"There are dozens of guys like Peter Anton out there. They—"

"That's not what I mean. I mean the timing. Don't you think it's strange that Peter Anton, someone who worked with Kayah before she disappeared . . . before she was killed, suddenly decides to go off to the Middle East just after she vanishes?"

Strom was silent a moment. "I see what you're driving at, Mr. Pearson."

"Do you?"

"You think Peter was involved in Kayah's death just because he takes a contract overseas around the time she vanishes."

"Seems suspicious, doesn't it?"

"Only if Peter hadn't done that sort of thing every year or two for most of his professional life. He's spent almost as much time in Saudi Arabia, Iran, Iraq, Egypt, Jordan—you name it—as he has here."

"Is he in the States now, or overseas?"

"I have no idea."

"Where does he live when he's in the US?"

Strom shrugged. "I think he had a place near Cortez, in Colorado. He loved Mesa Verde."

"You don't have a number for him?"

"We could ask Julie on the way out."

"Did you know that Peter Anton was *involved* with Kayah Wisechild?"

Now Strom's eyes registered surprise. "What? Peter? No way. He was a married man. He has a great marriage. No way was he messing around what that girl. I don't—"

"Before she disappeared she told someone about it."

"Who?"

"I can't say."

"Well, I don't believe it. If you ask me, that's nothing more than a rumor, the words of someone who had maybe been rebuffed and who wanted to get even."

"Can you think of anybody who would want to kill Kayah?"

Strom studied Silas a moment. "You seem to be asking a lot of the same questions the FBI was yesterday. You said you found the body. What's *your* interest here?"

"I don't know," Silas said, "I just can't get her out of my head."

"Look, I didn't know the girl. She was here for two summers. She did her work. She wasn't a spectacular archaeologist; just average. Young, you know? When she disappeared, everybody just assumed she went back to the Res. That's what these kids sometimes did."

Silas noted the xenophobic tone to his remarks. Somehow Kayah had gone from a valued employee to just "average" within a five-minute conversation. Strom had gone from having worked with her on projects to not really knowing her.

"What was she working on before she disappeared?"

"I honestly don't remember."

"Could you check?"

"What difference would that make?"

"Maybe none; might help me sleep better." Strom regarded him, his eyes narrow. He turned in his chair and pulled his computer over. Silas tried to read over his shoulder without being too obvious.

"Well, looks like she was working on a contract we had assessing some BLM lands. We were looking at the impact of off-highway vehicle use on trails east of Canyonlands. Nothing terribly exciting; just looking at how access to those areas was affecting low-value sites, such as those with minor rock art panels and flint scatter zones."

"Who was that client? Did you work for the BLM?"

"No, we were working with the Southern Utah Off-Highway Vehicle Club."

"Anything else?"

"Couple of projects doing site restoration in Arches. Park Service was the client."

From his chair, Silas could see at least four entries on Strom's screen. He squinted to read the final entry. There was something that Strom wasn't telling him; it was there on the screen.

"That's it," said Strom, closing the window and turning around. Silas quickly focused on him.

"You sure?"

"Like I said, nothing all that interesting. I don't see how that will help."

"I'm not sure either. I do have one last question," Silas said, reaching for his wallet.

"Sure." Silas handed him the picture of Penelope.

"Have you ever seen this woman?"

Strom looked at it longer than was necessary. "Who is she?"

"My wife. Her name is Penelope de Silva. She went missing in this area about three and a half year ago."

"You're *that* guy . . . the one who has been looking for his wife. You opened a bookstore."

"That's right. Have you seen her?"

"I don't know. Maybe around town, but that was five, maybe six years ago. I think I remember her speaking at one of the public land hearings then."

"Not more recently?" Silas asked.

"No, nothing. I haven't seen her."

"Thank you for your time."

"I'll have Julie get you that number, if she has it."

"Thanks," said Silas. Strom followed Silas out of the office.

"Would you find Dr. Peter Anton's number and give it to Mr. Pearson here?" he asked his assistant.

Silas left the building via the main doors. He was deeply engrossed in his thoughts about what he had seen over Jared Strom's shoulder. The last project that Kayah Wisechild had worked on before she disappeared had been for Jacob Isaiah.

14

SILAS DROVE BACK INTO MOAB. He parked at his store, and was tempted to walk the six blocks to Jacob Isaiah's office and confront him. He bet the developer knew a great deal more about the disappearance of Kayah Wisechild than he had let on. Instead, he unlocked the store and turned on the air-conditioning. Then he sat at his desk and considered his course of action. If he confronted Isaiah now, he'd likely learn little more than when the man had visited him just two days ago. In fact, Isaiah might use his considerable power and influence to create a barrier to Silas's ongoing clandestine investigation.

He needed another way to learn more about the project Wisechild had worked on. What he needed to do was talk to Penelope. She would know. Nobody lifted a finger to build something, dig something, log something, or drill a hole in something within five hundred miles of the canyon country without Penelope knowing about it. But he'd had his chance, and he had chosen to grade papers and give lectures to bored undergraduates instead.

Silas sat at the desk for a while, mulling over his options. The piece of paper with Peter Anton's number on it held a Colorado exchange. It rang three times and a woman answered. Silas sat up, surprised to reach someone. "Is Peter there, please?"

"Yes, may I tell him who's calling?"

"It's Silas Pearson, but he won't know me."

"Hold on, please." Silas heard the woman call her husband.

"This is Anton," came a deep, resonant voice.

"Dr. Anton, it's Silas Pearson calling."

There was a moment's pause. "Yes?" he finally said.

"I'm a friend of Roger Goodwin's. He told me I might be able to find you at this number."

"What can I do for you?"

Silas hadn't really considered how he was going to play this, so he decided to play it straight and see what happened. "It's about Kayah Wisechild."

"What about her?" asked Anton without hesitation.

"Did you hear that her body had been found?"

"I did. Down in Courthouse Wash. It was in the Denver papers."

"That's right. Dr. Anton, I was the person who found her."

"Okay . . . I'm sorry, it was Pearson? I'm not catching your point right now. Who are you again?"

"I'm the man who found her. I was . . . hiking. I run a bookstore in Moab. I'm just a regular citizen; I'm not with the police. I recently visited her family on Third Mesa. I spoke with Kayah's sister. She told me that you and Kayah knew each other. Well."

There was a moment's pause. "What do you want?"

"To talk."

"Start talking then."

"Can we meet?"

Silas could hear the man breathing. "You can come to Mesa Verde. I volunteer there two mornings a week, cataloging artifacts and working on their collection. I'll be there tomorrow. Call me and I'll meet you when you arrive." He gave Silas his cell number.

"Dr. Anton, have the FBI spoken with you?"

"No. Listen, do I need a lawyer for this? Or are you after something? Money?"

"No, I'm not after anything, and I'm not a cop or a private investigator or anything like that. I just want information. That's all."

"Come to Mesa Verde tomorrow."

"I'll see you then." Silas hung up the phone. He felt a mild electric buzz after the call, as if things were starting to click into place. He stood and stretched. His ankle was beginning to feel better. Soon he might be able to hike again. Maybe he'd test its limits with a stroll downtown to get a cup of coffee. Taking his cane, just in case, he locked up the shop and headed toward Main Street. He was sweating before he got there. He bought an iced coffee from a café and drank from the frothy concoction, then walked another block to the Visitor Center where he turned right and headed up Center Street.

Absentmindedly, Silas drew near to the Grand County Administration building, which housed the sheriff's department. He stopped twenty yards from the front doors. The tell-tale black SUVs the G-men drove might be parked around back. He was about to turn around when something occurred to him: the Sheriff's Office wasn't the only tenant of this building—so was the records department for the county. Feds or no feds, he decided to pay the registrar a visit.

The records department was on the second floor. Ten minutes after explaining his business he was seated at a table with a stack of development applications in various stages of approval. He had asked for all of the applications that Jacob Isaiah had filed in the last five years, and now he had a considerable stack of paper to work through.

Methodically, he read through them all, looking for connections to both Kayah Wisechild and his wife. As he worked his way through the paperwork, he grew horrified by how poorly grown men wrote, and he couldn't help but feel like he was reading term papers once again.

After some time, he found what he believed was the last project Kayah Wisechild had worked on. The application was on hold, pending a federal environmental assessment and completion of the requirements under ARPA for assessment of archaeological resources. Silas noted that Dead Horse Consulting was listed as one of several firms retained to do the preliminary assessment work, and that project lead had been transferred—around the time that Kayah had gone missing—from Peter Anton to Jared Strom. And while he didn't see any reference to Wisechild, he wouldn't expect to, given her subordinate status within the company. The dates matched, however. The location was listed as latitude and longitude.

He looked up at the clerk and asked, "Do you have a map of the county?"

He regarded Silas quizzically. "Of course," he said.

"Would you help me find this location?"

The clerk shrugged and brought a map over, unrolling it on the table in front of Silas. "What're the coordinates?"

Silas read them out. The clerk smiled. "What is it?" Silas asked.

"I don't need the coordinates for that one," he said. He pointed on the map. "Here. That one is mostly in San Juan County. We don't have all the records for that here."

"Why is there paperwork on it here?"

"Part of a bigger proposal spanning the two counties. Something about an all-season resort, condos, a golf course. It's been on the books for a while. You haven't heard of it?"

"My wife keeps track of these things," said Silas quietly.

"This is Canyon Rims. It's BLM land. A recreation area, about half an hour south and west of here."

"I've been there a few times," said Silas, thinking about the map on his wall. "I guess it's time I went for another walk."

15

HE WOULD KILL TWO BIRDS with one stone. He would meet Peter Anton Tuesday morning, and then return to look around the Canyon Rims region later in the afternoon. By 6:00 AM he was driving south, past Moab and over Hatch Wash and past the turnoff to the Canyon Rims region. The Outback was set up with his camping gear, hiking equipment, food, and libations. He figured he would camp in the Canyon Rims region while prowling around, to the extent his ankle would allow.

He made good time to Monticello, where he turned east on the notorious Route 666. This highway cut through some of the Southwest's most spectacular country, running east to Cortez and then swinging south through Shiprock, New Mexico, and the Navajo Reservation, to end at Gallup. The highway had recently been renumbered to 491 by the state's governor because of the bad publicity the number brought to the region.

Silas drove the route as far as Cortez, where he stopped for gas and a watery service-center coffee, then pressed on to the entrance to Mesa Verde National Park. He called Anton on his cell phone and received instructions to proceed through the park to the Chapin Mesa Museum, where the archaeologist was working that morning.

Though Mesa Verde was only three hours from the Red Rock Canyon bookstore, Edward Abbey's many books made only passing references to the area, so he hadn't considered looking there for his wife. Immediately upon driving into the park and flashing his park pass, he fell in behind a series of diesel-belching buses and lumbering RVs. The impressive view over the North Rim was effectively blocked by the oversized traffic, so he cursed briefly and turned his mind to figuring out the best way to approach Peter Anton.

The Chapin Mesa road wove its way along the high forested rim and then out onto the Mesa itself. After about half an hour of driving Silas arrived at the museum. Gratefully, he stepped from his car and stretched. At the museum entrance, a ranger ushered Silas to the back rooms. Silas knocked on the door they approached.

"Come," bid a voice from behind the door. The room he stepped into was crowded with artifacts, mostly pottery, but also cases filled with flint shards, spear tips, tools, cooking ware, such as mortars and pestles, and even bones. A strong scent of earth tickled his nose.

"Over here," came the voice again, and Silas found the source of the voice behind a tall stack of narrow drawers.

"Dr. Anton?" Silas asked.

"That's me."

"It's Silas Pearson." Silas limped around a large table containing numerous pots and pot shards. Anton was tall and lean with short gray hair and dark-rimmed glasses. His eyes were deep blue, and the hand that shook Silas's was firm and dry.

"So, how did you discover Kayah's body?"

After Silas told him, he asked, "Does that explain the limp?"

"Yes, but it's just a sprained ankle."

"You were lucky—you not only survived but you found Kayah . . . And now you think I had an affair with her?"

"Well, I understand the two of you knew one another—"

"That's right, we did," said Anton, leaning back on the cabinet of drawers.

"I mean, more than just professionally."

"We were friends. I suppose I was a mentor to her, a father figure, while we worked together at Dead Horse. Her own folks didn't really pay her much attention or give her the support she needed. She was the only member of her clan to go to college. She graduated in the top of her class. A very bright girl."

"Darla Wisechild told me that you and Kayah were in a relationship."

Anton suppressed a smile. "You think I was sleeping with my protégée and that I killed her in some lover's quarrel."

"Well, I suppose it does seem curious that Kayah Wisechild goes missing, and then, shortly afterward, you disappear to Saudi Arabia. And this information about an affair—"

"It's completely false; utterly and completely absurd. I've been happily married for forty-one years now, Mr. Pearson. I have never, never cheated on my wife and I would never even dream of doing so with someone as young and vulnerable as Kayah Wisechild. The timing is purely coincidental, and your accusations conjectural. I have been to the Middle East at least twenty times in my career. I wrote my doctoral dissertation on the lost city of Babylon. My trip to Saudi Arabia was planned six months before Kayah went missing. I was very sad to hear she had disappeared, but not because we were lovers. We were friends, and she was a good archaeologist, dedicated and thorough. Her whole life was ahead of her."

Silas listened to the man's rant. "Why would she tell her sister that you and she were lovers?"

"She was young, impressionable, and infatuated. I represented a figure of some influence in her life; maybe she simply had a crush and wanted to appear worldlier than her sister."

"In the Hopi tradition—"

"Yes, yes, don't try to school me on the Hopi traditions, Mr. Pearson. I know that in their tradition having this sort of relationship would be taboo. Where would it not, at least in modern culture, outside of France? And for the Hopi the implication is nothing short of witchcraft. For this young woman to disappear as she has—and to be murdered and left in Courthouse Wash, no less—would be considered the work of a witch. I assure you, Mr. Pearson, I'm no witch."

Anton's arms were folded defensively across his chest as he leaned back on the stacks of drawers. "Tell me about the work you did with Kayah."

"Does this mean you believe me?"

"It doesn't matter if I do or not, Dr. Anton."

"It does to me," Anton said. His voice was calm.

"Let's say, for the sake of argument, I do. I don't know what the FBI will say."

"The FBI is involved with this?"

"Of course they are. Kayah's body was found in a national park. The FBI field office in Monticello has joint jurisdiction."

"Do they . . . do they know about me?"

"I don't know. I think I'm about a day or two ahead of them in their investigation. I just happened to ask the right questions. It's only a matter of time, but if things are like you say—"

"Of course they're like I say!" Anton banged his fist against the cabinet. Silas felt uneasy. Anton drew a deep breath and seemed to calm down. "You know how things are. The FBI comes to my home in Cortez, or here, and I'm through. I'm done."

"Not if you have nothing to hide."

"That's bullshit, and you know it. People talk. My wife will hear people whispering at her bridge game on Wednesday night. It won't matter what the truth is."

"What if I told you the FBI won't hear it from me?"

"What do you want?"

"Just the truth."

"I've told you the truth."

"I want to know where you were working before Kayah was murdered." Silas used the word deliberately, to drive his point home.

"Have you got a map?"

Have I got a map, thought Silas. "Yes, in my car."

They walked out to the parking lot of the museum. Silas opened the back of his Outback and found the large-scale map of San Juan County and rolled it out on the hood of the car. Silas put on his sunglasses, and Anton squinted as the sun reflected off the map.

"Okay," said Anton, after a moment. "This is where we worked together. Right in here."

"Hatch Wash."

"That's right, and up here." He moved his finger north to Kane Springs. "And Behind the Rocks," said Anton.

"What were you looking for?"

Anton regarded him a moment. "You know, if the people at Dead Horse find out, I'll never work for them again."

"I was under the impression that you no longer worked for them anyway," said Silas.

"I don't know who told you that. I'm still involved, from time to time. I suppose not like I was before. Maybe that's what you mean. It's a little extra money. June and I, we take a trip or two a year on the money that comes in from these projects."

"You might have to stay home next year. But I won't be the one to tell them. What were you working on?"

Anton looked around. The parking lot was crowded with visitors. He seemed to be making rapid calculations in his head. "For as long as I can remember, Canyon Rims and Behind the Rocks have been hot spots for the debate over wilderness and development in this whole region," Anton said, circling the region on the map with his finger. "I don't know all the details; I try not to get involved with politics. I know that there have been some very public disputes between folks who want to protect these places and keep them wild and those who want more access to them."

"Access for what?"

"Off-highway vehicles like jeeps, motorcycles, quads, as well as oil and gas development. I guess there's a lot of interest in these lands for exploratory drilling, too, and some big companies are showing interest in making substantial investments in this area. There's a ton of money to be made if they can hit a sweet spot. And then, about five, maybe six years ago, a Moab developer . . ."

"Jacob Isaiah."

"Yes, Mr. Isaiah." Anton drew a deep breath. "He wanted to explore the idea of a year-round recreation village outside of Moab. I guess most of the good real estate in Moab had been bought up, so he started looking twenty, thirty, forty miles outside of town for something really spectacular. He looked all over the place; up in the Castle Valley, down toward Potash, on the Colorado, and around the Abajo Mountains. He started to zero in on this area." Anton poked at the map.

"The main reason was the water. Hatch Wash runs year round. It's BLM land, without much in the way of protection. They call it a 'recreation area,' but you can do just about anything you want there. It was at about that time that Dead Horse was brought on board, just to do some preliminary assessment of the values that we were dealing with. What plants and animals were there? What was the hydrology? What prehistoric sites were in the region?

"We didn't find anything at first. The Hatch region has been known to have some pictographs, but not much else. I was the team leader doing the inventory. Kayah was working with me as a field tech. We spent two, maybe three weeks working in the field and didn't find anything.

"Then, just about the time we were going to write a favorable report to Isaiah, telling him there wasn't much to be found, we stumbled on something. We—well, it was actually Kayah who found the cliff houses, granaries, you name it. They were totally protected—from the elements, and from view. She found them in a little pocket canyon off the main stream of Hatch, just a few miles from Kane Creek." Anton looked steadily at Silas, whose heart was racing. This was big news.

"It was significant. Nothing like here," said Anton, motioning to Mesa Verde. "But it was pretty impressive. Completely untouched. In the main kiva, there were still thousands of artifacts, hundreds of pieces of pottery, dozens of ceremonial artifacts. It was a gold mine for pot hunters."

Silas could hardly believe what he was hearing. "What did you do?"

"Nothing, at first. We didn't even tell Dead Horse. Not right away. We delayed our report and said that we still had field work to do. We spent a week there. It was like being Cortez himself, the earth felt so new. We camped down along the wash, and every day climbed up and did an inventory."

"Was it just the two of you?"

"No. I hired another guy, a young guy, from the NAU program too, to help."

"What was his name?"

"Kelly something. Williams, or Wilson. It was three years ago, and my memory . . . Anyway, we did the inventory and cataloged the site, then made a verbal report to Dead Horse."

"Who at Dead Horse?"

"Jared Strom. He's the head of—"

"I've met him."

"We did a verbal and told him that development in that area wasn't going to fly. No way. When the BLM found out, they would have to order a full environmental assessment. For that client, that would mean paying tens of thousands of dollars. Given the significance, the Park

Service would likely argue that the whole Canyon Rims area should be added to Canyonlands. They would contend that it was on par with the Grand Gulch Primitive Area, or the Horseshoe Canyon, which got tacked onto Canyonlands. That's what the enviros have been saying for a decade or more."

Silas looked at the map. "Can you give me the coordinates?"

"I don't see how that would help."

It might help very much with the search for my wife, thought Silas. "I want to see if I can retrace Kayah's last steps, get a feel for where she was before she disappeared."

Anton pulled a Blackberry out of his pocket and looked up the coordinates. Silas found his GPS unit in his pack and recorded them. "Thank you. What happened after you made your report to your boss?"

"Nothing. My guess is that Strom made a report to Isaiah and that was the end of it."

"That doesn't sound like Jacob Isaiah to me."

"I don't really know the man. Like I said, I do pots, not politics. Given the amount of money they had invested in the project already, I was a little surprised that they just dropped it, but who knows. Maybe Strom made his point. He's pretty persuasive when it comes to preserving finds like this."

"What exactly did they want to build?"

"An all-season resort. They would put an airfield up on Flat Iron Mesa, or maybe Hatch Point. They were planning as many as a thousand rooms in several sites, on Hatch, and on the Behind the Rocks Plateau, with a golf course, water pumped up from the creek, guided ORV trails, fine dining, a glass-bottomed sky walk off Hatch Point looking down a thousand feet into the wash. The whole deal. It would look a little like the worst parts of Grand Canyon Village, Aspen, and West Yellowstone, all thrown into one. They were talking about a five-hundred-million-dollar project over ten years. It would have been huge."

"Did word of this get out?"

"You mean to the greenies?" asked Anton. "I don't know. I think there were rumors, but because Isaiah was smart enough not to put anything on paper at the time, there was no smoking gun. You'd have to ask the enviros, though."

Silas nodded, knowing that something of this scale would have sent Penelope right off the chart. "What about this Kelly Wilson guy? Where is he?"

"I think it was Williams. I haven't worked with him since, but he's likely still in the Southwest. Remember, archaeologists get around a lot. He was young and keen, so I bet he's still in the community."

Silas straightened up. "Dr. Anton, my suggestion is that you go to the FBI and tell them what you know about Kayah. They're going to learn that you worked with her. They might not hear the rumors about a relationship, but they will want to talk with you about what you know. Better to call them."

"You're likely, right, Mr. Pearson."

"Thank you for your time. I appreciate it. This has been helpful."

"So you believe me?"

"About what? The ruins?"

"No, about Kayah."

"Of course I do," said Silas, though he didn't.

16

HE DROVE BACK THROUGH CORTEZ and on to Monticello. He waited until he passed through the town and then pulled out his phone and dialed Katie Rain.

"Rain," she said.

"Is that a greeting, or an invocation?"

"Ah, Dr. Pearson. What's up?"

"I told you I'd keep you in the loop."

"Yes, you did, and what have you learned?" He told her about his meeting with Peter Anton, and what Anton had told him about his relationship with Kayah Wisechild. He told her about the work they had been doing, but left out any details about where the work had been conducted.

"You think he's being straight up?" asked Rain.

"I don't think so. I think something happened between Anton and the Wisechild girl. I can't swear to it, but there was more going on with those ruins than he's letting on. I just don't know what."

"You're going to check it out, aren't you?"

"How did you know that?"

"I deal with bones, Dr. Pearson, but I'm a human being. You're easy to read."

"Yes, I'm going to go and have a look."

"Would you like to tell me where you're going? Just in case *you* pull a disappearing act?"

"If worst comes to worst, you can look for my car. With my ankle the way it is, I'll be within a day of it."

"That's not very helpful," said Rain.

"I'm trying my best," he said, smiling.

"Call when you get out. Your mother worries."

"Deal," he said, and hung up.

He drove past the entrance to the Needles section of Canyonlands National Park and turned onto the track that led off toward Hatch Wash. A plume of red dust followed his Outback, and he had to focus on navigating the rough, winding tracks. He had a recreation map open on the passenger seat, where he marked his turns. The country across which he drove was part of a vast tableland, on top of which a thin veneer of desert life existed, appearing amid swells of iron-red, blowing sand and in the lee of washes and arroyos. For more than an hour he coaxed the Outback over crests of sandstone and across tire-sucking, blowing sand. It was hard driving, working the clutch constantly, and his ankle pulsed. When he finally came to a point where he could drive no farther, he was glad to stop. He parked the Outback in the lee of a giant, twisted juniper, then found a flat rock to sit on, letting the desert's silence ring in his ears.

Silas looked at this watch: it was nearly five in the afternoon. Though there was enough daylight to descend the canyon, there wasn't enough to climb back out. And while he didn't mind hoisting a pack with a stove, food, and a sleeping bag, he felt that his ankle might not bear the additional weight.

He camped where he parked. Sometime shortly after he finished his dinner he heard the whine of a motor. Another vehicle was crawling across the tableland, but it stopped, and he forgot about it. As he curled up in his sleeping bag, his final thoughts were of his wife, and of the witch that Leon Wisechild invoked to lead Silas back to her.

In the morning, the going was much rougher than he expected, and he was glad he had taken his cane. The first half mile was a straightforward, gentle descent of the arroyo leading to Hatch Wash. But within half an hour he was forced to use his hands to down climb steep sections of sandstone, his legs spanning narrow fissures, his body pressed against the side of the perpendicular canyon. He zigzagged his way to the bottom of the side canyon, descending five hundred feet, according to his GPS, in little under a mile.

In another forty minutes he'd walked the length of the branch canyon, descended another five hundred feet, and arrived at the juncture with the main stem of Hatch Wash. A trickle of water ran over the slick sandstone exposed where the two arms of the canyon came together. He bent and soaked his hat in the cool water. He cupped a little to his lips and splashed his face. When he stood up, he regarded the land circling around him. He was a thousand feet below the rim, half of which was the sheer formation known as the Wingate Sandstone, the other half a jumble of sloping terraces and smaller cliffs, dotted with boulder fields and junipers. According to Peter Anton's coordinates, he was less than a mile from the ruins, so he walked very slowly down the central canyon, using his cane for support, and scanning the walls.

Other tracks, both human and animal, had left impressions on the canyon floor. His own distinctive three-legged trail joined the indentations of mule deers' cloven hooves, the frantic tracks of lizards, the impression made by heavy hiking boots.

He continued on. It was still just mid morning, so the light wasn't as harsh as it would be later in the day, the shadows not so deep. But he still walked right past the pocket canyon before he realized he'd missed it. Silas backtracked, his face now to the sun, shielding his eyes from the intense glare. In a few minutes he found the unremarkable side canyon, a jumble of fallen rock and a tangle of tamarisk appearing to cut it off from the main wash. He started in.

The narrow defile was covered in deep shadow and the temperature dropped. In places the side canyon was only twenty feet wide and deeply undercut, so that he could walk with one hand trailing along the wall, the canyon arched out above him like a tunnel. In places the canyon floor was a hodgepodge of boulders and Silas had to climb gingerly over car-sized rocks to avoid slipping on the slick stone. He was concentrating on one such effort when he looked up and was confronted by what Kayah had found. He stopped, stunned.

Laid out in three terraces along a nearly perpendicular section of the side canyon was a series of dwellings and granaries, and what appeared to be a central kiva or temple. He looked around, mystified that such a find could go undiscovered for so long. The upper structures were typical cliff dwellings, cemented into a soft recess of sandstone and protected from the elements by the overhang of cliff above them. Several of them boasted two stories, and all had windows and doorways opening onto a thirty- to forty-foot sheer drop to the canyon floor. The lower structures were laid out in a half moon along the terminus of the pocket canyon, and had intact log-supported roofs and several windows opening into the courtyard where the kiva lay.

Silas sat down on a boulder in disbelief.

He had been to ancient Pueblo ruins over the course of the last three and a half years. He had even found a couple that nobody had marked on a map or noted in a guidebook. He had seen large complexes of ruins, the evidence of a sophisticated civilization that had existed in the canyon country until seven hundred years ago, and then mysteriously vanished.

Sitting on this boulder in the shade of this box canyon, he felt as if he'd never seen a thing up until this moment. There was something about the design of this enclave that was in complete aesthetic harmony.

Hatch Wash was by no means remote. Peter Anton and his team had spent several weeks cataloging what they had found. Nevertheless, the ruins before him felt newly discovered, and in the backcountry of southeastern Utah, that counted for a great deal.

There was little reason to doubt the concern that Anton and Kayah Wisechild and this third man, Williams, would have had for the site's archaeological value. Was it significant enough to stop a major resort development from going up on the adjacent canyon rim? It might not be, but this density of construction suggested that somewhere else scattered through Hatch and its side canyons were other traces of ancient Pueblo civilization: rock art and artifacts. Taken together, and given the pressure to preserve the Canyon Rims region within Canyonlands National Park, it might give pause to the regulator.

Silas took out his binoculars and began to scan the multi-story ruins. The upper structures must have been accessible only by ladders because no handholds or footholds were visible. He examined the smooth surface of the slickrock and could see nothing to indicate another means of approach. In several places, near tiny ledges in front of the doors of the dwellings and granaries, the smooth surface of the stone had been scratched. It looked as if someone had jimmied their way up the slickrock walls to the granaries and cliff dwellings.

He stood and turned his attention to the central kiva. This was new for Silas. He'd seen sites of settlements in the Grand Gulch and Chaco Canyon, where the kiva was an impressively designed sacred space. But this one wasn't on anyone's map. Circular in shape, the kiva's still-intact roof was level with the surrounding canyon floor. The main structure had been dug by hand. The roof had then been constructed from timber dragged into the canyon, which would have been back-breaking labor. The roof had then been covered with chiseled stone. The small hole in the roof would have had a ladder descending into the sacred space. Another opening, not eighteen inches across, allowed fresh air to enter the structure.

At just twenty-five feet in diameter, it was by no means a grand structure, but it was beautiful in its symmetry. Silas peered in through the portal. There was no ladder, and no obvious way for him to get down. He walked to the ground-level portal of the closest building, a low-roofed adobe edifice with four sizable roof beams and windows facing the morning sun. Based on what Anton had told him, he expected a great treasure trove of discovery within, pots, shards, tools, maybe even a basket. With some anticipation he stooped and looked through the low door. It took a moment for his eyes to adjust to the dim light. He could smell the fecund odor of animal urine and stale earth.

It was empty. He fished his headlamp from the top of his pack and put it on, its powerful beam cutting through the dusty air and brightening the corners of the room. There was nothing in this dwelling. He went to the next, and the next, and found the same thing. There was nothing at all.

He felt a wave of disgust wash over him. Penelope had told him many times of how pot hunters and grave robbers plundered the Southwest of its rich archaeological, cultural, and spiritual history.

A resort on top of the mesa above wouldn't necessarily destroy this site, but the thousands of people who would be drawn to such a destination would demand trails, handrails, walkways, and even jeep access to something as spectacular as this ruin. It would be overrun, as Mesa Verde and Hovenweep had been. While its structures might be preserved by the Archaeological Resources Protection Act, the soul of the place would soon be shattered. Silas had heard the arguments before; had even had them from time to time with Penelope. Give thousands of people access to such a place and you allow them to view and maybe even learn a little from it; but in making it easy to reach, the feeling of discovery that he was now experiencing would be gone.

He hadn't fully grasped what Penelope, his own wife, had been arguing for all those years, until now. Silas wondered if she herself might have found this place. If she had, what would she have done about it? He had no doubt that such a discovery by his environment-avenging wife would have led to a tremendous showdown between her and those who wished to plunder this place. She and Jacob Isaiah would have had words, not all of them fit for family company. The BLM would have received an earful for even considering the proposal for a resort built near this delicate site.

Silas was drawn back to the kiva. She would have loved this. Penelope had told him about the kiva in Grand Gulch, and what she felt descending into that consecrated space of the ancient Pueblo people. Having searched the other structures, he decided that he would have to see the interior of this one too. It occurred to him, given the state of plunder, that he should look for further evidence of comings and goings, but now his own footprints in the sand covered the site. He would be more careful as he entered the kiva.

He slipped off his pack and took out the coil of eight-millimeter nylon rope that he carried with him. It was just eighty feet long, but for descending into slot canyons and safely getting out, it was perfect. Now he looked for a place to secure it.

Several boulders near the mouth of the structure would suffice. Silas doubled up the rope and looped it around a boulder a few feet back from the kiva. It left him with plenty of line. He put his weight on it and it held. He decided to play it safe and slipped on his climbing harness. He knew he could just drop into the kiva, but he didn't want to risk reinjuring his tender ankle.

He donned his pack again and stepped to the roof entrance to the ruin. He dropped his cane down first, then slipped the rope into his belay device and leaned back over the door. He eased himself down over the rim and felt the cool air inside the kiva beneath him. He pressed his back against the far side of the opening and carefully let his feet fall out below him and then played out the rope, delivering himself gently to the floor ten feet below the kiva's portal.

He stood a moment and let his eyes adjust to the dim light. He could turn his headlamp on, but wanted to get a look at the space in the natural morning glow first. He immediately noted that this room, too, had been plundered of anything left behind by the ancient Pueblo dwellers. The floor was bare and in fact appeared to have been brushed or swept clean. He found the sipapu, the hole in the floor that symbolized the portal through which the ancient Puebloans believed their ancestors first emerged to enter the present world. Next to it was the fire circle, and then the stone deflector, which kept smoke from being drawn up through the ventilation shaft at the foot of the kiva's wall. The deflector itself was constructed of four large stones, cleaved square, each measuring about a foot and a half by two feet. He looked up. The roof and its rectangular door, with his rope descending through it, ten feet above, seemed very high.

He unclipped his belay tool and walked around the room. To the ancient Pueblo people the kiva was the center of cultural and spiritual life. As he slowly circled the space, running his hand along the smooth stone walls, Silas imagined men gathered there, sitting on the low benches along the walls or gathered around the fire. He circled twice, his hand trailing along the cracks and fissures in the wall, as if searching for purchase there.

As he began his third revolution, his hand caught on something that wasn't stone. He stopped and turned on his headlamp. In one of the deeper fissures in the stone, a space almost large enough to be a ledge, something had been wedged. He hoped that maybe the pot hunters that had desecrated this kiva had missed something. Tucked into the two-inch-high crack, where a stone had been removed from the wall, was a red notebook. He put his fingers around it and gently pried it from its resting place. It came out easily. It was solid in construction, with a thick fabric cover and a delicate but faded pattern of leaves on the cover. It seemed familiar to him, as if he'd seen it before in a storefront or shop. It was covered in a thin layer of very fine dust, and was devoid of marks from fingers or hands. He brushed the dirt off of it and noticed that the dust hadn't soiled the cover.

He opened it, and a shiver went down his spine.

Inside the front cover were notes written in various pens and markers, but there was no mistaking the handwriting. He turned the page and there, at the top, was the familiar phone number. A cell number that he had called no less than a thousand times, almost all *after* his wife had disappeared. He turned the page again, and read what seemed to be a title page: "Notes on Ed Abbey Country," by Penelope de Silva.

He sat down in the dust, legs splayed out before him like a child. He flipped the page again, but there was no date, just several quotes as an end page to the book, and then page after page of descriptive writing. He flipped back to the start and looked again at the inside of the cover. Mostly notes to herself, it seemed. Silas turned to the page of quotations and read the first one:

> I come more and more to the conclusion that wilderness, in America or anywhere else, is the only thing left that is worth saving.

And then:

> I want to weep, not for sorrow, not for joy, but for the incomprehensible wonder of our brief lives beneath the oceanic sky.

They were aphorisms from Edward Abbey, the second having long been Penelope's favorite. It had been framed and mounted above her desk. It was from *The Fool's Progress*, her favorite novel. He was holding in his hands a great prize, his wife's record of her work here in the American Southwest.

Still holding the book, he began to scour the kiva for other signs of her passage. Crawling on hands and knees he examined every crack and crevice for anything else she might have left behind. There was nothing.

He sat down on the stone deflector, both deflated by disappointment and still breathless from what he had found. He opened the book and began to read. It was not prose—but merely a record of places that she had visited in the Southwest, a day or two from her Moab base, circling the Four Corners region that she had come to define as Ed Abbey Country. Her purpose soon became clear: these places that Abbey treasured, those within the national parks and monuments, along with many still unprotected across the vast swath of the Colorado Plateau, should become a single vast and sprawling national monument.

Reading the notebook, it was as if the great mystery of his wife's work was suddenly revealed to Silas. Her work, as she defined it, was to first catalog and then advocate for the preservation of these sites. Many, she noted in her entries, were threatened by such various development schemes: oil and gas, logging, mining, and dams. Others were threatened by such industrial tourism as Jacob Isaiah had planned, and others by off-highway vehicle use.

Silas reflected on his own maps and how they corresponded with so many of the entries in Penelope's journal. Now he would have to cross-reference the journal with his searching to ensure he hadn't missed critical locations. He had the best lead yet as to what his wife had been doing, and where she had been doing it.

He scanned the hundreds of pages of notes for any indication that the Canyon Rims region in which he now sat was on her list. Toward the end of the journal, several pages indicated that she had scoured these washes, based on rumors of a great Pueblo ruin, and had found several sites that were noteworthy in Trout Water, Hatch, and Kane Creek, but nothing that described the grandeur that surrounded him. He wondered how it was that she hadn't made any careful notation of the extraordinary scene that was just above him, outside the walls of this very kiva.

A chill swept over him. What if she had discovered it, and was preparing to make notes on it, when something had happened; when something *bad* had happened.

He thumbed through the final pages. They seemed to be a departure from her normal recorded observations and strategies throughout the journal. Here she did lapse into prose, and then his eyes caught his name.

> If only my darling Silas was with me now, I would hold him
> in my arms and help him see that this world of rock and stars
> and sky is all that we need. Here I am completely at ease, and
> with him in my arms I would be completely happy.

He put the book down and pounded his fist into the dirt. "Fuck!" he said. "Fuck, fuck, fuck!" he yelled, this time more forcefully. The sound was absorbed by the kiva's walls. In the silence, he heard the clink of rock against rock.

He stopped moving, his fist still in the dirt. Had his shout sent vibrations among the ancient ruins, causing a rock to drop from the cliff?

Not impossible; the whole place was just a pile of loose stone waiting for gravity to do its business. But he realized he had heard something else in the wake of his outburst. Voices? The Canyonlands often played such tricks: the trickle of distant water, the call of a raven high overhead or a black bird in the rushes; even the wind often sounded like voices. More than once he'd been shocked to hear his wife calling him from around the bend in a canyon, and when he'd rounded the corner, no one was there.

He heard another stone tumble, and then nothing more. He stood and tucked the notebook into his pack. He would take it back to his camp and read it cover to cover. Then he would drive home and spend the evening transposing the locations from the journal onto his wall maps.

He checked once more to see if he had missed anything. Satisfied, he took his jummars from the bag and clipped them to the line that hung from the opening ten feet above. He put his cane in his pack, and reached up as high as he could with the tools, meaning to make short work of his ascent. He gave a sharp tug to test tension on the rope, but instead of meeting resistance, he tumbled backward. A cloud of red dust floated up into the still air of the temple. He quickly stood up and pulled on the rope again. It was completely slack. He pulled some more and another five feet of rope joined him in the kiva.

The loop that he had secured around the rock had come undone. He pulled and now he guessed less than ten feet of rope remained on top of the kiva.

How had the loop come free? A final tug and the rope tumbled down onto the floor, another cloud of dust rising around him.

He looked around. The ten feet to the opening in the roof was the height of a basketball net. Even when he was young he had never once been able to touch the rim of a regulation net, no matter how much of a running jump he took. At fifty-five, with a sprained ankle, he doubted he could now. The walls of the kiva stood twenty feet wide, so the nearest point to the gap was ten feet away. Even the best climbers in Utah would have a hard time "pulling a roof" that steep. And his skills were far from those of a good climber.

He stared up at the opening, at the daylight beyond, and then down at the rope on the floor. The kiva's sanctuary had become a tomb.

17

HE DREAMT. THEY SAT IN the familiar comfort of Café Espress on San Francisco Street in downtown Flagstaff. He sipped his coffee and scrawled a note on a term paper. He became aware that Penelope was looking at him. "What is it?" he asked.

She smiled sweetly at him, and then her brow furrowed a little, her dark eyes becoming serious. "What is it that's haunting me, Si?"

"What?" he said.

"What is it that's haunting me? At times I hear voices up the road, familiar voices . . . I look; and no one is there."

Penelope stood and walked toward the front of the café. She reached the door and swung it open and stepped out onto the street. A moment later he was behind her; but she was gone.

He looked up and down the street but couldn't see her. "Penny!" he shouted. "Wait!" He ran toward the newsstand on the corner, but she wasn't there. He turned around, but she had vanished.

HE WOKE, HIS back aching, his ankle on fire with pain. He'd spent the afternoon and much of the evening trying to climb the walls of the kiva. His fingers were bleeding and he had fallen and landed hard on his side and bruised his ribs again. Finally, he had lain on a stone bench against the wall and fallen into a restless sleep. Awakening from this dream, he recalled its signature, the feeling of it, so familiar. And her words; he didn't even need to turn to a copy of *Desert Solitaire* to know that they were from the opening paragraph of "The Dead Man at Grandview Point."

It was dark outside. Beyond the roof of the kiva, he couldn't see any stars. He turned on his headlamp and realized that the batteries were growing dim. He had a spare set, but he decided to save them and turned the light out.

He would not, in all likelihood, die down there. He'd told Katie Rain that he was going to search for something. She also knew that he had spoken with Peter Anton. If he hadn't called in a couple of days, maybe three or four, she would begin to wonder and try to reach him. When she couldn't, she'd alert the authorities. Who, exactly? The BLM? San Juan County Search and Rescue? Unless Anton gave them the exact coordinates, however, it would be hard to find the box canyon he was in. Silas had walked right by it, and he was an experienced canyoneer.

There was no reason for Silas to believe that Peter Anton would provide the proper coordinates, was there? Maybe this had been his reason for giving Silas the location of the ruins in the first place—to lure him into this remote corner of Canyon Rims, to trap him here and leave him to die. He shook his head. It was a thin thread of hope to believe that Katie Rain would send anyone to his rescue.

He reviewed the contents of his pack. He'd tried two dozen times to get a signal for his cell phone, standing on the rocks at the back of the fire pit and holding the phone high over his head. He had two more thirty-two-ounce bottles of water, and enough trail mix for a few days. He could do without food, but the water concerned him. Even though the kiva's temperature remained constantly at around sixty degrees night and day, the aridity of the southwest desert sucked moisture out of the body. Under normal conditions a person could last just three, four, maybe five days without water. If he drew out his ration he might last a week or ten days.

It would be a desperate week to endure. Finding Kayah had led him to this kiva, where he had found Penelope's notebook. Now the dream was enticing him to Grand View Point in Canyonlands National Park. In Abbey's day a dirt road wove across the Island in the Sky, rutted and pocked and inaccessible after a hard rain. Today you could drive it in any old jalopy; or more aptly, in air-conditioned comfort in your RV or tour bus. Of course, Grand View Point had been the very first place he had looked for her. Three and a half years ago he had gone there, camped at Green River Overlook for week, and walked a grid back and forth across the torturous plateau until his feet bled. He had found nothing.

Now his wife was clearly directing him toward the overcrowded rim at Grand View Point. Under this clear directive, and with the treasure trove of intelligence in the notebook he had found, he stirred with frustration. He paced around the darkened kiva and twice kicked the deflector stones, sending a spasm of pain up his leg.

An idea formed, providing faint hope. He bent down and tried to move one of the stones. If he could stack one on top of the next he might be able to reach the opening in the ceiling. He groaned with effort, his face turning red, the veins standing out in his neck as he labored to move a single massive rock. It was no good; he couldn't budge it an inch.

Sweating and exhausted, he sat back down. A cool breeze trickling across his feet directed his attention to the ventilation shaft. He bent down and turned on his headlamp. The opening was no more than eighteen inches wide, squared off with heavy, roughly hewn sandstone. He peered inside. It extended half a dozen feet, and then turned upward at a right angle. From examining other similar sites, he knew that the shaft vented into the courtyard that surrounded the ceremonial room. Shards of stone and a maze of spider webs choked the shaft, but it looked wide enough for his torso. He wondered, however, how tight the fit would be where the shaft made its pivot toward the sky. Anything less than a couple of feet and he wouldn't be able to wedge his body into that space. He peered into the darkness again. There was no way to tell in the inky night, even with his headlamp. He would have to wait until morning.

Silas pulled his light jacket from his pack, took a sip of water, and lay back down on the bench, again drifting into a fitful, claustrophobic sleep.

AT FIRST LIGHT he rose, took another drink and walked to the opening in the wall by the floor. It seemed much more confined when viewed in the harsh light of day. But the sharp turn was now illuminated by the daylight penetrating the top of the shaft. There were a few stones he would have to clear before getting too far into the shaft. He contemplated it for a good ten minutes and then decided he had to try.

The first thing he did was take off his hiking pants and his long-sleeved shirt. He needed to be as thin as possible, and didn't want to risk his clothing catching on a loose rock. Standing in his underwear, he tied the rope around his ankle. Should he be successful he would need the rope to lower himself back down into the kiva to retrieve his pack and the precious journal inside it. He took a sip of water and ate a handful of trail mix, and sipped some water again.

If this worked, he could back at the Outback by lunch. If he failed, sometime in the future someone, maybe the FBI or the San Juan Search and Rescue, would find him wedged in the ventilation shaft, in his underwear, likely bitten black and blue by scorpions and tarantulas and gnawed on by rodents.

He bent down and used his long arms to clear the spider webs and debris as far as he could reach. Then, drawing a deep breath, he lay on his back on the floor of the kiva and raised his arms above his head, in part to feel his way, and in part to guide his body up when he reached the vertical shaft. As he pushed with his feet, his head entered the dark space, and he closed his eyes to keep out the dislodged dust and debris. His shoulders followed. It was cold in the shaft. The stones scratched his back, and a sharp edge pierced his shoulder. He could feel the wet, tacky blood. He reconsidered the decision to shed his clothing but decided he could live with a few cuts; he could not live with getting stuck.

He continued to push with his feet, digging his heels into the floor, and his shoulders continued scraping against the sides of the shaft. Silas tried to breathe slowly, pulling the musty air into his lungs. His breathing became a staccato rhythm and he fought to control his spiraling fear. Silas pressed his eyes closed and forced himself to breathe normally. He worked his feet on the hard packed floor, his boots digging into the dirt. He pushed again and his chest was in the opening. He drew another deep breath and was relieved that his heaving lungs didn't press his chest against the top of the shaft.

His hands touched something; the elbow in the shaft where it turned upward. He felt around for something to indicate how wide the opening was. He managed to walk his hands back and forth above him and determined that the space was nearly as wide as the one he was in: eighteen inches. Would it be big enough to make the turn? He knew that if he got halfway into the vertical duct, he might not get back out. Once he had made the turn, it would be all or nothing.

More debris fell onto his face, and another rock dug a trench down his back. He imagined he felt something moving across his stomach. The urge to panic and push his way back out grew. He started to breathe faster, his chest rising and falling, tiny stones rolling off it. His feet fought for purchase. He was going to die in this hole in the earth and he would never find her.

He pushed with his feet and pulled on the ledge of stone where the shaft made its turn and felt his head touch the far wall. His hands holding the corner of the shaft were now by his sternum. He drew in and exhaled again. If he opened his eyes he might even be able to see the sky above him now. He felt a breeze on his face, air being sucked down the flue. He pushed again and as he did, used his abdominal muscles to bend his body as tightly as he could, his head banging roughly against the stone, his feet pushing for all he was worth. This was the moment. He wedged himself more tightly into the turn, his face pinched in a grimace, the air escaping his lungs in an involuntary cry.

He was stuck. He stopped, then wiggled his whole body like a worm, pushing his arms fully up again. His feet were now completely within the shaft and no longer able to gain as much traction. His head and vertebrae grated against the rock wall beneath him.

He only gradually realized he was sitting upright, the vertical shaft fractionally wider than the horizontal. He could feel blood trickling down his back, and his knees were bleeding too. He reached up high overhead and found a crack in the stones forming the walls of the shaft. Digging in his fingers, he pulled for all he was worth. He raised himself up a few inches at a time, fighting the overwhelming urge to thrash with his feet. He turned his hips, and therefore his legs and knees, sideways to make the turn. In a short moment he was standing. He could feel the outside world teasing his hair.

He was upright; his arms extended overhead, his body touching the walls all around him. From here there was nowhere to go but up. Silas realized that he was praying. He had no idea how to do this, or to whom, but he said to the stone walls all around him, "Get me out of this place and I will find Kayah Wisechild's killer, and find my wife. Or die trying. Get me out of this place!"

His fingers found another hold. They felt sticky and hot and he realized he'd cut them too. His back and chest felt like they were on fire. His feet could move, so he used his heels and knees to wedge himself into the duct and then push upward. He had done this before, shimmying through the narrow slot canyons that carved up the desert plateau. He moved up a foot then another. The opening was above him and with all the strength he could muster he pulled himself free and collapsed on the earth.

He reached up to dig the grit out of his eyes, then carefully opened them. The blue sky above was pocked with only a few tiny, high clouds. His first instinct was tremendous relief. His second was pure, unfiltered rage. He stood and went to the place where he looped the rope. He could see the track it had made when he pulled it down into the kiva. There was no way in hell it had come undone on its own. The stone he had looped it around was nearly three feet high. He would have had to snap it like a lariat to get it over that rock. It had been pulled up and over that stone by human hands. He drew it up from the shaft now and coiled it on the earth well back from the opening.

Silas hunched down on the ground to study the area for tracks. He could see his own prints leading to the kiva opening, but could not see them in the dust around the stones he had used as an anchor. Whoever had unhooked the line had brushed away their tracks, erasing his as well. It was sloppy work. He backed out a hundred yards toward the main stem of the wash and found sign of the intruder where they had dropped a scraggly bunch of rabbit brush they had used as a broom. He soon found boot prints in a sandy path of earth between two boulders. He would measure them after he retrieved his pack.

Thirst came on, now that his anger was ebbing and so he went back to the kiva and tied the rope off again. This time he tied two sets of knots and moved a heavy stone on top of the rope to provide further tension. When he wiped the sweat from his eyes, his hand came away bloody. The adrenaline that surged through him after his escape was also ebbing. He took note that his upper body, knees, and arms were crisscrossed with hundreds of tiny scrapes and cuts, some of which bled freely, while others were clogged with dirt. He brushed off his chest and legs, but that only caused several of the deeper cuts to bleed.

Silas quickly dropped back into the kiva, slinging the rope around his back and through his legs to create an effective break for his short rappel.

Back inside he put his clothes back on, gathered up his gear, reattached the ascenders to the rope, and without pausing hoisted himself back out of the ceremonial chamber.

AFTER TAKING CAREFUL measurements of the boot imprints, Silas photographed them with his point-and-shoot camera. He washed some of the blood from his body in the tiny creek and headed back to his vehicle. His ankle ached, but the urge to be free of the place propelled him up the canyon. The last mile, through the sandy upper reaches of the arroyo, he leaned heavily on his cane.

To his surprise, his car was where he left it. Whoever had followed him into the gorge hadn't bothered to sabotage his vehicle, probably believing he would never make it back. He opened the hatch and took a pound of bacon and some eggs from his cooler and set up his stove. He ate a grease-laden breakfast, accompanied by a cold beer, while he sat overlooking the dendrite-like grottos where he had been left to die twenty-four hours earlier.

Only one person knew where he was going and that was Peter Anton. Silas had a good mind to drive straight back to Cortez and confront the man that afternoon. When he considered the journal, and his dream, he thought better of it. He fished his binoculars from the chaos of his pack and scanned the country around him. It was conceivable that whoever had left him to die in the kiva might be watching him now. He turned three hundred and sixty degrees but could see no sign of other people on the plateau. Whoever had wanted to entomb him with the ghosts of the Pueblo ancestors was likely long gone.

Silas packed up his car, and opening another beer, turned over the ignition and cranked up the air conditioning. He began the long drive back to Castle Valley. He had work to do that involved a room full of maps.

THE SUN WAS setting over the Castle Valley and he had been staring at the maps on his living room walls for three hours. His body ached and his head hurt but he had managed to go through much of his wife's notebook and transpose the areas she called Abbey's Country onto the walls. Many of the locations he had already searched: Arches, Canyonlands, Natural Bridges National Monument, and Capitol Reef National Park. Others, like Dark Horse Canyon, Canyons of the Escalante, and Grand Canyon, he had made superficial explorations of, but had much legwork left to do. Areas such as the depths of Glen Canyon, now a fathom below the fetid waters of Lake Powell, the unprotected lands of Labyrinth Canyon on the Green River, and the vast tableland of the Kaiparowits Plateau he'd scarcely begun to explore.

Silas went outside to sit in the evening air and opened his wife's notebook again. He'd been so absorbed in the details of it, maybe he had missed something important. His raw fingers fumbled with the pages and he dropped it. Grumbling, he picked it up again. It had fallen open to the inside cover. He looked it over with bemusement. A series of random scribbles by his wife: notes about groceries, locations for finding various supplies in towns like Escalante and Kanab, a few phone numbers heavily underscored. "Call Hayduke" was scrawled across the top in a thick Sharpie marker. Next to it was a number with a Utah exchange.

Hayduke was the creation of Edward Abbey that Silas least liked. Silas knew that Hayduke was a name Abbey applied to a variety of protagonists in unpublished stories before the character emerged as the misanthropic eco-saboteur who led the *Monkey Wrench Gang*. He was a Vietnam vet and a desert rat, and spent the bulk of the novel slurping cheap beer, littering the highways with his empties and cursing and cavorting with the Gang's somewhat loose heroine Bonnie Abbzug. He supposedly died in a hail of gunfire in the Maze district of Canyonlands on a dead-end mesa above Horse Canyon.

Call Hayduke. It wouldn't surprise him to learn that his wife had a friend who went by that name. Silas didn't know much about the people she ran with while she was on her crusades in the canyonlands. He wondered just how well his wife had known this Hayduke.

He got the cordless phone from the house and sank back down. He dialed the number. It rang five times and then a woman's voice came on telling him that the party he had called was out of the service area. He hung up. That didn't surprise him: half of Utah was out of the service area for cell phones.

He put the phone down and after a minute it rang. He jumped. Hayduke calling back?

"Hello?" His voice was hoarse. He realized he hadn't spoken to a soul in thirty-six hours, much of which he'd been below ground.

"Dr. Pearson, it's Katie Rain."

He cleared this throat. "Hi Katie."

"You sound like you've been gargling with flood water again, Silas."

"Thanks. I look like it too."

"More adventures?"

"No, just a quiet day out here at the home place," he said.

"I told you I'd check in, so I am."

"I appreciate that. Nice to be looked in on."

"I have a little news. Agent Taylor paid Peter Anton a visit. Taylor knows about the rumored affair, and went to talk with him today. Anton was, shall we say, uncooperative. He did, however, give *you* up pretty quickly. Notes in Taylor's file say that he now has grounds to bring you back in for another interview."

"Guess I'll have company tomorrow."

"I'd expect so."

"Thanks, Katie. Why are you helping me?"

There was a long pause. "I don't really know. I don't figure you for the death of the Wisechild girl. Nobody gets themselves knocked around in a flash flood just to cover up a two-year-old murder. So I guess I trust you."

"I had a dream, you know. That's why I was there. In my dream my wife *sent* me to Sleepy Hollow; to Courthouse Wash. That's why I was looking there."

The line was silent for a time. "I think you've been under a lot of stress, Silas. For a long time. You should see someone about it. Talk to someone, you know?"

"I am talking with someone. You."

"I'm a forensic anthropologist. I'd be more comfortable with you if you'd been dead for a few hundred years."

He smiled. It made the cuts on his face hurt. "You think I'm crazy."

"I think you're . . . dedicated."

"You think I'm obsessed."

"Silas, you've undergone a terrible loss. You're feeling guilt and remorse. It's common in these situations. You're brain doesn't know how to handle it. So it creates these . . . manifestations. Dreams."

He drew a deep breath. The sun was down and the sky was the color of the ocean after a storm. "Okay, well, thanks for the information. I guess I'll pack my pajamas for my trip to the clink."

"Are you okay?"

"Yeah."

"Good luck."

He thanked her and hung up. He hadn't dared tell her about his Grand View Point dream. She would have thought him certifiable.

18

IN THE MORNING HE FELT the pull of two competing priorities, find Hayduke and venture out to Grand View Point. Standing in front of the maps, Silas fiddled with the notebook for a few minutes and then made a decision. He would re-pack the car for camping and head into Moab to see if he could locate what might merely be a fictional character. Knowing that the FBI would likely be requesting his presence at the Sheriff's Office, he took the back road into town.

He parked by the Red Rock Inn and walked the single block to Main Street. He used his cell to dial the number in the journal again. Still no response. He knew exactly where to look for someone calling themselves Hayduke in the town of Moab.

For more than twenty years Back of Beyond Books had been the unofficial headquarters for Edward Abbey groupies. Silas opened the door and stepped into the store. Even if the shop was organized around an Edward Abbey section, Silas still loved it. He heard a voice call from behind the counter, "Oh-oh, Janet, better look out; the competition is in the store." Silas couldn't help but smile. Mary Avery, one of the owners, always ribbed him when he came in.

"Long time no see stranger . . ." and then, getting a look at him, "Jesus, Silas, what happened to you?"

"That bad?"

"You look like you hitched yourself to a horse and let it drag you clear across Poison Spider Mesa."

"Had a little argument with gravity," he lied. "Gravity won, as usual."

"Come here," Avery insisted. He did as he was told. From behind the store counter she put a delicate hand to his face. "Well, taken on their own they aren't so bad. It's just that all together you look to be a little worse for wear."

"I'll live."

"I hope so."

"I suppose with me out of the way—"

Avery laughed. "We'd sell at least three or four more books a month. When was the last time you were open?"

"I was open for an hour the other day . . ."

She laughed again. "What can I do for you, Silas? Or are you just here to spy?"

He leaned on the counter. "I'm looking for someone. He goes by the name of Hayduke. Maybe you guys would know him."

"Half the environmentalists in Moab fancy themselves some kind of Hayduke doppelganger, all big beards and long hair and leather sombreros."

"I think this guy might have known my wife, Penny."

Avery's smile faded. "No luck yet?" she asked respectfully.

"Nothing yet."

"I heard about the girl in Courthouse Wash."

Silas remained implacable. At least the media didn't know about his involvement yet. "I feared the worse. I still hope Penny will turn up in some little backward town like Hanksville, raising somebody else's kids."

Avery shook her head. "You know, I saw her a lot before she . . . before she disappeared, Silas. She never once had eyes for another man. Don't listen to that jackass Jacob Isaiah. He's a class A prick and is just getting under your skin because of how rough your wife was on his development plans."

"Do you know anything about what Isaiah was up to out at Hatch Wash?"

"He's got big ideas for just about every place within a couple of hours of Moab," she said. "But I don't recall anything. Doesn't mean much; *this* place is a full-time effort."

"What about this Hayduke?" Avery's colleague Janet Dempsey had come to the counter during the conversation, her arms loaded with books needing to be stocked. "I think you're talking about Josh Charleston." Silas looked at her. He had recently met a Josh.

"You know him?" he asked.

"Yeah, kid about twenty-eight, maybe thirty. Calls himself Hayduke. Has the beard and the hair. Not really a serious enviro. Just makes a lot of noise. I do remember seeing him with your wife once or twice, Silas. In here, and once on Main Street."

"Were they friends?"

"I don't know," said Janet.

"Don't suppose you know how to find this guy? He live here in town?"

"Winters he does. Summers he camps out in the Manti-La Lal National Forest."

Silas knew exactly where to find Hayduke.

THE ROAD TO Oowah Lake was rough and winding, but within two hours of leaving Back of Beyond Silas was driving through the aspen parkland that rimmed the La Sals. Mount Tukuhnikivatz rose prominently on the skyline, its symmetrical summit still dappled with patches of winter snow late in August. At over twelve thousand feet, summer never got a hand-hold on this prominent crest.

Silas parked at the gate to the campsite and unfolded his sore body from the car, holding his cane for support. He began to walk around the lanes, looking for Josh Charleston's Jeep. He asked about Josh when he saw other campers, but nobody had seen him or his machine. Finally, near the back of the site he found an older man who had been there on and off throughout the summer. He told Silas that Josh had moved to nearby Warner Lake.

Silas returned to his Outback and drove for half an hour on the winding, rocky roads, and pulled up at the Warner Lake trailhead. The blue Jeep Wrangler was parked among three or four others. Taking his cane again, Silas started up the trail, but when he reached the campground, it was empty. Josh could have ventured into the high country and might not be back for a week. He could be climbing Haystack Mountain or crossing Burro Pass and be ten miles from here. Frustrated, Silas turned and walked back to his car. The breeze rustled the leaves so they sounded like wind chimes made from rice paper.

When he got to the dirt parking lot he stopped in his tracks. The man he had met earlier in the week—who had introduced himself as Josh—was digging in the back of his Jeep.

"Mr. Charleston?" said Silas.

The man raised his shaggy head from the back of his machine and looked at Silas.

"We met up in Miner's Basin. I'm Silas Pearson."

Josh looked around. "Not blocking you in this time, am I?"

Silas approached him and stuck out his hand. "You're not. I wonder if you have time to chat." They shook, and Josh's hand eclipsed his own.

"'Bout what?"

"Would you like a beer?"

"Fuck yeah."

Silas went to the back of his vehicle, opened the hatch, and took two Canadians from his cooler. He handed one to Josh, who popped the top and drank the foam from the can. Some caught in his beard. He wiped his mouth with the back of his hairy hand. Silas wondered if this young man had been genetically altered to look like his alter-ego somehow; it was eerie, and he watched in fascination.

"What is it you want to talk about?" Josh said after swallowing half of his beer.

"I think you must have known my wife," Silas said.

Josh stopped drinking and looked at him. "Listen, there have been a few girls, but . . ."

"Not like that. I think you must have done some work with her. Some conservation work. Her name was Penelope de Silva. Did you know her?"

As Silas watched, Josh's face changed from mirthful to dark and somber and back to contentment. "I knew Penelope. She was a kick-ass and take-no-prisoners activist, man. She was rock solid, like rock fucking solid," he said, and to emphasis his point, stamped his booted foot on the ground.

"When did you see her last?"

"Oh man, it's been years. Like, four years? I heard she had gone missing. I heard *you* were looking, you know, it was in the papers and online. I haven't seen her in so long."

"Do you remember exactly when?"

"I'd need to think," said Josh, and as if to facilitate that, he put the can of beer to his lips and drank, his hairy Adam's apple bobbing as he tilted his head back. "I think it was in Moab, maybe May, just before she went missing. Maybe two months, three months before?" he said, and then belched. "We met at the bookstore and talked about issues. Man, she knew so much. She was really amazing."

"Thank you, I know she was," said Silas, realizing that he didn't really. He reached into his bag and took out the notebook and flipped it open. He showed Josh the book. "Is this you?" he asked, pointing to the scrawled note, "Call Hayduke."

"Yeah, that's me! Penelope insisted on calling me that. *She* gave me that name. I sometimes called her Bonnie. But we were never, you know, like in the book. Nothing like that, man."

"It's okay. I know. Do you know why she would have written that there?"

"Well, like I said, we worked a bit together. I helped her out. You know, with protecting this place," he said, holding his arms up. "The canyons, the deserts, the mountains. We did some good work together."

"Why would she have needed to write this?"

"I don't know."

"Can you remember what she was working on before she disappeared?"

"She didn't tell you? Man, sometimes it was hard to shut her up about stuff."

"We talked about a lot of other things. Can you remember?"

"I'd need to think about that. It was a long time ago."

Silas offered another beer.

"Hey," said Josh, "Why didn't you find me before and ask me this? It's been a long time."

"Well . . . I didn't know about you. You see, I just found this journal."

"Where?"

"Well, it sounds crazy."

"Try me."

"I found it in a kiva."

"Like, an Anasazi kiva?"

"Yeah, ancient Pueblo . . ."

"Which one?"

"Well, that's what I wanted to talk with you about. You see, it was in a set of ruins in Hatch Wash. In a little box canyon off the main stem. There's an amazing set of ruins there. Supposedly unmapped."

"Can you believe it? And so close to town. It's fucking crazy. They're only thirty miles from Moab."

"So you know about them. I agree, it's crazy. That's what I thought. But I talked with Peter Anton the other day—"

"Bad news, man. That guy is bad fucking news."

"Why do you say that?"

"He's working for the developmentalists; you know, people who are obsessed with paving this place. He's working for that fucker Isaiah."

"Not anymore."

"Once you're in, you never get out, man. Never."

"What do you mean, you never get out?"

"Those fuckers, they're like the mob, man. You take a blood oath. You don't get to just walk away."

Silas started to wonder how much sun Josh had gotten recently. He changed the subject. "Peter Anton told me about the ruins in Hatch. It seems that a young woman found dead in Courthouse Wash was working with him there before she disappeared two years ago."

"I heard about her. Found by a hiker."

"That was me."

"Fuck off, no way."

"Yeah."

"What were you doing there?"

"Well, I was . . . I was looking for my wife."

"You found this other chick instead. That is too much of a fucking coincidence."

"I think so too." Silas told him about his search, and the maps, and the dream about Sleepy Hollow.

"Right out of *Solitaire*, man. That is too fucking creepy."

Silas sipped his beer. "I went into Hatch, and there in the kiva is this notebook."

"You think Pen might have left it there?"

"Pen?"

"Yeah, sorry, it's what I called Penelope. Pen suited her better. You know, the pen is sharper—"

"—than the sword." Silas tried to keep the sadness of not knowing this nickname from registering on his face. He waited for Josh to take another long drink from his beer.

"This Canadian shit is pretty good," he said, belching. He crushed the can in his powerful hand. "Look, I have no idea how Pen's book got down into Hatch. Maybe she was there working on stuff and forgot it."

"I don't think so. It was not like Penelope to forget something this important. The notebook had laid out her plans for something she was calling Ed Abbey Country."

Josh stopped and looked at him. "You found *that* notebook?"

"Yeah, so?"

"It's just that, man, that was a really important bit of work."

"Tell me about it."

"Well, me and her, and some others I guess, we had this big idea to introduce a bill in the US Senate calling for the creation of Ed Abbey National Monument. It would protect a whole bunch of important places from further development, and restore a bunch of places the shitheads have already trashed. Stuff that's not already protected, like Canyon Rims and Back of the Rocks, as well as designate more capital W wilderness in the parks and monuments like Grand Canyon and Escalante, under the Wilderness Act."

"What was happening with this plan?"

"It wasn't going well. Pen was looking for a senator to introduce it. She met with that asshole Thorn Smith—well, with his dick-head assistant Nephi—and she was getting nowhere. She was going to look elsewhere for a friendly senator; you know, maybe back east where they have no wilderness. That's when she disappeared."

"And what about Canyon Rims? Was that part of the plan?"

"Yeah, it was part of the plan. Canyon Rims and Basins, they call it. The whole thing, right from 191 all the way to the park, and including Back of the Rocks. We were going to kick all the OHV crowd out on their ass."

"What about the plans for the golf course, for the hotels."

"Jacob Isaiah's fucking wet dream? We knew about it. Pen was all over it. She gave Jacob Isaiah a serious ear full."

"Did she talk about the ruins?"

"No. We didn't even know about them then. It wasn't until we started to prowl around down there that we learned about them."

"How? Did you find them?"

"No, there was a leak. Someone in Isaiah's camp let it slip."

"Do you think it could have been the young woman I found in Courthouse? She worked with Peter Anton at Dead Horse Consulting."

"I never knew the source of the leak. When it finally happened, I was away. I've got projects going on all over the Southwest, you know what I mean? Pen was handling that one on her own."

"Do you think it's possible that Jacob Isaiah found out that Penelope knew about the ruins and that they would be the nail in his coffin, so to speak, and, you know—"

"What, had her bumped off?" said Josh. "Man, it's always possible. That guy is a bad fucking dude. It's possible."

"And then, after the fact, learns that it was the Wisechild girl who was leaking, and so takes her out as well?"

"Like I said, I wouldn't put it past him."

"Who else do you think would have wanted my wife out of the way, Josh?"

"Why you asking me that, man? I don't know." He suddenly sounded defensive.

"Look, Josh, you're the only person I've met who actually worked closely with my wife. The other enviros in town, they all knew her and respected her, but nobody really worked closely with her. Now I find this," he said, holding up the book, "and it leads me straight to you. Do you think that's a coincidence?"

The young man shook his head. Something fell out of his hair; a twig or a leaf. "No, I don't. I don't know what happened to her. I'm as busted up about it as anybody."

Silas regarded him. "Josh, I need your help. I think that my wife wanted me to find Kayah Wisechild because the girl would lead me to this," he said, again holding up the book, "and that would lead me to *you*. I think you're my best shot at finding my wife."

"You still think Pen is alive, don't you?"

"I don't know."

"Where do you think she might be hiding?"

"I don't know."

"What *do* you know?"

Silas contemplated the scraggly stranger sitting next to him. "I know that my wife loved this place and that this is where she went missing. I know that against all the odds, I found the body of a young woman who had helped discover a set of ruins my wife was exploring. If I know anything about how Penelope thinks, she was hoping to use them to shut down a development that would have destroyed a place she loved. Somehow they are connected and I have been led to find *you*. Believe me, I'd do this on my own if I could, Josh. I would. No offense, but I really prefer my own company to just about anybody else. But I *can't* do this by myself. I need you. You knew her. You helped her. I need you to help *me*."

Josh turned away and looked up the mountains. A sly, wolfish grin came over his face.

"What is it?" asked Silas.

"If I'm going to help you, you're going to have to start calling me Hayduke."

Silas shook his head. "I don't know if Penny told you, but I don't really like Edward Abbey."

"Oh, yeah, she told me, alright."

JOSH CHARLESTON—HAYDUKE—HAD AGREED to sleep on Silas's request for assistance and call him in the next couple of days. He said he needed to get his shit together before he could jump back in with both feet.

Driving down into the Castle Valley, Silas turned his attention to his next task: finding out exactly what his wife wanted him to discover at Grand View Point. Maybe, he thought, a knot forming in his stomach, he wouldn't need Hayduke's help to find Penelope after all.

19

IT WAS 4:00 PM BY the time he approached the narrow peninsula of land known as Grand View Point. The night before he had re-read "Dead Man," and had used a fifteen-minute topo to carefully pinpoint the possible locations where Abbey, or more appropriately his brother Johnny, had found the cadaver at Grand View Point. He couldn't imagine a body remaining undiscovered for more than a few days, or even a week, on the point itself. Less than a mile across, it was the most heavily visited part of Canyonlands. Even though 90 per cent of the visitors to the Point only walked from their tour buses and RVs to the overlook and back, there were still a few who prowled around, aroused by the extraordinary view, seeking a moment of blissful solitude.

Instead of driving to the end of the road, Silas parked at Mesa Arch, where the plateau begins to narrow, and began walking north and east toward Gray's Pasture.

He carried his backpack, complete with light camping gear. He figured if he didn't find what he was looking for, he could camp illegally in one of the washes and be up at first light to continue his search.

After four hours of constant walking, crawling, and slithering through brush and narrow defiles, he had found nothing. His GPS said that he had walked almost ten miles, but he was only two miles from his car. He was caught by surprise when the sun sank below the western rim of Island in the Sky. He wondered if he should walk back to his car and drive to the Willow Flat Campground or simply sleep where he was. He chose the former, and finding the road just a few hundred yards away, tramped down the blacktop to his Outback and then drove to the parking lot at Green River Overlook. Ignoring the No Camping sign, he lay down in the back of the car, the tailgate open, listening to coyotes yap and yammer in the distance.

In the morning he rose before dawn and, foregoing coffee and break-fast, set out again with his pack. This time he wandered back and forth through a square mile of twisted earth that was closed in by the park access road on one side and the fifteen-hundred-foot drop into Soda Springs Basin on the other.

As the sun came up, he emerged from a broad pothole and crested a ridge to see chunks of Navajo sandstone formed into a bench shape. Drawn to the cluster of rock, he walked up the side of the depression and stopped where the earth vanished before him. Silas could see that the stones amassed before him, hedged up against the juniper, had not fallen there naturally; they had been piled.

Taking his pack off, Silas donned the pair of leather gloves he used for rope work and heaved a few of the stones aside. His ankle, healing well, held up for the heavy work, and in a moment he'd moved half a dozen of the giant rocks, each weighing a hundred pounds or more. After five minutes, he had shifted half the pile. Another five minutes hard labor provided him with his grisly reward.

THE CRIME SCENE encompassed all of the Green River Overlook parking lot, which provided space for the command center involving the Park Service, Sheriff's Office, Medical Examiner, and FBI Critical Incident Response Unit. Silas had made his call around 9:30, and by 11:00 AM Agent Taylor and his team had arrived and taken command of the vicinity. The media arrived, too, and were herded into a corner of the overlook where they milled about, spreading rumors. Just after 1:00 PM a helicopter landed on the access road and Katie Rain and another agent from the Trace Evidence Unit walked down the recently paved road.

Silas was sitting on the tailgate of a Park Service pick-up truck, drink-ing a bottle of water.

"Dr. Pearson," she said when she saw him.

"Dr. Rain."

"What have we got?"

Taylor appeared from between two FBI vehicles, Special Agent Nielsen at his side.

"Dr. Rain, this way please," said Taylor.

"Did Dr. Pearson find the body?"

"He did," said Taylor.

"I need him along, then," she said.

Taylor looked at Silas. "Let's go."

Silas stood and the four of them walked across the parking lot. Flagging tape ran along a roughly marked trail that cut across the slick-rock to the juniper where Silas had made his discovery. Nobody spoke. The afternoon sun was merciless and they were all soaked with sweat by the time they arrived at the tree.

A broad white tent had been set up around the site. Half a dozen FBI agents looked busy, and Chief Ranger Stan Baton, along with Sheriff Dexter Willis and Kiel Vaughn, the San Juan County sheriff, were there too. Derek Penshaw was on the scene once again to represent the Medical Examiner.

"What have we got?" asked Rain, stepping into the tent and taking off her bag.

It was Penshaw who spoke. "Intact skeletal remains; human."

"Condition?" asked Rain.

"Looks pretty much complete. Some fragments of clothing, though not much. No skin, but some hair fibers. Not much else. No identification."

"Dr. Pearson," said Rain. "Did you move the body?"

"No. I moved about two dozen stones from on top of it, however. Some shifting may have occurred when I did that."

"Okay," said Rain. "Let's see what we've got here." She looked at Huston, who pulled back the shroud that had been protecting the corpse. The skeleton was laid out carefully between rows of red sandstone boulders. Silas hadn't seen it since he found it that morning, and then he had only moved enough stones to discover a foot. The bones all lay flat against the earth, but they had held their shape.

"Okay," said Rain again. "We've got some of the smaller bones in the hands and feet missing. Not surprising. Rodents could get between these stones pretty easily. And this area is very open to the elements: snow, rain, and sun. Surprising, actually, that there is so little missing." She slipped on a pair of rubber gloves. "Has Janet done everything she needs to do with her camera?" she asked and received a nod. "Okay, let's see what we can determine. Silas, I guess you'll be interested to know that we are dealing with a male."

Rain pointed to the pelvis. "No room for babies. And it looks like we're dealing with a young man," she said, pointing to the skull. She gingerly moved it to point to the fusion points on the back of the cranium. "I'd say, twenty-five." She put the skull back down and examined the length of the body. "A little residual hair on the skullcap, and some clothing fragments, but not much else. Bones still intact but no muscle tissue. I'd guess—and I'll confirm this when we get the body back to Salt Lake—that this body has been here around two years. Maybe a little more."

"That's the same time as the Wisechild woman," said Agent Taylor. "Cause of death?"

"I would suggest, at the moment, blunt force trauma, but I haven't done a proper examination." She carefully picked up the skull again and pointed to a concave indentation on the right side of the head. "I don't see any other evidence of trauma. No bones broken. The hyoid is intact. No nicks or scrapes to suggest a bullet or a knife. I'll look more carefully once we get clear of the crime scene."

"Different MO," said Taylor.

"Opportunity knocks," said Nielsen.

"Come again, Agent Nielsen?" said Taylor.

"The Wisechild girl was strangled. Our friend here was likely hit in the head. Both about the same time, and the MO of leaving the body in a natural place fits. We could still be dealing with related crimes and the same perp. This person—let's call it a man, because I don't know of too many strangulations and bludgeonings committed by women—this man could be simply taking advantage of whatever situation arises."

"Somebody was paying attention on their last incarceration at Quantico," said Rain, continuing her examination of the body.

"The Wisechild woman was found buried in the sand, and this body has been neatly laid out as if some kind of ceremony was performed," said Willis.

"Remember," said Taylor, looking at Silas. "Dr. Pearson found the girl after the site had been disturbed by the flood. Everything, including the body, had been moved around. Isn't that right, Doctor?"

"Wait a minute," said Rain, and everybody fell silent. "What have we here?" she said, reaching down and moving the pelvis bone to pick something up from the ground. She held it up.

"It's a goddamned arrow point," said Agent Taylor.

"You think this guy was shot with an arrow?" asked Huston.

"Get out of the bloody office more often, John," said Nielsen. "It's a thousand years old. Maybe older. It's stone, chert, to be exact. You can see where the stone has been chipped away. The Anasazi would have used a tool made from deer antler to work the arrow point. Something as well preserved as that is worth money to the right collector. Most arrow heads from these parts have been stolen by pot hunters."

"Two points for Agent Nielsen today," said Taylor.

"Doesn't explain what it was doing there, under the guy's ass," said Huston.

"It was in his *pocket*." Everybody turned to look at Silas.

"Makes sense," said Rain. "That's about where the pocket of his jeans, or whatever he had on, would have been."

"And what was it doing in his pocket?" Huston asked again as he straightened up and looked at Silas.

"Do tell?" said Taylor, crossing his arms.

"He was a pot hunter," said Silas. "You do your dental work, Dr. Rain, but I am willing to bet we are looking at Kelly Williams right there."

"Just how the hell do you know that?" said Taylor.

THEY HAD A lot to talk about. They split up, with the Evidence Recovery Team and Penshaw working with Doctor Rain to prepare the body for transportation to the Medical Examiner's office. The two sheriffs, Chief Ranger Stan Baton, and agents Taylor and Nielsen sat with Silas in the parking lot at the Green River Overlook. There was no time to appreciate the view that afternoon.

He told them about his conversation with Kayah Wisechild's family and with Peter Anton, and told them that another hunch had drawn him to the edge of Island in the Sky and the discovery of a second corpse. He didn't tell them about his dreams, about Penelope's journal, or his entombment in the kiva. And he held back on revealing Hayduke's involvement in all of this. Hayduke was his ace in the hole to finding Penelope, and he didn't want to spook the young man.

"How did you know where to look? There must be two hundred square miles of tableland out here," said Taylor.

"Passages from *Desert Solitaire*," said Silas.

"You've got to be kidding me," said Nielsen. "Goddamned media will be calling these the Ed Abbey murders."

Silas shrugged.

"Okay," said Taylor. "Let's just suppose for a minute that we were to take your word about all this. Then what?"

"Go and talk with Peter Anton again. If this is in fact Williams, Anton worked with him as well. He and Wisechild and Williams worked on the mapping of the ruins in Hatch Wash. Talk with Jared Strom and Jacob Isaiah. They worked with all three of these people on the development proposed for Hatch Wash and the Canyon Rims region. I've been led to believe that Williams and Wisechild knew about plans to push Isaiah's development and maybe someone, you know—"

"Bumped them off?" Taylor raised an eyebrow. "Come on, Dr. Pearson. What do you think this is? A banana republic? This is the United States. Lots of people get killed here, but not because someone wants to build a golf course."

"Really?" Silas continued, "I'm not so sure about that."

"Eugene," said Taylor, looking at the FBI man. "You know the local politics better than I do. What do you think of that as a motive?"

Nielsen shook his head. "Isaiah is a pretty motivated fella, but I've never heard of him taking things that personally before. I don't see it as a motive."

"You think that *I* had one? I've never heard of these people before in my life."

"Did your wife?" asked Taylor.

Silas's face grew red. "Not that I know of."

"We'd like to search your home and your store," Taylor said.

"You'll need a warrant."

"We can get one. It will be easier without it. You just found two bodies inside of two weeks, Dr. Pearson. I don't think I've ever heard of that before. Have you, Agent Nielsen? What about you, gentlemen?" He looked at the sheriffs of Grand and San Juan Counties and at the park ranger. Everybody shook their heads. "So if making our investigation easier right now isn't your principal concern, what the hell is?"

Silas smiled for the first time that day. "Finding out how these two bodies are connected to the disappearance of my wife, of course."

HE WAS RELEASED on his own recognizance to run the gauntlet of reporters and get in his car and drive out of Canyonlands National Park. He would have loved to be able to have a few minutes alone with Katie Rain, but she would accompany the remains back to Moab, and he didn't see her again that day. He was certain that a reporter from the scrum at Green River Overlook was following him, so he drove into Moab before heading back to Castle Valley. He stopped to visit Ken and Trish Hollyoak.

When he got out of his car a man stopped and jumped out of a red SUV and asked if he could talk about his discovery. Silas kept on walking and when he rang the bell on Ken's door, the reporter was right behind him, still asking questions.

"You don't live here?" asked the reporter. Ken answered the door, naked except a pair of flowery shorts.

"Silas," he said, and then he saw the other man. "Who the fuck is this?"

"Reporter," said Silas, irritation showing on his face.

"Hold on, I'm going to get a gun." Ken turned and walked toward his den.

Silas turned. "He's serious." Something on his face told the man that he was.

"YOU CAN STAY here until all this blows over," said Trish. They were sitting behind the adobe house under the pergola.

"I need to get home," said Silas. "My maps, my gear, it's all there."

"Stay here tonight. We'll go together to the sheriff's office in the morning. I'll be with you when they serve you with the search warrant."

"Can you hold onto this?" Silas reached into his backpack and pulled out the notebook. He handed it to Ken.

"What is it?" he asked. Silas told them the entire story of his entrapment and escape, and about finding Josh Charleston, AKA Hayduke.

"No wonder you're looking so handsome," said Ken. Trish got up and looked at his cuts. "You know, a few of these could have used stitches."

"I didn't want to spend any more time or money at Moab Regional."

"We'll hold it. If push comes to shove you can say you gave it to your lawyer for safekeeping. Now tell me more about this Hayduke character."

"That's what he is. He's like a caricature of himself. It's almost as if every night he reads the *Monkey Wrench Gang* to find out what he's supposed to say next."

Ken laughed. "I don't like the idea of you getting too close to him. This boy sounds like a loose cannon."

"I need him, Ken. He worked with Penny. He's the only person I've met so far who had any real knowledge of what she was up to."

"Do you believe what he's saying about Jacob Isaiah? Do you think that he had a reason to want Kayah Wisechild dead?"

"I don't know what to believe right now. To me, it seems that Peter Anton had the best reason for wanting Kaya Wisechild dead—to keep her quiet about their relationship. He adamantly denies having been involved with her, but I think he doth protest too much, you know what I mean?

"And I don't think Anton knew Penny, at least not personally. Unless his involvement in Jacob Isaiah's land development scheme was deeper than I understand it to be, I just don't see a motive for his involvement in Penny's disappearance."

"Wisechild and Williams were killed two years ago, you said, Silas. Penny has been gone for over three and a half years, so why the big gap?" asked Ken.

"She could still be out there, Ken."

"I know, amigo. I know."

IN THE MORNING Ken drove Silas to the Sheriff's Office, which had once again been taken over by the FBI. The San Juan Sheriff's Office and the Park Service had both waived jurisdiction, but insisted on remaining present for the investigation, so members of all four policing bodies were present when Silas and Ken walked into the office.

Taylor looked up. "Who are you?"

"Dr. Pearson's attorney. Kenneth James Hollyoak. I understand you are to execute a search warrant on my client's home today. We will insist on being present."

Taylor looked from Ken to Silas and back. "We're just heading out there now."

An hour later there were six vehicles parked in Silas's driveway in the Castle Valley. The search team consisted of eight FBI agents, including Nielsen and Janet Unger and John Huston from the Evidence Recovery Team. Katie Rain was there too. She smiled at Silas when she stepped out of the black SUV.

"Didn't expect to see you this morning." Silas sounded disappointed.

"Taylor wanted me along."

"Why is that?"

"In case we find anything."

"Dr. Pearson, would you unlock the door?" asked Taylor.

Silas did as he was asked, and the agents stepped inside. It was hot and musty but otherwise looked exactly as Silas had left it. Ken Hollyoak followed the agents around with his iPhone, videoing them as they went about their work. Two agents walked around the backyard with a ground-penetrating radar unit. Silas watched them from the pergola. Next to his annual visit to his doctor for his physical, having his home searched by the FBI was the most violating experience of his life.

Half an hour passed before he heard his name being called from inside the house. He went in through the laundry room and found Taylor and Nielsen in the living room, along with Sheriff Willis and Ken Hollyoak. Silas looked at his friend.

"They found nothing. I made sure they put everything back where they found it."

Silas felt his anger rise as relief washed over him. "Of course they found nothing! There's nothing to find!"

"I'll say that again," said a voice from beyond the room. Katie Rain walked out of the kitchen. "Jesus, Silas, just beer and frozen dinners in the fridge?" He stared at her a moment and then laughed and shook his head.

"The agents want to ask you a few questions. I told them I wanted to be present. We agreed to do it here rather than back in Moab. Maybe we can sit outside where we might be more comfortable." Ken pointed to the two wooden chairs at the table in the middle of the living room.

They assembled under the pergola. Ken and Silas sat with Katie Rain on one side, and Taylor and Nielsen and the sheriff on the other.

"We're prepared to share some information with you this morning, Dr. Pearson. We hope that you might do the same," said Taylor. Silas just stared at him.

Rain began. "We have a positive ID on the remains found at Grand View Point yesterday. The dental records were in Moab, so it was simple. It was Kelly Williams, as you indicated. Mr. Williams was working on and off for the same firm as Ms. Wisechild. He was with Dead Horse for about two years. He worked with Dr. Anton and with Jared Strom. According to Mr. Strom, the last project Williams worked on was out on the Navajo Reservation. According to their records, he didn't work on the Hatch Wash project."

"That's a lie," interrupted Silas. "Peter Anton told me that he, Williams, and Wisechild spent two weeks together at Hatch."

"We'll talk with Dr. Anton again," said Nielsen.

"What I was hoping you might be able to help us with, Dr. Pearson, is connecting these two murders. You seem to have . . . a special relationship with this set of crimes that, frankly, I don't really understand."

Silas looked at Ken, who said, "As Dr. Pearson has nothing to hide, he can talk about this with you. But if you somehow think you're going to get a confession here, you're fucking crazy."

Taylor remained implacable. "Dr. Pearson, I know you don't like me. Maybe you don't appreciate how much work the Bureau has done in the past to try and locate your wife. Maybe it's just personal. Right now, you seem to believe that these two bodies are somehow linked to your wife's disappearance. We're your best bet to find out what that link is. You've got to tell us what you know."

"I don't know. You're going to think I'm crazy," Silas responded. His eyes caught Katie Rain's and she watched him with empathy.

"Dr. Pearson, whether I think you're nuts or not has nothing to do with this." Taylor continued, "We're banging our heads against the wall. We need to know what you do."

"You were warned." He took a deep breath and told them about his dreams. He told them how a dream had led him to Courthouse Wash, and how that led him to Darla Wisechild on the Hopi Reservation, and then about his descent into Hatch Wash after his visit to Peter Anton. The agents listened in silence.

When he was done, Taylor asked, "How about those cuts on your face, and the one on your head?" Silas told them about his twenty-four hours in the kiva.

"We're going to need GPS coordinates. We're going to have to send a team in there," said Taylor. "Would you be willing to submit to a polygraph test?"

Silas looked at Ken then back at Taylor. "Are you saying you don't believe me?"

"A lie detector test will help eliminate you as a suspect."

"That's not going to happen, Agent Taylor," stated the retired lawyer. "If you seriously think my client is a suspect, then arrest him, charge him with a crime, and we'll do what needs to be done."

Taylor was silent for a moment. He regarded Silas across the table. "We won't be charging Dr. Pearson right now, but don't leave the state, please."

20

SILAS STAYED WITH KEN AND Trish Hollyoak for two nights, sleeping in the same room that Penelope had used so many times. Half a dozen members of the media had camped out at his Castle Valley home, angering his neighbors and interfering with his ability to plan his next series of searches. Silas laid low, spending his days pouring over a series of topographical maps he'd brought with him when he and Ken had left his home after the conference with the FBI.

Despite Silas's refusal to grant interviews, newspapers from across the state and from neighboring Arizona, Colorado, and New Mexico ran pieces about the *"Desert Solitaire* murders." They dug up a photo of him from the NAU website, where he was listed as professor emeritus. Several of the papers, including the *Salt Lake Tribune*, wrote background stories on the disappearance of his wife. By day three, however, most of the regional media had lost interest, turning their attention to a series of gruesome murders in Provo. Silas was able to return home.

Within ten minutes of stepping into his house, his cell phone rang. It was Hayduke.

"Does this mean you're going to help me out?" asked Silas, by way of greeting.

"Yeah, fuck, I'm going to help you," grumbled Josh.

"Can we get together? I want to try and reconstruct a map of where Penny was, what she was doing, right before she disappeared. I need to know what she was working on."

"Yeah, we can do that. But I've got a better idea. Meet me in Blanding tomorrow afternoon."

"Why?"

"Because C. Thorn Smith, AKA Shithead, is going to be in his district office there making an announcement to his constituents that I think you might find interesting."

"I don't like games, Josh. Get to the point please."

"Call me Hayduke."

"I don't like games, *Hayduke*. Tell me what's going on."

"The senator will be in town to announce some new project that involves a massive fucking oil and gas development project for the canyonlands. It's going to be gigantic. You've heard that the feds have opened up a whole new slate of BLM lands for this sort of activity. They are calling it 'energy fucking security.' It's harder to argue with, when they can paint you as a fucking terrorist for wanting to keep drilling rigs out of the canyons. The senator is the big champion for this in congress. He's staked his political career on it. He's going to be in this lonesome little corner of his district to make a big announcement tomorrow afternoon at 1:00 PM."

"Do we know what the announcement is going to be about?"

"You're Canadian, right?"

"Yes, so?"

"Ever heard of Canusa Petroleum Resources?"

"No."

"Fuck, man, they are huge. This is the mega-machine that is devouring half the wilderness in the west. They do oil shale development, fracking, and traditional oil and gas projects, all across Utah, Wyoming, and Montana. Up in Canuk-ville too."

"Penelope would have—"

"Fucking right Pen heard of them. She knew these motherfuckers, knew them well. Knew what they were up to. She had their number. Dug up all the dirt on them, but they're good, really good. They have learned to burrow into the belly of the fucking beast, lay their little fucking eggs, and just wait. Now the eggs are about to hatch."

"You're saying you think my wife was getting between these people and what they want?"

"Pen got between a lot of people and what they want. A lot."

"Tomorrow at 1:00 PM?"

"That's right."

"Okay, I'll see you there."

"I'll see you first."

SILAS SAT IN the shade of the pergola and looked across the valley at the mesas and monuments beyond. He tried to unravel what it was that Hayduke had been telling him. His wife had gotten between a lot of people and what they want. *A lot*, Hayduke emphasized. The question seemed to be, had she come between the wrong person and what they wanted? He needed to learn more about Canusa Petroleum Resources and what exactly they were up to, and where.

If a company like Canusa was seriously considering large-scale development across the canyon country, he reasoned, they would need to do a lot of legwork before they could make an announcement. They would need to hire someone, or some company, to help them clear all the regulatory hurdles, such as the National Environmental Policy Act and ARPA, before they could announce a project like this. And who better to hire, reasoned Silas, than Dead Horse Consulting.

"MR. STROM IS in a meeting," said the woman at the front desk.

"This won't take long. I'll just wait." He sat down in the reception area and read the six-month-old magazines. From time to time he noticed the receptionist looking up at him, and after an hour he inquired again. With an exasperated look, she picked up the phone and spoke quietly. A few moments later Strom appeared by the counter, looking considerably less interested in talking with Silas than he had the last time. Undaunted, Silas rose to shake his hand.

"I only have a moment. Walk with me to my truck." He was carrying a thick white binder with the Dead Horse logo on it and several rolled up maps.

"I really just have one question for you, Mr. Strom." They stepped out of the air-conditioned office just as a semi-truck was gearing down on the outskirts of town. Silas waited for the sound of its engine brakes to recede. "Is Dead Horse working with Canusa Petroleum Resources?"

Strom stopped and looked at him. "You know, it's very unusual for any consulting firm to disclose who its clients are. This information is considered a trade secret to some."

Silas studied Strom, who was getting into his car. "I'm going to take that as a yes, Mr. Strom."

"You can take it however you want."

"Is Canusa exploring in the Canyon Rims region?"

"I have to get to a meeting, Mr. Pearson."

"They want to drill on Flat Iron Mesa, don't they? And Hatch Point and Behind the Rocks?"

"Good luck with your search . . ." Strom closed the door and turned over the ignition. He didn't wait for Silas to step away before he drove off.

Silas stood in the parking lot in the searing heat. One thing he knew, and knew well, was maps. A quick glance at the topographical sheets that Strom carried rolled up with this binder told him that they were one-degree sheets covering the vast, unprotected region on the eastern side of Canyonlands National Park known as Canyon Rims.

SILAS STEPPED OUT of his car at the San Juan County municipal building on South Main Street, Monticello. He had done the hour-long drive from Moab with the air conditioner cranked up high, the maps under Jared Strom's arm emblazoned in his mind. He walked quickly up the steps of the building and went inside.

"Hot one," said the clerk from behind the desk, not looking up.

"I'll say."

"What can I do you for?"

"I'm wondering about looking at land records."

"Municipal, state, or federal?"

"BLM lands."

"Federal. What quadrants?"

"The Canyon Rims area."

"Hold on a minute." She stood and went through a wooden door and came back with a map tube.

"If I give you a quadrant, can you tell me who has applied for any kind of development permit?"

"If it's come through the county, I can. You'll need to go to the BLM office in Moab to look at any environmental assessments."

She opened the map tubes and pulled out the one-degree sheets. She placed a couple of paperweights on them to keep them from curling up. County boundaries and other things were marked.

"Right here." He pointed to a quadrant on the rim above the Hatch Wash ruins that he had been within days before.

"Let me look, hon." She sat down at her keyboard and typed in some numbers. "Okay, let's see. Well, *I* don't have anything for that area."

"You sure?"

She looked at him. "Yes, I'm sure."

"Can you check the surrounding quads?"

She typed again. A few minutes passed. "Okay, if I get about five miles back, to the south, and another five miles, to the north, then we get some applications for exploration."

"Does it say who? The name of the company?" Silas was holding his breath.

"All I get is a number, hon."

"Can I have it, please?" He pulled a sheet of scrap paper toward him and wrote it down. "Is that the number of a company?"

"Must be," she said.

He thanked her, and perplexed, stepped back out into the midday sun. If there were no applications to drill in the immediate vicinity of the ruins in Hatch Wash, Silas simply couldn't see how Canusa's development applications could in any way be linked to Kayah Wisechild and Kelly Williams, or his wife, for that matter. The existing applications for exploration—for seismic testing, where the petroleum company would send shock waves into the ground and listen for oil or gas deposits far beneath the earth— were for important and beautiful areas, the Back of the Rocks region and the vast Hatch Point mesa. These were nearly ten miles from the ruins in the box canyon. Still, he would need to track down the players behind the numbered company to determine if they were connected with Canusa.

Back in his car, he let the motor idle as the air-conditioning kicked in. He had convinced himself that Kayah Wisechild and Kelly Williams's involvement in the discovery of the Hatch ruins was connected to their murders. He knew when he held this proposition up to the light that it was thin, based more on intuition than evidence. His own experience in Hatch suggested that he was getting too close to the truth for someone's comfort. But who?

If it was the case that the murders were related to the ruins, then why wasn't Peter Anton also dead? The only explanation he could come up with was that somehow Anton was involved. Had the FBI made that same connection? Why, then, wasn't Peter Anton behind bars? He would have to find out. He would make a call to Katie Rain later in the day.

On the drive back to Moab, something else occurred to him. If Kayah Wisechild or Kelly Williams had learned something about the Hatch ruins, had they left anything behind that might lead him to what they had discovered? He didn't know anything about Williams, and would have to find out. He did know Darla Wisechild. He would see if Kayah had given her anything that might be helpful. He picked up his phone and dialed Roger Goodwin's number.

"Roger, it's Silas."

"Dr. Pearson, how are you today? I read in the local newspaper that you're developing quite the reputation across the Four Corners."

"I try not to read the papers," he lied.

"What's next? Open a curio shop on Main Street in Moab? Souvenir T-shirts, '*I found a body in Arches National Park?*'"

"Funny. Listen, does Darla Wisechild have a phone? A cell?"

"Sure. Of course."

"Can you give me the number?"

"I can. What's up?"

"I want to know if Kayah sent her anything before she died."

"Do you want me to run over there for you? I'm out on Third Mesa later today."

"Would you?"

"Yeah, no problem. What are you looking for?"

Silas told him the story of the ruins and the kiva. Goodwin whistled, "Jesus, Silas. I need to come and check them out. This could be a class one find."

"If it isn't, it's close. There's not a lot of art, but the ruins themselves are in good shape. They look like they've been totally cleared out of artifacts.

Peter Anton told me that they were brimming when he went through them, but they're barren now."

"Does the BLM know about them?" asked Goodwin.

"I don't know. Anton told me that Dead Horse put a lid on the find after he made his report. There's no paperwork on it either. He told me that he was doing work for Jacob Isaiah at the time. I've also got wind that a big oil giant called Canusa wants to drill in the same area, though farther away from Hatch Wash, up on the Point, on Flat Iron, and in the Back of the Rocks region. It's ten miles away at the closest point. I'm still looking for the connection—"

"If Anton claimed that the ruins were thick with artifacts when he went through them three years ago, and they are cleared out now, I'd suggest you go back to the source."

"What do you mean?" asked Silas.

"Artifacts from ruins of that nature could be worth thousands, maybe tens of thousands of dollars. More if there was anything like a woven basket preserved there."

"You think that Peter Anton cleared them out?"

"Maybe."

"He could have killed the girl and this Williams fellow to cover his tracks."

"I didn't say that,"

"No, but it's a possibility."

"I'll run over to see Darla Wisechild this afternoon. I'll call you if I learn anything."

"Thanks, Roger. I owe you."

"I'll collect the next time I'm in town. I hear you're quite the chef," said Roger. Silas laughed and they hung up.

SILAS STOPPED AT the Red Rock Canyon bookstore on his way through Moab. He sat in the back at his computer and searched for the name Kelly Williams. It returned more than 8 million results. He narrowed it down: "Missing Kelly Williams." He found what he was looking for at the top of the page. The first three or four stories were about the recovery of the man's body at Grand View Point. After that, the stories went back over two years, and he slowly read through them.

It turned out that there was more to Kelly Williams than a simple undergraduate student on a dig as a summer job. Williams had been twice charged with grave robbing under ARPA. Once he'd been charged with disturbing an ancient Pueblo site in the Grand Gulch area, west of Monticello. A second time he'd been accused of pilfering a grave on the Navajo Reservation. In both cases the district attorney didn't have enough evidence that Williams was directly involved to win a conviction, so the case was dropped. What was Williams doing working on a highly sensitive site like the Hatch Canyon ruin?

Silas began to wonder *when* the site had been cleared out. Peter Anton mentioned hundreds of artifacts. Were they stolen before or after Williams and Wisechild were killed? Did Williams play a role and somehow pay for it with his life? If Williams and Wisechild had been involved with the grave robbing—which is taboo for the Hopi—and paid for it with their lives, there might not be any connection with Canusa, with Jacob Isaiah, or with Penelope. He knew that this *shouldn't* bother him, but it did. He *wanted* there to be a connection.

The stories on Williams mentioned the charges against him only in the context of his disappearance and recent unearthing. He would have to look back through the records in San Juan and Coconino Counties, where the charges had been laid, to determine the timeline. He also decided that it was time to press Peter Anton for more information. Cortez was only an hour and a half from Blanding, so before going to Senator Smith's announcement tomorrow, he would pay Anton a visit.

The bell to his shop sounded. He looked up to see Jacob Isaiah walking down the center aisle, looking at the shelves packed with books as if he were simply browsing. Silas stood up.

"Sit, sit," said Isaiah, "I don't need no help picking out a title." Silas remained standing.

"I understand," said Isaiah, as his stroll down the shelves brought him to the desk, "that you went and got yourself in *another* heap of trouble, Pearson."

Silas opened his mouth to speak, but Isaiah cut him off with a pointy finger in his face.

"That's a nasty-looking cut, Silas, nasty. Now, what were you up to *this* time that got you all cut up like you've been in a knife fight with a Mexican?"

Silas closed his mouth. He wasn't going to play this game.

"Poking your nose into the wrong people's business, it seems."

"And what business is that, Jacob?"

"Business is business. That's what your wife never could understand. Seems like you're going down that same sorry path, nothing but trouble. Look at you! You look like something that the dog up-chucked in the yard." Flecks of white saliva formed at the corners of his mouth.

"Jacob, I don't have time for your insults today."

"Maybe you have time for this, smart guy," Isaiah barked, poking Silas in the chest with his finger. "A warning. You think that what you got in your professor head is going to help you find your wife. I'm here to tell you that's not the case. Nothing you know means what you think it does. Your wife ran off, plain and simple. There's nothing more to it. Not a goddamned thing. So get your head out of your ass and everybody else's business. Leave well enough alone."

"You seem awfully agitated, Jacob, for a man who doesn't have any-thing to hide."

"I've got nothing to hide, Pearson. I do have a lot to lose, and I'm not going to let you get in the way of a good business proposition that's going to put a lot of people around here to work, and put some money into this economy—"

"And into your pockets?"

"Maybe you don't like to make money up in Canada. Maybe you're all a bunch of fucking communists with your free health care and your socialist ways. Down here in America, we believe in the free market. We don't like people like you, or that wife of yours, poking your nose into our business. Fucking foreigners, Mexicans, Canadians, you're all the fucking same. Now your wife has gone off, and that's all there is to it. Them others, well, they had a run-in with some bad men, maybe. Lots of people on the road who would be happy to throttle you or bang you on the head with a stone as soon as look at you; sick people, sick times. I'm telling you, Pearson, this has got nothing to do with your wife, so you go back to your hiking and leave us to do our business. You got it?" He poked Silas with his finger again, his eyes wide and wild.

Silas drew in a sharp breath and exhaled. "Jacob, if you ever come in my store again and put that finger of yours in my face, I swear to God I'll break it off."

Isaiah laughed, a speck of spittle landing on Silas's desk. "Son, there's nothing about *you* that scares me. I'll do whatever I goddamned well please. This is my town, *my* town, not yours. I'll be back and I'll put my finger where ever I damn well want to. Now, you mind what I just told you. It might keep you from getting that homely face of yours looking any worse."

Isaiah turned and walked out of the store, leaving Silas as hot as if he'd been sitting in the heat at noon.

HE CALLED THE Salt Lake City FBI office when he arrived back at his Castle Valley home. It was late afternoon and he sat under the pergola, watching the thunderheads build along the tops of the cliffs above the Adobe Mesa. Heat lightning flashed across the mesa as the clouds boiled with electrical currents. After a few minutes Katie Rain came on the phone.

"Hi Silas."

"Hi Katie."

"You're getting quite the reputation around here you know. We're calling you The Dreamer."

"Really?"

"No, that's just me. What do you think?"

"Perfect," Silas said. "What have you guys learned about Kelly Williams?"

"I'm a forensic anthropologist. I'm not an investigator, at least not for a long time now. Talking with you could get me in trouble. I mean, not trouble with a capital T . . ."

"It could. But not talking with me is going to get us nowhere. I think your guy Taylor is a good man, but he doesn't see the big picture."

"And you do?"

Silas was quiet a moment, then he said, "It's starting to come together." He told her his theory about Wisechild and Williams working together on the Hatch Wash ruins and somebody, maybe Peter Anton, maybe Jacob Isaiah, killing them to keep them quiet about the site.

"Tell me something," he said, remembering his exchange with Jacob Isaiah. "Did the FBI release to the press or the public the cause of death of either Williams or Wisechild?"

"No way. We hold that pretty close."

"Jacob Isaiah knew how both died. He told me so today. He was threatening me at the time, mind you, but he knew that Kayah had been strangled and Kelly bludgeoned. There are only two ways he would know that."

"Somebody told him."

"That's right, someone on the inside of the case. It sure as hell wasn't me."

"Nor me," said Rain.

"You have a leak. And of course, the other way he could have known was . . ."

". . . if *he* killed them both."

"That's right," said Silas.

21

BY EIGHT THE NEXT MORNING Silas was parked outside of Peter Anton's home in Cortez, Colorado. He had found the address through a contact in the administration department at NAU, and had left his home a little after six to make it across the border. He wanted to catch Anton off guard. He sat across the road from the two-story false-fronted adobe house just off Main Street. The rest of the neighborhood was 1950s-style bungalows, so Anton's modern home stood out. Just after Silas arrived, the front door opened and Anton came down the rust-colored steps and walked to his Chevy SUV. Silas stepped from his car and walked across the street. He left the cane behind, knowing that it reduced the effect of physical intimidation he wanted to convey. He called Anton's name.

The man looked up, startled. "Oh, it's you Dr. Pearson."

"A little jumpy this morning, Dr. Anton?"

"Just a wee too much coffee is all. I've been up for hours working on a new project for Mesa Verde."

"Are you off to the park now?"

"Yes, as a matter of fact, I am. What are you doing here in front of my house, Pearson?"

"This will only take a moment," said Silas. He leaned against Anton's Chevy. "You know that Kelly Williams—"

"Is dead? Yes I know. I read the newspapers. Even here in Cortez, we get the news."

"I found him."

"Yes, I read that too."

"You don't seem too upset or shocked by this."

"Well, I suppose I'm not . . . not really surprised."

"And why is that? Are you going to try and tell me he had it coming?"

"Kelly played pretty fast and loose. He took what he wanted and I suppose someone got tired of it."

"You hired him to work on the Hatch Wash ruin."

"Yes, that was before Kelly got sticky fingers."

"I was there. I went to Hatch Wash."

"I assumed you'd go. It's really quite amazing, isn't it? It makes the ruins in Grand Gulch look like a something a child would build."

"It's been cleared out." Silas watched Anton very carefully.

"What do you mean?" He put a hand against his SUV. His face seemed to register the shock.

"There's nothing left. The structures are there, but they are completely empty. Who do you think would have done this?"

Anton looked confused. "It could be anyone. There are hundreds of pot hunters in the Southwest. They steal what they can and sell it online or to unscrupulous collectors. There are literally tens of thousands of artifacts in circulation today that have been robbed from ruins like Hatch. I'm just sorry now that we didn't do something to prevent this."

"You or Strom didn't report the find to the BLM?"

"We felt that by keeping it quiet we would stand a better chance of protecting the site."

"That theory didn't really hold up, did it?" asked Silas. Before Anton could answer, he cut him off. "There might be hundreds of pot hunters, but who knew about Hatch?"

"I don't know. Just because we found it and cataloged it doesn't mean that some redneck on an ATV didn't drive up Kane Creek and happen to stumble into that box canyon. It was only a matter of time."

"People have been stumbling around that canyon for more than a hundred years and haven't found it, at least not that we know of. It seems improbable that someone would find it now. Who knew about the ruins?"

"Me, of course. Kelly and Kayah. Jared Strom, and a few others at Dead Horse Consulting."

"Do you think Kelly might have returned after you finished your work to clear the place? Sell it off?"

"It's possible. Even *probable*, given what he's alleged to have done."

"Might that have—"

"Gotten him killed? Dr. Pearson, that is pure conjecture. Really, I have no idea why Kelly Williams, or Ms. Wisechild, got killed. No idea."

Silas changed tacks. "Someone tried to leave me for dead in the Hatch Wash ruin. Did you know that?"

"My God, you're kidding. No, I had no idea. What happened?"

"I climbed into the kiva. I wanted to see if there was anything left. There wasn't, of course. When I tried to climb back out, I couldn't."

"What do you mean?"

"There was no ladder. I used my rope to rappel in. But when I tried to climb out the rope had been tampered with."

"How did you get back out?"

"Through the ventilation shaft."

"Jesus Christ, man. You're kidding. I never would have imagined that it would be big enough. It can't be more than a foot and a half . . ."

"Almost exactly eighteen inches square. The elbow was the tough part." Silas pointed to his face and showed Anton the marks on his arms.

"What happened to your rope?"

"When I was down in the kiva someone unlooped it from the belay point. Dr. Anton, you're the *only* one who knew I was there."

"Are you suggesting that I did this? Are you accusing me?"

Silas shrugged. "I'm not accusing you—"

"You are. You're suggesting that I followed you out there and . . . and what? Untied your rope? Left you to die there? And for what? You think *I* killed the Wisechild girl? What motive did I have? Because you think I had an affair?" He was hissing now, leaning into Silas. He wasn't a big man, and Silas towered over him by at least five inches.

Silas shrugged again. "Nobody else knew I was there. *I* told nobody. Did you?"

Anton looked at Silas a while. "I didn't tell anybody. *I* didn't follow you. You can ask my wife. She's in the kitchen right now. You can ask her. I was home all day that day."

Silas regarded the man. "That won't be necessary."

"I can read you, Pearson. You didn't believe me about Kayah, and you don't believe me about this."

"Let me ask you this," Silas interrupted. "If anybody else was trying to develop a project in the Flat Iron Mesa or Hatch Point region, or even at Behind the Rocks, would Dead Horse likely get the nod to do the EA work? And the archaeological assessment? Would another developer know that you've already done a baseline survey and rather than turning to some other firm, would they just say, Dead Horse has the data, let's use them?"

Anton was still clearly flustered. He shook his head. "I don't know. There are a dozen firms in Utah doing this sort of work, maybe two dozen. If the developer had local connections and knew that Dead Horse had a bead on what was going on in that area, they might try to save some money."

"Have you ever heard of a company called Canusa Petroleum Resources?"

"No, I haven't. I'm tired of getting the third degree, Dr. Pearson. Step aside. I'm late for a meeting."

"They plan on drilling for oil in the Hatch Point area, Flat Iron Mesa, and Behind the Rocks."

"I said I haven't heard of them. Now get the hell out of my way before I call the police."

"You know what I'd be worried about, Dr. Anton?"

"What? What should I be worried about?" He had pulled his cell phone from his pocket and flipped it open.

"Well, if *you* didn't kill Kelly Williams and Kayah Wisechild, then you're likely next on the list." Anton stared blank-faced at him. "I think you know a lot more about this than you're telling me, Anton. If I find out you're behind any of this, you're going to regret not having sealed *yourself* in that kiva. Do you understand me?"

Anton started pressing numbers into his phone. "I'm calling the cops."

"Be my guest. I expect you'll be getting another call from the FBI soon anyway."

22

THE OFFICE OF C. THORN Smith was on South Main Street in the town of Blanding. When Silas arrived, there were already more than fifty people there from the local constituency, along with a bank of television cameras and a gaggle of reporters. The senator's office was in a historic red brick building that also housed other government offices. A crisp new American flag sagged on its pole in the noonday sun. Silas stood across the street and scanned the swelling crowd for Hayduke, but he could not see him.

As he watched, a chartered bus arrived and several dozen people disembarked. Silas regarded this new group of supporters: typical middle-aged, middle-class Americans; most were overweight and had trouble walking along the flat sidewalk. He was absorbed with his observations when a voice startled him.

"Bussed these fuckers in."

Silas turned and Hayduke was next to him, a ball cap on his shaggy head, a wide, toothy grin on his face.

"Brought them all the way down from Price, near Smith's hometown of Huntington. Miners and their families, mostly. Out of work now, because the greedy bastards who run those mines have been bringing in cheap labor to replace the local workers. Guess they think they might get jobs in the new oil patch if they wave that flag for our senator."

Silas looked back at the growing group of supporters. Indeed, someone was circulating through the audience handing out flags. "Is that Charles Nephi?" asked Pearson, pointing to a man standing near the stage in crisp tan slacks and a white button-down shirt.

"It is," grumbled Hayduke.

"How much do you know about him?"

"Only what Pen told me. She did all the political work. Nephi's been around on and off for a while, works with the senator as a special constituency assistant or something. His whole gig is resource development in Utah. He stage-manages the senator's interests in forestry, mining, oil and gas, water. He's the brains behind Smith's relationship with the resource industry. A lot of people say that he's a dirty fucker, on the payroll of industry lobbyists, working the inside of the system for the petrochemical industry. There's no proof. He's never been registered as a lobbyist in Utah or in Washington. Doesn't mean he's not in their fucking pockets."

"What is *this* all about?" Silas looked around the small crowd. "I don't see how this relates to my wife."

"Patience, man, patience. Let's hear what the senator has to say."

Silas looked at his watch. A few moments later C. Thorn Smith walked out of his office with several men in casual business attire behind him. The senator was a tall man with a narrow, handsome face and well-groomed salt-and-pepper hair that gave him a presidential air. Casually dressed, he walked to the podium with a poised confidence and quickly got down to business.

"Good afternoon, friends," Smith said calmly. "It's one hell of a hot day, and I'm glad you all have come out to hear what we have to say. I'll get right to it and then let you find some shade. This afternoon I'm here with leaders of several of Utah's leading resource companies to tell you about an economic stimulus plan that will put the people of Utah back to work. It's called the Utah Land Stewardship Fund, and these companies have agreed to invest one hundred million dollars into our great state over the next ten years to ensure that what made Utah the best state in the Union continues to sustain and support our communities and families for the next generation."

The senator looked to the men at his side and continued. "Now, I'd like to introduce you to just a few of the leaders who will be investing in this program. Come on, step forward, gentlemen. This is Frank Palmer, of the Rainbow Bridge Coal Corporation. He's born and bred here in Utah, and his company now operates across the United States, in South America, and all over Asia. He's one of Utah's favorite sons."

There was a spatter of applause.

"This is T. Dermit Calhoon, vice-president of Forestry Operations for Tillicum Forestry. And last but not least, this is Tim Martin, president and CEO of Canusa Petroleum Resources. Tim was born and raised in the Great White North, in Canada, but he's since relocated to our great state and is residing in Salt Lake City to be closer to Canusa's main oil and gas play here in the Four Corners region. I want you to meet these forward-looking business leaders who will help ensure this state's future."

The senator stopped talking and nodded to his assistant, Charles Nephi. "The senator will take a few questions from the press now," said Nephi.

"Senator, tell us what you mean by the harmonization of development permits?" asked a reporter.

"I'm glad you asked about that. Did you know that right now, for a company like Canusa to help this country develop energy security by drilling for oil deep beneath our feet, they have to jump through no fewer than a dozen regulatory and licensing hurdles? BLM, EPA, Park Service, Agriculture, state regulators, county commissioners, water boards, you name it! It's easier for these companies to go to Saudi Arabia or Iraq and drill for oil than it is for them to supply our domestic demand with oil and gas right here, under our feet!" The senator jabbed his finger on the podium to emphasis his point. "That's going to come to an end with the Utah Land Stewardship Act, which I will introduce into the Senate when we sit again next week. I have co-sponsors for this bill and we're going to make it easier for companies to do business here at home than it is for them to do business overseas. We *can* protect the environment while we do it."

"How will this protect the environment, Senator?" asked another reporter.

"We'll simply ensure that the highest standards of environmental protection are considered, while not burdening these companies with excessive red tape. We'll cut through that red tape," he made a cutting motion with his hands, "and let American businesses do what they do best. Support this great state and this great country."

One reporter addressed Tim Martin: "Where will you be concentrating your oil and gas development?"

Martin looked at the senator, who stepped back and gestured to the microphone. "Thank you for that question. We have a number of options we're exploring. The Kaiparowits Plateau, the region north of the Grand Canyon along the Kaibab Plateau, and nearby in the Canyon Rims region. We believe these are three areas where we can support local employment and community while supplying long-term energy security to the nation."

The reporter put up his hand. "A quick follow. Energy development on the scale you're considering will require a lot of water. How will you address your water needs without compromising the water supply for wildlife or communities?"

Martin looked at the senator and then stepped to the mike again. "That's a good question. Part of the harmonized process the senator has been discussing here today is the streamlining of water storage and withdrawal permits for these projects. We'll be working with the BLM and the Bureau of Reclamation to address our water needs, as well as those of other stakeholders."

"You hear that fucking shit," spat Hayduke. "Now they've got the fucking dam builders involved. That's just what I was fucking concerned about. Those fuckers are talking about building dams to supply water to these projects. I fucking knew it!"

Silas noticed several bystanders were casting concerned looks at the rough-talking Hayduke. "Listen, let's get out of here so we can discuss this."

"I've heard enough from these fucking bastards," agreed Hayduke.

AFTER SOME DEBATE Silas followed Hayduke north on the 191 toward Moab. When Hayduke turned off the road to take the dirt track where Silas had ventured just a few days ago toward Hatch Point, he began to wonder what the renegade young man was up to. Hayduke soon pulled his jeep off the road where the main stem of Hatch Wash was just a hundred feet deep. They were still in sight of the road. He got out of his machine and walked to Silas's car. Silas opened the window.

"Wasn't sure how far your station wagon would make it," he patted the hood. "I wanted you to see what they are talking about. This is what they will dam." He pointed to Hatch Wash, with its thin trickle of water.

"Not here, though, surely?"

"No, down by Kane Creek. It will be a small dam, but it will flood Hatch Wash so they can draw on the water for injection drilling on Flat Iron Mesa and in Back of the Rocks."

Silas got out and looked down at the trickle of water. "It will take a long time to fill a reservoir."

"You think fuckers like Martin and Smith give a shit? They will take all the time in the world to destroy this, and not think twice."

Silas started to piece things together in his head. "How long has this been in the works?"

"I don't know. Maybe years."

"You don't think Penelope—"

"I don't know. I think if they were planning it, she knew. Maybe she was on to them."

"Lot of money at stake," said Silas. "Penny talked about water a lot in her notebook, about the dams that destroyed these places, Glen Canyon, especially."

Hayduke shook his head and spat. "We should have just blown that fucker up and been done with it." He spat again. "Now they want to dam this one. It don't look like much here, but you've seen it. The canyon's a thousand feet deep, and with those ruins in them. They flood this and it's game over."

"You can't flood a canyon that's got such an important archaeological site in it, can you?"

"If nobody knows about it, you can."

"Somebody should document it. Get in there and photograph it. Take the press down there."

"Maybe that's what them other two, Williams and Wisechild, were doing, and it got them killed. I know that I'm not going to let them destroy this place. Not after all the work me and Pen did to protect this area."

"Look." Silas kicked a clot of sand on the side of the road. "I respect your passion, but I've got to stay focused. I'm trying to find out what happened to my wife. This whole business with Kayah Wisechild and Kelly Williams, well, I can see how it might help lead me to Penny. I'm not in this to stop somebody from building a dam or drilling for oil. I'm trying to find my wife."

"That's exactly what I thought you'd stay. You want to find your wife, and then find out why Kelly Williams and Kayah Wisechild died. If what you tell me is true, maybe that's what Pen is trying to tell you. Don't be such a stupid fuck. The answer is staring you in the face. Those other two died because of something they knew about the ruins at the mouth of this here fucking canyon," cursed Hayduke, pointing to Hatch Wash. "You find out what, and I bet you'll find your wife."

23

SILAS HAD JUST PULLED INTO Moab when Roger Goodwin called.

"Silas, I went to see Darla Wisechild last night. I was out on a project and just got back to my place now."

"It's no trouble Roger. I really appreciate you doing that."

"I don't mind. They're good people. It seems like Leon in particular is having a pretty tough time with this. He's convinced that Kayah was killed by a witch."

"I don't think it was a witch, Roger. More likely flesh and blood. Did you find anything that might be helpful?"

"I guess the FBI had been by again asking something similar. There was no cell phone, no incriminating letters sent home. They had someone working on Darla's computer to see if there was anything from Kayah there. I don't know if they found anything. But they overlooked something, and Darla gave it to me."

"What is it?"

"It's a memory card from a digital camera. It might be nothing. Darla doesn't have a camera at home and it never occurred to her to look at it after her sister died. She just put it in a drawer with some other stuff that had been cleared out of her sister's apartment after she had gone missing. Kayah mailed it to Darla—"

"When did she say it was mailed?" Silas turned off Main Street and headed for his bookstore. He checked his mirror to see if Hayduke's Jeep was following him, as they agreed. The young man was still behind him.

"Two weeks before Kayah disappeared," said Roger.

"Have you looked at it?"

"I'm almost back at my trailer. I'll look at it on my camera, and if there's anything worthwhile, I'll call you."

"I'll be at my store, Roger. If there is anything good, you can email it to me and I'll look at it there."

"Will do."

"Thanks, Roger," said Silas, his hope growing that there might be something of value on the memory card.

"No trouble. I'll call you one way or another."

Silas parked on the street across from the shop and Hayduke nosed in behind him. The young man got out of his Jeep and offered Silas a beer, which he declined. Hayduke opened one for himself.

"You going to start measuring distances in cans of beer?"

Hayduke grinned his wide grin and tossed an empty into the back of the Jeep. "Maybe I will. That your place?"

"Such as it is."

"You got any Edward Abbey in there?" Silas opened the door of the shop. "Hey, what a great store!" said Hayduke, sounding like a kid. They walked in and Silas turned on the lights and the air conditioning. Hayduke wandered the aisles. Silas sat in his desk chair and pressed his fingers against his temples.

Hayduke called, "Where *is* the Edward Abbey section?"

"There isn't one."

"Fuck off, you're kidding me."

"I'm not an Abbey fan."

"This is a Red Rock Canyon bookstore."

"They're *my* books."

Hayduke looked around him. "You're shitting me."

"Nope."

"Every one of these books—"

"Came off my shelf in Flagstaff when I moved here," said Silas, his fingers still massaging his head.

"Fuck me," said Hayduke. "Why did you have so many books?"

"I taught literature."

"That's right, Pen told me about that."

Silas closed his eyes. This young man and his wife had shared stories about his life. He opened his eyes and asked Hayduke, "What exactly was my wife working on before she disappeared, Josh?"

The young man looked at him. "It's Hayduke," he grinned and put his beer can down on a shelf so he could pick up a book. "She was working on a lot of things. This whole Ed Abbey Country idea had totally possessed her. She wanted to lobby Congress to pass an act declaring most of the wilderness left in Utah, Arizona, and New Mexico as all part of an Ed Abbey Country National Monument. She spent most of her time traveling around, hiking in the canyons, making notes on locations."

"And getting under people's skin."

"And that. Pen figured if the developers were going to fuck everything up before she could get her bill passed, well, she was going to fight back."

"Right before she disappeared—what was she fighting? And who?"

Hayduke shrugged. "Lots of stuff."

"Come on, what exactly?"

"That whole Hatch Wash thing, really. She wanted Canyon Rims included in the bill. She wanted it added to Canyonlands National Park. That wasn't going to happen if it got fucked up."

"Who was she fighting? Jacob Isaiah?"

"Yeah, *him* for sure." Hayduke, beer can in hand, sat in the chair next to the desk. "This whole oil and gas thing was rearing its ugly fucking head back then too."

"Was Canusa the proponent back then?"

"I don't remember. We'd have to do some digging."

"Then let's. My assumption is that Penny learned about the ruins and was documenting them so she could stop whatever development was planned for the Hatch Wash area, whether it was Jacob Isaiah's resort or Tim Martin's oil play—"

"Or both," said Hayduke, drinking from his can.

"Or both? I hadn't considered that. I can't really see how having fifty oil derricks as your view would be all that enticing to people in a resort setting—"

"It's a big fucking piece of country out there. They could have the resort sitting on one side of the wash, and those fucking jackknife derricks scattered all across Flat Iron Mesa and Back of the Rocks. Those people don't give a shit what they look at. They just want to stuff their faces, get a massage by some pretty girl, and chase a little white ball around. Hell, if Canusa dammed up Hatch Wash then it would be easier for ol' Jacob Isaiah to water his fucking golf course."

Silas agreed. "Penny was onto something and she was documenting the kiva. Something must have happened, because she left her notebook behind, and then I found it."

"And then you found me."

"That's right. I found you."

"Now we're partners!"

"Listen," Silas said, "we're partners, but only as far as it helps me find my wife. I'm not an environmental crusader. That was Penelope's job. Look where it got her!"

Hayduke shrugged. "Suit yourself. So you think this Wisechild girl and this Williams guy were onto whatever Pen might have found out?"

"The timeline is weird. If Penny found out about the Hatch Wash ruins, that was at least eighteen months before Wisechild and Williams went missing. That doesn't make sense to me."

"It does to me," Hayduke continued, "I think that Pen knew about the Hatch Wash ruins. She could have been prowling around there even if someone like Isaiah, or maybe Martin, had only the slightest inclination of developing the region. She would have been documenting the place for her Ed Abbey Country bill. She would have been building her case so when it came to a hearing, she could blast away at them." Hayduke pounded his fist on the table. He belched, then smiled and said, "That's the way Pen did things."

"You think it's possible she was onto the Hatch ruins before Peter Anton started documenting them, along with Williams and Wisechild, and long before Dead Horse Consulting deep-sixed the report on the site."

"I'm fucking certain of that."

"That means we've got three people who might very well have wanted Penny—"

"Dead," Hayduke finished his sentence. Silas felt a wave of nausea wash over him.

Silas mused, "Jacob Isaiah, because he stood to lose millions—tens of millions—if his mega resort was quashed because of some ruins. Tim

Martin because he stood to lose hundreds of millions if he couldn't drill for oil. And Peter Anton—"

"Why Anton?"

"I think that he must have been in on things with either Isaiah or Martin. Look, he's the one who claims to have discovered these ruins. What if he did? He tells his boss, Strom, and they decide they would tell their client—"

"Either Isaiah or this Canusa company—" added Hayduke.

"That's right. Instead of making a report to the BLM about the archaeological value, the client decides to keep it quiet, and clear the place out."

Hayduke was sitting up and leaning on the table now. "That's right! Clear the place out, destroy all the evidence—"

"Keep the pots and bowls and baskets and arrow points and sell them. There was likely tens of thousands of dollars' worth of antiquities in those ruins. When it came time for the client to file for a development permit, they could say there was nothing in the way of archaeological value, and the development permit would sail through the regulators."

Hayduke was silent. He had finished his beer and was looking around the store as if another can might materialize amid the McCarthy and DeVoto and Doig.

"That means we have five suspects," Silas added.

"Five? Who else?"

"Jared Strom. Anton worked for him. What if Anton went to him and told him about the ruins and they decided to cut a deal. Anton could clear them out and keep the proceeds in exchange for keeping quiet."

"Strom finds out that Pen knows. She confronts him, the way she often would—"

"So he—"

"Fucker kills her." Silas looked down at his hands. "Sorry, fuck. I'm a fucking jackass. I know it. Sorry."

"You're right. I need to get my head around that possibility. All this time I keep expecting to get a postcard from France saying, 'Sorry, Si, just couldn't stand you being such a prick all the time.' Or maybe worst case, she pulled an Aron Ralston and got pinned by a rock in a canyon somewhere but didn't have a pocket knife to cut her own arm off. I think both of those possibilities seem less likely now, knowing what we know."

"Maybe it was Anton, or maybe Strom, trying to prevent Pen from fucking things up for one of their clients."

"Maybe one of the clients themselves, Isaiah or Martin."

"That's four," said Hayduke, holding up his fingers.

"C. Thorn Smith, Senior Republican Senator for Utah."

"Fuck off," said Hayduke, by way of agreement.

"The last thing Senator Smith would have wanted was Penny, or anybody else, doing something that would have scuttled his much trumpeted Utah Land Stewardship Fund. I bet if we dig around, we're going to find that the good senator from the 'great state of Utah' has a significant financial relationship with both Jacob Isaiah and Tim Martin, and the others who were on the podium today. Do you know how to look up political contributions?"

Hayduke grinned. "Fuck yes. I'm not just another pretty face, you know," he said, as he pretended to groom his gamey beard.

"Alright, let's start there. See what kind of financial relationship these guys have with one another. I'm going to pay a visit to the other men on our list of suspects: Isaiah, Martin, and Strom."

"I want to come too!" shouted Hayduke, sounding like a little boy.

"Due respect, but I think I'll get farther if it's just me. I don't want to intimidate these guys . . ."

"You're probably right. Just the sight of these guns and they're likely to wither . . ." The young man flexed his not insubstantial arms. "When do you want to, you know, compare notes?"

"How about we meet tomorrow, around noon, back here?"

"Yeah, that sounds good."

"Okay, then—" said Silas, just as his cell phone rang. He answered. "Yeah, I'm in front of my computer right now, actually . . . Okay, hold on." Silas opened his web mail and Roger's email containing a link. He turned to Hayduke. "It's a video. I've got to download it. Hold on." In a moment a grainy image appeared on his screen. Hayduke leaned over the desk to watch.

A high set of cliffs came into focus. The camera panned and the bottom of the box canyon off the side of Hatch Wash came into focus, complete with the courtyard and entrance to the kiva where Silas had spent a night. Above it were the ancient Pueblo ruins laid out in tiers across the back of the canyon wall. The camera focused in on some activity taking place around one of the dwellings. A man could be seen emerging from the small door, his arms cradling something. A second man walked into the frame and approached the first man, taking whatever it was he was holding.

"It's a pot," said Roger Goodwin on the phone. "It looks like early Pueblo design to me, as best I can tell."

The first man disappeared back into the ruin and a moment later emerged again, this time with what was clearly a basket. He handled it gingerly. The second man entered the frame and took the basket and disappeared off frame again. The camera panned back and Silas could see that the two men had rigged a ladder to reach the second tier of ruins.

"That's what made the marks on the canyon walls," Silas said.

"It goes on like this for a bit. They finish this dwelling and move onto the second."

"Where was the camera?" asked Silas.

"Hold on a minute. You'll see." Silas and Hayduke watched. After another few minutes the camera jiggled and turned around to face a young woman. She had a narrow face with light-brown skin and dark, almond-shaped eyes. She smiled sadly.

"So," she spoke into the camera, "This is how I spent my summer vacation." Then the camera was turned off.

"*That* was Kayah Wisechild," said Roger.

"Is there a date on this file, Roger?" asked Silas.

"Yeah, it was shot June 11, two years ago."

"That was right around the time that Peter Anton said he was doing the work for Dead Horse," Silas added.

Silas clicked his mouse and the footage started again near the beginning. "I don't know who the man in the ruin is, but I'm willing to bet that the man taking the artifacts is Anton. It looks like him for sure. Just the way he walks . . ."

"I think the other man is Kelly Williams. I only met him once," said Roger over the phone, "but I'm sure that the FBI could enhance this."

"Roger, thanks for this. Do you think anybody knew Kayah took this?"

"No. I don't. If whoever killed her knew about it, they would have come looking. Given the date, she took it a few weeks before she disappeared . . . was killed . . . and sent it home for safekeeping. Maybe she was in on it and needed an insurance policy in case things went bad. Maybe she caught onto what Williams and Anton were up to and wanted evidence."

"It's hard to tell where she is in this video."

"I don't think she's on the rim above; there's Navajo sandstone behind her when she turns the camera around."

"I think there is a ledge across from the ruins," said Hayduke.

"Who's that?" asked Roger.

"That's Josh Charleston. Josh, meet Roger. Roger, Josh."

"Call me Hayduke."

"I don't think I will," said Roger.

Hayduke shrugged. Silas asked, "You've been there?"

"Of course, with Penny."

"You didn't tell me that."

"Thought I did, sorry. I think I remember a talus slope and a ledge. I bet the girl was hiding there, making that video."

"You think she might have been in on the raid?" asked Silas to Roger.

"I don't know. If you look at the expression on her face, it shows real sadness. I don't think she was in on it. I think she found out about it and took the video."

"But didn't tell anybody? Just sent it home to end up in a sock drawer?" asked Silas.

"Maybe she told Anton that she didn't like what he was up to," Roger speculated.

"He whacked her," said Hayduke. Silas looked at him hard.

"What about Williams?" asked Roger.

"What if this Anton dude finds out that the girl is going to rat him out, kills her, and then to cover his tracks does the guy as well. No loose ends," said Hayduke.

"One loose end." Silas pointed at the screen.

SILAS DROVE HOME to the Castle Valley in the dark. He and Hayduke had spent another two hours together pouring over the video, talking about the motivation of their possible suspects. Now he had to decide if he would let Katie Rain in on what he knew. He knew he should. He knew that the FBI would have far more resources to investigate the five suspects. How seriously would they take him when he went to them and said that two powerful business men, and a senator, were among those he suspected of killing not just Williams and Wisechild, but Penelope too?

He had only been in the door a few minutes when his phone rang. It was Katie Rain.

"You're still in Moab?" His call display said she was calling from Dexter Willis's office.

"You people are keeping me busy. I kind of like it here."

"I was just debating whether to call you or not."

"Well, I guess that debate is over. How are you doing?"

"I'm doing well. You mean, after having my place sacked and being interrogated on my picnic table, not to mention my culinary choices scrutinized—"

She laughed and then stopped. "Taylor went pretty easy. I've seen a lot worse."

"I know he's just trying to do his job, and so are you, for that matter. Did you call to console me, or have you got something on Williams?"

"Obviously, we've looked into his past. He's an only child; both of his parents live in Durango."

"How'd they take the news?"

"Relieved and grateful, I think. It's really hard on people when something like this drags on for years . . ." Silas was silent. "Said they wanted to meet the man who found their boy."

"I think I've had enough of grieving parents for a while."

"Williams was under investigation by the Antiquities branch of the BLM. You probably know that. He'd been on both sides of the law when it comes to Pueblo artifacts. The BLM was going to be turning a file over to us when he disappeared. Of course, we investigated, but didn't find him or anything conclusive."

"Do you remember the location of the investigation?"

"You mean, which office? It was Taylor's—"

"No, I mean, where he was alleged to have been pot hunting?"

"Some place called Grand Gulch. You know it?"

"Oh yeah, I know it, big canyon full of ruins. It's what the government calls a 'Primitive Area.'"

"Well, apparently it was believed that he was removing artifacts; not many—"

"The Gulch has been pretty picked over by legitimate, bona fide grave robbers from major universities over the years. Do you remember anything about Hatch Wash in his file? He worked on that site with Peter Anton and Dead Horse Consulting."

"I don't remember the details. I'd have to look."

"Can you?"

"Silas, what do you know about this?"

"Katie, I don't know if I can trust the FBI. You know, we've got a bit of a history, and frankly, I think that Taylor and Nielsen would be pretty happy to hang this on me and wash their hands of it."

"You can trust me, Silas."

"I *feel* like I can, but you're still the G."

"You say that like it's a bad thing." He could hear the smile in her voice.

"Alright, listen, I've got something that I think you guys are going to want to see." He told her about the video, its origins, and what it contained. He told her about his list of suspects, and how each tied to Wisechild, Williams, and possibly even his wife.

It was Rain's turn to be silent. "Wow, you're damn right we're going to want to see it. Do you have it with you right now?"

"The memory card is with a friend down on the Hopi Reservation. He emailed the video to me. My computer is at my store."

"Silas, this is important evidence. Taylor is going to want this. He's not going to be happy you got it before him."

"It feels like nothing I do makes Agent Taylor happy."

"This is serious."

"Okay, what do I do?"

"Would you give me your friend's name? I'll call him and ask him to turn over the memory card. Taylor will likely find out you've got a copy sooner or later, but in the meantime this will help us learn more about what these three individuals were up to."

"How about I call him and get him to call you?"

"Okay, deal. If I haven't heard from him by say, ten tomorrow morning, I'm going to have to take steps."

"Kick in my door?"

"Something like that."

"Fair enough."

"We're likely going to have to go to this box canyon you're talking about. Can you give us the coordinates for it?"

"I could, or you could brace Peter Anton for them. He's the only one left alive from that video, and he seems to figure prominently in all of this."

"We won't have enough to charge him, and relying on him for this info would risk long delays. His lawyer will try to make a deal. Can you help me out here, Silas?"

"How about I take you there?"

"Oh, a field trip."

"Don't get too excited. I doubt there are any bones for you to play with."

24

HE WANTED TO GET TO Tim Martin and Jacob Isaiah before the FBI got hold of the video file from Roger Goodwin, so he started early. The night before, he'd called Roger, apologizing for getting him into such a mess, and asked that he arrange to turn over the file at 10:00 AM sharp. He then called Katie Rain back and told her that Roger would meet the agents in Bacavi, on Third Mesa, to give them the memory card. That would give him enough time to confront both Isaiah and Martin, if he could find them.

Silas was in Moab by seven-thirty. He had carefully planned his first encounter. He parked at the Visitor Center and walked the two blocks to the Moab Diner. He knew Jacob Isaiah ate breakfast there most mornings, so he waited outside. Isaiah emerged a few minutes later.

"Good morning, Jacob," he said.

The old man started. "Jesus Christ, don't sneak up on people like that. What the hell do you want, Pearson?"

"Just a minute of your time."

"You going to pester me about your wife again?"

"Not this morning, Jacob. Come on, let's walk."

"I'm going to my office. Some of us work for a living. You've got two blocks to state your business." They walked north on Main Street.

"I'll get right to the point then, Jacob. I've seen a video of Peter Anton working with a man named Kelly Williams, the same man whose remains I found at Grand View Point. They were clearing a set of ruins in Hatch Wash, moving out pots and even baskets. I think they were working for you."

Isaiah shook his head. "More goddamned accusations from you. First your wife, now you. What the hell is it with you people?"

"Did you know that Peter Anton and Kelly Williams were clearing that site? Did you ask them to?"

Isaiah was staring straight ahead when he answered. "No, I don't know what the hell you're talking about. There are no ruins in Hatch Wash. There's nothing there. People have been down in that canyon for years and never found a thing. If you think you're going to try and back me into a corner because I want to develop a resort on Hatch Point, you're out of your mind. Ruins or no ruins, it's no matter. I could care less. So could the BLM. It don't make a bit of difference to me. And no, I never asked anybody to clear a ruin I never heard of."

"Dead Horse Consulting did the preliminary work for your environmental assessment. You weren't counting on them finding anything because nobody ever had, but they did. When they reported this to you, you told them to clear it out so that it wouldn't be an issue."

"You must think you're pretty damn clever, Pearson. You seem to have that all figured out. So then what? I tell them to clear the ruins. So what? The ruins are still there. You think that if the BLM was so worried about disturbing Pueblo sites that just clearing them out of pots would make a difference?"

Isaiah stopped and looked at Silas.

"If there are Indian sites there, it wouldn't make a damn bit of difference if they had pots or arrows in them. It wouldn't matter one fucking bit to my project up on the Mesa. Not one fucking bit." Isaiah jabbed a crooked finger at Silas.

"So you didn't order Anton to clear them—"

"You're not listening to me. Your wife never listened either. I don't care about Indian sites. What I'm going to do up on that mesa won't matter one bit, even if you found the goddamned Cliff Palace there. You think that the kind of people who are going to come to my resort to play golf are going to hike down into that canyon?"

"I've heard you want to build some kind of gondola—"

"You've been talking with the conspiracy theory people, Pearson."

"I read it in the documents you filed at the Grand County offices."

"You spell out every possibility, but it's pie in the sky now—"

"Now that Canusa has found oil under Flat Iron Mesa?"

"That won't make a damn bit of difference either," he said. "We'll do tours of the oil fields. Do an interpreter show about energy security. People will love it."

"Here's what I think, Mr. Isaiah. I think you hired Dead Horse to do the assessment for your project, and when they came back and told you they'd found a class one archaeological site, you sat them down and asked what it would take to clear that site so you could build your golf course and your resort. They said no problem. It will cost you, but we can get the job done. Somebody found out, maybe even my wife. Maybe Kayah Wisechild got cold feet when she realized what she was doing, desecrating *her* ancestors' ruins. Maybe she was cut out of the deal because she was Hopi and Peter Anton thought she'd be a liability. She found out, anyway. When you or maybe Anton got wind of it, she disappeared. There were too many loose ends so Kelly Williams disappeared too."

Isaiah threw his head back and laughed. He sounded like a jackal. "The stories I heard about you were *all* true. You've been out standing in the desert looking for your wife for such an awful long time that you've gone and baked your fucking head." He tapped his finger on the side of his hat. "I sure like hearing your stories, Pearson. I sure do. I need to tell you this, though. If hear that you've been telling this story around town, or to the feds, I'm going to sic my lawyers on you and they will eat you alive. We understood, Mr. Pearson?"

Silas leaned forward. "It's Dr. Pearson, Mr. Isaiah. As soon as I get a chance I'll be telling this story to the FBI. I intend to show them where Kelly and Kayah were working before they were murdered." He turned on the sidewalk and walked back toward the Visitor Center, leaving Jacob Isaiah boiling in the coolness of the morning.

HE RETRIEVED HIS car and drove south on 191 to an industrial complex close to the offices of Dead Horse Consulting. He'd learned that Canusa Petroleum Resources had a local operations office in the complex and he gambled that Martin would be there bright and early. His gamble paid off. The receptionist in the windowless office took his name and called Martin on the intercom. Martin emerged from the back of the building and extended his hand to Silas.

"I'm Tim Martin."

"Silas Pearson."

"What can I do for you?"

"I have some questions about your operations in this area. I was at your press conference the other day—"

"Quite the pomp and circumstance, wasn't it? You Americans sure like your fanfare."

"I'm Canadian, Mr. Martin. I moved here twelve years ago, but I don't really understand the place yet either."

"Come on back. You know, in Calgary or Houston I'd have a wall of PR people between me and the environmentalists, but down here it's just me, a few engineers, and Samantha." They walked through a tangle of cubicles to the kitchen. "Coffee?" Martin asked.

"Sure, that would be great. I should tell you, I'm not with an environmental group."

"I just assumed you were here to bust my ass about our plans for drilling—"

"Not today."

Coffee in hand, Martin led Silas to his office. A window provided a view of the Moab Rim, but the office was otherwise unremarkable.

"You have a big presence elsewhere?"

"We're in the top twenty producers in conventional oil and gas in Alberta."

"Conventional?"

"Old-fashioned. Our main businesses is not in the oil sands, though we have a stake on a play—a development—there. Most of our business is in exploration and drilling. We're small-time in Texas and Oklahoma, but growing. We're building our American team and that's helping us get into the game down here."

"Hence the name Can-USA," Silas concluded. Martin nodded.

"What was it that you wanted to ask me?"

"I want to know about your plans to drill in the Canyon Rims region; Flat Iron Mesa, Hatch Wash, and Back of the Rocks."

"As you might have read in the papers, we're entering into the exploratory phase of our project. Any actual drilling is several years out. We're applying to the BLM for a permit to search for oil reserves in several areas in and around the place you call Canyon Rims. It's a designated Recreation Area, so we have to be sensitive to other uses."

"There are also half a dozen areas within the Canyon Rims complex that are Wilderness Study Areas."

"That's right. The BLM has those off limits, at least until Congress makes a decision on them. Who knows when that might be."

"You don't see your drilling plans as incompatible with the other uses in Canyon Rims?"

"Our operations will have a pretty small footprint."

"I'm no expert, but won't there be roads and pipelines and a lot of traffic?"

"Some, but we can bury parts of the pipeline and regulate road traffic."

"So . . . drilling would require a lot of water. Am I correct?"

"It does take some water to get the oil out of the ground in most cases."

"How does that work?"

"It's pretty simple, really. We mix water with clay—all perfectly harmless—to force the rock we're drilling through, and then later the oil, up to the surface. The water gets cleaned up and is returned to the watershed."

"Cleaned up?"

"We set up portable water purification systems that clean the solvents and residual oil out of the water before returning it to the source."

Silas could only imagine what his wife would have to say about that. "How much would you need?"

"Depends on how many wells we drill, and how much oil each produces. We won't know that for some time. We're only at the preliminary stages. We haven't received regulatory approval yet."

"That's what the senator was talking about yesterday, streamlining."

"We think of it as *harmonizing*." Martin took a sip of his coffee.

Silas shrugged his shoulders. "Call it what you will, the idea is to make the process of getting approval for a project simpler."

"Sure, but without taking shortcuts when it comes to protecting the environment."

"Everybody talks about protecting the environment, Mr. Martin, but talk is cheap. You know that you're going to get a truckload of opposition if you push ahead with a drilling project in the Canyon Rims area."

"I thought you said you weren't an environmentalist?"

"I'm not. Not really, but my wife is. I do like this part of the world. There're lots of others who are going to line up against you."

"Maybe they will, maybe they won't. Sure, Canyon Rims is a nice place, but it's not *extraordinary*. There's not much that is exceptional about it."

"I understand the groups like the Southern Utah Wilderness Association have been lobbying to have it added to Canyonlands National Park for more than a decade. They say that Hatch Wash is of particular importance." Silas watched for his reaction.

"Hatch Wash is pretty, like a thousand other places in the Southwest. You can't lock everything up and throw away the key and keep everybody out except young, fit people with Vibram-soled boots. We either find places where we can drill responsibly, or we import all of our oil from Saudi Arabia, where they don't have any laws at all. I've worked there, and in Iraq, and Kuwait. You think things are tough here? Over there they just cut your head off if you give them any grief."

"Have you done any kind of preliminary environmental assessment of Hatch Wash?"

Martin shrugged. "I'd have to check with my engineers, but I don't think so. This is just at the early stages right now. We know from the government's own reports that there is oil there, enough to make this worth our while. Once we get things rolling forward we'll have a look at the details."

Silas watched the man answer his questions coolly. He tried to remember some of the things that Penny would ask. What about the wildlife? What about the impact the traffic and the noise and the flaring would have on people who wanted to experience the wilderness?

"Where are you planning on getting your water from if you drill in Back of the Rocks, Flat Iron Mesa, or Hatch Point?"

"Well, we've got options."

"Do you? Really? I mean, the place is pretty dry. Kane Creek and Hatch Wash are rare—they have year-round water."

"Well, that is one of the things that makes the area appealing. We can also pump it in, if we have to, or truck it in, but that makes things expensive."

"Not as much return to the investors, eh?"

"I don't think that's a bad thing, do you? Making money is what a business is supposed to do."

"I don't really know. Would you consider building a dam?" asked Silas.

"It's way too early for us to be thinking about things like that," answered Martin, making a dismissive wave with his hands. "Tell me, Mr. Pearson. You're pretty curious—what's your interest? I take it you're a hiker and you like Hatch Wash?"

"Well, I'm not really much of a hiker. Maybe an explorer would be more accurate. Let me tell you what I'm getting at, Mr. Martin. Did you read about the FBI finding a body up at Grand View Point, over in Canyonlands?"

"Sure . . . wait a minute . . . that was *you*! *You* found that body. Now I recognize you. I've got to tell you, you don't look much like your picture."

"A lot of miles have passed since it was taken. Mr. Martin, do you know who it was that I found?"

"No. I can't remember the name. I think it was in the papers—"

"Kelly Williams—"

"That's it. Should I know it?"

"You should. I understand that he worked for you, albeit indirectly. He was on the payroll for Dead Horse Consulting. They were doing some of the preliminary environmental assessments that are required for you to consider drilling in that area. He was an archaeologist, working with another man named Peter Anton. The two of them had another colleague. Her name was Kayah Wisechild—"

"*Was?*"

"Was. She turned up dead, about two weeks ago now. I found her too."

"You found both bodies—"

"I did."

"What are the odds?"

"I'll be spending some time in Vegas after this is through."

"How did you . . . I mean, how did you find both of them?"

"Purely coincidental. You see, I was actually looking for someone else. Someone *I* lost. My wife. Three and a half years ago she went missing in this region. She went out to explore . . . somewhere . . . and never came back. I've been looking for her ever since. In the last two weeks I've found two bodies of people who were working on an archaeological evaluation of Hatch Wash. *Both* where *your* company wants to build a dam and draw water for your oil developments up on Flat Iron and in the Behind the Rocks region."

"Now wait a second—"

"Hold on, Tim, it gets better. I think my wife was also onto your work. I think she knew about it before either Williams or Wisechild, and she was about to blow the whistle."

"That's not possible." Martin stood up and turned to look out the window.

"I think it is. Her name was Penelope de Silva. Does that sound familiar?"

"I've never heard of her. Never." Martin turned and looked at Silas. His face was pale, but his eyes were narrowed.

"Are you sure? She was pretty doggedly determined not to let a place like Hatch and the Canyon Rims fall into the wrong hands."

"Back up a second." Martin sat down and played with his coffee cup, showing an agitation that hadn't been there five minutes before. "You said these two people, this Williams and—"

"Kelly Williams and Kayah Wisechild."

"When did these two go missing?"

"A little more than two years ago."

"And your wife? When did you last see her?"

"Three and a half years ago."

"What exactly are Williams and Wisechild, and Dr. Anton . . . what exactly *were* they looking for in Hatch?"

"I don't know if they were looking for anything in particular. They were doing an antiquities survey. What they found will keep you out of Hatch Wash, maybe forever. It will shut you down."

"What are you talking about?"

"Ruins. Ancient Pueblo ruins, Mr. Martin. Surely the consultants have told you about this."

"We haven't discussed it. I understood that there were no significant sites in Hatch or anywhere else in that vicinity."

"Who told you that?"

"Well, the senator's office, to start with. Jared Strom backed it up."

Silas was silent a moment. "When did they tell you this?"

"When we first hired them."

"When was that?"

"You see, that's what I'm getting at. I have no idea who these Williams and Wisechild people are. No idea. I'm very sorry to say I've never heard of your wife. Canusa just got involved with this play a little over . . ." —he looked at the ceiling, counting—"fourteen, no fifteen months ago."

"I find that hard to believe. Dead Horse has been working on this area for years, at least three or four."

"Not for us. We were invited in about fifteen months ago. *They* approached *us*."

"Who is they?"

"The BLM, and others. The senator actually made the rounds of all the midsized operations looking for suitable partners to work on his Utah Land Stewardship Fund. It was a good opportunity. We have people here in the US, of course, who speak on our behalf . . ."

"Lobbyists."

"We call them government relations specialists, but sure, lobbyists. They make sure that when someone like Senator Smith is looking for partners, he finds *us*. Nothing wrong with that. He approached us and we evaluated the play and decided to jump in."

"Was a report on the environmental and historical significance of the area part of that evaluation?"

"A small part. We looked at the petroleum reserve reports and the financial reports, but yes, there were those considerations as well. I have to assure you, there was nothing there to indicate that Hatch had anything more than a steady water supply."

"You know what I hate?" asked Silas. Martin looked confused. "I hate being lied to."

"I think it's time we put an end to this—" Martin stood.

Silas remained seated. "I think you have been lied to. Either that or you are lying to me. It's one or the other, Mr. Martin."

"Well, *I'm* not lying, and I've got to tell you that it's time for this conversation—"

"If that's the case, then I'd ask some hard questions of your consultants. *They* knew over two years ago, and maybe longer, that Hatch Wash would be off limits to the kind of development you are considering to support your . . . what did you call it? Your oil play?"

"I intend to ask those questions. I assure you, nobody is being lied to. Not you, and not me."

Silas stood and shrugged. "I'm afraid you're in for a rude awakening, Mr. Martin." Silas held out his hand. "Welcome to Utah."

SILAS WAS BACK at his bookstore when his cell phone rang. It was Katie Rain. "We've picked up the memory card from your friend Roger."

"Did you watch it?"

"Yeah."

"What do you think?"

"Agent Taylor has sent the file to the FBI's Digital Evidence Labratory in Quantico for analysis."

"What do you think?"

"I think Peter Anton is in trouble."

25

HE WAS AWARE THAT HE was dreaming but couldn't stop the pageant of images. "Si, it's like an installation from Mars or Saturn—vast, complicated, sinister, an alien presence," Penelope said to him.

A sinister, alien presence. He could see tears running down her cheek, but when he reached to push them away, he could no longer touch her.

THE BOOK WAS *One Life at a Time, Please*; not one of Edward Abbey's best known works. Not *Desert Solitaire*, not *The Monkey Wrench Gang* nor even *The Fool's Progress.* Abbey himself wrote somewhere that he preferred it, and his other books of essays, to those more commercially popular works. Silas found the line on page ninety-six. It was in the essay "River Solitaire: A Day Book," chronicling Abbey's ten-day solo trip down the Colorado River. The writer had launched his skiff just upstream of Highway 191 and floated past the Atlas Mill and then Potash. The Potash plant was a massive industrial complex on the banks of the Colorado about fifteen miles from Moab, and to most observers, it did indeed appear like a sinister, alien presence on the red rock earth.

It was a good place to hide a body. Silas considered if he wanted to find a third corpse. Maybe it was time to let the feds earn their pay.

It was six thirty-five. Most sensible people were still fast asleep on the first day of the September long weekend. *What the hell*, he thought. He found the cordless phone and dialed the now familiar number. It rang four times before she answered.

"Do you have any idea what time it is?"

"Yes."

"Silas, what is it?" Something in his tone had betrayed him.

"There's another body."

THE TEAM MET near the Atlas Mill, just off the highway. Silas stood next to his Outback, a cup of coffee in his hands. Two black SUVs pulled up, followed by the Grand County sheriff in his patrol car and then Derek Penshaw from San Juan County. Silas watched as Dwight Taylor first got out of the driver's side of the lead SUV, then Agent Nielsen and Katie Rain emerged from the passenger doors. They walked over to him.

"Are we ready?" asked Taylor. He had his hands on his hips and wore his inscrutable aviator sunglasses that morning.

"Just a minute. We're waiting for one more."

"Who?"

Silas peered over his shoulder toward the bridge that spanned the Colorado where it emerged from Hal Canyon. He pointed at the Lincoln Navigator rolling across it, slowing down for the sharp turn near the Atlas Mill. "My lawyer."

When Ken Hollyoak rolled down his window, his hair was standing on end and he had heavy bags under his eyes. "The next time you want to find a body, Dr. Pearson, try to do it during regular business hours, will you please?"

Silas got back in his car, leading the convoy, Ken behind him, followed by the cavalcade of law enforcement agency vehicles. They drove along the twisting curves of the Colorado River, the road hemmed in on one side by five-hundred-foot cliffs of Navajo sandstone and the slick red back of the river on the other.

Silas had no idea what he was leading everyone to, except that in his dream Penelope had been quite specific about where she wanted Silas to search. But for what? For her, or for another body somehow connected to her own disappearance? Silas felt his stomach twist further into a knot. The constant motion, the feeling of living on the razor edge of a cliff, was taking its toll on him. He checked his reflection in the mirror and realized he was rapidly becoming an old man.

Another twenty minutes of the winding road, the river, the acid green hue of the late summer cottonwoods, and they came to the gate of their destination: the Intrepid Potash Corporation's Moab mine. Silas got out as the other vehicles pulled up. In a minute a pick-up truck bore down the paved road beyond the gate and a man in a hard hat got out. He waved and unlocked the gate. Agent Taylor walked up and the two men shook hands.

"I'm sorry about this," Taylor apologized. "We'll do our best to not get in the way."

"You said on the phone that you believed there was a body on site?"

"That's right. We have reason to believe someone may have dumped a body here."

"When?"

Taylor shrugged. "We don't know that."

"Okay, well, the place is all yours. We ship about a thousand tons of potash a day out of the site, mostly by rail, so there is some activity going on," the mine manager said.

The convoy followed the manager up the Potash Road, and in a moment the main mine site came into view. The mine manager handed them hard hats.

Silas ignored them all as he scanned the site. The Colorado River slipped quietly by. That would be the obvious place to start. The entire mine site might end up being part of his search, though.

"What is this place?" Katie Rain asked.

"Intrepid Potash," said the manager.

Ken Hollyoak, now more awake, cut in. "Used to be Texas Gulf when it opened in 1963. The Saskatchewan Potash Corporation bought it in 1995, and Intrepid bought it in 2000."

"Mine's unique in all of our operations. We pump Colorado River water three thousand feet underground to dissolve the potash and push it to the surface through pipes. We use settling ponds to separate the brine from the marketable potash, which we either bag or ship out as raw product."

"What's it used for?" asked Silas.

"Everything from water softeners to fertilizer to drilling rig solutions."

"It used to be an underground mine when it opened," added Hollyoak helpfully. "An accident that very year trapped twenty-five men twenty-seven hundred feet below the surface. Only seven survived."

"We've come a long way since then." The manager leveled a stare at Hollyoak.

"Okay, Dr. Pearson," Taylor interjected. "Where do we start?"

Silas looked back at him. "You know, the last two times I did this I was alone, without a bunch of people looking over my shoulder asking me questions—"

Taylor held up his hands as if in surrender and turned and leaned on his truck.

Silas walked toward the river, the sheriff, Agent Nielsen, and Katie Rain following him. He crossed the road and stood on the banks and then looked back up at the mill as if seeing the plant from a boat midstream. "Let's spread out. Start on the bank of the river and just work our way up to the plant."

"Not many places to hide a body," said Rain.

"We might need to bring in the ground X-ray machine if we don't find anything on the first pass," said Agent Nielsen. Silas was impressed; they were taking his lead seriously.

Eventually Taylor and the two ERT agents joined them in their skirmish line. Within an hour they were soaked with sweat, and standing up in the shade of the hulking mass of the processing plant.

"What's next?" asked Taylor, taking a drink from a bottle of water.

"Inside?" asked Rain.

Silas shook his head. "I don't think so." He closed his eyes to remember the dream.

"What else is there?" asked Taylor.

Silas looked around, his hands hanging loosely at his sides. "The settling ponds."

They drove in a convoy behind the mine manager again. Half a mile from the plant, high on a bench of sandstone, were four hundred acres of settling ponds laid out like rice paddies. Massive earth movers were perched on the edge to scoop out the settled salt and potash from the slurry that filled the ponds. The ponds were electric blue. Set against the red earth they were startling.

"This is really the most amazing part of the operation," the manager boasted. "Mother nature does most of the work. We get three hundred days of sunshine, and the relative humidity is 5 per cent, so we don't need to use any energy. We just let it sit."

"Why is it so blue?" asked Rain.

"We add a blue dye, like food coloring, to aid in the evaporation process. The color absorbs more heat. The ponds are lined with heavy vinyl to prevent leaking. When we're ready to extract the final product we use laser-guided equipment," he said, pointing to the giant earth movers, "to scoop out the potash and salt so we don't rip the lining." He stopped and realized that nobody was listening any more. All eyes were on Silas.

"Which ponds have been recently excavated?" Silas asked.

"These three here." He indicated the ones by the two massive excavators.

"So that leaves us with—"

"Another fourteen," the manager said.

Silas looked around him, feeling defeated. He turned and looked at the manager. "How hard would it be for someone to get in here, say, after dark?"

"The gate is locked. We've got a team of security, night watchmen who make their rounds of the main plant and all the auxiliary facilities. I'd say it would be tough to come in the main gate—"

"Are there other accesses?"

"Well, there are other roads in the area."

"Have you got a map?" asked Silas.

They stood around the hood of the manager's pick-up and compared the map of the mine with Silas's USGS fifteen-minute topographic sheet. Silas turned and looked above him at the cliffs that fronted Dead Horse Point State Park, and below them at the crumbling Paradox Basin. He traced several routes on the map with his bone-dry finger, then he stopped.

"Let's start over here."

They followed the manager around the massive ponds to where the road threaded between two reservoirs and then crossed a level plane to another set of tanks. They drove to the far side of the ponds and parked.

"This road," said Silas as they gathered around the map again, "is called the South Fork Road. It winds along the river and connects with the Grand View Point Road way up on the mesa. From here you could drive up and be on Island in the Sky in about an hour."

They turned and looked at the settling ponds. "Alright, let's get to work," said Taylor. "Remember, if we find anything, we're going to be looking for forensic evidence, so crime scene rules are in effect. Janet, I want full video documentation before we start here."

They waited for half an hour while Unger walked a complete perimeter of the series of settling ponds, videotaping the entire scene. Meanwhile, Silas, to the consternation of Taylor, walked up the road toward Island in the Sky half a mile, looking for tire tracks.

When he came back, he said to Taylor, "Half a dozen vehicles have been over this road since the last rain. Tough to tell which was the most recent."

"Leave the forensics to us, Dr. Pearson. You concentrate on whatever it is we're here to find. Okay?"

Silas moved to the ponds. Huston had returned from his SUV with an infrared camera and began to scan the ponds, slowly walking along the narrow banks. Silas walked with him, more out of interest than his ability to be helpful. He had to admit that at this point, with the sun bearing down on them, and the afternoon looking like it would turn into some kind of biblical storm event, he was prepared to admit that Penelope had led him astray. There were more than seventy miles of Colorado River in the essay in *One Life at a Time, Please*. Maybe he'd misread the dream.

Half an hour passed with the team methodically searching along the banks of the electric blue ponds. The heat radiating off the water was dazzling and for a moment Silas imagined passing out and falling into the corrosive liquid. His hallucinations were interrupted.

"Got something!" called Huston. "Got something, right here."

"Nobody touches anything," ordered Taylor, "especially you, Dr. Pearson." The big man walked carefully to the edge of the pond. "What you got, Huston? Talk to me."

"I . . . got . . . yup, I got a body, right here." He lowered the camera. Silas could see nothing through the bright blue dye in the slurry of river water, salt, and potash.

"How far into the pond?" asked Taylor.

"Not far. Ten feet." Huston put the camera to his eyes again. Silas was aching to look through its lens.

"Alright," said Taylor, looking around. "We need the Underwater Search and Evidence Response Team on site. Everybody back to the vehicles. Huston and Unger, you're on documentation and evidence recovery." Taylor turned to the mine manager, who looked worried. "We're shutting this section of the site down. This whole area is a now a crime scene."

26

SILAS SAT ON THE REAR bumper of his Outback in the shade of the only cottonwood in the vicinity. Ken Hollyoak had opened a folding lawn chair and set it up nearby. His eyes were closed, his head lolling in the oppressive heat. Thunderheads boiled above, shot through with radiant incandescence. Silas drank a Dr Pepper and reread *One Life at a Time, Please*, because there was nothing else to do.

It had been five hours since the discovery of the body in the settling pond. Taylor had told them to leave the crime scene but to stay in the vicinity. An hour and a half after the body had been found additional agents arrived from the FBI's Monticello office, along with two additional members of the Grand County Sheriff's Office. They had set to work collecting evidence.

A helicopter had arrived two hours after that and four men had disembarked carrying massive cases of gear. Silas suspected this was the underwater recovery team, but he hadn't been allowed on the site.

Silas was summoned by one of the Monticello agents around five. He nudged Ken, who woke with a start.

"Ken, they want me to head up to the site." Ken struggled to his feet and rubbed his hands over his face. They walked up to the settling ponds where a dozen and a half people were in various stages of the investigation. Taylor and Rain approached Silas before he could reach the location where the body was being examined.

Rain stopped in front of Silas. "It's not your wife, Dr. Pearson."

Silas looked down and drew a deep breath. He could smell the ozone in the air.

"We want you to have a look, if you're willing. What we've got here is a woman, looks to be in her late thirties, early forties, but it's pretty hard to tell," she continued. "There has been considerable burning from submersion in the potash, as well as a lot of tissue loss due to dehydration from the salt. The preliminary assessment is that the remains have been here for less than a month. Maybe as little as two weeks."

Ken put his hand on Silas's shoulder and looked at his friend. "Silas, you don't have to do this—"

"It's okay, Ken. I don't mind."

"Okay, Dr. Pearson," directed Taylor. "This way."

They walked along the narrow pathway between settling ponds. The dive team was shedding their heavy gear and being hosed down just below. Other agents continued to collect possible evidence in the vicinity. Silas could see them making molds of tire tracks on the road that led up to Island in the Sky.

Sheriff Willis was hunched over the corpse. A white shroud covered her. He looked up as Silas approached. "Thanks for doing this, Silas."

Silas walked up to him. The man pulled the shroud back. The ghastly sight that met Silas took his breath away. The woman's face looked as if it had been eaten by acid. It was covered in dark red sores that in places exposed bits of bone. Her lips and much of her nose was missing, and her eyes were empty sockets. Her long hair was matted with thick knots of salt. Her earlobes were missing, and what was left was raw and red. What skin hadn't been burnt off by the potash was sucked dry of moisture so it appeared as if in the early stages of mummification. Despite this, he recognized the face.

Silas stood up and felt dizzy. The sheriff stood and steadied him. Silas pressed his eyes shut. A crack of thunder overhead made people look up. The sky was dusky black and a strong wind was picking up, blowing upstream. It smelled like rain.

"I know this is hard," said Rain. "Do you know who—"

"Her name is Darcy. Darcy McFarland."

"You know her?"

"My wife did. Penny did. They were friends in Flagstaff. She . . . Darcy . . . was a water rights activist. The Colorado River was her specialty." He looked down from the terraced bench of red rock at the river as it swept patiently by.

27

"NONE OF THIS MAKES ANY sense," said Silas. He was sitting on the back porch, under the pergola, of Ken and Trish Hollyoak's home. It was after eleven in the evening and the stars lay thick over the Moab Rim. After the brief rain, the desert now smelled fresh, as the first bloom of autumn's wildflowers emerged from the cracked and baked summer soil.

Ken drank an ice tea and ate a sandwich. Silas sat in a recliner and watched the flicker of candles that Trish had lit. He was exhausted, but he didn't want to retire to the guesthouse where he had agreed to sleep for the night so Ken and Trish could keep an eye on him.

"None of this makes any sense," he repeated.

Ken wiped his mouth with a napkin. "Hombre, none of this is meant to. We're talking about people killing other people. Now, where is the sense in that?"

"Three bodies," mused Silas, almost talking to himself. "Three bodies, two of them just bones. One of them fast becoming a skeleton. Good God, the state of that poor woman."

"Your girlfriend at the FBI said she would know the cause of death tomorrow?"

"She's not my girlfriend. She'll like me more after I've been a skeleton for a few years. Anyway, she said that because this wasn't anthropological she wouldn't be primary on the determination of the cause of death."

"If you're insinuating that very fine specimen of woman is not interested in you, I think you'd better think again, Dr. Pearson. I detected noticeable chemistry between you two."

Silas looked up at Ken, his face caught in the dance of light from the candles as he took a sip from his beer. "We were in an interview room with two other feds who were raking me over the coals about how I keep finding bodies, Ken. She was the only one not trying to hang me out to dry for three murders. Of course there was chemistry."

Ken shrugged. "Suit yourself."

"I will. Why do I keep dreaming about Penelope pointing me in some direction and when I follow her lead, instead of finding *her*, I find someone else?" Silas's hands were shaking.

"Silas, I am a happily retired lawyer from the great city of Salt Lake now living a quite retirement in the desert with my fourth and final wife. I am your friend, and I am happy to act as your counsel, but alas, I am not a psychologist, let alone an expert on dreams. For that, you will need to consult the experts. What I can surmise is this: for the better part of three and a half years you, my friend, have been wracked by guilt."

"Wait a minute—"

"Hear me out, Professor. When it came to Penelope, you were not particularly uxorious in nature as a husband. It's not that you were a cheating scoundrel. You just had . . . other priorities. When your dear Penelope disappeared, your guilt over being an absentminded professor more interested in the masochistic gloom of Cormac McCarthy than your elegant and, I must say, very sexy wife, got the better of you. You've been carrying that guilt around with you for coming on four years now. It's only a matter of time before our minds need to expunge some of that guilt. I'm amazed that Canadian beer and TV dinners are your worst acts of self-mutilation."

"You think this is just my guilt-addled mind opening a pressure release valve?"

"Like I said, I am a lawyer, not a head shrink. I could make you an appointment with my own witch doctor, but somehow you don't seem the type."

"It may come to that, Ken. You see, when I had that first dream, and even the second, I couldn't help but think that maybe somehow, through my subconscious, Penny was leading me to her."

"That is what you wanted to think."

"The first two bodies have both been dead for two years, and had been buried. They were both archaeologists, though their pedigree is certainly in question, as it appears that at least one of them, and maybe both, was involved in raiding the ruins in Hatch Wash. Both worked for Peter Anton, and through him Dead Horse Consulting. The consulting group worked for one or maybe both of the proponents of competing development proposals at the same location, out on the Canyon Rims: Jacob Isaiah's heatstroke-induced dream of a golf and destination resort, and Tim Martin's vision of energy security.

"I don't know if Penny knew either of these people, but I do know she knew about the ruins, because that's where I found that notebook you're holding onto for me. It stands to reason she knew the ruins, and the wash—and the whole Canyon Rims area, for that matter—were threatened. The Canusa Petroleum Resources boss Tim Martin tells me that he's only been looking at the Canyon Rims area for less than eighteen months, and those bodies are two years old. Penny has been missing for much longer than that."

"He could be lying."

"That has occurred to me," said Silas, "but that doesn't help me understand what happened today. Darcy McFarland has been a water rights activist for twenty years. She lived in Flagstaff, and her thing was the Colorado River Compact—that whole muddled mess of laws and policies that govern the Colorado River. She and Penny knew each other. I remember her coming over for dinner once, and the two of them sat on the porch and talked about politics. I think she believed that Penny had strayed over the last few years, but I can't say . . . I was an inattentive husband."

"Silas—"

"No, it's okay, Ken. Darcy was not an archaeologist, and she has no *apparent* connection with Isaiah—though to be perfectly honest I suspect Isaiah has pissed off every environmental activist in the Four Corners states with one project or another over the years. Darcy has no obvious connection to Canusa Petroleum. Nor does she have any connection with any of the *other* people I suspect might have had involvement in Williams's and Wisechild's deaths—Anton, Jared Strom, or even Senator Smith, at least none that I can see."

"*Yet*. None that you can see *yet*."

"Why Darcy? What is the connection to these other two that I'm just not seeing?"

"Maybe there is no connection. Maybe we're talking about completely different situations; different . . . cases. Maybe there is no connection whatsoever between the murders of Kelly Williams and Kayah Wisechild and the murder of Darcy McFarland."

"What about Penny?"

"No connection between any of these situations."

"There is a connection," said Silas.

"What's that?"

"Me. *I'm* the connection. I found Kayah and Kelly, and now Darcy. If I could figure out who between these players was most likely to want Williams and Wisechild out of the way, I'd feel like I was getting somewhere."

"You know, when I was a prosecutor, like forty years ago, before I learned that money could buy things and before I had gone through a few wives, I learned something profound. If you want to get to the root of all evil, follow the money. 'Men die and worms eat them, but not for love,' I think your friend Abbey once said. Most often it's for money, and for power, which money can easily buy, especially in Utah."

"I don't know the first thing about following a money trail."

"I bet you know someone who does. Isn't one of your suspects in all of this mess Canadian?"

"WHAT ARE YOU doing, calling so early?" asked Robbie Pearson.

"I'm sorry. I forgot about the time change. Do you want me to call back?"

"No, it's okay, I'm awake now. Is everything alright?"

"I'm fine. I mean, well, I'm alive and in one piece . . ."

"Dad, what is it?"

"Well, remember when you emailed me about the body in Courthouse Wash?"

"Yeah, you said it wasn't Penelope."

"It isn't. Wasn't. What I didn't tell you was that I found the body. And now I've found two more bodies. Neither of them Penny, but all entangled some-how with something that Penny was working on before she disappeared—"

"Dad, hold on. Did you say you've found three bodies?"

"Yes."

"Holy shit." Silas could hear banging in the background.

"Look, if it's a bad time, I'll call you back."

"No, I'm just making coffee. I think I'm going to need it. Tell me what's going on, Dad." Silas told him the whole story. Robbie asked questions, and Silas answered them as best he could.

"What can I do?" asked Robbie.

"I need some help following a money trail. This company, Canusa, is based in Calgary. I suspect that we might be able to learn a lot about what they want to do in the Canyon Rims area, and for how long they've wanted to do it, if we could just learn more about how they are financing the project. Can you do that?"

"Are they publicly traded?"

"I don't know." Silas could hear his son at his computer.

"Let me look into this," Robbie said. He was clearly typing. "Tell me more about some of the other people involved." Silas told him.

"There's one more thing. A numbered company is involved in some of the drilling proposals. I have no idea if they are connected with Canusa. If I give you the company number, can you do your internet thing with it?"

"Yes, I can do my internet thing. I don't know how much I'll be able to find out, but I should at least be able to get you the names of the people behind the number. I'll call you back in a couple of hours. It's going to be alright, Dad. You'll see."

They hung up the phone. Silas sat still for a moment. He felt better than he had in weeks, having spoken to Robbie, so he couldn't figure out why he wanted to weep.

HIS CELL PHONE rang. He was on Main Street buying a coffee.

"You want to know?" asked Katie Rain without saying hello.

"Of course." He stepped outside the coffee shop with his americano.

"She was drowned."

"She didn't drown, she *was* drowned?"

"That's right. We found a hairline fracture on the back of her head and bruising on her neck. Her lungs were full of that slurry of potash, salt, and water. She died after she'd been submerged."

"Jesus Christ." Silas looked down at the sidewalk.

"Yeah, it wasn't very pretty. A lot of burning on the internal tissue from the potash. We know for certain that her lungs filled up before she was dead. Anyway, I thought you'd want to know."

"Are you still in town?"

"Yeah."

"Do you want to split my americano with me?"

"Is this a date? You know I can't fraternize with a person of interest."

"Information sharing."

"Okay. Where are you?"

SILAS SAT AT his desk, Katie Rain in the chair across from it. She looked around the room. "This is nice."

"It's just a ruse."

"Come again?"

"It's for show. I don't really want to run a bookstore. I don't really care about selling books. In fact, these are all mine—"

"Pride of the small-business owner—"

"No, I mean, these were all from our library in Flag. When I moved here I didn't have any place to put them. You've seen my place."

"All maps, all the time." Katie smiled.

"Right. And I thought that I might go a little, you know, crazy"—he twirled his finger beside his ear—"if I didn't have something else to do, so I rented this place, put in some shelves and track lighting, and put my library in here. Nobody ever comes in. I sell maybe a dozen books a month. When I'm here, which isn't very often."

"I can't imagine what would make someone believe you were crazy."

He studied her. She was solidly built, with powerful arms that looked as if she could do more chin ups than he could. She wore her gun on her hip and her badge clipped next to it. "You really are an FBI agent, aren't you?"

She looked down at her sidearm. "I don't wear it very often, but Taylor insisted that if I was going to be on the team, I had to take it out of my travel bag and strap it on."

"I didn't think FBI science types carried weapons."

"I was an agent first. That was almost fifteen years ago. I was in the field for two years in Los Angeles and then Oregon. I finished my PHD and went into forensics. The Bureau put me through my doctoral program, and then post-doc work. I still have field agent status . . . *What?*" His face had fallen while she spoke.

"For some reason I thought I wasn't talking with a 'real' FBI agent."

She pinched herself. "Yup, real as it gets. I just don't do investigation work these days. You know, Silas, getting out of Salt Lake City and out into the real world has been a relief."

Silas let out a long breath and managed a smile. "We said information sharing. Share away."

"We spent the morning on the line with our people in NCAVC. We're coming up with a working theory—"

"NCAVC?"

"The National Center for the Analysis of Violent Crime. It's part of the federal Critical Incident Response Group. Part of their job is behavioral analysis in mass, serial, or spree killings."

"You think this is a serial killer?"

"We don't. Not now, at least. Unlike Wisechild and Williams, we think Darcy McFarland was killed on site. We think she knew her attacker; that he—or much less likely she—was someone Ms. McFarland trusted. We found some small flecks of sandstone consistent with that surrounding the potash site embedded in the skin on the back of her head, and one very small piece in the bone fragments there. It's possible this happened elsewhere. Navajo sandstone isn't exactly hard to come by around here. But there were trace amounts of crystallized salt on the stone, and we believe that means it came from the potash site.

"The blow didn't kill her, just stunned her, may have blinded her, as there was some damage to the optic nerve. There was also bruising around the hyoid bone, which indicates a violent struggle. We believe she was lured or possibly driven to the site, strangled violently, knocked unconscious, and then submerged in the water."

"The killer in all likelihood would have gotten some of the slurry on him."

"That's right. The body was ten feet from the shore of the lagoon, and in almost eight feet of water. The killer—or maybe killers—would have had to be very strong to heave the body into the slurry."

"What about tracks? If the killer drove Darcy to the site, then there would be tire tracks."

"There were eight different sets of tracks on the road leading to Island in the Sky. We took imprints, and will be running them through our database. It might not help us find the killer, but it might help convict."

"You're going to want to look at my car, aren't you?"

"Silas, Taylor still considers you a person of interest, but *I* don't."

"*He's* in charge."

"True, but this is what I need from you: motive. We're not getting anywhere and we can't determine what motive ties these three individuals together."

"What if they're not tied together?"

"That's always a possibility. But we need to eliminate the possibility of a link between them all first."

"Katie," said Silas, "I'm frankly stumped as to how these three people are connected, except by the frustrating fact that *I* found them all."

Just then the doorbell chimed. Silas looked up. Josh Charleston—Hayduke—was at the door. Katie turned to look at him. "You have a customer!" she said, grinning at Hayduke.

"Yeah—"

"I should let you attend to him. Rent to pay." She stood and offered her hand. He took it. "We'll be in touch." She turned and walked to the door.

Hayduke picked up a book by Charles Bowden and ignored her. "Nice piece on the fed," he said after she left.

Silas sat down. "What did she want?" asked Hayduke.

"To talk with me about my propensity for finding dead people."

"I can see why she would be interested. Fuck, nice-looking piece of—"

"Enough." Silas was weary of the Hayduke act.

Hayduke grinned. "So you found another corpse. I go away for one fucking day and look what kind of trouble you end up in!"

Silas signed heavily and brought Hayduke up to speed.

"I didn't know her," said Hayduke. "I mean, Pen talked about Darcy, but we never met. I've only been to Flag once, and that was years and years ago."

"Did you know her work?"

"Not really."

"What does a water rights activist do?"

"Fucked if I know," exclaimed Hayduke, looking around the store.

Silas drew a deep breath. "I guess I'll have to find out. Can you tell me if you've learned much about political contributions?"

"It's a fucking shit-show of corruption. I can tell you this, both Jacob Isaiah and this countryman of yours, Mr. Timothy *T.* Martin are up Senator Smith's ass so far they can't see daylight. Both of them are huge contributors. Isaiah has been handing him bags of green since the senator was governor in the 1980s. Your friend Isaiah ran this whole district for Smith when he was first elected to the Senate twelve years ago. He's backed off since, but still gives a fucking load of cash to him every year. We're talking about the federal limit for both individual and corporate contributions. Not to mention soft money. That fucker funds every industry group he can find that supports what Senator C. Thorn Smith backs in Congress."

"What about Martin?"

"He's newer to the giving game. Started four years ago."

"Well, he told me that his financial stake in this area started less than eighteen months ago."

"Fuck, man, he might have only bought the leases then, but his contributions to Smith started four years ago. He gave the limit, and then some!"

"Soft money?"

"No, but some of his senior VPs also made personal contributions."

"Don't you have to be American to donate?"

"Easy to get around if you own an American-based business, which Canusa qualifies as, given that it has offices in Houston, Salt Lake, and here. Don't forget, in America corporations are people too."

"Yeah, in Canada too. Do you have a list of who inside Canusa made donations?"

"No, but I can run that fucker down."

"Do, please." Silas's cell rang and he held up a finger and answered. It was Robbie. "It's my son."

"I can go—"

"No, it's related. Hold on. What have you got, Rob?"

"Well," said Robbie. "You told me to follow the money."

"Funny, I'm just talking with someone here about campaign contributions."

"Well, it's likely to get funnier."

"Do tell."

"I looked at the money trail and it's just what you'd expect: lots of cash moving around between Canada and the United States on this project. Canusa is 51 per cent American, so they can skirt all sorts of domestic ownership laws in the US. There's been about twenty-five million pumped into the Canyon Rims project so far."

"Twenty-five!"

"Yeah, mostly for geotechnical work and consulting fees."

"These guys are way further along than they are letting on. Let me guess, most of that going to Dead Horse?"

"Yup, about half of it to them. The rest was divided up among half a dozen firms that do seismic testing, that sort of thing. Also, Dad, there's been at least a million spent on lobbying."

"That's a lot of money. Certainly worth killing over."

"Maybe," said Robbie. "I don't know anything about that sort of thing. But here's something else I found. There's a revolving door between Canusa Petroleum Resources and the federal governments on both sides of the Medicine Line. We're talking about staff from Canusa working for the Department of Natural Resources in Canada and Alberta's Energy Minister, and in the US staff moving between management at the company and senior levels of the EPA and the energy department. It's not just within the bureaucracy. One of Canusa's senior managers has been doing a stint with one of your prime suspects, Dad. A guy named Charles Nephi."

"Say that again?"

"Charles Nephi has been with Canusa on and off for almost a decade. It looks like he's from Utah, worked in Texas for Canusa, went to the EPA, next to Canada as a junior VP with the company for two years, and then four years ago, right around the time that Canusa started putting money in the hands of your senator? It looks as if they gave him Nephi, because he showed up back in the senator's office. I guess his official title is District Assistant, but according to some bloggers with the Natural Resource Defense Council, the guy is like Smith's bag man for the energy industry in Utah. He's basically running the trapline, bringing more energy business to the senator's home state. The biggest investor in both the petroleum business and in Smith's coffers is Canusa. Nephi is also an officer of the corporation you asked me to look into. It's a Utah company, and all I could get were the officers, which are your man Martin, this Nephi fellow, and Peter Anton."

They finished the call and Silas looked at Hayduke. He filled him in on the developments.

"I think we had better go and have a talk with Mr. Nephi," said Hayduke.

"And Peter Anton," added Silas.

28

THEY AGREED TO SPLIT UP. Silas had argued that Hayduke might actually prove beneficial in a confrontation with Charles Nephi. Hayduke believed otherwise, arguing that bums like him usually got thrown out of a senator's office. Instead, Hayduke would try and learn as much as he could about Darcy McFarland's work and if there was a connection with either Kelly Williams or Kayah Wisechild. He would make the seven-hour drive to Flagstaff, camp up in the Coconino National Forest, and in the morning see what he could learn. Silas warned him to exercise some sensitivity, given that it was only yesterday that she had been discovered dead. At that, Hayduke smiled and explained that he was a "fucking paragon of restraint and sensitivity."

Hayduke departed for Flagstaff, leaving Silas to determine the best way to get both Charles Nephi and Peter Anton to come clean about their relationship with Canusa Petroleum Resources and the Canyon Rims project. Failing to think of anything better, he decided that the direct approach would be best. He would start with Nephi.

The senator's southeastern Utah offices were in what was once Blanding's post office and library. A small reception area led to offices of various government departments built into the open space that had once housed the library. An armed security guard sat behind the reception desk. He looked up as Silas entered.

"I'd like to speak with Charles Nephi, please." The guard picked up his phone and spoke a few words. Silas signed in, producing his water-stained, sand-encrusted driver's license as ID.

"How can I help you?" Silas turned and saw Charles Nephi standing at the door to the senator's office.

"I'm Silas Pearson." Silas clipped on a visitor pass.

"I have about ten minutes before my next meeting." Nephi looked at his watch.

"Should we talk in your office?" asked Silas.

They walked through a large open room with a desk for volunteers or a receptionist, and three offices running along the eastern wall, each with a glass window looking into the common space. Each room had a window facing west onto an alley behind the government building. In one Silas could see a conference table and six chairs. The room was occupied by half a dozen people stuffing envelopes with what looked like campaign propaganda. The middle office appeared to be the senator's; it housed a desk, a flag, a nearly empty bookshelf, and a picture of the Republican Speaker of the House. Nephi stopped outside the third office. Through a large window Silas could see it was a cramped affair. A stack of papers occupied the visitor's chair and a small tower of bankers boxes sat behind his desk.

Instead of inviting him in, Nephi stood at the closed door and crossed his arms. "What can I do for you, Mr. . . . ?"

"It's Dr. Pearson. I used to teach." Silas stood so he had a clear view into the office.

"What did you say your name was?"

"Silas Pearson."

"And you own a bookstore?"

"That's right."

"You're the one looking for his wife."

"Yes, so?"

"You found the bodies, that young Hopi girl and the other one. I saw you out on the reservation a few weeks ago."

"Yes, that's right. What of it?"

"Mr. Pearson—"

"Dr. Pearson."

Nephi ignored him. "I don't mind talking with people about the work our senator is doing, Mr. Pearson, but I like to know who I'm dealing with."

"It's true that I'm looking for my wife. She's been missing for three and a half years. That's not what I want to talk with you about. I wanted to ask you a few questions about the Utah Land Stewardship Fund."

"What's your line of business?"

"I own a bookstore."

"Dr. Pearson, I think we're wasting our time here."

"Tell me about the projects. I heard the senator talk about Canyon Rims."

Nephi shifted his body to block the window into his office. "Listen, I don't mean to be rude, but—"

"When did you quit working for Canusa Petroleum and come to work for the senator?"

"That's not anybody's business but my own."

"About four years ago, right? About the same time that Canusa started making significant contributions to the senator's PAC."

Nephi studied him. "You're with those environmental bloggers, aren't you?"

"I've never written a blog in my life," admitted Silas, "but I do recognize pork-barrel politics when I see them."

"I think this conversation is over, Mr. Pearson."

"You're still on the payroll, aren't you?" asked Silas. "You never left. The penny drops. I bet if I did the math I'd see that the campaign contributions Canusa is making to the senator's office are a pretty close match to your highly inflated salary as a constituency assistant. They're paying you to be the inside man and open doors for them. Canyon Rims is the first project, isn't it?"

Nephi went into his office and picked up the phone. "Would you please escort Mr. Pearson out of the building?" Silas's eye roamed from Nephi to the stack of bankers boxes. Nephi hung up and came back out.

"Did Wisechild and Williams learn about your project? Did Darcy McFarland? Did my wife?"

Nephi crossed his arms and shook his head. "I heard you'd gone a little nuts. Paranoid delusions are what you are experiencing, Pearson. Look it up in a book."

The security guard appeared. "Come with me, sir."

Silas looked at the security guard and back at Nephi. He left the building without a fuss.

SILAS SAT FOR an hour in his car, alternately turning it on to run the air conditioning and turning it off to save gas. It seemed likely that Charles Nephi was still being paid, albeit indirectly, by Canusa Petroleum. His job: clear away obstacles to development of oil and gas across the Canyonlands. If that was the case, how might he be tied to the deaths of Wisechild, Williams, and McFarland? How might each of their deaths be tied to the disappearance of Penelope? And what was in his office that he was hiding?

When he reached Moab, he decided to stop at the offices of Dead Horse Consulting. The receptionist told him that Jared Strom would *not* see him. Silas decided that he would go for broke and simply walked past her. She was right on his heels when he arrived at Strom's door. The man was on the phone and looked up when he saw Silas at his door, the receptionist behind him.

Strom hung up and opened the door.

"I'm sorry, Mr. Strom, he walked right by me. Do you want me to call the police?"

"I'll do it, Darlene. It's okay." He turned to Silas. "You're making quite a fuss, aren't you?"

"People are dead, and I think you know why."

"You're here to accuse me of murder?"

"I'm here to tell you that if you know who is responsible, this is a perfect opportunity to come clean. You might escape accessory charges."

"Really, Pearson, please, educate me."

"I think one of your clients has taken his greed too far. I think that it all started as a simple plan to develop a place that nobody thought was worth protecting, and has resulted in the murder of two and maybe as many as four people."

"Canyon Rims. Hatch Wash, is that what this is about? There's nothing there worth protecting. I know myself. I reviewed the survey. I've been to the site. There's nothing there to find."

"What have you done?"

"I haven't done anything, Pearson. It's what you've done that I'd be worried about."

HE DIALED RAIN'S number as he was making his way into town. When she answered he said, "You fed types still up for a field trip?"

THE CLOSEST HELICOPTER landing pad was at Moab Regional Hospital, so that's there they converged. Eugene Nielsen, Dwight Taylor, Katie Rain, the two evidence recovery experts, and Silas were crammed in the back of a UH-60 Black Hawk helicopter. They flew low over Moab and out across the Spanish Valley to where it broadened and opened into the Canyon Rims area.

Silas sat with his eyes turned to the landscape beyond. He'd never seen the canyon country from the air and the unfolding view of the cracked and fractured landscape fascinated him. At Bridger Jack Mesa the helicopter veered west and started following the defile of Kane Creek, flying five hundred feet above the canyon rim.

Over his headset he heard Taylor speaking. "Dr. Pearson, tell me again exactly what Jared Strom said." Silas told him. "Did he say if he or anybody else had been into this canyon in the last few days or even weeks?"

"No, but he didn't have to." Silas's eyes caught Rain's and she smiled at him. He nodded and looked back out the window. The helicopter banked up and over Kane Creek lookout and the point of land that separated it from Hatch Wash. They flew south and east again, just along the elevation of Flat Iron Mesa.

The helicopter pilot's voice came over his headset. "We're going to fly over your coordinates, Dr. Pearson, and see if we can't find a place to touch down."

They flew up Hatch Wash and at the box canyon banked east and flew over the tiny entrance of the canyon. From above Silas couldn't see anything that would indicate there were ruins there, the overhanging cliff protecting the site not only from rain but from aerial observation. He pressed his face against the window to try and spot the opening in the kiva but could see nothing.

"We're going to circle and do a soft-touch landing back in the main wash," said the pilot. A moment later the Black Hawk was descending perpendicular to the canyon walls, dropping straight down into a wide point in Hatch. Silas looked away from the canyon walls just a few hundred feet on either side of the helicopter and noticed Taylor watching him with practiced nonchalance. Silas forced himself to look back at the vertical landscape outside.

"Okay," the pilot said over the din. "When we touch, Agent Nielsen is on the door and everybody moves to the west of the Black Hawk, heads down. We'll dust off and stay on station on Flat Iron Mesa. We're only two minutes away if you need us."

"Roger that." Nielsen hunched down and grasped the handle of the door. The helicopter touched down and Nielsen threw the door open with experienced ease. Taylor jumped out first and reached back to offer Silas a hand. Heads down, they moved away from the helicopter. A hundred yards up the wash, toward the box canyon, they stood up and watched the others join them. The helicopter lifted off, straight up, and out of sight over the rim of the canyon. The world was silent once more.

"Lead the way, Doc." Rain adjusted her backpack. Silas led them up Hatch Wash five hundred yards and then found, amid the tangles of tamarisk, the side canyon that contained the ruins. The afternoon sun bore down on the small group of hikers as they picked their way up and over the rocks. Silas noticed that Nielsen and Rain handled the terrain well, while the others seemed to struggle with the difficult ground.

"If you don't mind my saying," Silas said to Taylor, "you're looking a little out of place."

Taylor looked up at him, a pearl of sweat caught in one eyebrow. "Why is that, Dr. Pearson? Because I'm black?"

Silas laughed. "No, because you're clumsy." Nielsen and Rain both grinned.

"I left Special Forces so I wouldn't have to tramp around in the desert anymore, and what happens? I get assigned to a jurisdiction that's nothing but desert . . ."

"We're almost there." Silas pointed to the amphitheater where the canyon boxed up, protecting the ancient settlement.

Katie took a few quick steps and walked next to Silas, her eyes up and alert. "Let's stop here," she said. Taylor came up beside them. "Let's treat this whole location like a crime scene." They made arrangements for Janet

Unger to begin to document while John Huston started the laborious hunt for physical evidence.

"Alright, Dr. Pearson, let's see these ruins."

They moved forward slowly, Taylor searching the cobbled canyon floor for footing as much as for evidence. They stepped out of the tiny wash and followed Silas up the talus slope and came out onto the small plateau. Silas stopped dead in his tracks. The canyon was silent in the midday heat. The ruins were not there.

"YOU SURE THIS is the right canyon?" asked Taylor, looking around.

"I'm sure."

"There's nothing here."

Silas walked along the floor of the canyon where the kiva had been; where a week before he'd been left for dead.

"This is the place." Where the floor had once been a smooth terrace, it was now jumbled with talus. He looked above at the alcove where the three tiers of ruins had once been nestled into the sandstone, but the walls were now vacant. "Someone's demolished the ruins."

Taylor looked at Nielsen, who stepped up beside Silas. "Show me where." The two men walked across the plateau and Silas pointed.

"Well, the kiva was here. The opening . . . about here, and up there, where you see that hollowed-out alcove, that was the third tier of the granaries and dwellings." Nielsen looked around the canyon floor and stamped his cowboy boots down in a few places. He moved off toward the canyon wall and examined it. He rubbed his hand against the smooth stone and then put his fingers to his nose to sniff, then to his tongue to taste the gritty residue.

"No doubt about it, this place has been blasted. You can see where that streak of varnish, that black line, has been interrupted recently. That big piece right there," Nielsen said, pointing to a slab of stone on the canyon floor, "has come off right there and has been moved. I can smell *and* taste TNT. I suspect that whoever did this had some mechanical help, so John should be looking for tracks, maybe even some diesel. We're also going to want to get someone from the BLM down here who knows these artifacts to tell us what *might* have been here. And we'll need the ground-penetrating radar so we can get a clear picture of Dr. Pearson's kiva. See if anybody might be home."

Taylor looked around again. "Alright, let's get to work. I'll radio up for the necessary reinforcements."

BY 4:00 PM there were half a dozen additional agents and BLM officers in the box canyon. Silas sat in the shade, his back to a giant boulder, surveying the busy scene. The ground-sensing equipment had been lugged up the canyon by two of the new FBI agents and two BLM field officers and they were now making an image of the kiva. There was nobody home. An archaeologist with the BLM, who had talked with Silas when he first arrived, was now making a map of what the ruins may have looked like. Huston had talked with Silas, too, about where he thought Anton, Williams, and Wisechild had been in the video they had recovered.

In all it was a chaotic scene, taking place where just a week before Silas had discovered his best lead in his search for Penelope. Left on his own for a moment, he contemplated the loss of the ruins. Had his wife discovered this site? If she had, it surely would have been her crowning moment of exploration in what she called Ed Abbey Country.

Taylor approached Silas. "Our scan clearly shows the outline of the kiva you told us about," Taylor said, adjusting his FBI ball cap. "There is no sign of any bodies within. It appears to have had its roof caved in, maybe with a small explosive charge. John says he's found traces of TNT residue all over the place. After that someone moved a lot of material from these surrounding cliffs into the hole and tamped it down. We've found lots of pieces of the adobe from the granary walls. They may have had some small pieces of machinery in here, maybe a hand-held unit. We haven't found any tire tracks, and I don't think they could get a rig up here no matter how hard they tried. Our guess is that a crew of half a dozen men came down here. We've found some boot imprints along the cliff that we might be able to match."

Silas looked back at Taylor from his scan of the cliffs. "Did you check those ledges along the opposite wall?"

"We did. No tracks, but remember, the video Ms. Wisechild made would have been two years ago—"

"Do you think that whoever did this might be the same people who left me for dead?"

"From the evidence, there's no way to tell."

"Are you going to be able to find out who did this?"

Taylor gazed at him levelly. "We think we may already have."

29

SILAS SAT IN THE DARK of Red Rock Canyon Books. It was 11:00 PM; he hadn't been home in two days and was still wearing the same clothes, now caked with dust and soaked with sweat, he had on when he left to talk with Charles Nephi. His hair stood on end, brittle from the parched air, baking sun, and salt of his brow. He drank a can of Molson's and waited.

When his phone rang he almost jumped out of his chair. He grabbed the receiver. "Yes?"

"Hey, fuck, you're there. Wow, okay, that's great." Hayduke. Not who he had been expecting. "I wasn't thinking I'd get you."

"Yeah, well, it's been quite the day."

"What happened?"

"Well, the FBI sent a team down into Hatch Wash. I went and braced Jared Strom and he let on that somehow I had done something to destroy the ruins there. Sure enough, they're gone."

"What do you mean, gone?"

"Someone got in there with some TNT and a jackhammer and destroyed them."

"Motherfuckers! I find the fucker who did that and they are going to be sorry—"

"Well, you're going to have to get in line. The FBI took Peter Anton and Jared Strom in for questioning this afternoon. I'm waiting by the phone to hear from Agent Rain. She said she'd call to let me know what they had found. Are you still in Flag?"

"Those sons of bitches—" Hayduke was still raging. Silas thought he sounded like he was reading from a script for *The Monkey Wrench Gang*. "Nothing in this goddamned desert is sacred. Nothing is holy to those people! No, *not* people. Fucking animals. No, not even animals . . . I don't know what they are, but they aren't from this fucking planet."

"Where are you?"

"I'm in Flag. I wanted to ring and tell you what was up with that lady, Darcy McFarland. I found someone who worked with her and she filled me in on what Darcy was doing. You know how she was into water rights? Well, according to this source, Darcy McFarland was digging up a whole bunch of dirt on your buddy Tim Martin. It turns out that he was in thick with the political elite of the state and with some dirty people in the federal government, greasing the fucking wheels with political contributions—"

"We knew this—"

"Keep your shirt on, man. It looks like the contributions went beyond just paying for Nephi. It turns out they were rigging water deals. All over the state, and down along the Kaibab Plateau in Arizona, north of the Grand Canyon, and over in the Escalante, the places where Martin wants to drill. He needs water, and the only way he was going to get what he needs, according to the work Darcy McFarland was doing, was to bribe his way through the fucking system. He's funneling money through that fucking senator's office to pay off half of the Bureau of Reclamation and the BLM and the Park Service and who the fuck knows who else—"

"And it all begins—"

"That's right; it all begins in Hatch Wash. There's enough water coming down that little canyon to operate a hundred fucking drilling rigs, but only if they dam it up. I guess Darcy McFarland found out."

"You think someone killed her because of it?"

"Seems like."

"Jesus. Did this friend of Darcy's . . . did she say anything about Penny?"

"She knew Penny alright, but she says that Pen wasn't involved in this."

"I can't believe that."

"Well, maybe this friend didn't know Pen all that well. I mean, I didn't know who she was."

"The FBI is going to want to talk with her, this friend. I'm afraid you as well—"

"Fuck, man, I don't want to get mixed up with the feds."

"You're going to have to tell them what you know."

"Can't we leave me out of this? Just tell them that you made some calls? I mean, I've got a bit of a history . . ."

"What do you mean?"

"Nothing serious. Listen, you know I served, right. Desert Storm. Afghanistan. I did my time, but when I came home, I got in some trouble. My head was pretty messed up. I got in a couple of fights, and well, someone got hurt, and fuck, well, it wasn't me. I just think that if you drag me into this, well, they're not going to believe me."

"Alright." Silas leaned his face on his hands. "Can you give me the woman's name, I'll call her and go over all this and see if the feds can interview her themselves."

"Oh man, I don't know. How about if I just give you the files that I got here and leave it at that?"

"You've got paper on this?"

"I got a smoking fucking gun. Darcy had a bunch of records on this whole deal that she was going to go public with before she disappeared. I'll get them to you tomorrow or the next day, as soon as I get back."

Silas cradled the phone to his ear. "Okay. I think this can wait. In the meantime, I'm going to try and learn more about how Charles Nephi was connected to all of this."

"How you going to do that?"

"I don't know." There was something about that office that spoke to Nephi's contempt; what was it?

"You there?" asked Hayduke.

"Yeah, hold on. It was the boxes."

"What the fuck?"

"Boxes. Nephi had boxes in his office. He's been here longer than I have. Yet there are still stacks of boxes in his office. From Canada. They had been shipped from Canada."

"What are you talking about?"

"I've got to figure out how to break into a senator's office."

"Fuck, yeah! Count me in!"

"You said you didn't want to get tangled up with the FBI. You get caught, and you've got a record, it's not going to be pretty—"

"Yeah, but fuck, man, imagine the damage we could do."

"Listen, Hayduke. I'm not going to torch the place and I'm not in this to stop a dam or save a canyon. I'm trying to find out what happened to my wife. If I have to expose cronyism in the process, well, that's fine."

"Yeah, okay, I get it. Pen always said you didn't give a shit about the cause. I guess she was right."

"You listen to me, Hayduke." Silas's eyes felt like they were on fire in the dark of the bookstore. "Penelope might have been your pal, and maybe you guys shared a passion for the desert, but she was *my* wife. Got it? In all the years I've been searching for her, two weeks ago was the first I ever heard of you. Got it?"

The line was quiet a moment. Silas could hear the man breathing on the other end of the phone. "Yeah, I got it," Hayduke finally said.

"Call me when you get back from Flag. I'll get the documents from you and turn them over to the FBI. You can disappear if you want to. Alright?"

"Whatever you say."

HE WAITED IN the dark for another half hour. He drifted into a restless sleep sitting in his chair, his head propped on his hand. When the phone rang again he started and knocked over a stack of books.

"Yes?" he croaked into the phone.

"It's Katie." She sounded as tired as he felt.

"How'd it go?"

"Not bad."

"Did you, well, arrest anyone?"

"No. We may still. The district attorney and the US state attorney agree that we don't have enough to lay charges yet."

"I see."

"Listen, we're three blocks apart and there's a bar in the middle. Buy a girl a drink?"

"Okay. Eddie's in five?"

"I'll be half a beer up on you."

THE BAR WAS nearly empty and it was half an hour to closing when Silas walked through the door. Katie Rain was sitting at a table, her coat on,

215

concealing her sidearm and badge. She had a pint glass in front of her and stood up when she saw him. "Thanks for coming."

"No trouble. You sounded tired on the phone."

"Well, it's been a while since I was on a field investigation. Long hours."

"Taylor has you fully integrated on the team?"

"The trace evidence is going to be so critical he wants me in on all of the interrogations."

"That makes sense, I guess. What happened with Strom and Anton?"

"I can't tell you everything, you understand. Strom admitted nothing, told us that his comments to you were merely made out of frustration with your trespassing at his business. He said he was going to file a complaint with the sheriff. I told him that the sheriff was on the other side of the one-way glass and that he'd take notes."

Silas ordered a beer when the waitress appeared.

Katie continued. "We're going to get a search warrant and will likely case his place tomorrow looking for explosives and the like. But I think that's pretty much a dead-end. We may get lucky and find residue in a vehicle or in a backpack or something, but by now he'll have been able to cover his tracks."

"What about Anton?"

"We did a little better there. He didn't admit to anything, but he was a much less practiced liar than Jared Strom. We asked him about his relationship with Kelly Williams and Kayah Wisechild first. Like before, he admitted that he'd worked with them. That's pretty hard to deny, given the paper trail with Dead Horse. We put some pressure on, you know, thumb screws, water-boarding—"

"Really?"

"You Canadians really think we're all malevolent masochists, don't you?"

"No. Well . . ."

She took a drink. "Here's the kicker. He admitted to having 'relations' with the Wisechild girl, an affair."

"I guess that lands him in pretty hot water, doesn't it?"

"Gives him clear motive. We pressed him some more, but he wouldn't confess to murder. He was in tears before the interview was over. I think he would have given up his mother if he thought it would help."

"Did you get anything on the ruins?"

"He started off saying he had worked with Dead Horse on the assessment. Said he didn't know who the client was; explained that this was part of the procedure: minimized conflict of interest. He said that he had discovered the ruins and reported it to Strom, and that Strom had ordered him to back off."

"Doesn't sound right. If you were a professor of archaeology and you discovered a new set of ruins, wouldn't you tell everybody? Publish a paper?"

"This is where it gets interesting. You see, we knew we were going to want to interview him before you called this morning, so we had the paperwork done up with our Durango office and had them standing by with a judge. As soon as we got him to confess on the Wisechild affair, we pushed the paperwork through and searched his home. We must have found five hundred artifacts there. There's no way of knowing which are legit and which were stolen, but we've got the BLM's top archaeologist on her way to Cortez in the morning. We were able to tell him this about four hours into the interview. We also told him we had the video. That helped."

"*Just* helped?"

"We're going to need our facial recognition expert to match his face with the image on the Wisechild video, but he didn't know that."

"So he rolled over?"

"He admitted to clearing the site, but not to destroying it, and insisted he had nothing to do with Wisechild's and Williams's deaths."

"You believe him?"

"No, but he wouldn't give anything else up. Not yet."

"Did you guys look into Kelly Williams's history?"

"Agent Nielsen did. Williams had two charges but no convictions against him for offences under ARPA. He was a pot hunter and a grave robber, but nobody could prove it. Not hard to imagine him working with Peter Anton to clear the site and then things getting out of hand between them. You talk with the enforcement people at the BLM and they'll tell you that they've never seen a more violent culture than the one around the illegal artifacts trade. I guess these grave robbers make poachers look like a bunch of Sunday school students."

Silas had heard the stories too. "Who was Peter Anton working for?"

"We went back to Strom at that point. We have accessory after the fact at the least with him, and the clearing operation, and maybe conspiracy. So we pressed him. He told us that when the ruins were discovered, Dead Horse was working for Jacob Isaiah—"

"That doesn't mean that Isaiah was in on it."

"No, of course not." The waitress appeared and Rain pointed to both of their glasses. "My shout. It doesn't necessarily mean that Isaiah was involved. It was four years ago." She paused and then said, "I *know* what you're thinking."

"Tell me."

"You're thinking that your wife discovers the ruins while she's out doing her environmental thing. She learns that Jacob Isaiah has this evil plan to develop a resort on the Canyon Rims area, and she confronts him. He kills her to shut her up. When the same thing happens with Williams and Wisechild, he kills them too."

The waitress brought their beers. "Sure, okay, so you do know what I'm thinking. Here's the trouble. Canusa was *also* a client of Dead Horse. They come on the scene around the same time. That's when Charles Nephi moved from corporate head office to backwater USA to help pave the way for a massive expansion of petroleum development into the canyon country. They contract with Dead Horse to do similar environmental and archaeological work as they did for Isaiah, and they come up with the same results. Instead of shutting the project down, there's enough money in the oil play to warrant taking some risks. Canusa needs the water from Hatch Creek, which will mean flooding the ruins, and not just exposing them to some flat-footed tourists."

Katie picked up his train of thought. "Canusa says to Jared Strom, 'clear out those ruins so we don't have to deal with ARPA.' They get their man Anton, who has a penchant for being light-fingered, to do it. And he brings Williams along, as we see on the video. Anton is allowed to keep or sell the pots in exchange for his silence."

"Something goes wrong. Kelly turns on them, or maybe the Wisechild girl threatens to expose the whole shop and Kelly goes along with her rather than going to jail," finished Silas.

"Tim Martin kills them?"

"Or has someone else do it."

"Either way, it's murder one. Life without parole. More likely a date with the executioner." Rain looked thoughtful for a moment.

"There's one more thing."

"There's a hundred more things. This is a tangled mess."

"Yes, but there's one more thing that provides clear motive."

"What's that?"

"A numbered company. When I was digging around, trying to find out who was behind the applications for drilling out in Canyon Rims, I found a numbered company. There are three directors: Tim Martin, Charles Nephi, and Peter Anton."

"How did you—?"

"My son is studying criminology."

"Handy and helpful. We'll look into this."

"But it provides another link."

"Damn right it does. It ties both Nephi and Anton to Canusa."

"You know, there's someone else here who stands to lose a lot."

"Who's that?"

"The Senior Republican Senator from Utah."

"C. Thorn Smith."

"His Utah Land Stewardship Fund is big money. It's going to funnel vast amounts of dollars into companies for hiring. They will all be beholden to the good senator for his pork-barrel largesse. It consolidates Smith's power, not just in Utah, but across the West."

"Are you telling me that you think a US senator could have killed these people, including your wife, because they found out about dirty dealings that would have prevented one petroleum project in the middle of nowhere in his home state?"

Silas shrugged. "Could have been the tip of the iceberg. Remember, Penelope wanted to protect this whole region. Penny would have fought him every step of the way. With her out of the picture . . ."

"Silas, environmentalists aren't exactly fleeing the state just because one of their own went missing and another turned up dead. You read the headlines of the *Salt Lake Tribune* recently? There was a rally with over five hundred people outside of Thorn Smith's office two days ago, protesting drilling around Canyon Rims."

"I'm not saying that it's likely. Maybe Penelope had something on Smith, something other than Hatch Creek."

"How does Darcy McFarland fit into all of this?"

"I've done a little digging with the help of a friend in Flagstaff who knew Darcy. Apparently she had a file thick with information linking the senator with a scheme to give away water permits all across the Southwest. I haven't seen the info yet, but it's conceivable that this information might be the smoking gun to tie the death of McFarland to the senator's office."

"When will you have the file?" She leaned forward, interested.

"Tomorrow, day after next. It's on its way up from Flag."

"Taylor will want to see it when it arrives. Despite the fact that he's a pompous ass, Smith has a clean record in office. The Bureau has never had to investigate him for anything."

"There's a first time for everything."

Katie finished her beer and looked around. The bar was nearly empty. "It helps me to talk this through with you."

"Really?"

"Taylor and Nielsen and the rest of the team, they're smart but they look at things in a linear fashion."

"While I'm all over the map?"

"Literally. Remember, I've seen your living room."

Silas wanted to tell her what he was going to do next, but he hesitated. "I know you go right back to Taylor and tell him what we discuss."

"Not everything, just the stuff that's going to help us catch a killer. Are you okay with that?"

Silas finished his beer. He felt it gurgling in his stomach. "I think if you were a little less charming, I'd be put out, but for now, the relationship works."

"And when it stops working?"

Silas stood up and fished a twenty-dollar bill from his pocket. "I go back to taking long walks in the desert, looking for my wife."

30

SILAS SAT IN THE LIVING room of his Castle Valley home and stared at the wall. Such a vast swath of country; even in his three and a half years of wandering he hadn't covered half of the landscape that he wanted to. He had brought the portrait of Penelope from the bedroom and put it on the table. "What do you want?" he asked the wall.

There was no reply.

He went and stood by the map of Arches National Park. He picked up a yellow sticky note from the small bookshelf and wrote "Wisechild" on it, then stuck it on the map at the junction of Sleepy Hollow and Courthouse Wash. He wrote "Williams" on a second and pasted it near Grand View Point, next to the Green River Overlook on the map of Canyonlands. "McFarland" went on a third and went up near Potash, on the Colorado River. When he stood back and looked at the panorama of maps on the wall, the three yellow notes formed a rough triangle. Did *that* mean anything? He couldn't tell. He went over and wrote the approximate dates of each person's death on the notes.

Kelly Williams and Kayah Wisechild were both killed two years ago. Wisechild had been reported missing in October, but Williams hadn't been reported missing for several months after that, though according to the FBI, his whereabouts were unknown for a period of time leading up to the missing person report. His family thought he had just gone off on an archaeological project, as he often did, and hadn't kept in touch.

It was reasonable to assume that both had been killed about the same time, according to the information provided by Katie Rain. If they were killed by the same person, why was the method of murder different? Why were the bodies buried in different locations? Why go to all the trouble?

Kelly Williams was bigger than Kayah Wisechild, and had been found closer to a road, but it was still a long way from the parking lot at Green River Overlook to the promontory of land where he had been buried under stones. It seemed only reasonable to believe he too had walked to his grave, though unwittingly. That meant he too must have known his killer.

What about Darcy McFarland? The ME report estimated that she had been dead less than three weeks. That meant that she had been killed *after* he had found Kayah Wisechild, but *before* he had found Williams. Had the killer of these first two learned of the discovery of Kayah's body and panicked, thinking he had not tied up a loose end?

McFarland's body was dumped a matter of feet from a roadway. The ME report clearly indicated that she had been drowned in the slurry. There had been a struggle.

To Silas it felt as if somehow the floodgates had opened, but for all the deluge of information that was pouring in, he didn't feel any closer to finding Penelope. He'd gone from a sedate existence where he searched the backcountry for his wife and sold the occasional book to being at the center of three murder investigations. The sensation was not unlike what he felt as he was swept down Sleepy Hollow.

He turned to look at the picture of his wife. "How does any of this relate to *you*? What are you trying to tell me?"

HE PLANNED THE evening carefully. He'd never broken into anything before, so he did his homework. He didn't remember seeing an alarm in the building, but that didn't mean there wouldn't be one. He also didn't know if there would be a night watchman, but he doubted it. The most difficult task would be to get into the building in the first place. He decided going through the window directly into Nephi's office would be the safest. He remembered that the building backed onto an alley, and he surmised that there would be little traffic after dark. He packed his bag with a thin pair of leather gloves, a headlamp and extra batteries, a digital camera, and a small box of tools that he might need to pry open the window. Out of habit he added his first-aid kit, a couple of bottles of water, and some food.

He put the bag in the car and walked back into the house. As he was walking through the living room, his phone rang. He grabbed it on the fourth ring. It was Katie Rain.

"Having regrets about talking with me last night?" he asked.

She laughed. "No, not yet, at least. I wanted to give you an update. I spent my morning working with some of my advanced equipment I had shipped down from Salt Lake. Moab Regional is starting to look like my office. We haven't sent the Williams remains up to the Medical Examiner yet, so I spent my morning examining the wound on the back of his head. He was bludgeoned with the butt of a pistol. I'm about 90 per cent certain of that. I can tell by the shape of the wound. I'm running a test with sodium rhodizonate to see if there is any trace of gunshot residue on the skull."

"It could still be there after two years?"

"We have some pretty sophisticated tools for measuring this sort of thing. There's a new test that we can run with gas chromatography and a nitrogen phosphorus detector to separate and identify components. If there was any gunpowder on the grip of the pistol used to attack Mr. Williams, it could have left a trace on the skull. All we need is a single particle using this new test."

"Can you tell what sort of pistol?"

"Not with any certainty. Certainly nothing dainty. Likely a large-caliber weapon such as a .44 or .45. If we recover a pistol during our search today, we may be able to match them up."

"How is it going?"

"I haven't heard anything yet. You're not just sitting around the house waiting, are you?"

"Oh, you know, I'm trying to catch up on my housework. Place needs a vacuum in case I have guests again."

"We bring our own, you know?"

"Funny. Not that kind of vacuum. Anyway, no, I'm not just sitting around. I am waiting for the arrival of the info on Darcy McFarland. My friend is supposed to bring it up today. I was thinking about maybe going for a little drive. Do some thinking."

"Dangerous."

You don't know the half of it, he thought to himself.

HE CALLED HAYDUKE a couple of times but got no answer, so around 2:00 PM he left the Castle Valley and drove south to Blanding. The afternoon heat piled cumulus clouds on top of each other along the rounded backs of the Abajo Mountains. He parked half a block up the street from the small government building and rolled down the window. From time to time he raised his field glasses and studied the structure, but he was aware of how conspicuous this looked, so he kept his surveillance to a minimum. After an hour most of the building's employees had left, and at five-thirty the security guard exited too, locking the door behind him. No other night watchman appeared.

He went for a walk and found himself at the Edge of the Cedars State Park. The museum was open and weary, heat-stroked tourists wandered throughout the grounds. He walked past the tour buses and fifteen minutes later found himself on the edge of the park, past the Pueblo ruins and the gift shop, looking over the broken landscape toward the Abajos. He slipped off his pack and ate a meal of beef jerky, trail mix, and water, and waited for dark. He mulled over the great mass of convoluted information that was jostling around in his head.

It seemed to him as if *everybody* was somehow involved in the death of these three people, but that was too spectacular to be possible. Silas hoped that the risk he was about to take would be worth it. If he got caught, he could go to jail.

He was startled when his cell phone rang. He dug it out of his pocket and looked at the call display. He snapped it open. "Where the hell are you?" he asked.

"Got delayed. Sorry. Fuck, man, I hate Flagstaff."

"What happened? No, wait, I don't want to know. Are you on your way to Moab?"

"Yeah, I'm on my way. Where are you?"

"I'd rather not say."

"I got those papers. I went through them again today. You know, your compatriot Martin is in really fucking thick with the senator's office. McFarland got some emails through Access to Information that basically show complicity between the two offices. Old C. Thorn's name isn't on them, just his lackey Nephi, talking like they are old friends. Why the

224

fuck do people still carry on that way knowing that somebody, sometime, is going to get their hands on this stuff?"

"Greed makes people stupid."

"You want me to drop these off? I could meet you at your shop."

"How 'bout I meet you there when I'm done."

"You're not going to tell me what the fuck you're up to?"

"Best that I don't."

"You're doing the thing with the senator's office, aren't you?"

"Listen, Josh—"

"Hayduke, man—"

"Listen, Hayduke, I've got to go. Why don't we just meet in the morning? I'll buy you breakfast and we can compare notes."

"Alright, fine. Fuck, I'm going to go sleep up in the La Sals. I'll see you at, say, 9:00 AM at the Moab Diner?"

"Sure. See you then." He hung up.

No sooner had he hung up than the phone trilled again. He figured it was Hayduke calling back. "No, you can't help—"

He heard Katie Rain laugh. "Well, I *wasn't* really offering, but seeing how you asked so nicely."

"I'm sorry. I thought you were someone else."

"I just wanted to let you know that Taylor has pulled up stakes here in Moab. The bunch of us are on our way down to the thriving metropolis of Monticello."

It was Silas's turn to laugh. "I simply don't know what to say."

"Tell a girl where she can get a decent cup of coffee in the morning."

"No can do. I'll buy you a drink on my way back tonight if you want. All the 3.2 per cent beer you can drink before your bladder explodes."

"Where are you?"

"I'm . . . I'm out for a walk near Blanding."

"You're not going to find any more bodies tonight, are you? I could really use some time to get caught up. I've got half a dozen bone bags waiting for me back in Salt Lake too."

"As long as I don't fall asleep out here, I'm sure you'll be fine."

"You're just going for a walk?"

"That's right."

"Okay, well, call when you're coming through. It's been twenty-four hours since I got a lecture from Agent Taylor, so—"

"He busting your—I mean, giving you a hard time?"

"Fraternizing with the enemy, you know."

"Didn't think you cared. Thought I was just a source of information."

"Keep dreaming. Literally."

"I've got your cell on speed dial, now."

"Be careful, Silas."

He looked around to see if she might be watching him. He was alone, sitting on the edge of the desert, the sun nearly down behind the Abajos. "I will." He broke the connection.

31

HE WAITED ANOTHER HOUR AND then stood stiffly, his ankle sore, and walked the first few steps back toward the center of town. It had been completely dark for the better part of an hour. He made his way along tree-lined streets and past San Juan County Hospital until he reached South 100 Street.

Looking around to see if he was being observed, he slipped into the alley behind the government building. There were no lights on, but to be sure he paused and watched for a moment, his heart beating in his chest, his hands sweaty. He dropped the pack and reached into the top pocket, pulling out his leather gloves and headlamp. He slipped the light on over his forehead and then re-shouldered the bag. Pulling on the gloves, he waited and watched again: nothing.

Silas made his way to the window of Nephi's office and stood beside it, scanning the alleyway and the cluster of other buildings around him. The quiet little town felt nearly deserted at 10:00 PM. He slipped the dusty bag off and pulled out a small crowbar. Slipping the tool into the crack at the bottom of the window, he leaned his weight on it. The old window moaned and creaked, then popped open, a piece of wood splintering off from the base of the jam. He heard something hit the floor in the office. He scanned again, then hoisted himself up and into the room, head first.

He landed on a stack of papers, which cascaded to the floor. He listened a moment. Hearing nothing, he turned and tried to shut the window behind him. It wouldn't budge. In wrenching it open, he had jammed the wooden runner too tightly to close easily. He bent down and restacked the newspapers. He drew the curtains that covered the now open window, switched his headlamp on, and went immediately to the boxes stacked behind Nephi's desk. He opened the first box. It contained dozens of fat file folders, all stuffed with project reports, assessments, records, and other papers on oil and gas projects around the Southwest. He closed that box and looked in the second one. Again, files on oil and gas projects, but this time their location was in Canada: Alberta, northern British Columbia, Saskatchewan.

He opened the third box, his headlamp playing around the room as he paused, listening for signs of trouble. More folders were crammed in the box, but this time each bore a person's name. He scanned through them, and felt his heart race as he saw three familiar names: Timothy T. Martin, C. Thorn Smith, and Peter Anton. He pulled those files out and sat down on the floor to read.

He started with Anton's file. It contained a long record of correspondence, mostly printed emails, all pertaining to the exploration of Hatch Wash. Most of the correspondence was unidirectional: Nephi probing Anton as to the state of the archaeological assessment of the wash, eagerly inquiring as to what had been found, if anything. Silas scanned through the documents, noting the dates as they advanced from a period starting four years ago up to the present. There was no mention of his wife's name in any of the correspondence, but about two years back, Silas's eye caught the word "Wisechild." He read more carefully:

"*This business between you and the Wisechild girl is compromising your ability to operate objectively,*" said Nephi in an email to Anton. "*Her unwillingness to undertake the planned activities is going to be a problem unless you sever the relationship and ensure she is excluded from the operations.*"

Silas read on down the page for Anton's reply: "*Mind your own damned business. Kayah will not be a problem*" was all he had to say. Obviously she was. The video footage she shot from the cliff above the ruins in Hatch attested to that.

He flipped through more pages containing detailed descriptions of the contents of the ruins. Anton had reduced the wealth of artifacts into statistical lines of text: "*24 pots, intact with various designs; 22 pots, with some structural decay; 6 woven baskets, intact; 4 woven baskets, with some structural decay; 3 pairs of sandals; 67 arrowheads; 4 bows with decorative arrows; 2 ceremonial mounds . . ."* It went on, reading more like a stock-room inventory than the contents of an undisturbed archaeological find.

Silas kept scanning through the pages. He was sweating in the darkness. His eye caught the words "numbered company": *"We're setting up a subsidiary that will manage drilling contracts in the Canyon Rims project. Mr. Martin has agreed to give you a 10 per cent stake in return for your services."* The email was sent from a Gmail account to Anton. No wonder Anton was so eager to clear the ruins. With them out of the way, he had removed a major obstacle to the development of the Hatch Wash project. He now stood to profit not only from the sale of the artifacts, but also from the drilling contracts.

Why, if he stood to lose so much by their discovery, would Anton send Silas there in the first place? Why lead him to the place they had worked so hard to keep secret? Did he believe that the ruins, cleared of their artifacts, would no longer pose a threat to a dam on Hatch Wash? Or was there something more sinister at work? Did Anton send Silas into that canyon only to follow and leave him for dead in the ceremonial kiva? If murder was Anton's intent, why not just club him on the back of the head like Kelly Williams?

Only briefly did Silas consider that maybe Anton had gotten cold feet himself.

He returned to his review of the files. The correspondence with Anton returned to its businesslike tone. If Nephi had been employed as a project engineer for Canusa Petroleum Resources, it could have all been very routine, but of course, two years ago he had already been long installed in Senator Thorn Smith's office.

Next Silas turned his attention to Smith himself. His file was thicker, and Silas patiently read, starting five years back. Nephi and the senator discussed his employment, his absences working on again and off again with Canusa, and the handling of the Utah Land Stewardship Fund development.

By the end of the file Silas's eyes were bleary from reading in the poor light, and he felt he was no closer to a link between Nephi, his wife, and the three bodies he had found. His stomach felt queasy from the depth of the collusion between the senator's office and the petroleum business, but nowhere in any of it had he found the hoped for smoking gun that tied any of this to Penelope. Yes, there was circumstantial evidence tying Anton and Nephi to Wisechild, and by tenuous extension, Williams, but nothing explicit.

He finally opened the file on Martin. Like the file on Smith, it began five years ago, but unlike the other two files, this one merely contained a series of newspaper reports and stories from trade magazines associated with the petroleum industry. Silas flipped through them, looking for anything relating to Hatch Creek, but all he found was a piece written in Moab's *Canyon Country Zephyr* from the previous week covering the announcement of the Land Stewardship Fund. He closed the file, disappointed.

He felt as if he'd taken a terrible chance for next to nothing. It was time to get out. Silas stood and listened again. The alley behind the office and the building itself seemed quiet as a tomb. He decided to search the rest of the office and then leave. He began to open the desk drawers: pens, markers, paper clips, a stapler. In one drawer were three cell phones, but none had any battery power left, and their SIM cards were missing. The bottom drawers were empty. He closed them and turned his headlamp off and was about to make his way to the window when he heard a noise in the lobby of the building. It was the sound of a heavy door, opening and then closing.

Silas's heart began to pound and he immediately felt flushed. He turned to look through the broad window into the common area. He could feel blood coursing in his ears. He heard something else through the trembling stillness: keys. Someone was jingling keys outside the senator's office. Silas's first thought was to bolt for the window, but as he was about to move toward it, the door to the outermost office opened and he saw a flashlight through the window. He ducked, the beam playing across Nephi's desk.

On hands and knees, conscious of his pack's bulk, he crawled to the wall beneath the window that faced the common room. Suddenly all the lights in the space came on. His heart beating in this throat, Silas pressed his body against the wall, willing himself not to breathe. A year would be a long time in a US prison, he kept thinking to himself. And if it was Nephi himself . . .

He waited, feeling naked and exposed in the bright fluorescent lights. A movement across the room caught his eye—the curtains in the office were moving ever so slightly. Where the window had been jammed open, a delicate breeze entered the room. He watched the curtains as they shifted; if the night watchman—or whoever was in the office—noticed the movement, he was sunk. He crouched there, unable to breath, and then, without warning, the lights went out and he heard the door close. He bent over and drew a deep breath and shook his head. He laughed to himself, the wave of relief washing over him like a hot flood.

Get out, was his only thought. He cased the room and returned its contents to their places. There was nothing that clearly pointed to Nephi as a killer, though he believed now that somehow he and Anton had been in collusion with Martin to destroy the ruins in Hatch Wash to make way for Martin's development scheme. He felt he had no choice but to tell Rain and Taylor what he suspected and let the FBI do what they could to draw the link. Ken Hollyoak was a good lawyer, even if retired, and might get him off on house arrest.

He sighed as he approached the window, looking over his shoulder to ensure that the office was in fact clear. To make sure he could close the window after he slipped through it, he grabbed the top of the frame, pushing down to force it through the runners. When it budged he felt some hope. With his crowbar, he pried between the sides of the window and the frame, then pushed on the window again. Reassured, and with the crowbar back in his pack, he slipped out and dropped to the ground. He reached up and closed the window easily.

He might actually get away with this, he mused, as he scanned the alley. Relieved, Silas took a circuitous route to his Outback, parked four blocks away. The streets were empty.

He'd call Katie Rain and make arrangements to meet in Monticello on his way back to Moab and then wash his hands of this whole mess. He reached his car and unlocked the door and sat down in the driver's seat and fished his cell phone from his pocket and then his keys. He had inserted the keys in the ignition and hit speed dial on the phone, when he glanced in the rear-view mirror. Someone was sitting in the back seat.

"Jesus Christ!" He tried to turn, but the nose of an automatic pistol clipped his right cheek and he reached up to feel the hot stream of blood there. He looked at the face in the mirror again.

"Find anything interesting, Dr. Pearson?" asked Charles Nephi.

32

"PUT THE CAR IN GEAR and drive." Nephi had the barrel of the pistol pushed into the side of Silas's neck.

"Where?"

"Just drive. I'll tell you when to turn."

Silas looked in the mirror. Nephi was sitting in the middle of the back seat, a 9mm Browning pistol held tightly in his right hand.

"Where are we going?"

"Out of town."

"Where out of town?"

"We're going for a drive, Dr. Pearson. That's all you need to know."

"I didn't find anything in your office. Why are you doing this?"

"There was nothing there to find. There's nothing to find anywhere, Pearson. Shut up and drive."

Silas shifted up into fourth. They were approaching the municipal airport.

"Don't speed. You attract any attention I'll kill you."

"You'll get caught."

"Maybe."

"Why are you—"

Nephi pressed the pistol into Silas's face.

"If you keep this up, Pearson, there's going to be nothing left of you. Now slow down and turn right up here."

"Highway 95?"

"Turn." Silas slowed and made the turn onto Route 95 and started across the darkened desert landscape. His headlights cut a narrow hole in the blackness, and from time to time the eyes of some nocturnal desert creature appeared by the side of the road.

"What are you going to do?" Silas risked asking.

Nephi sat back, relaxing, and sighed. "You're going to have an accident, Dr. Pearson. An accident."

"Did you kill Kayah Wisechild? Williams and McFarland too?"

Nephi laughed. "If this was a Hollywood movie or some second-rate paperback, this would be the part where the bad guy spills his guts, right? You run a bookstore, you've read that trash. You think I'll confess all my sins because you're not going to be around to do anything about it, but then somehow you escape my evil grasp and heroically return to use my confession against me—"

"I haven't read any of those books. Not my thing."

"Maybe not, Pearson, but you're not going to get any confessions from me."

"What about my wife? Did you kill her?"

Nephi laughed again. "I never even *met* your wife, Pearson. Too bad—from what I've seen she was a good-looking woman. Now, just drive and keep it under the speed limit. I'd hate to have to shoot you a few times before you actually have your tragic mishap."

They drove on in silence for a few minutes and then began the long, steep incline of Comb Ridge. Silas could feel his hands growing sweaty. "You're going to do this on Comb Ridge, aren't you?"

"Just drive, Pearson."

"That's fitting. Penny was such an Abbey freak, and Comb Ridge was where *The Monkey Wrench Gang* did their first job."

"I hate Edward Abbey."

"Me too."

They drove up the long back of Comb Ridge, the blacktop hissing under the Outback's tires. Silas's mind raced. He had seen in movies where, in a situation like this, the driver had crashed the car deliberately, so that the unbelted assailant in the back seat would be injured or killed, and he could walk away from the accident, saved by his air bag. He looked for a likely place to do it, but the road was hemmed in between walls of sandstone on one side and guard rails on the other. He feared that at worst, he would enrage Nephi and get himself shot in the process.

"Was this really all about oil?"

"I'll tell you this much, Pearson, only to shut you up. It's about power. Oil is just the tool you use in this country to get it. It's about power."

"Power for who? For your boss? Martin?"

"Tim Martin is not my boss. Never has been."

"Smith? Senator Smith?"

"You almost got me to confess there, Dr. Pearson," said Nephi.

"But I didn't find anything."

"You really think I would leave something sitting around in my office? I'm not that stupid. But you have demonstrated a surprising level of determination that frankly has to be interrupted before you stumble on something truly important."

"I was just about to give up—"

"Too late now. Stop the car there, in the weeds by the side of the road."

Silas pulled the car over. His eyes darted from the mirror to the world caught in his headlights and back to Nephi. The crest of the roadway over the ridge was cut deeply into the ancient sedimentary stone, so they were parked in a narrow pull-off. On the south side, where the highway opened up and began its long precipitous descent toward Comb Wash, the slope opened roughly and led up to the top of the ridge.

"We've stopped on top of Comb Ridge," Silas said, glancing back in the mirror. As soon as Nephi got out he was going to gun the engine and race down the steep side of Comb Ridge. He'd drive all the way to Natural Bridges National Monument if he had to.

"Turn the car off," ordered Nephi.

Silas turned off the engine but left the keys in the ignition.

"Hand me the keys," said Nephi sardonically. Silas grabbed the keys out of the ignition.

The pistol clipped Silas in the jaw just below the ear, and he felt more blood trickle down his neck. A bead of perspiration leaked from his hairline and settled in his brow. Next plan, drop the keys at Nephi's feet and hope he looked down. Before he could reach back, Nephi hit him with the butt of the pistol behind the ear. Silas heard the crack before the world went black.

HE WOKE LYING on the ground, his hands tied in front of him with twine, his head aching. He could taste blood in his mouth. He was staring heavenward and his first thought was how extraordinary the desert sky was. The stars were pasted across the black cosmos in layers that receded into infinity. He rolled onto his side and immediately wanted to vomit. He suppressed the urge, breathing in through his nose. He smelled something mechanical, oil or grease. He focused his eyes and saw Nephi's legs protruding from under the front of the Outback. The legs wiggled and Nephi emerged.

"Don't even think about moving." Nephi patted the pistol in his waistband.

"What are you doing?"

"Cutting your brake lines. These vehicles are a bitch to work on. You got any tools in the back, Pearson?" Nephi wiped his hands on his jeans.

"Fuck you."

"I would have expected more from a professor of literature. Something more . . . well, *literate*, I suppose." Nephi walked to the back of the vehicle and opened the hatch. He found Silas's toolbox and rummaged through it for a large enough pair of wire cutters.

Silas tried to sit up, but his stomach turned over and he returned to his side. He realized that his legs were also bound. He scanned the car and the rocks beyond, seeking some salvation, but he could find none.

Nephi found what he was looking for. "This should do."

Silas detected movement ahead, beyond the car, something in the rocky cliffs on the side of the road. A coyote?

Nephi walked back to the front of the car and was preparing to duck under when a voice boomed from the rocks.

"Drop the fucking gun!"

Nephi dropped the wire cutters instead and pulled his Browning from his belt. He fired twice in the direction of the voice, into the rocks. A muzzle flash and the roar of a .357 Magnum responded, the bullet whizzing past Nephi and ricocheting off the rocks behind Silas's body. Nephi fired three more times into the rocks.

Silas thought he saw a bulky figure move amid the boulders. Realizing his precarious position, Silas struggled to stand, but instead fell face forward into the dirt. Desperate, he began to roll toward the back of the car. Nephi wheeled on him and fired twice in his direction, both shots hitting so close to Silas that he felt their impact reverberate through the blacktop.

Silas heard another blast from the .357 and the windshield of his Outback exploded. Nephi turned toward his attacker and fired two more rounds.

Nephi jumped into the car. It roared to life. Silas, prone behind the rear wheels, feared Nephi would back over him. Instead, Nephi spun the wheels, kicking rocks and dust into Silas's face, and the car raced down the steep slope of Comb Ridge.

A stout figure emerged from the rocks. Silas watched the man take aim with a revolver and fire at the speeding car. The man turned and Silas could see the hairy visage clearly. Hayduke.

"Holy fuck," roared Hayduke. "You okay? You hit?"

"Fine, I'm fine."

"Sweet motherfucker!" he yelled again, his pistol at his side. "Let's get that cocksucker!"

"He's gone."

"I got my Jeep a hundred yards back."

Silas sat up. "Go get it!"

Hayduke rushed off into the night as Silas struggled with his bound hands. He heard the Jeep roar to life and a moment later it crested the road that cut through the ridge. Hayduke jumped out, a bowie knife in hand, and deftly cut the twine off Silas's wrists. Silas could smell the sweat and fear from Hayduke and see the wildness in the man's eyes.

"Let's go!" he yelled as he cut the twine on Silas's feet. They raced to the Jeep. Hayduke spun his tires and they sped off in pursuit.

"Sure you're okay?" asked Hayduke as Silas buckled his seatbelt.

"My head aches like a bitch, but otherwise okay. You got a cell phone? Mine's in my car."

"Yeah, here." Hayduke pulled his phone from his pocket as he held the Jeep in a steep downward turn to Comb Wash. He gave Silas the phone, then shifted into fourth and red-lined the engine. They could see the lights of the Outback a mile ahead, already cross Arch Canyon Wash.

Silas dialed the familiar number. It beeped, and then Katie Rain's voice came on.

"Who is this?" she asked.

"It's Silas."

"Hold on." The line went silent, and then Rain came on again. "You okay?"

"Yeah, I'm alright."

"Where are you?"

"I'm descending the west side of Comb Ridge. I'm chasing Charles Nephi. He's in my Outback."

"I just lost your cell signal. I've had your phone line open since you left Blanding."

"I thought you might. I wasn't sure if my call had connected. You heard everything?"

"Yeah, and so did Agent Taylor. We're on our way now. We're maybe five or ten miles behind you and coming in fast. We've called the ranger station at Natural Bridges and we have state troopers and local police coming up from Mexican Hat. We're dropping the net on this guy."

"I'm just a mile behind him."

"Who's driving?"

Silas looked at Hayduke. He was concentrating on the road, revving the Jeep up to over a hundred miles an hour, the black desert passing in a whir. "You'll never believe it, but just some guy out camping. He came up Comb Ridge just in time, and Nephi spooked. He saved my bacon, and now we're following Nephi."

"Do not engage," ordered Rain. "Just observe. If you see him turn, tell me and we can radio it in. We've got roadblocks being set up above the Mokee Dugway on 261 and outside Natural Bridges on 275. There's nowhere for Nephi to go."

"You want me to keep the line open?"

"It's okay. You can hang up. Just dial back if there is any change."

Silas hung up. He checked the line to make sure it was disconnected. Hayduke was smiling at him. "Thanks. Fuck, I really don't want to get mixed up with the feds, you know?"

"You saved my life."

"Guess I did, hey?" Silas could see Hayduke grinning by the dashboard lights.

"The FBI says they've got roadblocks going up on 261 and 275."

"There's a hundred places he could go between here and there. Fuck, the Hidden Splendor Mine is just over there." Hayduke waved his hands toward Dry Mesa.

"The Hidden Splendor Mine is fictional."

"Fuck no, I've been there. It's real."

"Look, we're coming up on the junction of 261. He goes straight, the park rangers get him. He turns left, the state troopers." They were a mile behind, racing across the desert. Silas clung to the roll bar as they banked around a corner.

"He's taking 95, toward the park." Silas dialed Rain back. "He's heading toward Natural Bridges."

"We can see you ahead of us. We'll catch you in a few minutes. I'll call it in to the Park Service."

"Okay." Silas hung up.

They watched the tail lights in the distance for another few minutes, and then the brake lights went on and the Outback veered violently to the south.

"Where the fuck is he going?" asked Hayduke.

They came to the road the Outback had turned down. "Grand Gulch," said Silas.

"He goes into the fucking Gulch, he could disappear."

"Let's see if we can cut him off!"

"Fuck yeah." Hayduke shifted into second on the gravel road and gunned the engine. The Jeep leapt forward and jumped over rocks and loose gravel.

"The road splits up ahead," observed Silas.

"You been here?"

"Of course."

They came to the fork and could see no sign of their prey. "Which way?" yelled Hayduke.

"Stop a minute." Silas jumped out of the Jeep as it skidded to a halt.

He climbed up on the hood and looked across the midnight landscape. In the distance, leading to the head of the main stem in Grand Gulch, he could see tail lights blinking as his Outback jostled over the rough road.

He jumped down and directed Hayduke to the correct path. He dialed Rain.

"Where are you?" she asked.

"Grand Gulch." He heard her speak to Taylor and then heard Agent Nielsen's voice in the background.

"Silas, Agent Nielsen says that's a dead-end. We've got him trapped. Break off pursuit. We'll be there in five minutes."

"Okay," said Silas to Rain. Then to Hayduke: "Feds want us to stop."

"Fuck that, we almost got this motherfucker." Hayduke geared down to run through loose sand. The road had been recently driven over and the sand was soft but the Jeep performed well.

"Josh, let's stop. The feds will be here any minute."

"That fucker was going to sell out Hatch Wash, man. He was going to sell out Flat Iron Mesa and Back of the Rocks. You want him to get away?"

"He's not going to get away. There's nowhere to go."

"Grand Gulch is massive, man. You could hide there for a year."

"He's in jeans and dress shoes and has no water, no food."

"He could live for two weeks if he finds Collins Spring."

The Jeep bounced over an outcrop of slickrock and then the Outback loomed in front of them, sideways to the dirt track.

"Fucker!" Hayduke yelled and veered off into the brush on the side of the track. A spray of sand like a wave enveloped the Jeep, the tires bogging down in the dirt.

Silas saw a figure move in front of the Outback and had no time to yell a warning. He saw a flash and heard the pop of a pistol and the windshield of the Jeep exploded, showering glass across the two men. Hayduke was out of the vehicle in a second, hitting the soft sand and crawling on his knees to the front of the vehicle. Thinking it better to follow Hayduke to the safe side of the vehicle, Silas crawled across the broken glass and dropped to the sand. He heard two more pops and the metallic plunk of the rounds striking the Jeep.

"That cunt is going to kill my machine." Hayduke pulled his revolver from his belt and took aim at the Outback.

"Wait, I hear engines." Silas looked back over his shoulder and saw two sets of lights coming down the trail, red and blue signals blinking in the darkness. "It's the feds."

"I want this cocksucker." Hayduke took aim into the darkness.

"Don't—"

"It's a matter of honor," Hayduke hissed. Nephi rose from behind the Outback as the two FBI Yukons pulled to a stop near the slickrock outcrop. Nephi began to run down the dirt road toward the drop off into Grand Gulch.

Hayduke squeezed one eye shut and steadied his massive revolver with one hand under the other.

"This one's for Hatch Wash." Hayduke started to squeeze the trigger as Silas pushed his arm up. The roar of the pistol and the flash of the muzzle pierced the night but the shot went off harmlessly into the darkness. Nephi's shadow disappeared toward the rim.

"FBI!" came a voice behind them. Eugene Nielsen and another agent appeared behind Silas and Hayduke.

"It's me—Pearson."

"Drop the weapon," ordered Nielsen.

Hayduke looked at Silas out of the corner of his eye. The dark, malevolent moment passed and he put the revolver down in the sand. Both men stood up, hands in the air.

"Nephi is heading toward the canyon."

"We'll get him," Nielsen held his pistol toward the sand as he approached. Katie Rain ran up behind him, her Sig Sauer in her hand. She smiled when she saw Silas.

"You alright?" she asked.

"Fine. Nephi is getting away. That way," he nodded toward the Outback.

"Taylor is chasing him down. We've got two teams on their way in now, plus the park rangers and state troopers. We'll get him." She holstered her pistol. Nielsen picked up Hayduke's weapon and put in on the hood of the truck.

"I got a permit for that," Hayduke said.

"Good thing," said Nielsen.

"Who's your friend?" asked Rain, looking hard at Silas.

Silas watched her eyes as she shifted her gaze from him to Hayduke and back. Silas looked at Hayduke and asked, "What *is* your name?"

Hayduke looked back at him. "Josh. Josh Charleston."

Silas looked at the two agents. "This is Josh Charleston. Good Samaritan."

33

SILAS HADN'T BEEN ABLE TO sleep. He lay on the cot inside the small wall-tent provided by the Park Service for a few hours. Around 4:00 AM he walked out onto the mesa, pulling on a heavy fleece for warmth, and sat on a rise of sandstone close to where the Subaru Outback had come to a halt. He looked out over the draw that led into the main stem of the Gulch, toward the vast plateau that ringed it. It was dark and cold when he sat down, but it was by no means still.

The manhunt had begun around midnight, and by 2:00 AM there were fifty law enforcement officers from half a dozen jurisdictions in the Gulch area. Now, with first light, more were inbound by helicopter so that every ten minutes or so the morning air was cracked by the rattle of more team members arriving.

Nephi had vanished into the catacombs of the canyon, and if he had any sense at all, would bolt straight to Canyon Springs for water. The Park Service and the BLM and the FBI knew that, and were converging on that position. All Silas could do was sit and watch, and wait.

Hayduke had stayed for two hours, and then, temporarily cleared by the FBI, had nonchalantly bid farewell to Silas and accepted a ride back to Blanding. His vehicle would be towed there later in the morning, where he could retrieve it after the Evidence Recovery agents from the FBI concluded their crime scene investigation. For now, yellow tape surrounded the Jeep and the Outback. The Outback's front two tires were flat; Nephi had driven over the slickrock ledge and blown them out. The vehicle had ground to a halt a moment later in the sand accumulated across the road.

Silas felt a tap on his shoulder. He had drifted off to sleep. He opened his eyes with a start and saw Katie Rain with two cups of coffee in her hands.

"Sorry to wake you." She handed him a cup.

"If I was asleep, it was only for a minute."

"You're going to be stiff as hell if you fall asleep on that rock."

"I've used it as a pillow more than once." He remembered a line from *Desert Solitaire*: "Rocks softer than sand . . ." He accepted the coffee. Katie sat down next to him. Her hair was tied back in a ponytail and she wore a heavy sweater and an FBI windbreaker over her bullet-proof vest. Her sidearm protruded over both garments. She sipped from her coffee cupped between her hands, looking in the same direction as Silas: the vast Grand Gulch Mesa and the canyons of the San Juan River beyond.

"You're not on the manhunt?"

"Only interests me if it involves bones." She took another sip of her coffee.

"Hopefully they'll find this guy before it comes to that."

"We will. There's really nowhere for him to go. He's on foot, no food or water or protection from the elements. As soon as the sun hits the canyon floor he'll come crawling back to us, begging for water."

"You think he'll confess?"

"We can be very persuasive. We've got him on kidnapping, at the very least," she said. "We can charge him and hold him and go to work on him over the next little while . . . But there's something else. I didn't get a chance to talk with you about it last night, in all the excitement."

"What is it?"

"Peter Anton and his wife, they've disappeared."

"How? I thought you were watching him?"

"We had two units watching the house. Front and back. When this went down with Nephi last night, one of the units went in to check on him. He wasn't there."

"He gave your guys the slip?"

"That, or—"

"Or someone got to him."

"It's a question we'll be asking our canyon-exploring friend when we find him."

Silas shook his head. He felt a terrible sadness welling inside of him. So many lives erased by this foolishness. So much waste.

Katie looked at him. "You okay?"

He nodded but didn't say anything.

"Sometimes when I'm doing my thing, you know, with the bones, I let my guard down and imagine what these people's lives were like when they were flesh and blood and oxygen. I imagine what the people they love might be thinking when I'm reassembling a crime scene, or searching for cause of death. It keeps me from building too many walls between me and the vic."

Silas sipped his coffee. "I didn't ask for any of this. I just want to find my wife. I didn't ask to find these people. I don't know any of them, but now I can't get them out of my head. I just want to find Penelope and maybe, I don't know, find some peace."

"I think you'll find her," Katie finally said, after they watched in silence a moment. "I think you'll find peace, and finding these others will help bring some peace to their families too."

They heard a radio crackle. Katie turned to the park ranger who came up on the slickrock behind them.

"Agent Rain, Agent Taylor was just on the radio. They've got him."

34

SILAS SAT IN THE RED Rock Canyon bookstore. It was the Saturday of a mid-September weekend and he had sold three books that day already. Sales were brisk, on pace to set a record. He drank a cup of coffee and scanned the headlines.

It had been five days since Charles Nephi had been captured in the Grand Gulch. He had been hiding in a set of ancient Pueblo ruins, out of bullets and out of places to run.

The chime at the door sounded and Silas looked up. It was Josh Charleston.

"You got your Jeep back?" Silas asked by way of greeting.

"Fuck, man, what a mess. Never let the FBI do your repairs for you. Jesus, it took them three days to get the windshield replaced. But yeah, fuck, I got it back. I told them to leave the bullet holes, adds character."

"Were they hard on you?"

"Me? Fuck, man, they raked me over the fucking coals."

"Really? I'm really sorry—"

"I'm just busting your balls. No, they were okay. They accepted that I was just driving by and stopped to aid a fellow citizen . . . or whatever the hell you are."

"You saved my life."

"Yeah, fuck, I guess I did. Guess you owe me now, don't you."

"How did you know?"

"I was driving through Blanding, on my way back from Flag. Remember? We talked that morning."

"The documents."

"Yeah, well, fuck, at first I couldn't find you and then I remembered what you were up to. I wasn't going to let you have all the fun, but I didn't want to blow it for you either, so I waited. I saw your little car. I drove around and when I came back, around ten, I saw you drive off with that other motherfucker in the back with you, so I followed."

"We didn't see you."

"I know. Pretty fucking smart, right? Lights out. Just like Hayduke in the final chase scene in *The Monkey Wrench Gang*. Like I said, you owe me now."

"I guess so. What *did* happen with the documents you had?"

"I had to dump them. I didn't want the feds to know you and I were in cahoots, you know? So I trashed them. There was nothing there we can't dig up again if we need to."

Silas was clearly disappointed. Darcy McFarland's death was the loose end in this whole terrible debacle. The FBI had left it open and unsolved for the time being.

He shook off the discontent. "I got you something."

"Really? What is it?"

"It's a gift. Open it." Silas reached under the counter and brought out a small, book-shaped package. He handed it to Hayduke, who tore the paper off with excitement.

"Holy fuck, man, where did you get this?"

"It was Penelope's."

"Fuck, would you look at that." The cover of the book was purple and tan, with a strange rendition of a Puebloan rock art mountain lion and clear, white lettering: *Desert Solitaire: A Season in the Wilderness.*

"It's a first edition. Open it."

Hayduke did. "Holy sweet motherfucker. It's signed."

Silas smiled. They sat in the air-conditioned comfort of the store. It was only 11:00 AM, but Hayduke was drinking a Molson Canadian and Silas had a Dr Pepper.

"I don't think they know we're working together," said Hayduke.

"You're worried about that?"

"I just want to save the fucking wilderness. I don't need to get tangled up with your fed friends."

"I just want to find Penelope. I could do without the rest of this."

"Has that fucker confessed to anything? Has he said anything about Pen?"

"Nothing. Nothing yet."

"What about that guy over in Cortez? The one who was doing the Hopi girl."

Silas winced. "Peter Anton? Nothing on him yet either. The working theory right now is that Nephi got to Anton and his wife before he came for me, but until Nephi talks, or the feds turn up a body, or some other evidence . . ."

"We're shit out of luck. What next?"

"Sell some books. Keep looking for Penny."

"They're still going to fuck up Hatch Wash."

"Maybe. This whole mess is going to turn ugly when Nephi is formally charged. Tim Martin and Canusa are already backing out of the Utah Land Stewardship Fund, distancing themselves from the good senator's office. So far there's nothing to tie either of them in an official way to any of the deaths, but that doesn't make a bit of difference. The media is all over them. They'll be lucky if the dust on this settles in such a way that lets them go ahead with their Hatch Wash project."

"Fuck, man, that's naive if I ever heard it. You really think that this gets Hatch Wash and Back of the Rocks off the hook? Fuckers will be back. It's just a matter of time. Americans forget fast. They want that oil so they can drive their fucking SUVs to the Big Box Store and buy more Twinkies."

"Maybe. We'll see. The one thing that keeps me up at night right now is something that Nephi said to me: that he had *never been* working for Canusa. The whole time I thought that he had been on their payroll and had gone to work for the good senator to try and grease his palms for the company, but it was the other way around. He was always on the senator's payroll and was dropping into companies like Canusa to bring them on board with the Land Stewardship fund."

"Slippery motherfucker. Got any proof?"

"No. C. Thorn has distanced himself from Nephi, obviously. Called on the courts to render swift and ultimate justice. Send the man to the gallows before he can spill the beans on his own furtive arrangements, I guess."

"You want to go after him?"

"Who?"

"The senator?"

"Jesus, Hayduke, I just want to find my wife."

Hayduke took a swallow from the can of Molson's. He finished it and looked around, as if seeking a place to toss the empty. Silas reached out and took it from him. "You want another?"

"Nope. Got to hit the road. Two six packs to . . . well, wherever the hell I end up."

Silas wanted to change the subject. "Where *are* you going to spend the winter, Josh?"

The young man shook his shaggy head. "I don't know. Maybe down along the Arizona border. Or New Mexico. Fuck, I might go down to Baja. Old Cactus Ed liked it down there too."

"Well, amigo. I owe you. You let me know if there's anything you need." Silas stood up.

Hayduke stood too and the two men clasped hands, mountain man style, palm on wrist.

"I guess this is goodbye."

"Fuck that, I'll see you again. This thing isn't over, and we still got to find Pen . . . Penelope."

Silas watched as Hayduke turned and walked toward the door. He spun around at the door and held up the book and then was gone.

"THIS DOESN'T HAVE to be formal, you know," said Sheriff Willis. They were in a room at the Sheriff's Office. Silas sat across the table from him. Ken Hollyoak sat next to him, his hands neatly crossed on the table, a look of bemusement on this face.

"Anytime you fellas want to talk with my client here, I'm going to have to insist on being present. Too messy any other way."

It had been two weeks since the shootout on Comb Ridge and the pursuit across Comb Wash and into the Grand Gulch.

Taylor said, "The Office of Senator Smith has decided not to pursue a breaking and entering charge against Mr. Pearson . . . Dr. Pearson, I mean. The peace bond is still in effect. You're not to be within a hundred yards of the senator or his office."

Hollyoak turned to Silas. "We'll have that matter cleared up shortly, I assure you."

"Be that as it may," said Agent Taylor, "I for one am still not satisfied with your client's explanation for all that has happened in the last month. I'm going to request that you take a lie-detector test and undergo a physiological examination to help the FBI get a better handle on your claims of . . . well, your claims of extra-sensory perception."

"Neither of those is going to happen," Hollyoak said, his face growing dour. "The FBI is just going to have to live with my client's explanation." His voice rose an octave, taking on its courtroom tone. Silas put his hand on Hollyoak's arm.

"It's okay, Ken."

"These jokers said this was going to be information sharing. Now they want to strap the lie-detector cuff on you. I say we get up and leave."

"Do you have anything that you actually want to share today, Special Agent Taylor?" asked Silas.

Taylor leaned back in his chair and looked at the sheriff. Willis shrugged his shoulders. "I guess you must know by now that we've charged Charles Nephi with the death of Kelly Williams," Willis said.

"Has he confessed?" asked Silas.

"No. He's not making it easy on us. But the DA has enough to charge him. We believe Dr. Rain can provide us with enough forensic evidence that we can make this stick. We've followed the paper trail that we found in his office back to the time when Mr. Williams disappeared, and the dates add up."

At the mention of her name, Silas briefly lost his focus on the hulking man sitting across the table from him. Rain had left for Salt Lake just a day after the showdown in Grand Gulch. He hadn't had the opportunity to say goodbye, and it left him feeling unsettled.

He struggled to regain his focus. "What about Kayah Wisechild?" he asked.

"We don't believe Mr. Nephi is responsible for her death," said Taylor.

"Then who?"

"Peter Anton," said Willis.

Taylor held up a hand. "Here's what we think. Dead Horse Consulting was working for both Canusa Petroleum Resources and Jacob Isaiah. During their work for Mr. Isaiah, they dispatched an archaeological team that included Dr. Anton, Ms. Wisechild, and Mr. Williams to investigate resources in the Hatch Wash area. After several weeks of intense investigation, they discovered the ruins and artifacts in the box canyon and reported their findings back to Jared Strom. You understand that there's no paper on this. The only records we've been able to discover—and we've taken Dead Horse apart over the last week—is a cryptic reference in the notes in their files about archaeological finds relating to Mr. Isaiah's project. In our discussions with Mr. Strom he confirmed what you originally told us, Dr. Pearson—"

"About the ruins."

"That's right. And what we were able to extract from Dr. Anton before he disappeared. What happened next, I'm afraid, is still conjecture. But it adds up, based on the video footage shot by Ms. Wisechild. The discovery of the ruins didn't slow Mr. Isaiah down. That's when Canusa *also* hired Dead Horse to undertake their preliminary environmental assessment. Dead Horse already knew there were class one ruins in Hatch, but went ahead anyway, and we believe that someone, likely Dr. Anton, would have gone to Canusa to explain to them what they were dealing with. The ruins wouldn't have stopped Isaiah's proposal to build a resort. They would have slowed down, and maybe even stopped, depending on the courts and the Department of the Interior, the building of a dam on Hatch Wash. There was no official paperwork at that time—"

"Someone involved in the project ordered the ruins cleared and razed."

"Yes. Sometime after the initial discovery—and we've got people working to extract an exact date from the digital file—Dr. Anton, Mr. Williams, and Ms. Wisechild returned to Hatch Wash to pillage the ruins. We believe that they were acting on orders from Mr. Nephi at this point. The records you pointed us to regarding the creation of the numbered company, with Nephi, Anton, and Mr. Martin involved, suggest that these three men stood to lose the most in the event that the project was halted."

"I was under the impression that Nephi was working for Canusa all along and that he was doing time in the senator's office just to advance the interests of the oil and gas company. I was wrong. He told me so himself. He was working for the senator all along."

"That may be true. We can't prove it yet. Senator Smith has put a mile of bureaucratic hurdles between Nephi and himself in the last two weeks."

"He said it wasn't about money. It was about power," said Silas.

"It's always about power in Utah." Nielsen was leaning on the door. "Money is just *one* of the ways we get to hold onto it."

"Anton, Williams, and Wisechild were acting on orders from Nephi to clear the ruins so they could report that Hatch Wash had nothing of value to prevent Canusa from proposing a dam. They could use the water for drilling on Flat Iron Mesa, along Hatch Point, and in Back of the Rocks."

"Dr. Anton's affair with Ms. Wisechild got in the way," said Silas.

"That, and the fact that Ms. Wisechild got cold feet. It was a deadly combination for her," said Taylor. "Nephi found out and put pressure on Anton."

"And he killed her."

"That's right."

"He took her to Courthouse Wash and killed her there. They walked down the wash and he strangled her and buried her body under the cottonwood log."

"Charles Nephi simply cleaned up the rest of the loose ends. He killed Kelly Williams," said Taylor. "The story that Mr. Williams tried to blackmail him and he killed him in self-defense doesn't wash. The wound is in the back of the head. We believe that he asked Mr. Williams to meet him out at Canyonlands National Park and hit him with the butt of his pistol. That was a mistake. We're testing it for Mr. Williams's DNA. We've tracked down some of his possessions from his family and will test them in the next couple of days, but we're pretty certain we've got him on that."

"If Nephi was closing up loose ends, why not kill Anton?"

"Well, expedience, for one," Taylor answered. "For Wisechild and Williams to disappear was one thing. The girl was young, and her family Hopi, and unfortunately, her disappearance didn't raise too many alarm bells. Young people from the reservation sometimes just wander off. They go to Flagstaff, or Durango, or Phoenix. And Williams, well, he was in trouble for his activities in Grand Gulch, and elsewhere it turns out, and the antiquities trade is surprisingly violent. The fact that he wasn't reported missing by his family for some time after Ms. Wisechild didn't trigger a connection between the investigations—"

"You dropped the ball."

"Yes, we did," admitted Taylor.

"Nephi didn't need to kill Anton. Not yet, at least. He had him by the economic balls, tens of thousands of dollars' worth of artifacts, and a 10 per cent stake in the profit from drilling all across the Canyon Rims region. After the bodies turned up, and his relationship with Wisechild, and then with Canusa and the senator's office was revealed, he became a liability."

"That's what we suspect. We haven't found the bodies of either Dr. Anton or his wife. Mr. Nephi has nothing to say on the subject."

"They could have run."

"It's possible, but unlikely, unless they went their separate ways and got some very good advice on how to vanish. Once they are in our system, the only way they could disappear is to do so on foot. They couldn't get on a plane, rent a car, use a credit or debit card, nothing. No, Dr. Anton and his wife are dead. We just haven't found their bodies yet."

"Speaking of bodies," Silas said, looking at the sheriff. "Did you ever find out who told Jacob Isaiah that I was the one who found Kayah Wisechild?"

Willis looked down. "I'm sorry about that, Silas. No, I haven't. Short of dragging ol' Jacob in here and putting the lamp on him, I'm afraid that one is simply on my head. I'm sorry about it."

Silas let it go. "What about Darcy McFarland?"

"Dr. Pearson, to be honest, we don't know. The tire tracks on the road to Island in the Sky might be helpful once we've apprehended a suspect, but right now, they are not much use to us. We've eliminated your vehicle."

Silas shook his head.

"Any vehicle we can tie to Charles Nephi, Peter Anton, and Tim Martin have likewise been eliminated, but we haven't been able to narrow the search for a suspect with that evidence. It's a possibility the work Ms. McFarland was doing to protect the Colorado River and other waterways throughout the Southwest brought her into conflict with

Mr. Nephi at some point. We're going over her files, and his, but so far we've got no connection with the deaths of Williams or Wisechild, or Darcy McFarland. We think that Darcy McFarland's murder is unrelated. It's 'open-unsolved' at this point."

"But you're still working on it?" asked Silas.

"Of course."

"Any person of interest?"

"We have people we're watching."

"Me?"

The room was silent except the hum of the overhead fluorescent lights. "Dr. Pearson, this brings us back to the question of how it is you have been able to lead us to three bodies over the course of a single month."

"Gentlemen," said Ken Hollyoak, "that's where I get to earn my generous fee. You can either charge Dr. Pearson, or we are going for breakfast."

"There's no charge at this time," said Willis. "Silas, you're free to go."

"What about Penelope?" Silas asked after a moment.

"What about her?" asked Taylor.

"Don't you think that before all of this started, before Anton discovered the ruins, she must have found them? Don't you think that Nephi maybe—"

"Killed her too?" asked Taylor.

"Surely you can see it's possible." Silas was almost pleading.

"It is possible, Dr. Pearson. We haven't ruled that out. Nephi had already moved back to Utah at that time, but there is absolutely nothing to suggest that anybody, including your wife, had set foot in the ruins until Dr. Anton made his detailed survey of the canyon. Given that these ruins have since been destroyed, well, it's going to be impossible to determine if your wife ever had anything to do with them."

Silas remained silent. He contemplated the journal that was still in safe-keeping at Ken and Trish's home. He decided against mentioning it to Taylor. If he told them about it, the FBI would seize it as evidence, and he would lose the only thread that tied him to his wife.

"You told me when we were in the ruins that you knew who had destroyed them," Silas said to Taylor.

"That's right. We are building our case along with the BLM."

"It was Jared Strom, wasn't it?"

"He did the dirty work; Nephi gave the orders."

Silas asked, "What about whoever left me for dead in the kiva? Have you got that figured out?"

"I'm guessing Peter Anton could illuminate that mystery, if he hasn't already taken the secret to the grave with him."

Anton seemed like the only possibility. He was the one who sent Silas there in the first place. In doing so, he must have known that he was setting himself up, and so his best hope for evading detection as Kaya Wisechild's killer was to follow Silas there and wait for the opportunity to kill him.

That didn't put Silas's mind at ease. None of the explanations did. He figured at best the FBI had a fifty-fifty chance of winning a conviction against Charles Nephi on anything besides his own kidnapping. To win that conviction, Silas would likely have to incriminate himself in the break-and-enter at the senator's office. He knew that he could make a deal for immunity, but as a Canadian in the United States on a long-term work visa, he might risk being sent home. That would mean an end to his search for Penelope.

While the line of inquiry they were discussing made perfectly good sense to him, there was little or no actual evidence to lead to a rock-solid conviction against Charles Nephi. It was like the country that surrounded them. Even the most solid thing in it—bedrock—sometimes was slick with paradox.

35

SILAS CAMPED ON THE RIM of Hatch Wash for three nights. He combed the ledges and benches of the wash, scoured the canyon bottoms, ticking off the miles with his GPS. Each evening he returned to his camp, cooked a simple meal, kindled the fire, and studied his topographic sheets. Before going to bed each night he read the journal Penelope had left in the now ruined kiva at the bottom of the canyon, tucked away in a hidden alcove, unseen.

Every day he searched, but she was not there.

On the fourth morning he heard a pick-up truck grinding across the Point in low gear, four-wheel drive. He put the pot of coffee on and prepared to greet his guests. Five minutes later, as he brewed a dark blend of coffee, he watched as Roger Goodwin piloted his truck over an outcrop of naked red earth and came to rest near Silas's new Outback. Two men and two women sat in the truck's king cab with him. Roger waved and got out and opened the passenger door for his guests. He helped the women down, and the men followed.

Silas had been practicing for the last two days. He smiled at the woman and extended his hand and said: "*Um pitu?*" You have come.

She took his hand in hers. "*Um waynuma.*" Yes, we have come. It was a traditional greeting for the Hopi of Third Mesa.

"*Owí,*" said Silas and he greeted each member of the Wisechild family in turn: Leon, his wife, Evelyn, and their daughter, Darla. Roger introduced Silas to the fourth member of the party, a member of the Kykotsmovi Council named Frank Quochytewa.

"Mr. Quochytewa is here to help the family put Ms. Wisechild's memory—and her ghost—to rest," explained Roger.

They had coffee, sitting on folding lawn chairs that Roger pulled from the bed of his pick-up. As the sun chased the morning chill from the landscape, Roger and Silas donned heavy packs filled with extra clothing, food, water, and ropes, and the six companions started down the dry arroyo toward the drop-off into Hatch Wash. The procession was quiet and somber, with Leon Wisechild asking the occasional question about the ongoing investigation into his daughter's murder, and Silas doing his best to answer.

When they were at the rim of the canyon Silas rigged a rope and helped each member of the party descend the tricky sections. Soon they were all on the canyon floor, making their way through brightly colored tamarisk and willow to where the box canyon opened onto the main stem of the creek. They came to the head of the canyon where it opened into a semi-circular amphitheater, once filled with ancient Pueblo ruins, now choked with emptiness.

"This is the place?" asked Leon, taking off his ball cap and running the back of his hand across his forehead. The old man looked around him. Evelyn sat down on a large rock and looked up at the cliffs rising three hundred feet above them, their painted walls streaked with desert varnish, the rim leaning over the alcove where the ruins had been.

"You say that someone took these places from our ancestors and destroyed them?" asked Leon again.

"That's right."

"So they could build a dam on that little creek back there?" Leon picked up a piece of adobe and tossed it in the dust as a raven wheeled overhead, turning cartwheels as the air warmed in the canyon and rose up the sheer cliffs. He shook his head and put a weathered hand against his face.

"Do you think that our daughter—" started Leon and then stopped, looking down at his hands.

"I don't think so. I think she tried to stop them. She made that film Darla found because she wanted those men to be stopped."

"They killed our little girl because of it?" Leon had tears streaking across his dark brown skin.

"That's right," said Silas. The group was silent for a while. The morning had warmed up and they sat in their shirtsleeves while Silas and

Roger passed around water. The light shifted throughout the box canyon, shadows of clouds passing across the cliff faces, the changing mood of the stone world ebbing and flowing like a tide.

Leon sat very still for a very long time. Silas watched him and his family, wondering what passed through their minds as they sat here in the blank shadow of the ruins their daughter had discovered. After more than an hour of silence Leon waved Silas over to his side. Silas sat down next to Leon on a boulder.

"You know, our ancestors left these canyons when *they* were threatened with a terrible violence against which they could no longer defend themselves. They fled. They left almost everything behind. People seem to think we don't want it anymore. So they come and they take it. The memory of this place, and many, many others like it, has all but been erased by time and by greedy hands that take what they want and leave nothing of our story. I think Kayah was trying to learn that story. But she got caught up in the echo of that violence. I think that's why her ghost has been troubling you. I think that's why her ghost *chose* you."

"I don't understand," confessed Silas.

"Did you stop them from destroying this place?"

"I don't know. I'm not *trying* to save Canyon Rims, or anything else. I just wanted to find my wife."

"You followed our girl to this place. And what did you find?"

"My wife's journal—"

"She won't trouble you anymore." The raven wheeled overhead, its body black as obsidian against the azure sky. He turned once more and then disappeared beyond the canyon rim.

THEY SAT TOGETHER on a dome of Navajo sandstone above Green River Overlook on Island in the Sky. The mesa behind them was dusted with the first snowfall of the year. The sky was streaked with cirrostratus clouds forming broad fans of translucent white that allowed the pale November sun to reach the red rock earth.

They both wore heavy jackets and sat on a worn, duct-taped foam pad that he carried in his pack during the colder months. Silas's hair was uncharacteristically washed and bore only a passing resemblance to a nest of porcupine quills. Long shadows reached toward them over the vast, vertical earth.

Katie accepted the cup of steaming hot chocolate and held it to her lips before taking a sip. They had spent the day searching Upheaval Canyon and the Buck Mesa region of Canyonlands National Park, and had taken a detour on their way back to Moab to watch the sun set.

"Does this mean you get to color in another section of your map?" she asked.

"Yup. I searched this area once three years ago, so it's been cross-hatched. Now I get to color it in."

"Does that help?"

"What do you mean?"

"Does it help you feel like you're making progress?"

"I guess, but only superficially. Really it just helps me keep track."

She sipped her drink. "Did you spike my hot chocolate?"

"Of course, otherwise it's just kids' food. Does the Bureau know you're out here?"

She shook her head. "No, but what I do with my vacation time is my own business."

"I don't know if Assistant Special Agent in Charge Taylor would see it that way."

"The information you've provided has been really helpful in bringing charges against Nephi. I doubt very much if Taylor or Nielsen would have fared as well without it."

"Are you saying you used your feminine wiles to coax information out of me?"

"Is that a protest?"

"No."

"Plus, I *like* you Silas. You're a *good* man. I want to help you find your wife."

He looked at her. The evening light painted her face the same hue as the crimson desert all around. She held the hot chocolate to her lips a moment and then took a sip.

He asked, "Why?"

"Why what?"

"Why do you want to help me find Penelope?"

"I was married once. I understand."

"You were married?"

"Yes, why is that so strange?"

"I just thought . . . I don't know. I don't know what I thought."

"I was married. He was in the air force. He died in Iraq."

"I am *so* sorry."

"I know what it's like to lose someone you love, Silas. I want to help you find Penelope. Maybe then you can move on."

He looked back out over the agoraphobic distance, down to the Green River where it snaked around the Anvil, and beyond to the Maze, the distant Henry Mountains, and the endless, searching sky. Silas felt an urge to put his hand on her arm and tell her that he was sorry once more, but instead changed the subject back to one they had discussed on and off all day.

"You know, the first time I saw Charles Nephi was on the Hopi Reservation."

"With all the media you can see how Taylor would have agreed to a ride-along by a senator's aide to console the family."

"Nephi was really just checking up on how much the family knew."

"Lucky for them, they didn't say anything."

"It's a good thing Nephi didn't speak Hopi."

"It's a good thing your friend Roger *did* or we might still be in the dark."

"What about Darcy?"

"That has us all scratching our heads. Different time frame, different MO, and we have only the thinnest thread of connection between her work and what was going on with Hatch Wash. The evidence of connection you mentioned to me that time—"

"It hasn't panned out." Silas looked away. The documents Hayduke claimed to have connecting McFarland to Canusa and Senator Smith never re-materialized, and he hadn't heard from the elusive desert rat for nearly two months.

"You still don't want to tell me who your friend is?"

"I'm still working on it. There is *no* friend, Katie. *I* was trying to get the info myself."

"This ever goes to trial you're going to be put on the stand, you know."

"I know."

"You know I saw your buddy Charleston in your bookstore, right?" Silas was silent. "Taylor and the others believe his being there that night on Comb Ridge was random. You and I know differently. We don't have anything hard connecting McFarland with Nephi, Anton, or any of the other players here. *If* she knew about the plans to dam Hatch Wash, then she might have threatened to cause trouble, and maybe Nephi might have zeroed in on her. Nephi killed Williams with a blow to the head. McFarland was drowned, and in potash solution, no less. This one remains "open-unsolved" in our books. I'm sorry to report, we can't tie either Anton or Nephi to Penelope. There is simply nothing in any of their homes, offices, records, emails, that even mentions your wife, Silas."

They sat in silence for a while. The sun disappeared. "What's next?"

Rain shrugged. "Taylor's team keeps the investigation into Darcy McFarland's death open. We keep looking for Peter Anton. And we keep looking for your wife."

"Who's we?"

"You and me."

SNOW FELL THE next night in the Castle Valley. It wasn't a blizzard; just a gentle dusting to cover the dry upland desert. He sat in his living room with the lights out, drinking a bottle of Fat Tire. He had decided to try something new and had bought a case of this micro-brew while in Colorado. It was good. Silas watched the snow fall like stars from the heavens across the baked earth. When it melted the desert would bloom again, even if just for a few days, and the earth would feel fresh and new.

He stood and put the bottle of beer down and scanned his maps. He took a colored pencil from the bookshelf and carefully colored in the section of desert around Upheaval Dome and Whale Rock. He and Katie had searched there that morning before he had driven her to Canyonlands Fields, the local airport, to fly back to Salt Lake City.

He missed her, and it made him feel confused and disloyal. He had been an awful husband all of his life, but he had never been disloyal. But now, strangely, with his wife missing for nearly four years, and with him scouring the desert for her, he felt as if he was cheating, even though he had never so much as touched Katie Rain.

He shook his head and turned his attention to the maps. He would have to lay out a plan soon for searching lower country. The snow would make travel in much of the high canyon country impossible. He considered his options: a week or two in Grand Gulch, a few weeks down in the inner gorge of the Grand Canyon? And maybe as far afield as the Escalante, before the Hole in the Rock Road was snowed under. It might be time to break in his new Subaru Outback.

Silas pulled Penelope's notebook from the shelf and sat in one of the hard-backed chairs, and drinking his beer, opened the book. He had waited a month after the capture of Charles Nephi to retrieve it from Ken Hollyoak, on the off chance that the FBI zeroed in on him again. He had read it every night since mapping out the parameters of Edward Abbey Country: Penelope's plan to preserve her heart's true home, the great American wilderness.

He opened it to the first page and read again, as he always did, the line from *The Fool's Progress* that his long lost wife had clung to as her mantra: "*I want to weep, not for sorrow, not for joy, but for the incomprehensible wonder of our brief lives beneath the oceanic sky.*"

He studied the journal until it was dark, and then he flipped on the overhead light and read some more, searching for the answers that he knew only these pages would contain. Exhausted, he stood and walked on stiff legs to the bedroom. He lay down, and touching his wife's face on the portrait beside the bed, fell into the darkness of sleep.

THEY SAT TOGETHER on a dome of Navajo sandstone above Green River Overlook on Island in the Sky. It was the brightest of mornings, in May, the earth verdant with wildflowers and the crispness of a new day. He held her hand. There was a breeze and it tossed his wife's long dark hair like the tail of a mare. The world was perfect. And he was dreaming.

"Silas."

No. Please no.

"Silas, it's okay. Trust me."

Just one more moment here. Please.

"There will always be one more river, not to cross but to follow. The journey goes on forever, and we are fellow voyagers on our little living ship of stone and soil and water and vapor, this delicate planet circling round the sun, which humankind call Earth."

He woke weeping. Blindly stumbling through the darkness of morning, he found the book, and after two hours, found the passage, the last lines of *Down the River*. He didn't bother to wait until dawn, but dialed the phone.

"Are you okay?" Katie asked by way of greeting.

"The Dolores River. It rises near Cortez. The Dolores River. You'll find Peter Anton there."

ACKNOWLEDGMENTS

I WISH TO THANK GREER Chesher for introducing me both to the ecology of the American Southwest, and to the mystery genre, when I worked for her as a volunteer at Grand Canyon National Park in 1993–94. Greer also read early drafts of my never-to-be-published attempts at fiction and gently pointed out that these stories would benefit from a plot.

Dirk, Darren, and Devin Vaughn of Tex's Riverways of Moab have been friends and guides to the Canyonlands region since 1997. I am deeply grateful for their effort to explain many facets of the region to me, as they shuttled me back and forth on various trips on the Green and Colorado Rivers.

Dr. Erik Christensen, the Assistant Medical Examiner for the State of Utah, Denny Ziemann, the Chief Ranger for Canyonlands and Arches National Parks, and Darrel Mecham, the Chief Deputy for Grand County provided helpful insight into investigative procedure for this book. Thanks also to the staff at the Grand County District Attorney's office. Any mistakes or errors of omission are mine.

I wish to express my gratitude to independent bookstores like Back of Beyond in Moab, and so many others across Canada and the United States, who have stocked my books and promote them among readers. It's because of you that I get to do what I love.

Without the enthusiastic support of my publisher, Ruth Linka, and editors Frances Thorsen and Lenore Hietkamp, *The Slickrock Paradox* would likely be a heap of unintelligible verbiage riddled with unpublishable tripe. One cannot underestimate the importance of fabulous editors and a visionary publisher.

My deepest thanks are reserved for all those I have traveled with in Utah, New Mexico, and Arizona. So many amazing adventures have led to the creation of the Red Rock Canyon Mysteries and there is a little bit of all of you between these pages. But most of all, my thanks go to Jenn, who, as always, supports me on the greatest adventure we share together.

STEPHEN LEGAULT is an author, consultant, conservationist, and photographer who lives in Canmore, Alberta. He is the author of five other books, including the first three installments in the Cole Blackwater mystery series, *The Vanishing Track*, *The Cardinal Divide*, and *The Darkening Archipelago*, as well as *The End of the Line*, the first book in the Durrant Wallace mystery series. Please visit Stephen online at stephenlegault.com or follow him on Twitter at @stephenlegault.

Other books by Stephen Legault

Carry Tiger to Mountain: The Tao of Activism and Leadership (2006)

THE RED ROCK CANYON SERIES
The Slickrock Paradox (2012)

THE COLE BLACKWATER SERIES
The Cardinal Divide (2008)
The Darkening Archipelago (2010)
The Vanishing Track (2012)

THE DURRANT WALLACE SERIES
The End of the Line (2011)

For information on new books in the Red Rock Canyon series,
the Cole Blackwater series, the Durrant Wallace series, or other books
by Stephen Legault, visit stephenlegault.com/writing.